THE SCIENCE OF
THE X-FILES

THE SCIENCE OF
THE X-FILES

JEANNE CAVELOS

BERKLEY BOULEVARD BOOKS, NEW YORK

THE SCIENCE OF *THE X-FILES*

A Berkley Boulevard Book / published by arrangement with the author

PRINTING HISTORY
Berkley Boulevard trade paperback edition / November 1998

The Penguin Putnam Inc. World Wide Web site address is
http://www.penguinputnam.com

ISBN: 0-425-16711-9

BERKLEY BOULEVARD
Berkley Boulevard Books are published by The Berkley Publishing Group, a
member of Penguin Putnam Inc., 375 Hudson Street, New York, New York
10014.
BERKLEY BOULEVARD and its logo
are trademarks belonging to Berkley Publishing Corporation.

PRINTED IN THE UNITED STATES OF AMERICA

10 9 8 7 6 5 4 3 2 1

To my father
who shared with me
the wonder of science

CONTENTS

ACKNOWLEDGMENTS

I WOULD LIKE TO THANK MY TWO RESEARCH assistants, Keith Maxwell and Anthony Collamati, who rolled up their sleeves and searched for information on the most bizarre topics. Without them this book would never have been completed.

Grateful thanks also to all the scientists and doctors quoted within, who generously shared their time and expertise and answered some rather outrageous questions.

I'd also like to thank the many people who offered information, insight, and feedback: Tom Thatcher, Dale and Michael Hoover, Maria and Ken Kinsella, M. Mitchell Marmel, Dr. Gary Day, Dr. Paul Viscuso, Dr. David Loffredo, Janis Cortese, Dr. Gail Dolbear, Megan Gentry, Dr. Stephanie Ross, Dr. Andy Michael, Britta Serog, Dr. Michael Blumlein, Elizabeth and Ben Dibble, K. Waldo Ricke, Marty Gingras, Joellyn Crowley, William Hartman, Judith Hardin, Patricia Jackson—who thought I should change the title to *Jeanne's Gross Science Facts*—John Donigan, Jacquie Miller, Michael Flint, Margo Cavelos, Crystal Campisi, Nancy "Sam" Urtz, Dr. Robin Marra, Dr. Robert Epstein, Dr. James Dill, Dr. Catherine Craven, Dr. Craig Hieber, and Richard Powell.

Thanks to Chris Carter and all the talented writers of *The X-Files*, who have provided the rich, fascinating food for thought for this book.

Thanks to my editors—Barry Neville, for his guidance and support, and Kim Waltemyer, for her enthusiastic follow-up—and to my agent, Lori Perkins, for her continued faith in me.

Thanks to my iguana, Igmoe, for not trying to mate with me during the writing of this book. And special thanks to my husband, for sustaining me and putting up with me, and for teaching me what it truly means to love . . . the Cigarette-Smoking Man.

INTRODUCTION

"That is the essence of science: You ask an impertinent question and you're on your way to a pertinent answer."

—Fox Mulder,
"Conduit"

"Nothing happens in contradiction to nature. Only in contradiction to what we know of it."

—Dana Scully,
"Herrenvolk"

"WHAT SCIENCE? ARE YOU KIDDING?" Those were my friend's first words when I told her I was going to write this book. She is a huge fan of *The X-Files*. In fact, her enthusiasm drove me to start watching soon after the show came on the air. Yet, perhaps like many fans, she felt the unexplained phenomena on the show flew in the face of science, and that a close examination of them would only reveal how impossible and ridiculous they were. But I believe that these unexplained phenomena often illuminate fascinating areas of science, that they explore frontiers science has yet to understand, that at their best they walk the line between what science can explain and what it can't. And like Scully, I believe that the lack of a scientific explanation does not mean that there is no explanation. Exploration of just such phenomena has been and continues to be the driving force behind scientific progress.

That's not to say that *The X-Files* doesn't occasionally screw up in its science. Scientific errors have certainly crept in over the years (perhaps the first being Scully's assertion in the pilot that time is a "universal invariant." Since she wrote her senior thesis on Einstein's twin paradox, which illustrates the theory of relativity, she should know that time is relative). And some premises, based on our current state of knowledge, seem unlikely in the extreme. But the purpose of this book is not to nitpick. The intention is to pursue the truth, in scientific terms, as far as we know it. Writing this book, I often felt a bit like Scully, typing up my reports late at night, seeking out the latest research on unusual subjects.

But I also, at times, felt like Mulder. The X-files raise many questions, most of them residing on these scientific frontiers. To get the answers to those questions, I had to consult the experts. This book includes the expertise, opinions, and reactions of over fifty of the foremost authorities in the disciplines discussed, scientists undertaking research that helps to illuminate these frontiers. Confronting them with Mulder's "impertinent questions" often led to fascinating answers.

A few words on how the book is set up. The discussions build on each other, so you'll probably find it most helpful to read them in order. I based all of my discussions on the episodes themselves (through the end of the fifth season and the movie), excluding any additional information given in *X-Files* reference sources. To refresh your memory of a particular episode, you may want to watch it or read the summary from an episode guide prior to reading the section. I apologize in advance for not covering every episode. Early into the writing of this book, I realized that the show had provided me with such a wealth of issues to discuss that the book as planned would be one thousand pages long! It was simply impossible to cover every scientific issue raised on the show. Instead, at the wise urging of my editor, I focused on the most interesting ones.

What I came to realize, in countering my friend's argument and writing this book, was that *The X-Files* is actually the television drama most concerned with science today, incorporating recent discoveries and exploring the limits and values of science. What you'll find within this book are the answers to many impertinent questions, an exploration of the truth as far as we know it, and a peek at what might lie beyond the shifting line that defines the limits of our knowledge.

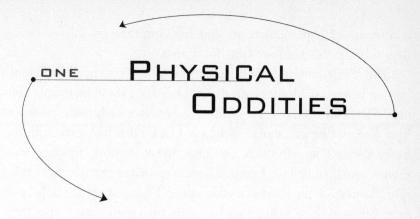

ONE PHYSICAL ODDITIES

"Nature abhors normality. It can't go very long without creating a mutant."

—Dr. Blockhead,
"Humbug"

EUGENE VICTOR TOOMS STANDS OUT-side a barred window at night. He's hungry for human liver. His prey is inside the house. The window is the only way in, but the bars are a mere six inches apart. He raises his foot, fits it and his calf through the narrow opening. The night air caresses his nostrils with the scent of a particularly tasty liver. He presses his head against the cold metal bars, his body alive with hunger. His skull is wider than the opening. He twists his head, grimacing, pushing, pushing. And as he pushes, hidden muscles engage, stretching pliant bone, nerves, tendons, causing his skull and the brain within to deform, elongating and narrowing like the image in a fun-house mirror, until his head slips through the narrow opening. His chest follows, ribs and internal organs flattening, stretching, the pressure on his heart making each beat resound with the power of a seizure. His pelvis flattens, stretches, and then his thighs. Tooms steps through the window. Time for dinner.

The X-Files abounds with genetic mutants, "genetically different" human beings, as Mulder calls them. They have some incredible abilities. They can stretch, grow younger, regenerate body parts, even perform fission. Life as a mutant might not be all that bad, except for the funky diets. These mutants consume livers, tumors, pituitary hormones, and liquefied fat. Leonard Betts is made entirely of cancer cells; John Barnett has the hand of a salamander; Flukeman is part fluke, part man. Some of these beings may have inherited their peculiarities from their parents, though most seem to be one of a kind. They raise a fascinating range of scientific questions, those "impertinent" questions Mulder believes form the essence of science. Could a man made totally of cancer survive and regenerate body parts? Could a salamander hand grow on a human? Could radiation spawn a mutant hybrid creature?

Mutants seem fairly commonplace in the world of *The X-Files*. How possible are such radical mutations? Could any one of us be a mutant? Before we can answer that last question, we need to take a whirlwind tour of the genome.

BIOLOGY 101 FOR FBI AGENTS PURSUING GENETIC MUTANTS

A quick refresher course. Genes are made up of DNA, molecules whose double-helical structure looks rather like a spiral staircase or a ladder twisted around and around. Each rung of the ladder is made of a pair of nucleotides. Since there are only four different types of nucleotides in DNA, and each type can only bond with one other type, the number of possible rungs is only four. If we number the nucleotides one through four, then the possible rungs are 1–2, 2–1, 3–4, 4–3. Just as a computer breaks all information into sequences of zeros and ones, or your printer prints out a picture by simple dots of black or spaces of white, these four possible combinations, in different long sequences, can convey very complex information. Like a four-letter alphabet, this genetic code spells out the assembly and operating instructions for your body. Since the work of assembling and running your body is done by proteins, your DNA is basically a recipe book, carrying the recipes for many different proteins. Each of these protein recipes is called a gene. A gene may contain as few as one thousand nucleotide pairs or rungs, or as many as 2,300,000 pairs. An entire DNA strand, or ladder, carries thousands of genes. These DNA strands are called chromosomes, and since they are several inches long, the cells often keep them wound in tight bundles.

ARE YOUR PARENTS MUTANTS?

If you want to know whether you might be a mutant, a good place to start your investigation is with your parents, since you inherited your DNA from them. You inherited your traits, some good, some bad, from them. Did you also inherit mutations? Each person, over the course of his life, accumulates mutations. Your parents, between the time they were born and the time they conceived you, underwent genetic mutations that may have been passed on to you.

How would they have acquired mutations? Actually, mutation is a way of life. Our genes are constantly under attack. Environmental factors such as radiation, smoke, and chemicals can create in our bodies free radicals, dangerously reactive molecules that damage DNA.

Nutrition also plays a critical role. The lack of a simple nutrient, such as folic acid, can cause chromosomes to break. If a segment breaks off, it may be lost entirely, or it may become attached to a different chromosome, interfering with that chromosome's genetic material.

Our very own life processes also cause genetic damage. Our bodies create energy by oxidizing carbohydrates and fats, a process that also creates free radicals. Oxidation occurs with every breath we take.

Growth can also accidentally cause damage. When a cell divides, the DNA must duplicate itself to create one set for each daughter cell. The nucleotides split apart, each rung of the ladder breaking in half, unzipping. Each half then recreates its missing side, resulting in two identical sets of DNA. At least, they're *usually* identical. Sometimes errors can occur.

But while those mutations are unintentional, others exhibit a disturbing sense of purpose. Sometimes the genes shuffle and rearrange themselves intentionally. Mobile genes, also called "jumping genes" or transposons, don't sit quietly on their chromosome as they should. Instead, they multiply and insert themselves into multiple positions on their chromosome, as well as into different chromosomes, bullying their way around. These genes have been called selfish, working only for their survival rather than for yours. They simply want to make as many copies of themselves as they can. In some plants, these selfish genetic elements account for as much as 60 percent of DNA. Transposons can also carry neighboring genes with them in their exploits, rearranging DNA. They may insert themselves into the middle of an otherwise healthy gene, disrupting that gene's functioning. Some forms of cancer, hemophilia, and other diseases may develop as a result of these rearrangements.

Genetic invaders can also alter our DNA. Some viruses, including retroviruses like HIV, actually insert their DNA permanently into our chromosomes, much like transposons, and can cause similar disruptions. Genes have even been found that jump from one species to another, again damaging existing genes.

A single gene in our DNA may be damaged ten billion times in a lifetime. The resulting genetic mutation may be small—the substitution of one pair of nucleotides for another in a single gene; or it may be large—damage to a chromosome that affects hundreds of genes at once. So why doesn't all this rampant genetic tinkering kill us or make us into grotesque, zombified mutants?

Well, on the positive side, there is a chance that these mutations could be beneficial, actually aiding in our survival. Such positive mutations are the driving force behind evolution. The chances of a positive mutation in the genetic lottery, though, are pretty small. While most mutations have no effect, those that do are much more apt to have a negative rather than a positive one. The severity of this effect depends on where the damage occurs. Remember that each gene codes for, or carries the recipe for, a protein that helps our bodies to work. If genetic damage significantly changes that recipe (instead of 1 teaspoon of pepper, it now calls for 1 *cup*), then it can seriously impair body functions, or perhaps improve them. If it doesn't significantly change the recipe (the genetic equivalent of a typo), then the mutation won't do any harm. The reason most mutations have no effect at all is that at least 50 percent—and perhaps as much as 90 percent—of our DNA doesn't code for a protein and so doesn't seem to do much of anything (for example, all those multiple copies of transposons). Even if a dangerous mutation occurs, it usually is not spread because the damaged cell recognizes its flaw and either repairs itself or heroically self-destructs.

But with so much damage occurring, sometimes dangerous mutations happen—and sometimes they go undetected. More than five thousand human disorders, including many common ones such as cancer and aging (yes, aging is a disorder), are linked to genetic damage and defects.

So your parents, like their parents and their parents before them, built up genetic mutations in their bodies. These mutations couldn't have been too severe, or they wouldn't have survived long enough to reproduce. Since they did survive, they pass their DNA on to you. Their defects and mutations, however, only pass to you if they occurred in the germ cells (the egg and sperm) that form you. Otherwise, those mutations die with your parents. Mutations in the germ cells are rare because the body protects and repairs those cells more carefully than the cells in the rest of our bodies, ensuring the survival of the species. But germ cells face one mutagenic process that regular cells do not: meiosis.

Meiosis is the process by which germ cells are made. The precursors of the sperm and eggs, like all regular human cells, have forty-six chromosomes, two complete sets, one inherited from each parent. Your father, for example, will have one set that he inherited from your grandfather, and one that he inherited from your grandmother. These precursor cells must split so that each germ cell has only twenty-three chromosomes, one set. That way, when your parents' sperm and egg join, the fertilized egg—you—will have the correct total number of forty-six chromosomes. To split, the two sets of chromosomes line up using the buddy system, two by two, with comparable or homologous chromosomes pairing off. While they're waiting, these pairs overlap and exchange genetic material in a process called *crossing over*, allowing new combinations to be formed. This means that the chromosome you inherit from your father may not be identical to the one he inherited from his grandfather. It can have some of your grandmother's genes on it too. Crossing over is the major source of chromosomal mutations. Humans average two or three crossovers per chromosome! That's why no two germ cells are alike, and you can be so normal, while your sibling is a fat-sucking vampire.

While most crossing over simply creates different combinations of traits, more radical mutations may also occur. Segments of a chromosome can be lost, duplicated, or moved. In addition, if transposons have changed the order of genes ahead of time, this crossing over can create a jumbled mess.

After exchanging material, the homologous chromosomes are pulled away from each other, drawn to opposite ends of the dividing cell. Sometimes, though, the forty-six chromosomes are not split exactly in half, and a germ cell may get an extra copy of a chromosome, or lack a copy of a chromosome. This condition causes many birth defects and the majority of all miscarriages. It is almost always fatal.

So the egg and the sperm that will soon be you are formed. The older your mother is at your conception, the greater chance for mutations in her ova. Women are born with all their eggs, so these eggs age and are exposed to the same internal and external threats that the body is. Men produce fresh sperm throughout their lives, so your father's age at your conception is less important. Yet as all systems deteriorate with age, so the system for producing sperm is more prone to errors later in life. If a fertilized egg has too many damaging mutations, it will be immediately miscarried, without the mother aware that any fertilization has occurred. This happens in up to 25 percent of all pregnancies.

Your mother's egg and your father's sperm meet and join. You're a fertilized egg in the womb. You've got your genes, for better or worse, and they're not so horribly mutated that you'll immediately die. Can you at least develop in peace? Not exactly. You're actually most vulnerable right now, during your first three months of growth, when your organs are forming. Of the four million infants born annually in the U.S., 3–5 percent are born with birth defects. Many environmental factors can contribute to developmental abnormalities, including drugs, radiation, smoking, and nutrition. If your mother gets sick, drinks alcohol, or even uses certain acne medicine, she can negatively influence your development.

You survive these various hazards and are born, the doctor holding you up before your proud mother. Does she sigh in relief, or scream in horror?

WILL YOUR MOTHER SELL YOUR BABY PICTURE TO THE NATIONAL INFORMER?

You surely are a mutant. We are all mutants, in that some of our DNA has suffered damage somewhere along the way. That's pretty scary all by itself. But because mutations are so pervasive, the world is filled with examples of what mutations can do, and what they can't. Most of us mutants are considered "normal," and we are, since mutation is a normal part of life. Some aren't as lucky. Although I've treated the subject lightly so far, the consequences of serious genetic or developmental damage can be tragic: illness, deformity, disability, death. But even with all the mutations occurring in the world, we've never seen living mutants as radical as those shown on *The X-Files*. Genetic mutations that would give rise to a radically different—and still viable—human being from normal parents are extremely unlikely. Major chromosomal screw-ups certainly occur, but sperm with such defects are unlikely to be healthy enough to win the race to the egg, and eggs with those defects are unlikely to produce a viable fetus.

But we know these oddities are unlikely; that's part of what makes them so fascinating. They may be one in a billion, but that doesn't mean they're impossible. If they did arise, how might they survive? And how might they have developed their incredible abilities?

CANCER MAN

Of all the oddities Mulder and Scully have encountered, Leonard Betts would have to be one of the oddest. Leonard's body is made up entirely of cancer cells. He loses his head in a car accident, but that doesn't keep him from walking home and—after soaking a few hours in iodine—growing a new head! Leonard enjoys snacking on tumors, and has a talent for sniffing out tumors in others. He's even able to split in two, forming a duplicate of himself—a handy ability to have. But can someone live if his entire body is cancerous, if he is, in essence, one big tumor? To answer that, we need to look at what cancer is and how it works.

We have three hundred trillion cells in our bodies. Over the course of a human lifetime, ten thousand trillion cell divisions take place. On average, this means that every second, twenty-five million cells divide in our body. There. Did you feel it? Normally cells divide at the right time, in the right place, in the right way—a perfectly choreographed minuet. But sometimes they begin to divide much too rapidly, forgetting their proper place and duties, shoving other cells out of the way, pushing into places they don't belong, recruiting blood vessels to satisfy their needs, fooling the immune system into ignoring them. Dr. Dvorit Samid, associate professor of medicine at the University of Virginia and former section head of differentiation control at the National Cancer Institute, describes it like this: "A cancer cell has lost its respect for proper growth control commands. It has no respect for the social behavior one cell should show another. It grows as if the rest of the cells don't matter, causing anarchy." So instead of executing a minuet, a renegade group of cells is slam dancing. And we have cancer.

How does a cell change from good citizen to anarchist? The change seldom comes all at once. Several steps must be taken to produce a fully malignant cell. During the course of our lives, billions of cells may take the first step toward cancer. But the likelihood that all of the steps will occur in any single cell is very low. And if they do, the body has defense mechanisms that will kill a damaged cell or cause it to kill itself. But if those several steps do occur in a cell and it somehow isn't killed, it will produce more cancerous cells.

What are the steps a cell must go through in order to become cancerous? Several different key types of genes must be damaged or impaired. The first is called a proto-oncogene. Remember that a gene carries the recipe for a protein that helps do the work of the body. A gene is said to "express" itself in a cell if it is making its protein. At different times, under different conditions, different genes will be expressing themselves in different cells. But how do the genes know when to express themselves?

Let's take a step back for a minute. We all come from an initial cell that divides and divides, creating duplicates of itself. But gradually the cells differentiate, taking on various roles and characteristics. Although all daughter cells carry the same genes, they don't all express the same genes. Muscle cells express different genes than bone cells or liver cells. These differences allow these cells to take on distinct identities, properties, and duties. A genetic mutation can cause a gene to express itself—to make its protein—when it normally should not, or to not express itself when it should.

Why is damage to proto-oncogenes so dangerous? They carry the recipe for a protein that stimulates cell growth and division. When these proto-oncogenes are damaged, they lose all sense of control and express themselves when they should not, pouring out growth-stimulating proteins like psychotic gourmets. Damage turns mild-mannered proto-oncogenes into megalomaniacal oncogenes. And like a stuck accelerator pedal in a car, the oncogenes drive the engine of cell division faster and faster. Every cell in our bodies contains over one hundred proto-oncogenes.

For a cell to become cancerous, damage must also occur to a second type of gene, the tumor-suppressor genes. These suppressor genes act like the brakes on a car, expressing themselves with proteins that slow or stop cell division when appropriate. Damage to these genes causes them not to express themselves when they should, and so the genes don't put on the brakes. The cell continues to divide, the cancer to grow, with the tumor suppressor genes asleep on the job. Seventeen of these tumor-suppressor genes have been identified, and damage to one or more of them seems present in almost all forms of cancer. One key tumor-suppressor gene is p53, which when functioning properly prevents a damaged cell from reproducing and causes the cell to destroy itself if the damage cannot be repaired. The p53 gene exists in damaged form in about 50 percent of all cancers and has been found in fifty-two different types of cancer. Among those who inherit an abnormal p53 from parents, 90 percent get cancer by the age of fifty.

Damage to both proto-oncogenes and tumor-suppressor genes seems to contribute to the formation of every cancer. There are two different ways in which this damage can occur. The damage may be genetic, as in the mutations we discussed earlier, or it may be epigenetic. Instead of changing the DNA sequence as genetic damage does, epigenetic damage changes the expression of genes. The recipe may be intact, but if you spilled a pot of tomato sauce onto it, you can't read it anyway. Dr. Samid explains, "Particular molecules, methyl groups, can sit on the gene. If you have a lot of groups sitting there, the gene can become silent. It is not expressed." If this happens to a tumor-suppressor gene, again the brakes will go out on cell division.

The cause of this epigenetic damage is not yet understood, but it can lead to even more problems. Cells go through several stages in the transformation from healthy to malignant. The most interesting stage for our purposes is the first, in which the cell either fails to undergo differentiation or it *dedifferentiates*. This means that the cell does not display the specific characteristics it should; the correct genes are not expressing themselves. A muscle cell stops acting like a muscle cell, or a liver cell stops acting like a liver cell. The cells begin to act like more primitive embryonic cells, not aware that they have a specific role to play in the body but only knowing that they should divide as often as possible. Dr. Henry Brem, director of neurosurgical oncology and professor of neurosurgery and oncology at Johns Hopkins explains, "The more mature or differentiated a cell is, the more it will behave as it is supposed to behave. The less differentiated a cell is, the more it will act as an embryonic cell." So rather than maturing and taking on their appropriate duties, these slam dancers remain perpetually immature. Since they have no sense of their place or role in the body, they proliferate out of control, growing into areas they don't belong and serving no useful purpose. Dr. Samid believes the epigenetic damage is more often a contributor to cancer development than genetic damage.

Leonard Betts's cells, however, seem to behave in a differentiated way, despite their cancer. His body does not grow out of control, like one gigantic tumor; it has structure. He has eyes, a nose, a mouth. He breathes through lungs; in order for his body to work, he must have bones and muscles. Mulder theorizes that the cancer cells are somehow being guided into a constructive pattern. But the very fact that they are not growing out of control, that they are conforming to patterns and performing functions, seems to disqualify them as being cancerous. As Dr. Brem explains, "Cancer cells don't do what they're supposed to do. A *glioblastoma* [brain tumor] cell can't help you think; it can't help you initiate motor functions, even though it originated from a brain cell." That's why cancer is so bad. The cells take up valuable space, crowding out productive cells and doing nothing in return. Since Leonard Betts's cells are differentiated, we might wonder why they are even called cancerous.

Dr. Samid believes she knows why the pathologist in the episode makes this determination. "If a pathologist looks at the tissues and cells, he may call them cancer cells by appearance." Since cancer cells divide so rapidly, they are crowded together. Also, cancer cells have an abnormally small skirt of cytoplasm around their nucleus. Normally after a cell divides, the two daughter cells will rest for a while, making more cytoplasm to fill themselves out. But a cancer cell will not. Cancer also provides evidence of cell division where there shouldn't be any. For example, brain cells don't normally divide, so evidence of cell division in Leonard's brain would clearly indicate cancer.

But if Leonard's cells are cancerous and dividing out of control, how can they possibly remain differentiated and functional?

The answer may lie in Dr. Samid's research. Dr. Samid is working with a class of chemical compounds called aromatoids, which includes phenylacetate and phenylbutyrate. These compounds exist in both plants and animals in small quantities. They are also formed in our bodies as products of digestion. Dr. Samid and her colleagues have shown that these simple, small molecules can change which genes are expressed in a cell. "The cancer cell is expressing the wrong combination of genes. If you think of the cell as a piano, it's playing a defective tune. The aromatoids make the cell play a new tune, correcting the defective tune."

Remember the methyl groups, sitting on the genes and inhibiting their expression? The aromatoids clear them away, allowing the genes to once again express themselves. Returning to our cookbook analogy, the aromatoids clean away the tomato sauce stain, allowing the recipe to be read once again. The cancer cell doesn't die, but it begins to behave more maturely. Dr. Samid describes the transformation. "In skin cancer or melanoma, the cancer cell doesn't look like a skin cell. But when we treat it with aromatoids, the cancer cell begins to look like a skin cell, and it starts to make melanin, as a skin cell should." The cell is differentiating into its proper form.

While this helps with the epigenetic damage, genetic damage may still remain. But since the cancer cells are now behaving better, they are no longer such a threat to the body. Their rate of division slows, and they no longer shove their way into areas where they don't belong. They are contained. Some of the cells even regain their ability to sense their own damaged condition and kill themselves. Dr. Samid describes the effect of treatment with aromatoids. "The tumors grow slower at first, then stop growing, then start shrinking. They may not shrink away completely, but the patient feels better." With such treatment, a person may be able to coexist with cancer.

Cancer cells that have been treated with aromatoids, then, are somewhat differentiated but still cancerous, just like the cells of

Leonard Betts. Dr. Samid agrees. "We can speculate that this person has a higher level of aromatoids or other differentiation-inducing molecules that will allow the cancer cells to function to some degree." So Leonard's cells might still be able to carry out their necessary functions, despite their cancerous mutations.

With aromatoid treatment, people may someday be able to live with their cancer. Leonard Betts has just reached that goal first.

I'D LIKE A NEW HEAD, PLEASE, SIZE LARGE

What about Leonard Betts's ability to regenerate a head? Is there a connection between cancer and regeneration? Could cancer cells allow us to grow missing body parts?

A salamander can produce a new tail and new limbs. A newt can even regenerate its jaws, spinal cord, and ocular tissues. This has puzzled scientists because the cells involved in regeneration seem to abandon their established roles—to dedifferentiate, just as in cancer—and to take on new roles.

When a salamander loses an appendage, epidermal cells, from the outer layer of skin surrounding the wound, crawl over the wound and seal it. Then fibroblasts from the dermis, the under layer of skin, come out from the perimeter of the wound and migrate to the wound's center. A fibroblast is a cell that makes connective tissue in the body. The fibroblasts and epidermal cells form a protective layer over the wound. The cells beneath this protective layer—whether they are bone, blood, or skin cells—then dedifferentiate to an embryonic type of cell, similar to cancer cells. These accumulate and form a bump, the blastema, which then grows into a limb bud.

The pattern of the new limb develops slowly. The undifferentiated cells in the blastema begin, under the control of the fibroblasts, to differentiate into the various types of cells needed: cartilage, connective tissue, bone, nerve, and so on. Oddly, the regeneration begins with the distal or far end of the pattern first. So if an arm has been cut off, the blastema differentiates "finger" cells first, meaning that the specific combination of genes whose expression will cause the formation of a finger are activated. These finger cells notice that they are beside shoulder cells, and realize that in a healthy arm, this meeting should not be taking place. Dr. Susan Bryant, principal investigator at the Developmental Biology Center at the University of California, Irvine, stresses that this "confrontation and recognition" is critical. "If the cells recognize they have abnormal neighbors, then they will keep growing until they have normal neighbors." So the finger cells, realizing that they don't belong next to the shoulder, will stimulate the growth of cells to fill in the missing territory. In that way they will grow "hand" cells and "wrist" cells and "lower arm" cells and "upper arm" cells until at last all the neighbors are happy with each other.

According to Dr. Bryant, in order to regenerate a limb, "You have to have a group of cells that have information and can interact to make the appropriate shape, size, and pattern." The cells that hold the information are the dermal fibroblasts, which are different than fibroblasts found elsewhere in the body. These dermal fibroblasts have the ability to generate skin, bone, cartilage—everything but muscle, which must arise from broken-down muscle fibers and muscle satellite cells.

How do they do it? The initial migration of fibroblasts out from the dermis is critical to successful regeneration. If a flap of skin is grafted over the wound, the limb will not be regenerated, because the fibroblasts will see no need to migrate out over the wound. This migration, which leads fibroblasts from different spots around the circumference of the wound into confrontation, is essential. Like drug dealers from many different parts of the city running into each other at the same diner (as happens in "Kill Switch"), the meeting of these fibroblasts at the center of the wound tells them that something extraordinary is afoot. "It forces the cells to interact," Dr. Bryant explains.

In humans, the fibroblasts do not migrate from the dermis, which is one reason we are incapable of regenerating even a small hole in the skin. The human dermis does not regenerate itself; rather, cells from below come up to cause healing and scarring. Bryant states her belief that "our fibroblasts are a little defective in some way that we have to figure out." One exception to this rule appears to be the human fingertip. If the fingertip is cut off and the skin is not sutured up, it will often regenerate, even recreating the fingerprint. Dr. Bryant theorizes this may be because the distal part of the pattern regenerates first, and at the fingertip we are at the distal part of the limb.

As for how humans might gain the power to regenerate more than a fingertip, there are several possibilities. The option used by Dr. Ridley in "Young at Heart" involves grafting a salamander blastema to a human. On the show, this method results in a squishy-looking four-fingered greenish yellow hybrid human/salamander hand on convict John Barnett's wrist.

Experiments have shown that salamander blastemas can be grafted to different parts of a salamander's body and result in a new limb. This occurs because regeneration is caused by local cell interactions (that confrontation and recognition again), not by a body-wide decision that a new arm is needed. Salamanders don't even need a previously formed blastema to grow a new arm. A ring or cuff of skin from around the wound grafted to the new site will provide the necessary epidermal cells and dermal fibroblasts. Grafting either skin or a blastema to a human, though, poses more problems. First, there's the danger of the immune system rejecting such foreign cells. Second, there's the risk of transmission of diseases between animal and human. Third, there are the differences in physiology. Scientists have tried grafting tissue from salamanders onto mice, but the grafts don't take. The cool body temperature at which salamander cells thrive has thus far proved too different from the warmer body temperature of mice. The same problem would arise in grafting salamander tissue onto humans. So Dr. Ridley's technique seems not the most likely candidate for success.

What techniques might be more likely to have us growing new limbs? First, we might take human embryonic cells, which have not yet differentiated, and apply them to a wound. After all, back when we were embryos, we had the ability to form a leg. Although no such known test has been attempted, a similar process has been tried with frogs. A limb bud from a larval frog was grafted onto a frog that had a leg amputated. The frog with the graft grew a new leg. In theory, Bryant admits, it could work with a human, "though it's unlikely to be acceptable."

Another possibility would be introducing the genes that seem to be associated with regeneration and seeing if they elicit any response. Dr. Bryant and her colleagues recently identified one gene, *distalless*, which seemed to "turn on" in a regenerating salamander limb. She is now trying to introduce this gene into chicks.

Yet another possibility would be to discover how to make our own cells dedifferentiate. Dr. Bryant and her colleagues have discovered a protein, FGF-2, which seems critical in the process.

LET'S RETURN NOW to Leonard Betts. Regeneration and cancer are clearly connected, since both involve cells dedifferentiating, though the nature of the connection is not yet understood. Tumors in salamanders and newts are extremely rare. In addition, salamander limbs injected with cancer cells do not grow tumors. Instead, they grow extra limbs. The cancer is somehow guided into a constructive pattern rather than a destructive one, the cancer cells differentiating into the various types of cells needed. It was this precise fact that inspired Dr. Samid to begin her study of cancer. Dr. Bryant attributes the formation of cancer cells into a limb to the local cell interactions exhibited by salamanders. A cancer cell's inappropriate behavior would "alert the neighbors," who would make sure that any growth is controlled and channeled into a useful pattern. Since human cells lack these local interactions, this "confrontation and recognition," they are effectively blind, letting those neighboring cancer cells get away with murder.

Leonard Betts's cells, though, do seem to undergo these local interactions. His cancer does not grow out of control, but rather is guided into a useful pattern. The new growth generated on his neck is not a tumor but a head. Since the exact process through which these local cell interactions take place is not yet understood, it's difficult to say why or how Leonard may have developed this characteristic. But since certain genes seem critical in controlling regeneration, and cancer is caused in part by genetic damage, perhaps the genetic mutations responsible for Leonard's cancer are also responsible for awakening in his cells the ability to interact with each other.

Dr. Samid approaches Leonard's ability to regenerate differently, considering the differentiation process in chemical terms. The salamander's cells may differentiate because a chemical, such as an aromatoid, may enter the dedifferentiated cells and tell them, "Grow up! Mature!" The differentiation process would be triggered just as it is in the cancer cells treated by Dr. Samid. In the case of Leonard, when he needs to grow a new head, the level of aromatoids in his body may decrease, allowing those vital cancer cells to dedifferentiate and proliferate once again, and when his tissue has expanded sufficiently, the aromatoids may increase, causing the cells to slow their growth and differentiate into their proper forms.

But why would Leonard soak his headless body in iodine? Dr. Bryant knows of no connection between iodine and regeneration. Another chemical, though, does affect regeneration. Retinoic acid changes the regional identity of cells. Dr. Bryant states, "If you take a frog going through metamorphosis from larva to adult, amputate his tail, and treat the wound with retinoic acid, instead of growing a new tail, it will grow a bunch of legs." Obviously something Leonard Betts should keep out of the medicine cabinet.

DO YOU WANT TO LIVE FOREVER?

While we discussed Dr. Ridley's experiments with regeneration in "Young at Heart," those are really just a hobby. His main goal in that episode is to learn how to reverse the aging process, which he has apparently done in John Barnett. Ridley claims he made his breakthrough by studying children with progeria.

Hutchinson-Gilford Progeria Syndrome was first discovered in 1886. Children with it appear normal at birth, but their growth slows dramatically by the end of their first year of life. They will never grow larger than a five-year-old. Some die as young as age seven, though others live up to their late twenties. This slow growth may sound like a prolonged youth, but those with progeria actually exhibit many of the symptoms of premature aging. They suffer from arthritis, respiratory problems, atherosclerosis (the fatty blockage of arteries), premature senility, and repeated nonhealing fractures. And although they remain small in size, their appearances become aged: Their faces look old and wizened with wrinkles, beaked noses, receding chins, and prominent scalp veins; their corneas become clouded; degeneration of the hair follicles leads to baldness and loss of eyebrows and eyelashes; and their skin becomes thin and parchmentlike.

This rare disease is inherited, though the exact gene that causes it has not yet been identified. Some scientists believe progeria is a dominant trait. This would mean that one of the parents would have to suffer from the disease (which would be unlikely, because of their short life span, and is not borne out in the research) or that one of the germ cells of the parents suffered a mutation (which researchers find plausible since babies with progeria tend to be born to older fathers, where mutations would be more likely). Others believe progeria is a recessive trait, meaning that the child must inherit the trait from both parents in order to suffer from the disease. They point to a number of cases in which parents of children with progeria are cousins or otherwise related, increasing the chance that they would both carry the gene. There is no known treatment.

In "Young at Heart," Dr. Ridley claims he has been able to reverse aging by using the genetic components of progeria. Yet most scientists feel that a study of progeria would be limited in what it could tell us about aging. Since progeria does not really resemble normal aging, different mechanisms are most likely involved; as we discussed above, a single-gene mutation is likely responsible for progeria, but not for aging. While the study of progeria would be unlikely to lead us to a method of stopping or reversing aging, it could, however, help us understand various processes associated with aging, such as atherosclerosis.

So what possibilities do exist for slowing or stopping the aging process? Before we can answer that, we need to understand why exactly we age. Scientists are still working on figuring this out. At least eight major theories exist, and it now seems that they are all at least partially true, making aging the most complex disease we know.

Scully cites one of these theories in "Home" when she explains that our bodies are merely vehicles for genes needing to replicate. This theory is called the "disposable soma" theory of aging, the *soma* being the body. The human body ages and wears out because its purpose is not to live forever. Its purpose is to reproduce. We are not nature's end, but its means, its means to continue the species. We are germ cell producers, storage banks, and maters. Once we mate, our job is done. Nature likes to create us so that we can mate as early as possible, to minimize the risk of death from outside forces before mating has occurred. This rapid maturation may work against a long life span, but that is not nature's concern. Scientists see nature as a careful investor searching for a balance between investments in maintenance of the body, or somatic maintenance, and investments in reproduction. It's sort of like deciding whether to spend money repairing and maintaining your current car or to put all your money toward buying a new car. If nature invested all her resources in maintenance of the body, the body could be maintained perfectly, and we would be theoretically immortal, with no reproduction required; if nature put all her energy into reproduction, we'd be popping out kids like there's no tomorrow, and there wouldn't be, for our bodies would quickly fall apart.

Nature has found that the most successful investment portfolio puts some of her resources into somatic maintenance (keeping us alive at least long enough to mate), but doesn't waste resources by keeping the soma around longer than it's needed (those repair bills get awfully high, after all).

Dr. Michael Rose at the University of California at Irvine demonstrated the connection between mating and life span using *Drosophila*, the fruit fly. He did not allow the flies to breed until they were old. In this case, a long life span then became a critical component to reproduction. In just fifteen generations the life span of the flies increased by a third.

Another theory looks at old age from an evolutionary perspective. Evolution explains how species develop through the survival of the fittest. Yet survival of the fittest has nothing to do with how well you age. Fitness is a state judged at the time of reproduction. If you are "the fittest" at the age of reproduction, then you will reproduce and your traits will be passed down. If you later become infirm and sickly, those traits have no effect on the survival and reproduction of your offspring. So evolution does not select us for longevity or health in old age, nor does it eliminate genes that cause harm late in life from the gene pool. This suggests that genetic traits that cause negative effects at old age have spread unchecked through our species.

Probably the most well-known theory relates aging to the presence of free radicals in the body. At the beginning of this chapter we briefly discussed free radicals, dangerously reactive molecules that damage DNA. Free radicals are caused by oxidation, the process by which our body creates energy. All cellular energy in all creatures is generated by means of electron-transfer reactions, in which electrons move from one molecule to another. In metabolic oxidation, electrons are pulled from carbohydrates and fats and shuffled through a series of reactions that extract energy from them. That energy is stored in a fuel called *ATP* (adenosine triphosphate), which is used to power our cells. At the end of the process, the electrons are picked up by oxygen molecules. Oxygen is naturally hungry for more electrons, and it does a good job of retrieving the electrons. If the oxygen picks up four electrons (along with four protons), it becomes two stable water molecules, and all is well. But if it picks up only one, two, or three electrons, an unstable, highly reactive free radical is created; a molecule desperate to bond with anything else in order to become stable. This is what makes oxidation a dangerous process, the same process that causes fires to burn, iron to rust, and fat to go rancid. As Dr. Bruce Ames, professor of biochemistry and molecular biology at the University of California at Berkeley points out, "We're all going rancid in some way." A free radical may bond to

DNA, creating a big, unwieldy lesion. When the DNA attempts to replicate itself, this lesion can cause the wrong nucleotide to attach, thus creating a mutation. In similar ways, free radicals can damage proteins, deform the fatty membranes of our cells, and even cause DNA to break apart. Scientists have calculated that each cell in a rat's body gets hit by one hundred thousand of these toxic radicals each day. Since rats have a higher metabolic rate than humans, the rate in our bodies is somewhat lower, but it still amounts to a huge daily onslaught.

The free radical theory of aging states that these radicals cause random damage to the body that accumulates over time and plays a fundamental role in the decline of physiological function. The majority of oxidative damage, it is believed, occurs in the *mitochondria*, the tiny power plants in the cytoplasm of our cells where oxidation takes place. The mitochondria have their own DNA, separate from the chromosomes in the cell nucleus. Due in part to oxidative damage, this DNA mutates at a much faster rate than DNA in the cell nucleus, and the mitochondria in general decay faster than the rest of the cell. Since the mitochondria power the cell, and thereby the body, damage to their DNA impairs the function of the entire body. And when mitochondria are damaged by free radicals, they produce even more radicals, accelerating the rate of damage. Repairing the mitochondrial DNA takes energy, and yet damage to the mitochondria reduces energy output. This lower energy output could contribute to signs of normal aging: loss of memory, hearing, vision, and stamina.

Outside factors can produce free radicals as well, such as cigarette smoke, pesticides, and even exercise. Flies confined to a small space, which limited their flying, lived twice as long as flies in a larger space. As you breathe faster, you generate more free radicals and hasten aging (aren't you glad you're sitting down reading a book?). To counter this attack, we can take antioxidants, such as vitamins C, E, selenium, and beta-carotene, which neutralize free radicals and slow oxidative damage. In studies, the life span of mice has been increased 30 percent by antioxidants.

The good news is that the body itself produces antioxidants. We have now begun identifying genes that regulate the production of these antioxidants. Dr. Thomas Johnson at the University of Colorado has discovered a gene in *Caenorhabditis elegans*, a microscopic worm, that regulates the production of two enzymes, catalase and superoxide dismutase (SOD), which serve as antioxidants. Disabling the gene increased the production of these enzymes and increased the life span of the worms by 70 percent. A similar technique might be used in the future to increase the human life span.

Now for the bad news. The rate of oxidation increases with age, and antioxidant defenses decrease with age, the natural antioxidants becoming less active. Nature keeps the repair mechanisms working only as long as she thinks necessary to ensure our survival as a species.

More bad news. Each cell is allowed only a certain number of divisions, called the *Hayflick limit*, until it is reduced to an inactive state, called cellular senescence. At the end of each chromosome is a safety cap, or telomere, which holds everything together and keeps the chromosome from fraying or being damaged. Each time a cell divides, each chromosome loses a bit off the end of its telomeres. In germ cells, these telomeres are repaired by an enzyme called telomerase (nature's investing in reproduction). But in the somatic cells—the rest of the cells in the body—no telomerase is produced, and the telomeres erode, eventually preventing the cell from dividing again. Now prevention of overdividing is good if you're young; it can help prevent cancer. Yet as you age, an increasing number of your cells become senescent. It hasn't yet been proven how these cells contribute to physiological decline, and many scientists think they don't, but the number of these senescent cells does increase with age. This erosion of telomeres is just one of many processes that can be positive early in life and cause deterioration later on. Recent research has shown that somatic cells extend their life span by twenty divisions when given the gene to produce telomerase.

You can see what a complex series of issues we face in the attempt to slow or reverse aging. The body fails for many different reasons and in many different ways. So the possibility that Dr. Ridley would have discovered a simple method of reversing the aging process seems unlikely. He could, however, have discovered how to influence one small part of it. In fact, we already know that much.

Antioxidants certainly slow the damage due to free radicals. Also, eating 40 percent fewer calories has reduced age-associated diseases in rats and extended their life spans by 30 percent. Eating less seems to result in the production of fewer free radicals, increased antioxidant activity, and less mitochondrial DNA damage. Dr. Ames admits that constant hunger has a drawback. "The rats get a little testy and will bite you."

Dr. Ames believes he has just taken a major step toward reversing the decay of mitochondria due to aging. One major source of mitochondrial impairment is damage to proteins that help the mitochondria do their job. Dr. Ames has found a way to help one of these damaged proteins keep functioning. The protein promotes a reaction in a material, or substrate, called carnetine. "Oxidation damage loosens up the proteins," Dr. Ames explains, "and they need more of a substrate to work on." Since the body is limited in how much carnetine it can produce, Dr. Ames provides more, thereby increasing the amount of substrate available to the proteins. He also provides more lipoic acid, a coenzyme that helps promote the carnetine reaction. Both of these substances, by the way, are available in health-food stores. Dr. Ames describes this process as "tuning up the mitochondria." The results are dramatic. "When we give these two to old rats, they get up and do the maccarena. These are the liveliest rats you ever saw." This technique does not repair or reverse the age-related damage, but it does eliminate the negative consequences of that damage. While we're developing many methods for slowing deterioration due to aging, actually reversing aging, as Dr. Ridley claims to have done in "Young at Heart," remains far beyond our reach.

One additional area that may be important in future aging research is nutrition. Dr. Ames believes nutritional supplements are key to extending life span. "Each human requires forty substances to make all his biochemistry go around." While we know what these substances are, we don't yet know the optimal quantities of each to maximize our life span. Future research may provide a nutritional formula for longer life. But this formula may already lie hidden within another X-file.

EAT YOUR LIVER!

Eugene Victor Tooms, a prototypical *X-Files* oddity from the episodes "Squeeze" and "Tooms," is over one hundred years old, yet he looks to be only in his twenties. He enjoys making nests out of bile and news-paper, collecting trophies from his victims, hibernating for thirty years at a stretch (no pun intended), and finding that perfect liver. In addi-tion, he's able to squeeze through some incredibly tight spots. (Why do I feel as if I'm introducing him on *Love Connection*?) His social life aside, could Tooms's secret of flexibility, long life, and youthful ap-pearance lie in his gourmet diet of five human livers every thirty years?

Many people—mothers especially—tout the nutritional value of liver. While nutritional information on the *human* liver is unfortu-nately scarce, beef liver contains huge quantities of iron, vitamin A, folic acid, vitamin B_{12}, vitamin K, and many other valuable vitamins, minerals, and amino acids. Dr. Judi Morrill at the Department of Nu-trition and Food Sciences at San Jose State University says, "Liver is a really good source of iron, and for women who are anemic, it can be good. It's a high-cholesterol food, though, so people don't eat it much now. I don't particularly recommend people eat it at all."

Liver's nutritional fame arose in the 1920s, when scientists proved that patients with pernicious anemia, arising from an often fatal vita-min B_{12} deficiency, could be cured by eating a special diet including a half pound of fresh liver per day. Dr. Michael Field, professor of med-icine and physiology at Columbia College of Physicians and Surgeons and director of the Division of Gastroenterology at Columbia Presby-terian Medical Center, explains, "The liver stores vitamins, so it can provide many vitamins if you eat it. But vitamin pills are even better sources of vitamins." Perhaps Tooms has pernicious anemia due to a de-ficiency of B_{12} and is treating himself with the high-liver diet he heard about back in the '20s. There is a genetic component to pernicious anemia, so we might theorize that this deficiency runs in Tooms's family and has led to the development of these quaint family traditions.

The problem with treating pernicious anemia with huge quantities of liver is that this diet may mask the deficiency rather than curing it. Those with pernicious anemia lack a certain substance called *intrinsic factor*, which is excreted by stomach cells and allows us to absorb B_{12}. Scientists believe pernicious anemia is an autoimmune disorder, in which the body's immune system attacks itself. In this case, the immune system attacks the specific stomach cells producing intrinsic factor, destroying them. Without this substance, the B_{12} goes unabsorbed and a deficiency arises. While ingesting huge amounts of liver may allow some small amount of B_{12} to penetrate the intestinal lining by itself—and other nutrients, such as folic acid, may cure the anemia—the underlying B_{12} deficiency may very well remain. Prolonged B_{12} deficiency causes irreversible neurological damage that may result in unsteadiness, poor muscular coordination, mental slowness, confusion, delusion, and psychosis. The last four symptoms certainly seem present in Tooms. So Tooms may be trying unsuccessfully to eliminate his deficiency through diet and growing more and more delusional and psychotic. These days a B_{12} deficiency is easily treated with vitamin B_{12} injections that bypass absorption by the intestine.

Could this diet provide any explanation for Tooms's longevity? Within the human body, a person's liver releases enzymes that help to purify the blood. So, could eating a liver help to purify your system? Unfortunately, no. The digestive process breaks down enzymes into their building blocks, amino acids, so that any protective function they once had is lost.

A diet solely of livers would clearly involve serious nutritional deficits that would prove fatal to any normal person. We are forced to theorize either that Tooms's nutritional needs are different than a regular human's, or that he gets his calcium, fiber, and other nutrients from eating a variety of foods in addition to liver. Since the first theory prevents us from drawing any conclusions, let's explore the second. Even if he is eating supplemental foods, a diet so rich in liver would introduce a harmful excess of several elements. Too much iron causes intestinal bleeding and produces large quantities of free radicals in the body, which can cause extensive damage. Too much vitamin A, called hypervitaminosis A, causes toxic effects, including irritability, headaches, irresistible drowsiness, nausea, liver damage, bone and joint pain, loss of bone mass, bone fractures, and limitation of joint motion. Eating a lot of liver ironically damages one's own liver rather than enhancing its function. The drowsiness might in some small way be tied to his periods of hibernation, but how can Tooms possibly be as flexible as he is when this condition limits the mobility of his joints?

Now that I think about it, though, I don't believe I ever saw Tooms actually chowing down on a human liver. Yes, he did leave bite marks on a victim from gnawing one liver out with his teeth, but perhaps, after he got it out, he used it in some other way. Might he be able to create some sort of injection from the livers that would benefit his health and allow him to filter out excess vitamin A? Obviously nothing has been tried like this with the human liver. If he could isolate the B_{12} from the livers, he could treat his pernicious anemia with injections as described earlier (though wouldn't a trip to the doctor's be easier?).

In addition to curing an illness, might the livers also somehow enhance his health? The liver of the dogfish shark contains a recently discovered steroid called *squalamine* that kills some bacteria and helps stop the spread of cancer. For a tumor to grow, it needs to cause nearby blood vessels to produce new offshoots to connect to it. The blood will nourish the cancer. Tumors send a message telling the endothelial cells lining the blood vessels to divide and form new vessels. Squalamine can inhibit this growth by making the endothelial cells too acidic to divide. Recent studies show squalamine slowing the growth of new blood vessels near tumors in rabbits' eyes by 43 percent. Squalamine is currently being tested for treatment of breast cancer.

Shark livers also provide *Alkyglycerol* (AKG), a family of compounds that help to produce and stimulate white blood cells, which fight infection and disease. AKG is also found in mother's milk, and serves as a natural booster to the immune system. Some scientists claim that AKG is an extraordinarily potent antioxidant that can slow aging.

Do human livers have these same beneficial compounds? Dr. Jay Moorin, chairman of Magainin Pharmaceuticals, believes that the reason we have receptors that allow us to benefit from squalamine is because we make similar substances in our own bodies. Molecular biologist Dr. Michael Zasloff, who discovered squalamine, believes that we may very well produce squalamine or a variation of it.

So if Tooms is processing these livers somehow to derive beneficial chemicals from them like vitamin B_{12}, squalamine, and AKG and then injecting himself with them, perhaps he would benefit. Whether that would slow the aging process to such a level that a man over one hundred years old would appear about twenty is doubtful, but it might help minimize those tiny lines around his eyes.

SHOULD YOU BE EXPECTING VISITORS THROUGH YOUR TOILET?

Tooms's longevity and diet aren't even his most amazing characteristics. That honor goes to his extremely flexible body. He squeezes through a six-by-eighteen-inch air vent into a business office, slithers between bars on a window, shimmies down a six-by-twelve-inch chimney (are cookies and milk the wrong snack to leave for Santa?), and even seems to cram himself into a sewer pipe, nearly coming up through a toilet after a woman tries to Roto-rooter him (renewing a recurring fear I had as a child that a mummy would come up through the toilet while I was sitting there). So how small a space can a human being fit through?

Those most skilled in squeezing and stretching are, of course, the contortionists. Many contortionists are actually "genetically different" human beings. That's why, no matter how much we stretch, some of us still can't get our legs up behind our heads. The most important components in determining flexibility are our ligaments. Ligaments connect bones to other bones, and bones to tendons. They help to hold us together. The dominant element in ligaments is the protein *collagen*, which is made of three helices of protein twisted together into long fibers. When these fibers are relaxed, they are folded up like an accordion. When you pull on the fibers by bending your knee, they unfold and stretch. The collagen produced in different parts of our bodies differs somewhat, to make parts of us more elastic, and parts more firm. Some people, though, have the more elastic collagen throughout their bodies. Their hypermobility gives them the potential to become true contortionists.

For a few people, this flexibility can become a serious health problem, their collagen so elastic and loose that joints dislocate spontaneously. Dr. Gail Dolbear, assistant professor of obstetrics and gynecology for the State University of New York Health Science Center at Syracuse, says, "The bones can slide all over, being double-jointed so to speak." This condition, called *Ehlers-Danlos Syndrome*, arises from a dominant trait that can be inherited from just one parent. Ehlers-Danlos actually encompasses a group of disorders. In one, the joints exhibit severe hypermobility, but there are few other deformities. In other disorders within the group, the syndrome can also affect the skin, blood vessels, and intestines—which use collagen to maintain elasticity—and can make them dangerously pliable. Skin can be pulled inches away from the body. It tears, bruises, and scars easily, healing in thickened, wrinkled bunches. Gaping wounds are common and difficult to close. Arteries can spontaneously rupture. Bracing is sometimes necessary to stabilize joints.

Those for whom flexibility is not a health problem, though, are able to fit into some rather tight places. The Armenian Rubber Man, who has performed with the Jim Rose Circus Sideshow, can fit his entire body through the head of a 1970's tennis racket. As Jim Rose, who was featured in "Humbug," says, "If he gains a single pound or becomes constipated, his career is over!" Smaller than standard rackets used today, a typical 1970's racket is about eight inches wide and eleven inches long, with a face of about seventy square inches, making it comparable to many of the places Tooms squeezes through in his first episode. In the sequel episode, Tooms's powers seem to become more incredible. The barred window and the toilet are extreme examples of Tooms's ability that can't be explained by hypermobility. Those two openings are smaller than the adult human head, which tends to be rather inflexible, implying that Tooms's bones are actually able to deform and then reform. No fully formed animal with a skull has that kind of flexibility. That would defeat the whole protective purpose of the skull.

Children, though, have bones that are not fully formed. Some bones, in fact, are not completely formed until the late teens. Children's skulls are made up of several different sections that fit together like puzzle pieces, with small gaps, or sutures, in between. The soft spot on the back of a baby's skull is one of the larger gaps between these pieces. Dr. Dolbear explains how these pieces can allow deformation of the skull. "When babies squeeze through the pelvis at birth, these bone plates can come closer together, and even overlap. This is at some cost, because the brain underneath could literally be squeezed to death." More commonly, only slight brain damage occurs, and the brain compensates for the damage. As the child matures, these pieces of the skull fuse, increasing the protection to the brain and eliminating any possible compressibility. If Tooms's skull for some reason did not fuse, it would allow for some compression, though with associated brain damage (which may be why Tooms doesn't seem terribly brainy).

But could he get through a standard three-inch-diameter sewage pipe? Perhaps Tooms doesn't have a traditional skeleton. A shark's skeleton is made of *cartilage*, a tough, flexible tissue. Cartilage is actually the material that first forms our own skeletons when we are embryos, before it is replaced by bone. Cartilage is made of a network of collagen fibers embedded in a firm, gelatinous substance that has the consistency of plastic. Since we already theorized that Tooms has unusual collagen, theorizing that he might have a cartilage skeleton seems to carry a certain twisted logic. Humans do retain some cartilage beyond the embryonic stage, at the ends of growing bones, at the joints, in the nose, ears, and elsewhere. This cartilage varies in flexibility, just as collagen does. The cartilage in your ear, for example, is much more pliable than the cartilage in your nose. The cartilage skeleton allows the shark the flexibility to twist around and bite. A cartilage skeleton might allow Tooms to squeeze through the barred window.

A cartilage skeleton does present several drawbacks, though. The shark is more vulnerable, since it is less resistant to compression. A porpoise ramming a shark's underbelly can damage its internal organs, or ramming its head can actually break the skull apart. A cartilage skeleton would provide poor protection for Tooms's brain and internal organs. When Tooms, in his attempt to frame Mulder for assault, whacks his face with Mulder's shoe—hard enough to leave a tread mark—he probably would have cracked open a cartilage skull. Another weakness of a cartilage skeleton is that it can't support a lot of weight. Since a shark doesn't have to stand up and support its weight, that's not a problem. But for Tooms, it would be. To support our weight, we need the framework of a hard skeleton.

So while a cartilage skeleton might provide some hint of what is responsible for Tooms's distinct talent, his skeleton—and the rest of his body—must have a unique combination of properties, perhaps due to some unusual collagen his body produces. I still can't imagine how he could squeeze through a sewage pipe, but maybe he wasn't in there at all. That toilet may just have had a really wicked clog.

ARE MUTANTS BREEDING IN YOUR SEWAGE?

He's part fluke, part man—he's Flukeman! Our final, and most radical oddity, appears to be the result of environmental factors acting on genes. The beloved Flukeman in "The Host" arises out of the radioactive murk on a Russian freighter carrying waste from the Chernobyl Nuclear Power Station. Scully theorizes that the radiation caused radical mutations that allowed DNA in human sewage to combine with fluke DNA, creating one of the most delightfully disgusting oddities on the show: a hairless, vaguely man-shaped creature with pale wrinkly skin and a perpetually open mouth. Flukeman's main goal seems to be to reproduce. He injects his larvae into a human host through his bite.

The larvae mature, are coughed up by the human host, and appear to live out their adult stage in water. Is Flukeman just an oversized worm, or is he a true radioactive novelty? I can't wait to find out . . .

A *fluke*, or *trematode*, is a type of flatworm. There are six thousand different species of fluke, and they range in size from a few tenths of an inch to four inches in length. Flukes are parasitic, usually feeding off two or three successive hosts—including humans. In each host they mature further, going through several immature or larval stages before reaching maturity or adulthood. Some attach themselves to the external surface of a host, though most attach themselves to internal organs. They use muscular suckers and hooks to form a firm attachment with the host. Most flukes are hermaphroditic, with both male and female sex organs.

Like the fluke found in the dead Russian sailor, the human liver fluke, *Clonorchis sinensis*, spends the adult stage of its life in the bile duct of a human or other fish-eating mammal. It feeds on the tissue and blood there, causes a tumorlike proliferation of the cells and may cause cirrhosis of the liver and eventually, death. To reproduce, the adult—between snacks on your liver—releases larvae in your bile duct. The larvae leave your body through your feces, and then wait to be eaten by a snail. Inside a snail, the larvae develop further through several immature forms, and finally leave the snail to burrow into the flesh of a fish, enclose themselves in protective cysts, and settle down for a nap. If you eat that fish raw, the cysts break down in your digestive tract and the immature flukes develop into adults in your small intestine within three to four days. *Clonorchis* is common in the Orient, where eating raw fish is popular. Over five million people are infected with flukes in China alone, with over forty million infected across the globe.

Flukeman's origination in sewage, then, makes some sense, since a contaminated sailor could have passed fluke larvae through his feces. In fact, flukes are highly prevalent in Russia, though their government kept this information secret until a few years ago. Those fluke larvae in the sewage, though, if acting normally, would need a snail or some other animal as intermediate host. As far as we can tell, Flukeman came into being without a host.

Since we don't really know the details of his origins, though, let's instead examine how he reproduces. His life cycle seems significantly simpler than that of a fluke. He attaches himself externally to a potential host for his larvae and injects them into a human host, where they mature. But hold on a minute. If Flukeman is having babies, should we really be calling him Flukeman? Flukewoman seems more likely. Likelier still would be that Flukie is hermaphroditic, as most flukes are, in which case the most appropriate name would be the politically correct Flukeperson. Scully says Flukie has no sex organs, but I think perhaps she just doesn't look in the right place, or doesn't recognize them when she sees them.

Back to Flukie's life cycle. Its active involvement in inserting the larvae into the host is very unusual for a fluke. The adult fluke actually does the opposite, living within a host and ejecting the larvae through the host's feces. Flukie's larvae appear to grow inside the host by feeding off the liver, a common fluke activity. Then they're coughed up by the host. We see this with the sanitation worker, who hacks up a juicy worm while in the shower. Can we find any similar mechanism in flukes?

The lung fluke, *Paragonimus westermani*, has a similar life cycle to the human liver fluke, but it behaves differently inside its human host. To mature, this fluke migrates from your intestines to your lungs, where it grows to a half inch long and produces small cysts filled with eggs. The cysts rupture, and you unknowingly cough up the eggs and swallow them. The eggs travel through the digestive system, sheltered in a protective coat, and pass out through the feces.

This seems to partially mirror what happens with Flukie's babies. After feeding and growing in the liver, they migrate to the lungs where they are coughed up and out, hopefully escaping into water. If, instead, they were swallowed—like *Paragonimus westermani*—Flukie's babies would most likely die, since they are not sheltered within a cyst that would protect them from the stomach's digestive acids and enzymes.

Since the mammal or human host always functions as the terminal host for flukes (the place where the adults live), it's unlikely that Flukie's children would seek out another host after leaving their human home. This means the young Flukies use only one host, go through probably only one immature stage, and live their adult lives outside of any host. These are processes with no parallel among flukes.

So while Flukie has a number of characteristics in common with flukes, much of its life cycle is different. Could that be from the human influence in its genes? Scully calls him a "quasi-vertebrate," suggesting similarities with humans, who are vertebrates, but the extent of any skeletal similarities is uncertain. Humans do require only a single host to mature—our mothers. Flukie is able to survive out of water and to breathe air, suggesting additional similarities with humans. But attaching to a host to transfer children, and coughing up children, doesn't quite bring human beings to mind. Though either method seems easier than human childbirth.

WHAT EVER HAPPENED TO FLOWERS AND CANDY?

Researchers Nicolaas Michiels of the Max Planck Institute for Behavioral Physiology and Leslie Newman of the Smithsonian Institution made a bizarre discovery in their recent study of the hermaphroditic flatworm *Pseudoceros bifurcus.* When this 2½"-long worm wants sex, it just rears up and stabs its neighbor with its penis. If the penis scores a direct hit and penetrates flesh, which only happens about 15 percent of the time, it will inject sperm into whatever area of the body it has stabbed. The sperm find their way to the ovaries. If the penis does not score, which is more common, the neighbor, getting into the spirit of things, will jab its own penis back. This begins an unusual type of foreplay, which the researchers have named "penis fencing." This dueling can last up to an hour, with both parties intent on playing male and the jabbing causing severe wounds. Neither one seems to be in touch with its feminine side. Perhaps a little sweet talk would help.

IS IT JUST A FLUKE?

What about the underlying premise of "The Host"? Could radioactivity spawn a new mutant life-form? Radiation has been blamed for monstrous creatures from giant ants (*Them!*) to Godzilla. Are these flights of fantasy, or is the danger real?

The Russians provided us with our best recent test case when Chernobyl Nuclear Power Station blew up in 1986. Tons of radioactive debris were released over ten days and spread across the northern Ukraine and Europe, as far as Scandinavia, Italy, and the Atlantic Ocean. Seventeen million people were contaminated to some degree. Radioactive isotopes drifted through the air, infiltrated the food supply and seeped into the groundwater. In Byelorussia levels of radioactive strontium shot up to many times their normal quantities, increasing twenty-five times in white bread, ten in milk, and six in potatoes. Some entrepreneurs sold contaminated food in violation of the law until they were discovered, causing customers serious internal contamination. The total ionizing radiation released was ten times that of the atomic bombs dropped on Japan during World War II—with a far greater longevity.

Ionizing radiation is made up of high-speed particles and high-frequency electromagnetic energy. This radiation passes through matter and causes it to ionize, breaking apart molecules and atoms, forming positively and negatively charged particles. In the human body, such radiation hits molecules and breaks them up, creating free radicals, which we know damage DNA. Radiation can create so much genetic damage that the strands that make up DNA can actually be broken. Under normal circumstances, most of the damage caused by free radicals is repaired. But with radiation, the rate of damage accelerates so much that the repair mechanisms can't keep up with it. Damage to genes critical for a cell's survival goes unrepaired, chromosomes are damaged, and eventually cells die.

Cells that divide rapidly are the first to go. Since we have two copies of each gene, if a critical one is damaged, a backup still exists to keep the cell alive. But when the cell divides, only one cell will get the healthy gene, while the other with the damaged gene, may die. Broken chromosomes are not divided correctly between two daughter cells, causing further aberrations. Since blood, bone marrow, and spleen cells divide most rapidly, people exposed to radiation often suffer from leukemia. All this genetic damage can also cause cancer. The initial effects from Chernobyl included twenty-eight deaths due to huge doses of radioactivity, with skin lesions covering over 50 percent of the body; followed by hundreds of radiation-induced thyroid tumors, particularly in children; increased infant leukemia; and an increased level of birth defects. Over ten years later, thyroid cancer in children in parts of the Ukraine is now thirty times more prevalent than before.

Researchers anxious to measure the rate of mutation in the human population faced a difficult challenge. Since the normal, functional DNA in our bodies mutates extremely slowly, any increase in the mutation rate would be so small as to be unmeasurable. But as discussed earlier, we have other DNA in our bodies, "junk DNA," which does not code for any proteins and rarely has any effect on our bodies. Since junk DNA mutates at a much higher rate, changes are easier to detect.

Scientists studied blood samples of seventy-nine families living two hundred miles north of Chernobyl. Comparing the junk DNA of children born eight years after the explosion with their parents, they found that the mutation rate was twice as high as normal: The children had twice as many genetic differences from their parents as expected. Now these junk DNA mutations were not connected to any health problems in the children, and it's unlikely they would be, since they aren't changes to functional DNA. However, this acceleration may indicate that an equal acceleration in mutation is occurring in the functional DNA.

This finding surprised and shocked researchers, since studies of survivors of the atomic bombs dropped on Japan found only somatic mutations in survivors, with no evidence of mutations in the survivors' children. Mutations can only be passed on to children, remember, if they occur in the germ cells, and germ cell mutations are much more rare than somatic cell mutations. One important factor may be that the Japanese survivors received just one huge dose of radiation, while the

Chernobyl survivors have been exposed to radioactive contamination for twelve years. Another factor may be additional pollution from other sources in the area. Whatever the reason, humans living near Chernobyl have suffered genetic damage to germ cells, which has now passed on to the next generation. The full consequences of these mutations remain unclear for now.

But some scientists believe that radiation and toxic chemicals are affecting the long-term evolution of species. The study of such multigenerational effects has formed a new field: evolutionary toxicology. Rather than studying the direct effects of radiation on the individual, the scientists of this new discipline study the indirect effects on a population. Evolution requires a variety of traits to exist within a species. This variety allows natural selection to occur, the organisms with the more favorable traits thriving, and those with less favorable traits dying off. If radiation and pollution trigger genetic mutations, then they are introducing more variety into populations and so putting the rate of evolution into overdrive.

But what are the effects of this increased variety? In most cases, the mutations caused by pollution or radiation are not helpful to the species, and so those mutated individuals are not "the fittest." They die off, ultimately lessening the genetic diversity of the species. The few remaining animals, who have some quality favorable to survival, interbreed and repopulate the area, but now the population has a more narrow genetic base, which leaves them less able to adapt to new changes in the environment. Dr. John Bickham, professor of wildlife and fishery sciences at Texas A & M, explains, "You'll go to these places and you'll think, 'Great! The animals are still alive!' But what you see are the survivors, the ones that were genetically tested and were successful. The genetic constitution of those animals may be quite different than what was there before." You may think, "So what? Now they're better equipped to survive." The problem is that while these animals may be able to survive in radioactivity, their smaller genetic base makes them less able to adapt to future changes in the environment. Dr. Bickham says, "We're only beginning to understand what happens to populations exposed to environmental contaminations."

So how likely is Flukie to arise from "a primordial soup of radioactive sewage"? Dr. Bickham says that such dramatically different mutants are "not something we see in nature. Yes, radiation produces mutations, and yes, mutations can change organisms. The more different these organisms are from their progenitors, though, the less likely that they are going to be viable." The truth is that the results of radiation are a lot less fun than Flukie, causing deterioration, illness, and death. As for whether such mutants could endanger other life, Dr. Bickham says, "It's more likely that such an organism will get eaten by something that hasn't changed rather than eating something that hasn't changed."

And that's really the case with all of our physical oddities. When our genes are horribly mutated, the tragic results die before birth or shortly after. Yet we are all mutants, and new mutations occur constantly all around us and within us, part of every life process, every breath, every birth. And with each bit of genetic chaos that infiltrates our systems, the infinitesimal chance persists that a radically different creature may one day be born and survive.

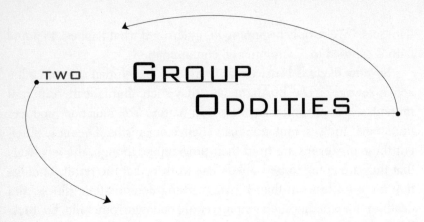

TWO GROUP ODDITIES

"They say three species disappear off the planet every
day. You wonder how many new ones are being created."

—Fox Mulder,
"The Host"

THE CLUMSY CRUNCHING OF HEAVY
boots through underbrush echoes beneath the dense canopy of trees.
Intruders have entered your forest. This is not allowed, has not been allowed for as long as you remember. They must be stopped. You move
silently on the balls of your feet, well familiar with every plant, every
fallen twig, every tree. As you stalk closer, colors play across the surface
of your skin, instantly adjusting to the light and hue of your surroundings, rendering you virtually invisible. All they might see are your red
eyes. The intruders are growing close now, heading straight toward you,
their voices strange and loud. You lay down on the ground in their path,
a living trap. You feel most comfortable here, your skin touching the
cool darkness. You close your eyes, rendering the camouflage complete, and the ground transmits the vibrations of their approaching foot-
falls. One has stopped, the second continues to approach. You will free

the woods of this scourge. You will secure your territory once again, and carry the infidels into darkness.

While some X-*Files* oddities appear to be one of a kind, others seem to be part of a group. They may be the crew of a ship isolated in an unknown land, they may be an interrelated clan or tribe, they may be members of a single family (and what family can't be described as a "group oddity"?). Traits can spread quickly through a small group, and these X-files have more than their share of bizarre ones. Eladio Buente and his brother spread fungi wherever they go; Samuel Aboah is one of the legendary "Teliko" who must suck the pituitary glands out of others; Eddie van Blundht and his father have tail-like appendages; Lanny and Leonard are detachable conjoined twins; and the Peacock family is just plain screwed up. Could humans hundreds of years old acquire camouflage pigmentation? Could a man without a pituitary gland survive by sucking the pituitaries out of others? Could conjoined twins separate at will? Let's explore how the forces of inheritance and evolution combine with genetic mutations to guide the development of groups.

IF YOU KEEP EATING THAT MUCH CHOCOLATE, YOU'RE GOING TO TURN INTO A GIANT PIMPLE

In the episode "Detour," Mulder and Scully discover some odd humanoid creatures living in the Apalachicola Bluffs and Ravines Preserve in the panhandle of Florida. This protected area is actually quite unique. Made up of two different sites totaling over 8,500 acres, this region around the Apalachicola river has unusual terrain. Bluffs of fine sand are broken by deep, straight-sided sandy ravines with streams at the bottom that drain into the river. These ravines are cooler and moister than the surrounding area and support a variety of plant life. Over twelve thousand years ago, glaciers from the last ice age were still moving south and plants native to the north were driven south before them. These plants found shelter in the ravines alongside subtropical plants. When the glaciers receded to the north, these plants remained, isolated from the rest of their species. The unusual conditions and this reproductive isolation caused them, over the course of thousands of years, to evolve into species unique to these ravines. One such plant is the Florida yew, a shrub found only in the ravines and in a single nearby swamp.

The humanoid creatures that Scully and Mulder find in Florida live underground, are intelligent, and defend their territory against incursions. They have five fingers on each hand and five toes on each foot, yet walk on the balls of their feet like animals. Aside from their red eyes, they're able to camouflage themselves, so that they are virtually invisible until they die, when they lose their camouflage coloring. In death they appear human but with prominent veins marbling their skin, almost like a leaf's.

Mulder theorizes that the creatures are Ponce de León and his crew, who came to this area in 1521 searching for the Fountain of Youth. Mulder believes they found the Fountain of Youth and, in living almost five hundred years in these woods, adapted perfectly to their environment. A trait developed in response to changes in the environment is called an *acquired character*. Could camouflage coloration be an acquired character?

We humans as a species may be very adaptable, yet the physiological adaptations we can make during the course of our lives are limited. We can become stronger or weaker depending on our level of activity, we can tan in response to the sun, we can put on more layers of fat to protect from the cold, we can develop protective calluses on areas prone to damage. But major, permanent adaptations to environmental changes occur over the course of multiple generations.

One of the few cases of possible individual adaptation, in which significant physiological changes may have occurred during an animal's lifetime, was observed in *Anolis* lizards in the Bahamas. Researchers took the *Anolis* lizards from their native island, Staniel Cay, and transplanted them to several nearby lizard-free islands. While their home island had tall trees in which the lizards lived, the new islands had only short bushy vegetation. Life in the bushy vegetation was easier for anoles with shorter rear legs, which provided increased agility. After fourteen years on the new islands, these lizards now have shorter rear legs than their ancestors. So far this sounds like a case of natural selection, in which the animals with shorter legs lived and reproduced while those with longer ones didn't. But some scientists don't believe the shortened leg lengths are genetic in nature. They believe that, as a muscle can be built through exercise, that the shortened legs could be caused by the different stresses produced on the legs by climbing over the bushy vegetation. In that case, the short legs would be an acquired character. Similarly, if the camouflage creatures began walking on the balls of their feet all the time, the muscles and tendons in their calves and thighs would adjust to these new stresses, and eventually they'd be unable to walk comfortably with their feet flat on the ground.

If aliens abducted me and took me to live on the Moon (I'll pass on the probing, thanks!), in time I would lose muscle and bone mass from living in the decreased gravity. If I happened to be pregnant while on the moon (by my husband, not an alien), my baby would develop more acquired character than I, adapting as much as physiologically possible to the new environment. Recent tests showed that pregnant rats taken into space gave birth to babies back on Earth whose inner ears had developed differently in the absence of gravity. Again, though, there are limits to how much we can change, determined by our genes, whether we live fifty years or five hundred. Living underground and walking on the balls of our feet as the creatures in "Detour" do are adaptations we could make if we had to, but red eyes and camouflage coloring aren't within the realm of possibility. Camouflage is simply not a skin-color option we have, which I'll discuss later. Mulder here seems to be reaching for the wildest theory, when one much more reasonable, and yet still amazing, is right at hand.

An alternate explanation seems implicit in the nature of the Apalachicola ravines and their plant life. Over twelve thousand years ago, when glaciers were moving south and Northern plants were moving south along with them, Indians lived in America, and they too moved south with the cold weather. Just as certain Northern plants were left behind in the ravines with the glaciers' retreat, perhaps a small group of Indians also remained in the ravines, breaking off from the rest of their tribe. Just as the plants evolved into unique species, the Indians, in this isolation, could also have evolved. If some of the Indians possessed traits advantageous in the new environment, they would be the ones to survive and reproduce, and those traits would be passed on to the next generation. Any new mutations that occurred that were helpful to survival would also be passed on. Natural selection in this unique environment would lead the evolution of the group in a new direction. These creatures appear so different from humans that they seem to be a different species. According to the evidence we have, it's unlikely that a new species can evolve in the five-hundred-year time span Mulder's theory gives us; but it could evolve in twelve thousand years. While Darwinists believed a new species took much longer than even twelve thousand years to form, the evolutionary theory of punctuated equilibrium supports the idea that the formation of a new species can happen much faster than previously believed.

Mulder cites the theory in "Leonard Betts," stating that evolutionary changes don't happen in small steps but in "huge fits and starts." Why Mulder thinks of punctuated equilibrium to explain the isolated case of Leonard Betts, rather than the long-term development of the group in "Detour," is one of those X-Files mysteries. Punctuated equilibrium describes changes occurring over many generations, not any single mutation.

The theory of punctuated equilibrium, or *punc eq*, as it's affectionately known, was first articulated in 1972 by two paleontologists, Dr. Stephen Jay Gould and Dr. Niles Eldredge. Their theory, based on fossil records, was that organisms did not necessarily evolve slowly and incrementally over tens of thousands of years, as had been thought, but instead evolved in rapid bursts over short periods that punctuated long periods without change. These short periods of change lead to the creation of a new species. This is actually what the fossil record had shown, but scientists had been convinced that the missing evidence of gradual changes—the "missing links"—were results of a flawed and incomplete fossil record. But Drs. Gould and Eldredge asserted that it was not the fossil record that was flawed, but their interpretation of it. A new species could form in a few thousand years—incredibly rapid compared to established thought at the time—and would then remain in stasis for millions of years. The theory was met with a great deal of skepticism and debate, though it's now supported by many scientists and studies.

A study of snails in the Bahamas revealed an actual transformation from one species to another in only ten thousand years. This represents a period of punctuation, or change. Other research has uncovered new species forming in as little as one thousand years. Dr. Gould, teacher of biology, geology, and the history of science at Harvard University, explains that there is no formula to calculate the time required to form a new species. "It's not like the inverse square law of gravity. There's an enormous range in time."

Other studies reveal that smaller-scale evolutionary change can occur in even shorter time periods. A study of Trinidadian guppies reveals major changes in a population transplanted to a different environment after only four years. The study focused on two different groups of guppies. One lived in pools with lots of predators who liked to eat large guppies. Another lived in pools with much fewer predators and a more secure life. Those in the first group matured more quickly and were smaller at maturity than those in the second group. They had more offspring per litter and had more litters overall. This makes evolutionary sense. The first group had adapted to reproduce more quickly, before they became big enough to be eaten. The second group was able to mature later and produce fewer children, each bigger and healthier. Guppies from the first group were then transferred to pools that had much fewer predators (and no other guppies). Within only eleven years, the guppies had become virtually indistinguishable from the second group, maturing later and having fewer children. After the guppy population adjusted to its new environment, it entered a period of stasis. There was no need for further change. The guppies evolved at a rate ten thousand to ten million times faster than that shown in the fossil record. While the guppies did not transform into a new species, they revealed that significant genetic changes can occur in short periods of time through mutations to germ cells, reproduction, and natural selection.

It can be quite easy, then, for small groups to evolve unique characteristics. These may become prevalent because they offer an advan-

tage in the local environment, or they may simply be random mutations with no particular benefit or drawback, what scientists call *genetic
drift*. The smaller the group, the easier it is for a new trait to spread
throughout it. The pressure of natural selection is stronger when the
change in the environment is greater. So, a small group of Indians, isolated in a unique environment that drives natural selection in a new direction, could be undergoing one of these evolutionary spurts. Dr.
Gould believes "Detour" comes closer to portraying a possible instance
of punctuated equilibrium than "Leonard Betts." Would twelve thousand years, or even five hundred years, be enough time to change so
drastically? Dr. Gould says, "Five hundred years is twenty to twenty-five
generations. The writers are making a reasonable attempt to come to
terms with what the theory means. They're closer there."

Would an evolutionary spurt leave them red eyes and camouflage
coloring? Probably not. But distinctive genetic traits could establish
themselves in the group. Studies of the frequency of sixteen different
genetic traits in Yanomama Indian villages in Brazil and Venezuela has
shown significant genetic differences between the small villages. Since
new villages usually form when a group of dissatisfied relatives breaks
off, the members of each new village would tend to carry similar genes,
and inbreeding would increase the chances that recessive traits would
manifest themselves in offspring. Such inbreeding increases the distinctive features of each group. One village has inhabitants much
shorter than the others, averaging only four feet, eight inches in height.
Inhabitants of another village have hazel eyes and light brown hair, in
contrast to the dark hair and eyes in the other villages. We might assume the "Detour" group was interrelated, increasing the chances that
recessive traits would manifest themselves in their offspring.

The Yanomama study also discovered some fascinating genetic differences between the Yanomama and other races. In some villages the
Indians completely lack some of the blood proteins found in humans
around the world. And in most of the villages the Yanomama have a
blood protein that exists in no other population in the world. Even so,

while the Yanomama have distinctive facial and physical features, they don't have anything as radical as camouflage coloring.

If you're wondering why a clan of genetically different American Indians in Florida might have a pole from a Spanish ship carved with the words "*Ad Noctum*," well, they could easily have killed and eaten Ponce de León five hundred years before.

PARDON ME, BUT COULD I STICK THIS METAL ROD UP YOUR NOSE?

Samuel Aboah, in "Teliko," is an African immigrant born with no pituitary gland. One of the legendary *Teliko*, or spirits of the air, Samuel must feed off the pituitaries of others. To do this, he retrieves a metal rod that he keeps down his throat, like a sword swallower, and sticks that rod up the nose of his victim. If Samuel does not feed, the pigment begins to drain from his body, patches of pale skin appearing among the dark, his hair turning blond and his eyes purple. As a kind of bonus skill, he can also fit into tight places, like drainpipes, much like Tooms.

All this fuss over a pituitary gland? Part of the endocrine system, the pituitary is a pea-sized gland—about a half inch in diameter—that secretes hormones in the body. The pituitary gland is divided into two parts, the anterior and the posterior. The anterior lobe of the pituitary secretes hormones that regulate a wide range of processes from growth to reproduction, including human growth hormone (HGH); adrenocorticotropic hormone (ACTH), which stimulates the adrenal glands; thyroid-stimulating hormone (TSH), which helps control the metabolism; and melanocyte-stimulating hormone (MSH), which affects skin pigmentation.

Could someone survive without a pituitary gland? According to Dr. Anne Klibanski, chief of the neuroendocrine unit at Massachusetts General Hospital, a person can lose pituitary function at any point in life, most commonly due to a pituitary tumor, or radiation or surgical treatments for any tumor on or near the pituitary gland. A patient may lose partial function of the gland, in which the release of just one hormone may be affected; or the function may be lost entirely, which would be equivalent to not having a pituitary at all. Dr. Klibanski says, "This condition is relatively uncommon, but certainly occurs." Even more uncommon is being born with a pituitary deficiency. But a birth defect called Multiple Endocrine Neoplasia I is a dominant inherited trait that often does not express itself until one is at least twenty, and often much later. It may give rise to a benign tumor in the pituitary, which would affect the pituitary function. Pituitary deficiencies are now treated fairly easily with synthetic hormones, which are widely available (if only someone had told Samuel!).

Since this trait is dominant, it could be passed from generation to generation within a small, isolated group, creating the myth of the Teliko. A similar situation has been documented among the Pennsylvania Amish, an isolated population that is extremely inbred. Samuel King, one of the founders of the community, introduced *Ellis-van Creveld syndrome* into the gene pool. Ellis-van Creveld is a recessive abnormality of the skeleton that includes extra digits, short limbs, a long, narrow chest, and a heart defect. The disorder is now more common among the Amish than any other group.

Could Samuel Aboah's technique of sticking a metal rod up someone's nose and somehow sucking the hormones out of the pituitary serve as an alternative treatment to that offered by modern medicine? Dr. Klibanski says, "In fact, this very technique of going up through the nose is employed in transphenoidal surgery to reach the *sella*—the bone in which the pituitary gland sits—to treat patients with pituitary gland tumors and other tumors in the sella." Taking hormones from the pituitaries of others is actually close to the treatment used in the days before synthetic hormones were available, as Dr. Klibanski explains. "Children with growth hormone deficiency were treated with growth hormone derived from human pituitary glands obtained at autopsy." The concentration of hormones is low, so that many pituitaries are needed for such therapy. Samuel would need some help to gather more victims.

Would Samuel's hormone deficiency cause him to lose pigmentation in his skin? The exact connection between the pituitary and skin pigment is still not completely understood. *Melanin* is the pigment that colors our skin, hair, and eyes. Melanin is manufactured in specialized cells, *melanocytes*, that look rather like nerve cells. They have long, branching appendages, or processes, that attach to nearby skin cells. Tiny granules of melanin are pumped out from the tips of these processes and into adjoining cells. One melanocyte can provide pigment to quite a large piece of skin.

Within the melanocytes, the production of melanin is long and complex. In mice, it is regulated by over fifty genes. The pituitary is involved in that it secretes ACTH and MSH, both of which have an effect on pigment. Overproduction of these hormones causes a darkening of the skin, while a lack of them makes the skin pallid. The skin color will not, however, become blotchy as Samuel's does. And sucking out the contents of another person's pituitary gland will not make that person lose all pigmentation instantly. First, pigment production will not completely stop in the absence of ACTH and MSH. And second, even if the stimulating hormones were sucked away, the already-produced melanin would remain in the skin cells, causing a growing pallor only over several days, like a fading tan. If the victim dies as a result of the attack, though, which is the case in this X-file, then the pituitary's lack of function would make no difference to the corpse, and it would never exhibit an unusual pallor (just the typical corpse pallor).

Now that we understand the mechanisms by which pigment is made in our skin, let's jump back to the camouflage creatures in "Detour" and explore why camouflage pigmentation is not an option for humans. Many different genetic defects can certainly lead to irregularities in human skin pigmentation, but none are anywhere close to the chameleon-like pigmentation we see in "Detour." Dr. Bryant explains that humans have only one kind of melanocytes, while lizards have many, producing pigments of radically different hues. Also, the pigment cells of lizards are connected directly to the nervous system, so that if a particular cue is perceived, the pigment cells can quickly react, extending or retracting their long processes, either making or breaking connections with surrounding cells. This can cause a gradual change in skin color. So in order to camouflage ourselves, we would need new types of pigment cells, and we'd need to wire them to our nervous systems, and we'd need the genetic instructions to operate them. Mutations that would cause this entire system to develop, unfortunately, would be unlikely in the extreme.

THE WALKING HUMAN FUNGUS

Scully and Mulder investigate a case similar to "Teliko" in *"El Mundo Gira."* A trait seems to exist within a population of migrant workers that has led to or encouraged the legend of *El Chupacabra*, the goat sucker, a creature with gray skin, a large head, and black eyes. Eladio Buente and his brother, Soledad, have this trait, which allows them to become carriers of a powerful fungus without being killed by it. Their heads swell and their skin turns gray with the infection. This superfungus secretes an enzyme that encourages the growth of any fungus it contacts. And so people begin dying from massive fungal infections. The fungi themselves are common: *Aspergillus,* which is found in compost, dust, and dead leaves; and athlete's foot. These common fungi, however, are growing at accelerated rates. So is it possible that a case of athlete's foot, jock itch, or a yeast infection could grow out of control and quickly cover our entire bodies, actually killing us?

Obviously this isn't a common occurrence. Fungi, however, are all around us. There are several hundred thousand known species of fungi in the world. They feed off of plants, animals, wood, cloth, electrical insulation, food, and even glass. Fungi break down complex products into simple ones, absorb these, and use the energy to create more fungus. About the only substances not attacked, broken down, and decayed by fungi are metals. Most fungi are saprophytes, consuming dead plant or animal matter. But some are parasites, consuming material that they take from living plants or animals that serve as their hosts. Usually fungi are found in soil, and they enter the human body through a skin puncture or by being inhaled into the lungs. Some also spread between humans or from animals to humans.

How dangerous are fungi? While some internal parasitic fungi live normally within humans and cause no harm, these fungi can sometimes grow out of control. Also, external fungi can cause infections in humans. These two different types of parasitic fungi cause about thirty different diseases. Since we have natural defenses against fungi, deaths due to fungi are rare, but they are seen in people debilitated by other diseases, a problem that is growing as the number of people with impaired immune systems increases.

In immunocompromised individuals infected with *Aspergillus*, mortality can approach 100 percent. The *Aspergillus* spores are inhaled into the lungs and the fungus grows there, invading the surrounding tissue. According to Dr. Michael R. McGinnis, professor and director of the Medical Mycology Research Center at the University of Texas Medical Branch, the fungus is attracted to blood vessels, and will often occlude or plug blood vessels, causing swelling, infection, and the death of surrounding tissue. By sending out filaments, or hyphae, *Aspergillus* can spread to other parts of the body, such as the brain.

People whose diabetes is not under control are also in danger of fungal infections, particularly by black bread molds. Black bread molds are attracted to sugar. The blood sugar level of diabetics is high, making them attractive hosts. The fungi "grow like a little rampage," according to Dr. McGinnis, and can kill a patient in twenty-four hours or less. Treatment involves surgically removing the fungus, administering antifungal drugs, and most importantly, controlling the underlying state—in this case, the diabetes—that allowed the fungus to flourish in the first place.

MISCHIEVOUS FUNGI

As Dr. McGinnis says, "Fungi have caused different kinds of mischief over the years." In nineteenth-century London, a rat infestation led to an interesting solution: add arsenic to the wallpaper paste to kill the rats. Unfortunately, the rats weren't the only ones that found wallpaper paste tasty. *Scopulariopsis*, a fungus feeding on the paste absorbed the arsenic, then released it in gaseous form and killed the occupants.

As jet airplanes were being developed, occasionally the engine would blow out and die in mid-flight. Eventually scientists discovered that *Scopulariopsis* also grows in aviation fuel, and the fungus would plug up the gas filters, eventually stopping the flow of fuel.

The threat from fungi can be more direct as well. In 1994, an earthquake near Los Angeles stirred fungi from the soil, sending spores into the atmosphere and causing 170 cases of disease. According to Dr. McGinnis, the same thing can happen on a smaller scale if you stir up your backyard compost heap.

Fungi grow relatively quickly, though not at the speeds witnessed in *"El Mundo Gira."* They can cover the surface of a three-inch-wide culture dish in two or three days, and can grow through a loaf of bread in a few days. A moderately fast-growing fungus will advance at the rate of about .0001 inch per minute. You can see it grow under a microscope. If fungi could grow as quickly as is shown in the episode—eating away the eyes and lips of Maria, Soledad's girlfriend, in mere minutes—then the health hazards would be much more serious, the fungi doing fatal damage before the immune system could mount any defense.

Fungi digest their food by means of enzymes, much as we do. The essential difference is that fungi digest most of their food extracellularly, outside their bodies, like fat-sucking Virgil Incanto in "2Shy." Fungi secrete enzymes and acids that diffuse out through the cell wall into the substrate through which the fungus is growing. These enzymes and acids then break down the substrate into simple compounds, which diffuse back into the fungus cells and furnish energy for growth. Most fungi are able to secrete a great variety of enzymes, each one breaking down a different material. Dr. McGinnis cites a case in which a patient's lungs were actually being dissolved by one of these enzymes.

Fungi reproduce by means of spores, which are so small and buoyant that a tiny current of air can carry them off and keep them airborne for miles. The smallest of these spores, less than .0002 inches long, can take up to thirty minutes to fall one foot. This means that they can commonly travel hundreds or even thousands of miles with a moderate wind. Spores of common fungi are so abundant that tons of them are drifting across the country in clouds at any given time. The most prolific fungi can produce hundreds of millions of spores within three to four days.

On the show, a mycologist discovers that the reason these fungi are growing so quickly is that they have been exposed to a new enzyme, unlike any ever seen before. Scully witnesses a startling demonstration of the power of this enzyme. When the mycologist puts two drops into a petri dish, the fungus overruns it in seconds. Scully gradually deduces that one man, Eladio, is spreading the enzyme. This means Eladio must have an unknown fungus that produces this enzyme. Unknown fungi are all around us, so that's not hard to accept (I'll discuss this more later). The next step we have to take is much harder. Eladio actually seems to be sweating or secreting this enzyme, since anything he touches experiences the rapid growth of any preexisting fungi on that surface. This means that the fungus inside of him is attempting to digest material outside of him — an impractical method of gaining food, since Eladio deposits the enzyme and then moves on before any material can be broken down and absorbed back into him. In essence, Eladio is a walking human fungus (no offense intended), secreting an enzyme that will digest material for him to absorb as food. But there's a good reason fungi don't walk. They need to hang around to collect their nutrition. Eladio's behavior is rather like that of the bulimic, who eats food and then vomits it up before it's digested. This behavior is okay for a fungus on a diet, but not for one that wants to grow. We also would need to assume that this new enzyme, unlike the enzymes we know, can digest all different kinds of materials, particularly humans and even metal (fungi grow on a water spout as a result of Eladio's touch).

The most interesting thing about this fungus is that its effect — perhaps unintentionally — is different than the effect of other fungi. The secretions of all known fungi contribute to their own growth. The secretions of this fungus contribute to the growth of other fungi. We could attribute altruistic motives to this fungus and think of it as a "helper" fungus, or we could interpret this as simply a case of the fungus trying desperately to gain nutrition and failing miserably (since other fungi are absorbing the products its enzyme has created).

Dr. McGinnis describes a patient who looked rather similar to Maria, the young woman who was the first victim of Eladio's enzyme. *Coccidioides immitis*, a fungus that lives in desert soils, infects up to 90 percent of the inhabitants of the southwestern United States and northern Mexico. Most experience flu-like symptoms and then recover, but in a few cases internal organs are infected, often fatally. In one unusual case, a patient had lesions on his skin, especially around his mouth, nose, and eyes, each of which were "jam packed" with fungus. These areas had a black, crusty look just as they do on Maria. Touching those areas or even breathing around the patient could conceivably have transmitted the fungus. The patient was kept in quarantine.

Could Eladio's fungus be of extraterrestrial origin? We'll discuss the possibility of alien life surviving on a meteoroid in chapter 5. For now, we can note that it's unlikely a fungus that has evolved on another planet would happen to find conditions in the human body favorable for its growth. In addition, if previous generations of this population of migrant workers had exhibited such characteristics, we'd have to postulate that meteoroids containing fungal spores had a habit of dropping near Eladio and his ancestors and no where else on the globe.

Additional evidence suggests that the fungus probably originated on Earth. While we have catalogued only several hundred thousand species of fungi, it is estimated that perhaps 1.6 million different species of fungi exist here on Earth. It would be much more likely that an unknown terrestrial fungus, disturbed by expanding agriculture or other changes in the environment, might enter the human population. Rain carries spores down out of the air, the first raindrops of a shower carrying many spores. So the yellow rain may have carried the spores down to Eladio.

But if the fungus is not extraterrestrial, if it is fairly common on Earth, why would Eladio carry the fungus and no one else? According to Dr. McGinnis, the genetics of a host system are linked to the genetics of a fungus. For example, in the 1970s, a new type of corn was introduced that had several desirable characteristics. What botanists didn't realize, however, was that this new type of corn was vulnerable to the Bipolaris fungus. This infection, called southern blight, nearly destroyed an entire corn crop. Changing the genetics of a host created a new opportunity for a fungus. One might imagine, then, a genetically altered crop becoming host to a previously unknown fungus. And if in place of the word *crop* we put the word *human*, then we are on our way to understanding this X-file. An inherited mutation could make someone vulnerable to a particular fungus that does not normally grow in a human host.

Might such a mutation be limited to a population of migrant workers? In fact, there is evidence that certain racial groups are predisposed to specific fungal infections. South Sea Islanders seem to have a recessive gene that allows a skin-eating fungus to grow, while other ethnic groups on the islands are not affected. The fungus *Coccidioides immitis* that we discussed earlier, common in the southwestern U.S., has a higher incidence among Asians, Mexicans, and Blacks than other ethnic groups, suggesting a genetic connection. During World War II, many Japanese-Americans were held in internment camps in the Southwest. Many of them became infected with *Coccidioides immitis*, and many died from it.

If there are genes that predispose an individual to getting a certain fungal infection, it seems fairly likely that there are also genes that might provide resistance to a fungal infection. Scully theorizes at the end of the episode that Eladio has an anti-enzyme gene, which apparently prevents him from being consumed and killed by the fungus to which he is host. Perhaps this gene—along with one predisposing him to infection—runs in his people, creating fungus carriers and giving rise over time to the legend of *El Chupacabra*.

I worry, though, that this new fungus may starve. Since Eladio's body is resistant to the fungus's digestive enzyme, the fungus is desperately secreting enzymes outside his body, trying to find something to eat. Yet other fungi are absorbing the fruits of its labor. Perhaps when Eladio sleeps or sits still, the fungus will have the opportunity to absorb some hard-earned nutrition. And then to release spores so that it can reproduce. Then who knows what will happen?

"THE FORCE HAS A STRONG INFLUENCE ON THE WEAK MINDED"

One of my favorite genetic mutants is the romantic janitor Eddie Van Blundht from "Small Potatoes." Like his father, Eddie was born with a thin layer of muscle tissue covering his entire body beneath the skin and a cute four-inch-long tail that could spin around like a piglet's. He uses the first trait to change his appearance to resemble anyone he wants, having sex with a series of women while disguised as their husbands, and with a *Star Wars* fan while disguised as Luke Skywalker. The women become pregnant, and the children are born carrying his second trait, the tail. Scully describes this caudal or tail-like appendage as a rare birth defect.

Human babies have been reported with fleshy growths on their backs ranging up to about two inches. Though these have been called "tails," they actually lack the bone and muscle characteristic of animal tails. Such a growth is basically a thickening of the skin over the sacrum or lower part of the spinal cord. This thickened area of skin can continue down over part of the buttocks, but it is attached to the surrounding skin and so lays flat against the body, unable to move. This can actually present a serious threat to the proper development of a child, since the skin mass can hamper the growth of the spinal cord. Surgery is usually used to remove the tissue connecting the skin mass to the spinal cord. Eddie's tail, then, is very unusual.

Even more unusual is the presence of a caudal appendage without any more serious birth defects. Caudal appendages usually appear in association with other genetically inherited birth defects, which involve serious deformities and are often fatal.

As for Eddie's ability to shapeshift using the unique layer of muscle beneath his skin, a muscle contraction will not change body mass, height, underlying skeletal structure, skin pigmentation, skin texture, hair color, eye color, and a host of other factors necessary for Eddie to do what he does, much as we enjoy watching it. We'll talk about this issue more in chapter 6, when we get to alien shapeshifters. Perhaps, rather than posing as Luke Skywalker, Eddie actually *is* Luke Skywalker, using the Force to make people believe he's someone else. It might be the best way to father a new generation of Jedi without anyone being the wiser.

YOU THINK <u>YOU</u> HAVE A DYSFUNCTIONAL FAMILY . . .

That prize, I'm afraid, has to go to the Peacock clan in "Home." They bury their latest progeny alive, beat the sheriff to death with clubs, and keep their paraplegic mother under the bed in a cage—and she prefers it that way. Inbreeding is a way of life for the Peacocks. They've been practicing it since Civil War times, cultivating a long lineage of deformities and disorders. They even inbreed their pigs and cows. While advantageous traits can spread quickly through a small population, as happens in "Detour," if the group is too inbred, disadvantageous recessive traits can become a serious problem. The drawbacks of a small, inbred group become apparent in "Home." The Peacock family has become horribly deformed.

Scientists have long known that the offspring of closely related parents often suffer from physical illness and mental disability. Current research confirms that these children have a higher incidence of genetic disease. Inbreeding doesn't create new genetic problems, but it reveals those that are already lurking in the gene pool. Since related couples may each carry the same negative recessive trait, the chances of a child inheriting two copies of that recessive gene—and so suffering from the recessively inherited disease—are greatly increased. How likely is it?

Each of your grandparents carries two copies of a specific gene. If only one gene in one grandparent carries a negative recessive trait, the chances of your carrying that trait are one in four. Your cousin, who shares the same grandparents, has the same one in four chance. If you marry your cousin and have a child, the chances of your child receiving the gene with that recessive trait from both you and your spouse is then one in sixteen. If your child does receive that trait from both parents, then he will express that trait.

A *consanguineous marriage*—marriage to a cousin or other close relative—was probably common practice for thousands of years, and even persists today in areas of Japan, the Middle East, and Africa (where between 20–50 percent of all marriages are consanguineous). A recent study by Dr. Muin Khoury and colleagues at the U.S. Centers for Disease Control showed that the offspring of first-cousin marriages are 1.41 times more likely to die before reaching adulthood. In a study of Japanese first-cousin marriages, Dr. James V. Neel, professor of human genetics at the University of Michigan, found that 11.7 percent of offspring of first-cousin marriages have some meaningful physical defect, whereas only 8.5 percent of the offspring of unrelated parents do. He explains, "This increase is statistically significant. It's considerably less than the popular imagination, though." Children of first cousins tend to be slightly smaller, slightly weaker, a few weeks behind in learning to walk and talk, and to score slightly lower on intelligence tests.

If parents are even more closely related than cousins, the chances of a child expressing negative recessive traits become even higher. Researchers studying cases of incest, where, for example, a father-daughter or brother-sister pairing produced offspring, found that about 20 percent of offspring died in childhood and an additional 33 percent suffered disabilities. Repeated incest over generations would only increase these numbers.

Inherited diseases can be debilitating—including hereditary deafness, blindness, cystic fibrosis, sickle-cell anemia, muscular dystrophy—or fatal. In a perverse twist of genetic fate, though, related couples are blessed with greater fertility. Scully lists some of the birth defects she sees in the buried Peacock baby, including Meckel-Gruber Syndrome and Neu-Laxova Syndrome. Both Meckel-Gruber and Neu-Laxova are believed to be caused by recessive genetic traits and so are more common in cases of parental consanguinity. Symptoms include a small, malformed head, which may be missing part or most of the brain and spinal cord, a skin-covered sac on the back of the head containing a malformed portion of the brain, and deformed limbs.

Scully suggests that the type and degree of mutations in the Peacock baby indicate that the inbreeding and the mutations go back for many generations. Dr. Neel explains, though, that it is impossible to make such a determination from the DNA of the baby alone. To find out whether mutations are new or inherited, "We would have to look at the parents."

But who are the parents? Mulder theorizes that each of the three Peacock men is father to the child. While no case of a single egg being fertilized by three sperm has been documented, there are other alternatives that would allow for more than a single father. Three fertilized eggs might fuse to form a single organism. The fusion of two fertilized eggs has been documented in a few animals, though never in humans. Or an ovum may, though malformation, have two nuclei, which may then be fertilized by two different sperm. These two fertilized nuclei then both grow and divide, contributing cells to the developing embryo, though these cells are genetically different. This condition, in which all the cells of an individual's body do not have the same genes, is called *genetic mosaicism.*

Such a case was recorded by Dr. Stanley M. Gartler and colleagues. They examined a two-year-old hermaphrodite who had one hazel eye and one brown eye. On studying the patient's DNA, the scientists found that about half of them contained female XX chromosomes, and half male XY. The left side of the body contained a normal ovary, while the right contained a hybrid ovotestis. The patient literally had the cells of two different people. This type of person, animal, or plant, which has tissues of two or more genotypes, is called a *chimera.* Chimeras may be created artificially by grafting, mixing cells of embryos, or through hybridization. Naturally occurring human chimeras are rare. In the case of the Peacock baby, we might postulate an ovum with three nuclei fertilized by three different sperm, though no such thing has been documented. And the only way Scully could make such a determination would be to find genetic mosaicism, with three different types of cells in the baby's body.

Some scientists, including Dr. Neel, believe that inbreeding does have a positive side. "Inbreeding brings to the surface and eliminates some of the bad genes that are accumulating through mutation in populations." Since many of the offspring who have inherited these negative traits do not survive, inbreeding over the course of many generations helps to eliminate these traits. However, we are now developing treatments for many of these diseases, which allows them to persist in populations. In Cyprus, beta-thalassemia, an inherited blood disorder, is so common that treating all the affected children will take up half of the entire health budget within the next ten years. Similarly, those with other inherited diseases such as sickle-cell anemia and cystic fibrosis can survive and procreate. In fact, the populations that are growing the fastest on Earth are those where marriage between first cousins is preferred. Perhaps the Peacocks will be moving in next door soon.

Or, looking at it in another way, perhaps *we* are the Peacocks. I'm near-sighted and have chronic back pain, both of which my parents passed on to me. My husband suffers from asthma and allergies that probably would have been fatal without modern medicines. I'm glad we have the medicines to treat him. On the other hand, illnesses and disorders are becoming ever more widespread in our world, as medicine overrides natural selection, and we might wonder at the long-term consequences of that.

THE EVIL TWIN

Mulder and Scully are drawn into another troubled family relationship when they meet brothers Lanny and Leonard in "Humbug." Lanny and Leonard are parasitic conjoined twins: Lanny is a full-grown adult, Leonard a child-sized, partially formed identical twin. Unlike the Peacocks' deformities, though, Lanny and Leonard's condition is probably unrelated to genetic factors. Conjoined or Siamese twins are thought to be caused by environmental factors in the womb, where a fetus is extremely vulnerable.

Conjoined twins are extremely rare, with an incidence of about one in forty thousand births—and 40 percent of those are stillborn. Conjoined twins occur when an embryo begins to split apart into twins too late to make a complete division. In all cases, conjoined twins are identical twins who develop with a single placenta from a single fertilized ovum. According to J. David Smith, dean of the School of Education and Human Services at Longwood College and author of

Psychological Profiles of Conjoined Twins: Heredity, Environment and Identity, "Any set of identical twins could have been born joined, if there had been incomplete separation." Monozygotic or identical twins occur when the zygote, the fertilized egg, completely splits in two. The zygote may split as soon as one day after fertilization. If it splits early, each embryo will be surrounded by its own protective sack of tissue. The later the zygote splits, the more surrounding tissue will be shared by the embryos. If the zygote doesn't split until after fourteen days, conjoined twins may result. By the end of the third week, either the process of normal twinning or the process of conjoined twinning will be underway.

The factors that control when the zygote splits are still unknown. One early theory posited that conjoined twins were caused when a woman wore excessively tight clothing during pregnancy. These days, conjoined twins are believed to be caused mainly by the environment within the womb, though genetic elements may also play a part. Seventy percent of conjoined twins are females, and they are more likely to occur in India or Africa. Areas of attachment can be small or large. The most common ways in which such twins are joined are at the buttocks, at the upper half of the trunk (with the two heads looking over each other's shoulders), or at the mid-trunk. Other more rare types include a cranial union only, a union of the upper halves of the body with two faces on opposite sides of a conjoined head, a lateral union of the lower half (two heads and chests, but only two legs), and a union of the pelvis. Two even more rare types are *fetus in fetu*, in which an imperfect fetus is contained completely within the body of its twin; and parasitic twins, such as Lanny and Leonard, in which one twin is incompletely formed and dependent upon the other.

As mentioned on the show, the most famous conjoined twins, Chang and Eng Bunker, were born in Siam (now Thailand) in 1811. They were joined only at the lower chest by a narrow band of flesh, 4½ inches long and 3½ inches across. Since the band was somewhat flexible, they were able to move about fairly well. Their pulses were not synchronous, and their digestive systems were separate, so that Chang, who had a drinking problem, could become drunk, and Eng would feel no effect from the alcohol—except irritation at his drunk twin. Chang was hard of hearing, while Eng had an acute sense of hearing. Chang and Eng married sisters and fathered a total of twenty-two children, with no twins, though some of the children were deaf-mutes. They all lived in the same house until the wives had a falling out and demanded two separate homes. Then Chang and Eng alternated homes, living at each for three days at a time. They lived until the age of sixty-three, when Eng was awakened in the middle of the night by a strange sensation and found Chang dead. He appears to have died from pneumonia, though some say it was a cerebral blood clot. Eng knew then that he would die. Some accounts say he died within five minutes of his twin, though others give the time as two hours. Eng complained of a choking sensation and horrible pain in his legs. As he lost strength, Eng broke into a cold sweat and asked his wife and children to rub his arms and legs. Eng's cause of death is unclear. At the time, it was attributed to fright, though scientists today feel he probably bled to death as the blood pooled in Chang's body. Doctors now feel that Chang and Eng could have been separated relatively easily, and Eng's life could have been saved.

While Chang and Eng exemplify the image most people have of conjoined twins, other types exist as well. The incidence of fetus in fetu is uncertain, since only a small percentage of these cases is discovered. The contained fetus forms a cyst in the body of its fully formed twin, usually in the brain, liver, or abdominal area. These range from complete fetuses to abcesses containing teeth and hair. In the early part of the century, a nine-year-old boy was found to contain the partly developed fetus of his twin inside his abdomen. The fetus grew too large and finally killed the boy. Last year, a sixteen-year-old teenager in Egypt who complained of stomach pains was found to actually have an undeveloped twin fetus in his abdomen. The fetus was seven inches long and weighed 4½ pounds. It had an arm and a head with teeth. Doctors operated and removed the fetus. Examination showed it had the teeth of a sixteen year old, meaning that it had been living and feeding off its twin for his entire life. An unusual recent case involves two sisters. One sister had a parasitic or partial twin conjoined to her buttock. The partially formed twin was surgically removed. Many years later, the other sister went into surgery for a bowel loop. The surgeon instead found a large fetus in fetu that had nearly filled her entire abdomen. It was removed.

Accounts of parasitic twins are rare. One documented case described a parasitic twin with a connection at mid-trunk, the head seemingly buried inside the complete twin's chest. In another case, Piramal, an Indian man who appeared in freak shows around the turn of the century had an under-formed, parasitic twin growing from the side of his chest. To spice things up, the twin was advertised as his sister, Sami, though it was actually male, since conjoined twins are always identical. Sami was made up of only two legs and an arm protruding from the side of his twin. The illusion, when you looked at them, was that Sami's head was buried inside his twin's body, but that was not the case. Sami was only a part of a body, as are all parasitic twins, not a whole.

Leonard appears to be acting more as a parasite than as a parasitic twin. Unhappy with his sibling, he's searching for a new host. Yet parasitic twins are not like a separate parasite and host; they are actually parts of the same single organism. Think of it this way: Your arm is a parasite on the rest of your body, living off the nourishment the body provides. Leonard detaching himself and crawling away is comparable to your arm doing the same. But that would be another X-file.

In our study of groups, whether as small as a family or as large as a tribe, we see that oddities needn't be lonely, and we, as mutants, have plenty of company out there. Groups can propagate negative traits for generations. They can also, though, spread positive traits and mutations. After all, mutations, over the course of generations, are what allow us to adapt, thrive, and evolve—into who knows what.

THREE UNUSUAL DISORDERS AND AMAZING POWERS

"I've had my head up my rear end for the past five years."

—Fox Mulder,
"Patient X"

AN ARREST IN A BALTIMORE WARE-house goes bad, and Special Agent Fox Mulder finds himself in the middle of a shoot-out. The dimly lit interior erupts with muzzle flashes as Mulder dives for the cover of nearby shipping containers. Bullets rip through the cardboard boxes, and multiple jets of gas shoot out. Pushing himself from the floor, Mulder inhales a huge dose of the gas. Instantly his lungs are on fire. He falls onto his back, ripping off his jacket, his shirt. He gasps for air, unable to catch his breath, his heart pounding. The floor seems to sway beneath him, the outlines of the boxes above him shifting. He rubs his burning eyes. The world seems uncertain, reality rearranging itself around him. A dark figure with a swollen, bulbous head hovers malevolently over him. Then more figures arrive, with small bodies and large heads. They move back and forth in a loudly grinding light, rearranging crates that contain his thoughts, taking them away one by one. He struggles to move, to stop them, but he cannot. They will succeed, he realizes, in emptying him completely of thought. He must warn others. A phrase comes to mind, a thought of great significance, which he must pass on to the world. "They're here. They're here. They're here."

The X-Files is filled with normal people suffering extraordinary illnesses or disorders. They contract bizarre diseases, are exposed to mind-altering substances, and are subjected to covert government experiments. The exposure or damage, which carries the amazing power to change the working of our minds and bodies, can come from all types of sources: radiation, a mysterious implant, a bullet through the brain, or alien DNA. Scully's abduction results in a nasopharyngeal tumor; Ed Jerse's tattoo causes hallucinations that ultimately drive him to murder; pesticides send the people of Franklin, Pennsylvania, on a series of spree killings; alien pheromones nearly make Scully do "the wild thing" with a stranger. These situations threaten our belief that we control our own lives and impulses. Could a tattoo drive someone to murder? Could the removal of a tiny implant cause cancer? Could aliens release pheromones so powerful that they are sexually irresistible? Might Mulder die of autoerotic asphyxiation?

CANCER WOMAN

The condition we care most about, of course, is Scully's cancer. We discussed cancer in chapter 1, in connection with our talented friend, Leonard Betts. Unfortunately, cancer now threatens Scully's life. In "Memento Mori," Scully discovers that she is suffering from nasopharyngeal cancer. She first seeks treatment from the untrustworthy Dr. Scanlon, who has unsuccessfully treated Betsy Hagopian and the other MUFON members. Later, in "Redux II," she receives an experimental treatment from Dr. Zuckerman and has an implant, identical to the one that was earlier removed, inserted in its place. Three possible theories are offered for the cause of Scully's cancer: It may be the result of having the microprocessor at the base of her skull removed, of radiation treatments received while she was abducted, or of her DNA being hybridized with DNA from chimera cells. Before we examine the possible causes, let's first take a look at nasopharyngeal cancer.

Behind the nose, the *nasopharynx* is the upper section of the throat, or pharynx. The nasopharynx is connected to the nostrils and also to the ears. Nasopharyngeal cancer is rare among those of European descent, with a rate of less than one case in 100,000, and it rarely occurs before age fifty. Early symptoms may include bloody nasal discharge (as Scully experiences), trouble breathing or speaking, frequent headaches, a lump in the nose or neck, and ringing in the ear or trouble hearing. This type of cancer most often starts in the throat near the mouth and then moves upward.

The prognosis for those with nasopharyngeal cancer is not good, because this cancer often goes undetected until it has spread to other areas, such as the lungs, liver, or bones. Treatment usually involves a combination of techniques, including radiation therapy and chemotherapy, as suggested for Scully by Dr. Scanlon, as well as surgery and immunotherapy. Although Scully claims surgery is not an option, surgery is sometimes used as part of a larger treatment plan, though the position of the tumor makes it difficult to reach. The survival rate for cancer of this type is around 45 percent.

Dr. Scanlon claims that he intends to treat Scully with gene therapy on p53. As we learned in our earlier discussion, p53 is a tumor-suppressor gene, which, when it is functioning correctly, monitors the DNA in a cell for damage or mutations, helps stop cancerous cells from dividing, and induces cell suicide if the damage cannot be repaired. A mutation in p53 that prevents the gene from working correctly is found in many different cancers; however, it has been found in only a very small percent of nasopharyngeal cancers. This makes Dr. Scanlon's treatment even more suspect than it already seems.

Let's put that aside for a moment, though, and examine how gene therapy might be used to treat cancer, since this technique becomes important in other episodes. Gene therapy is an experimental treatment in which doctors attempt to replace a faulty gene with a fully functioning one. If a healthy p53 gene could be inserted in place of a defective copy, it could cause cancer cells to destroy themselves, leaving only healthy ones.

To deliver the replacement gene, scientists need a vector, an agent that transfers genetic material from one location to another. Luckily, nature provides a very efficient vector: the virus. A virus is basically a set of genes held together in a protein envelope, and its job is to invade cells, express its genes there, and replicate. To use a virus for gene therapy, scientists first neutralize the virus, making it harmless, then insert the correct gene into the protein envelope, and the envelope into the patient. Theoretically, the virus then infects the patient, inserts the gene into the cells, and the new gene replaces the flawed version.

So far, though, the theory has outpaced the execution. In practice, scientists haven't yet figured out how to insert the new gene into our DNA exactly in place of the old. Instead the gene will attach itself randomly to a preexisting chromosome, leaving the flawed version in place. Though this theoretically may be enough for the treatment to work, there are other problems. The new gene may splice itself into existing genes at a spot that disrupts healthy genes, just like some viruses, creating a possible danger of cancer or other illness. Or it may splice itself into a dormant region of a chromosome where it will never be activated. Sometimes the gene may not splice itself to the old genes at all but simply sit separately in the nucleus. In those cases, the new genes seem to shut off after a while.

Another problem is that we cannot yet direct the vectors to the specific cells that need them; our protein envelope has the wrong address on it. Viruses can only enter a cell if the proteins projecting from the surface of their envelope find matching receptors on the cell (the round peg has to go into the round hole). That allows the envelope to attach to the exterior of the cell, and the viral DNA to enter the cell. Scientists are now working on altering the envelope to target the cells it can enter.

And there is yet another problem. In many cases the body's immune system recognizes the invasion of the viral envelope and attacks the virus and the modified cells, inactivating their new genes.

Scientists, though, are working to turn this problem to their advantage. Rather than using gene therapy to repair a flaw, they want to use it to mark the flawed cells so that they will be destroyed by the immune system. Since the immune system does not always recognize cancer cells as enemies, scientists would insert genes that "tag" them for the immune system, making them clearly visible as invaders to be destroyed. This sounds like the type of therapy Scully may be receiving from Dr. Zuckerman in "Redux II." While gene therapy remains quite experimental, isolated cases have shown tumor regression, so this type of treatment may be helpful for Scully.

But how did she get such an unusual type of cancer in the first place? From our "Leonard Betts" discussion we understand the general causes of cancer, but scientists are still struggling to discover what specific factors give rise to nasopharyngeal cancer. Researchers have linked its development to the Epstein-Barr virus (EBV), which grows in the salivary glands, theorizing that a single EBV-infected cell may initiate this type of cancer and may contribute to the abnormal growth of cells. I wonder if Scully's been tested for EBV. Other suspected contributing factors include genetic predisposition, smoky surroundings, foods— such as salted fish, sausage, or duck—and herbal medicines. None of these have been connected to the abduction experience thus far (although we might imagine it: "Prepare for the mind probe, Earthling! And eat this salted fish!").

One of the possibilities mentioned on the show is that Scully's DNA has been hybridized with viral DNA from chimera cells such as those found in "Redux." My guess is that the virus mentioned is the alien retrovirus. We'll discuss these chimera cells later in our discussion of hybrids; right now they're really unimportant. The important component is the alien virus that appears to be growing in these cells. The DNA of the virus matches DNA in Scully's cells, suggesting that she was infected with this virus at some point in the past. Since the Epstein-Barr virus has been associated with nasopharyngeal cancer, it's not too difficult to imagine that this alien retrovirus might have contributed to Scully's cancer. We know that retroviruses insert their genes permanently into our chromosomes and cause genetic disruptions and damage. All retroviruses also appear to contain proto-oncogenes, so their presence increases the number of sites that, if damaged, can lead to cancer. The possibility that the alien retrovirus caused Scully's cancer then seems reasonable.

Another possible cause mentioned for Scully's cancer is the high amplification radiation she was exposed to during her abduction. This radiation allegedly stimulated superovulation, allowing her abductors to harvest all her ova and use them for all sorts of mischief. How can we tell if radiation might lead to a nasopharyngeal tumor?

Well, the good old U.S. government has lent a helping hand. From 1943 to the mid-1960s, over 20,000 U.S. servicemen and up to 400,000 children and other civilians were treated with nasopharyngeal radium irradiation. The servicemen—U.S. Army Air Force flyers and Navy submariners—were treated to help them cope with changes in air pressure due to takeoffs and landings, diving and surfacing. These repeated changes often caused *otitis media*, or inflammation of the middle ear, resulting in pain and temporary hearing loss. Radium capsules delivering high doses of radiation were inserted into the servicemen's nasal passages to shrink adenoid and lymphoid tissues (Do I detect the Cigarette-Smoking Man's hand?). During this same time, children were also given similar treatments at a hearing loss clinic. A follow-up study of these children shows that they have suffered from 5.3 times as many head and neck cancers than the general population. So there seems to be evidence that radiation may have contributed to Scully's tumor. And if we combine the radiation with the retrovirus discussed above, Scully's chances of cancer are even higher. If the alien retrovirus introduces proto-oncogenes, and the radiation damages genes, it could convert the proto-oncogenes to oncogenes, sending Scully on her way to getting cancer. And there's more.

The children subjected to the government tests also suffered an incidence of Graves' disease, a thyroid condition, 8.6 times the normal rate. This suggests that the thyroid suffered radiation damage. But the thyroid, wrapped around the trachea in the neck, is relatively distant from the site of radiation. Scientists theorize that the Graves' disease may have been caused not by direct radiation damage to the thyroid, but by damage to the pituitary gland, which is much closer to the area of radiation. (Remember the pituitary can be reached by sticking a metal rod up someone's nose.)

The pituitary, as we know, regulates a number of other glands, including the thyroid. It produces thyroid-stimulating hormone (TSH), which controls the thyroid's secretions. Graves' disease occurs when the thyroid produces excessive amounts of thyroid hormone. Thus Graves' disease may have been caused by excess production of TSH by the pituitary. The radiation stimulated excess pituitary activity, which in turn stimulated excess thyroid activity.

Why do we care? Because if Scully's radiation treatments had a similar effect, the increased pituitary activity could have some very interesting consequences. TSH isn't the only hormone produced by the pituitary, and likely wouldn't be the only one excessively produced. Two others are follicle-stimulating hormone (FSH) and luteinizing hormone (LH), which in women work on the ovaries. In fact, these are the two critical "fertility drugs" used by doctors to stimulate superovulation in women. So radiation applied to the nasal passages could theoretically be responsible for both Scully's cancer and her superovulation.

When women wish to undergo in vitro fertilization, doctors treat them with high doses of the naturally occurring hormones FSH and LH. While normally FSH and LH, in their monthly cycle, cause the maturation and release of one egg, this hyperstimulation of the ovary causes about twenty-five eggs to mature. The embryonic eggs grow and mature within *follicles*, sacks that grow to about ¾ inch under the influence of FSH and LH. When the sacks reach this size, the doctor administrates human chorionic gonadotropin, which initiates ovulation. As ovulation is about to occur, the doctor goes in to remove the eggs. Dr. Michael Tucker, an embryologist at Reproductive Biology Associates in Atlanta, explains the process. "An ultrasound probe is brought up against the ovary and used to observe what's going on inside. You get a television picture of a gray area filled with fluid-filled dark sacks. These are the follicles. Then you pass along the probe a fine hollow needle. The end of the needle is attached to a pump that will aspirate fluid. Controlling the pump with a foot pedal, you rupture each follicle and suck the egg out. It's like a video game."

While there may be up to forty thousand primordial follicles, or potential eggs, within a woman, this hormone treatment stimulates only a small percentage of them to grow. Dr. Tucker recalls that the highest number of eggs he ever got from a patient was seventy-two.

After treatment, women commonly return to normal ovulation within a month. The superovulation procedure has no long-lasting effects.

Why Scully's abductors may have used radiation rather than fertility drugs is unclear. Even if radiation to the pituitary might prove an alternate method of stimulating superovulation, doctors currently find it easier to disable the pituitary during fertility treatments, so that the gland doesn't get confused by conflicting signals. Dr. Tucker explains that by first flooding the system with another drug, gonadotropin releasing hormone analog, the pituitary can be shut down, so "we can play our own tune on the woman's ovaries."

Radiation, in general, is "very, very bad for ovulation," according to Dr. Tucker. It can destroy the primordial follicles, which would prevent more eggs from maturing. Women undergoing radiation therapy for cancer have a high potential for becoming sterile, even if the part of the body radiated is far from the ovaries. Many are now having their ovarian tissue removed and frozen before radiation treatments, so that afterward their fertility can be reconstituted.

While the government's radiation tests seem to give some credence to the idea that radiation can stimulate pituitary function, in general the opposite has been shown to be true. Radiation generally cripples or destroys the pituitary, so that it would release less LH and FSH, not more.

Radiation, though, might work another way. Women can experience stress-induced ovulation, which is why many women get pregnant from rape. Dr. Tucker admits, "It's vaguely conceivable that some sort of radiation stress to the system might induce ovulation of that nature."

These eggs, by the way, can now be frozen for later use, as shown on the show. While sperm and embryos have survived freezing for some years, the first case of an egg remaining viable after freezing was reported just last year. Superovulation was induced in one woman, the eggs were frozen, then later thawed and used to impregnate an infertile woman.

The final suggested cause of Scully's cancer is the removal of the implant at the back of her neck. This suggests that the implant was providing some sort of protective effect, preventing or slowing the growth of cancer. When the implant is removed, the cancer grows. When the implant is returned, the cancer goes into remission. While we don't yet have such control over cancer, we do have implants that aid in the treatment of brain cancers and that are being developed for many different types of cancer.

For the past ten years, Dr. Henry Brem, director of neurosurgical oncology at Johns Hopkins, has been experimenting with polymer wafer implants. These dime-sized wafers contain drugs traditionally used in chemotherapy for cancer, such as carmustine, which interferes with DNA replication when cells divide. Since cancer cells divide more rapidly than other cells, carmustine causes the most damage to them. Dr. Brem inserts the implants as part of the surgical procedure that removes the brain tumor. He shaves the hair from just a half-inch patch of scalp, revealing the skull, and makes a small incision in the scalp. Then he drills small holes half the size of a dime in the skull, connecting the holes so that he makes a small door of bone in the skull that he can lift out. This exposes the *dura*, the leatherlike covering of the brain, in which he makes a tiny incision. If the tumor is not visible, he uses a computer system loaded with previous magnetic resonance images of the head. The computer system displays images of the exact area where Dr. Brem is working, serving as a guidance system to reveal the safest, shortest path to the tumor. Once he has reached the tumor, he uses a *Cavitron*, a device that vibrates the soft cancerous tissue, loosening and irrigating it. He then uses an aspirator to suck up the cancerous tissue, precisely guiding the instrument both visually and through the use of ultrasound. After removing as much of the tumor as is safe, Dr. Brem lines the newly created cavity with up to eight wafers. The polymer wafers biodegrade, slowly dissolving layer by layer, like a bar of soap, over two to three weeks, delivering time-released drugs to kill the remaining cancer cells.

Patients can go home four days after surgery, with only a tiny incision. Patients who receive the wafers have three times the survival rate of those who don't. So far, the use of the implants has been focused on brain cancers, because these are particularly difficult to treat with chemotherapy. Traditional chemotherapy, administered intravenously or by mouth, exposes the whole body to dangerous drugs like carmustine, which damage not only cancer cells but other rapidly dividing cells in the bone marrow, digestive tract, and reproductive system. In fact, the brain receives the least amount of these drugs. Chemicals entering the body through ingestion or injection have a hard time entering the brain because the endothelial cells that line our blood vessels are packed much more tightly together in the blood vessels of the brain, creating a protective shield called the blood-brain barrier. These cells regulate the passage of materials in and out of the brain. This means only a small amount of the chemotherapeutic drugs breach the barrier and reach the tumor in the brain. Implanting the wafer directly into the brain allows the full power of the chemicals to work on the tumor, and prevents the severe, negative side effects of chemotherapy on the rest of the body. Because the implants are a more direct and effective way of treating cancers, they can potentially be used on many different types of cancer, including nasopharyngeal cancer.

A variety of drugs are being tried in implants, and a variety of sizes, some much smaller, are being developed. Dr. Robert Langer, professor of chemical and biomedical engineering at Massachusetts Institute of Technology, who developed the polymer wafers in conjunction with Dr. Brem, has now developed nanospheres only forty billionths of an inch in diameter that can deliver as much dosage as a dime-sized wafer.

These nanospheres can be administered intravenously or possibly even orally. Dr. Langer is now working to develop a method of controlling the rate of release of the drugs and targeting the location of release.

So how do these implants compare to Scully's? Scully's implant is at the base of her skull not in her nasopharynx, and it doesn't appear to be impregnated with or carrying a chemical that might affect her cancer. According to Agent Pendrell, it's a tiny microprocessor. This implant might, however, send a signal to a second, undiscovered implant in the nasopharynx, only a few inches away, telling it to "release medicine" at regular intervals. This second implant could even be microscopic, like Dr. Langer's nanospheres, which could be why it has not yet been detected. There's an important advantage to inserting a controlling mechanism for drug delivery. If the implant is ever removed—meaning your abductee has caught on to you—the signal stops, the medicine is no longer delivered, and the abductee is killed. A handy device. Is it within our reach?

In fact, both magnetic fields and electric currents are being used to control release rates of implanted drugs. For magnetic control, a special elastic polymer implant is created that includes magnetic beads. When an oscillating magnetic field is externally applied to the patient, the pores in the polymer expand and contract, pumping out drugs. Dr. Langer imagines the magnetic field could someday be applied through a preprogrammed wristwatchlike device worn by the patient. Or perhaps a magnetic field could be applied covertly as an FBI agent passes through the metal detector at the entrance to the J. Edgar Hoover building.

In the case of an electric field, a small battery power pack is implanted in an easily accessible location, perhaps below the collarbone, and a wire runs from the power pack to an electrode attached to a specially designed polymer wafer at the site where treatment is required. Unlike the time-release implants, this wafer does not normally dissolve in the human body. The electric field breaks apart the body's water in contact with the surface of the wafer and causes a pH increase, triggering the disintegration of a portion of the polymer. The drug is only released when the electric field is applied.

While we're getting close to explaining how the removal of Scully's implant may have caused her cancer to grow, neither of the options on page 72 involves two completely separate implants, as we are postulating for Scully. Could an implant like the one on the back of Scully's neck be designed to control the release of a separately implanted drug, perhaps by periodically sending out an electric pulse? Such an implant would need a power source and a transmitter. Dr. Brem finds this arrangement perfectly reasonable. "Absolutely. That's being developed right now."

We'll discuss some examples of this technology in our final chapter, when we examine the other phenomena associated with *X-Files* implants. You'll be frightened to learn what is within our reach.

JUST BECAUSE I'M PARANOID, THAT DOESN'T MEAN THEY'RE NOT OUT TO GET ME

Implants are only the tip of the iceberg when it comes to covert government activities. In several episodes we see government experiments producing mind-altering effects on civilians. These experiments involve ergot, a form of the fungus *Claviceps purpurea*. In "Unusual Suspects," the government has created ergotamine histamine gas, which causes anxiety and paranoia and convinces Mulder that little green men have invaded a Baltimore warehouse. In "Blood," a pesticide derived from ergot, lysergic dimethrin, evokes intense fear in humans and causes normally mild-mannered people to become mass murderers. Ergot even manages to cause problems without the government's help. In "Never Again," Ed Jerse gets a tattoo with ergot-contaminated ink that seems to change his personality. He hears the tattoo, a winking woman's face, talking to him. The tattoo's words poison his mind, driving him to kill his downstairs neighbor and to nearly kill Scully.

Let's take the simplest case, of Ed Jerse's tattoo, first. Scully discovers that her potential boyfriend's blood contains an ergot alkaloid,

which causes hallucinations and bizarre behaviors—a documented
condition known as hallucinogenic ergotism. How did this ergot get
into his blood?

The Russian tattoo artist says he makes his special red ink from rye
and other grasses. The problem is that the ink not only contains rye, it
contains ergot. According to Gail L. Schumann, a plant pathologist at
the University of Massachusetts at Amherst and author of *Plant Diseases: Their Biology and Social Impact*, ergots are actually "hard, pur-
plish black, grainlike structures produced by *Claviceps purpurea.*" This
fungus grows as a parasite on grains such as rye, and when the grains
are harvested, the ergots are harvested with them. The Russian could
easily have collected both, creating contaminated ink.

The great threat of ergot historically has come not from tattoo ink,
though, but from rye bread. When the contaminated grain is milled,
the flour then contains toxic alkaloids produced by the fungus, alkaloids that can cause illness in people. While these days the ergots are
separated from the grain before milling, ergotism was a common disease in the Middle Ages, caused by the regular ingestion of contaminated rye bread. The rural poor, who depended on rye bread as a staple,
suffered from mass outbreaks of what they called Holy Fire or St. Anthony's Fire.

Ergot stimulates the medulla oblongata in the brain stem, and so
in its early stages causes psychiatric symptoms, such as auditory and
visual hallucinations, delusions, confusion, and bizarre behaviors.
Schumann describes these hallucinations as "rainbow visions and dis-
tortions. Like looking through a prism or looking at a road on a hot day
when everything shimmers." Ergot can cause temporary or permanent
psychosis. Common in these cases is fear of enemies, even panic.

Those with high levels of ergot suffer from nervous dysfunction, including muscle spasms, writhing, tremors, and frequently fatal convulsions. In a variant of the disease, Schumann says, "People described the
feeling of burning skin or insects crawling under their skin. Severe
cases resulted in gangrene infections due to constriction of blood vessels in the extremities; many victims lost hands and feet."

Since a family would eat from a common loaf of bread, often symptoms were shared by household members, suggesting to doctors that the problem was an inherited mental disorder. Others attributed the odd behavior to sinfulness, thus the name Holy Fire. Those suffering from these odd behaviors would often go to the monastery to repent, where, amazingly they would be cured of their affliction. The cure is not so amazing, however, when you consider that most people could afford only rye bread, while the monks, often somewhat better off, ate white. What puzzled the monks, though, was that all their acolytes would revert to their sinful ways as soon as they went home. Some historians believe that those accused of witchcraft in France, Germany, and possibly even in Salem, Massachusetts, at the infamous Salem witch trials in 1692, were simply suffering from delusions caused by ergot-infected grain. Sometimes an entire town would go mad for a few days. Dr. Mary Kilbourne Matossian, author of *Poisons of the Past: Molds, Epidemics, and History*, theorizes that ergotism helped trigger the Great Fear of 1789 in France, which contributed to the French Revolution. Ergot alkaloids have also been found in morning glory seeds used by the Aztecs in shamanic rituals.

Ergot's ability to constrict blood vessels makes it a useful drug, and ergot is used today in a number of pharmaceuticals, including methergine, which is given to most women after childbirth to stop postpartum bleeding; and ergotamine, which is prescribed for migraines because it contracts blood vessels in the head. But ergot is most famous for its hallucinogenic properties. As Peter Webster, librarian at the Psychedelic Library website, explains, experiments conducted to synthesize the various alkaloids in ergot led to the creation of d-lysergic acid diethylamide, or LSD. "*Lys* means to split, and *ergic* means acid of ergot, thus lysergic acid is the acid you get when you split ergot."

LSD is one of the most potent mind-altering chemicals known, distorting perception and causing profound visual and auditory hallucinations. How exactly does it work? Scientists remain uncertain. LSD somehow leads to accelerated firing of the neurons of the locus coeruleus, a region of the medulla oblongata, where the effect of ergot is centered. A similar though less dramatic acceleration occurs with any kind of sensory stimulation. Thus LSD somehow acts like a super sensory stimulant. This would explain why LSD seems to heighten sensory experience and why senses sometimes seem to blend together, so that people "see" sounds and "hear" sights. The locus coeruleus is a unique structure, containing the nuclei of a mere three thousand neurons, compared to billions in the cerebral cortex. Yet these neurons have long axons that reach into every part of the brain, branching numerous times to touch at least one third of all brain cells. The accelerated firing of these neurons releases large quantities of norepinephrine, one of many neurotransmitters that allows neurons in the brain to communicate. These neurotransmitters carry neural signals across nerve synapses and muscle connections. Norepinephrine changes our level of awareness, causing a state of extreme alertness that might feel like a transcendent state to the user. It is also believed to have a strong influence on our emotional response to environmental stimuli.

While LSD only remains in the brain for twenty minutes, the effects of LSD, triggered by the chain reaction described above, begin twenty minutes after that and last up to twelve hours. At doses of only one hundred to two hundred billionths of an ounce, it significantly alters perceptions, mood, and psychological processes. Light seems brilliant, colors vivid, details sharp. The user often feels flooded with experience and sensation. His sense of self may be altered, so that he feels one with an object, or with the universe, or feels completely empty. Physical effects also occur, including muscle weakness, numbness, nausea, increased blood pressure and heart rate, and impaired coordination. At these low doses, though, the user is aware that any hallucinations are just that.

But on a "bad trip" or at high doses, the user can lose that awareness. Hallucinations can then become terrifying, causing confusion, anxiety, paranoia, panic, aggression, and possible violence. Time, distance, the senses, past and present can all become confused. Dr. Albert Hofmann, the chemist who discovered LSD, describes his first accidental contamination: "Everything in my field of vision wavered and was distorted as if seen in a curved mirror. . . . Pieces of furniture assumed grotesque, threatening forms. . . . The lady next door, whom I scarcely recognized, . . . was no longer Mrs. R. but rather a malevolent, insidious witch with a colored mask." Sounds a lot like Ed Jerse's perception of his downstairs neighbor, who he believes is trying to drive him crazy. To the user, seconds may seem like hours, or an old memory may seem as if it's happening now. Pathological mental conditions or latent psychoses can be intensified, sometimes leading to accidental death, suicide, violence, and murder.

A bad trip is a temporary reaction, lasting less than twenty-four hours; LSD psychosis is a more long-term reaction, lasting days, months, or even years, that can be triggered by just one exposure to LSD. These long-term reactions may include paranoid delusions, hallucinations, overwhelming fear, and schizophrenic breaks. A history of mental illness or a greater exposure to psychedelic drugs makes LSD psychosis more likely, but they are not necessary. LSD psychosis can occur in previously well-adjusted people.

Could ergot in tattoo ink cause Ed Jerse to believe his tattoo is talking to him and drive him to murder? Webster believes the quantities in a tattoo would be far too small to have any effect. But if the ergot was present in sufficient quantities, could it create such a reaction? Schumann admits, "It's possible. People do a lot of weird things on LSD too."

IT'S GOT TO BE GOOD FOR SOMETHING

One of the weird things people tend to do on LSD is to tell secrets when asked. The CIA discovered this in 1951 when they began testing LSD. Since they'd been looking for a truth serum to use during the interrogation of spies for many years, they embraced LSD enthusiastically. Soon they learned, though, that the "truth" obtained from those on LSD didn't have much relationship to reality. And overwhelming anxiety would sometimes keep their subjects from speaking at all. The CIA then looked for alternate uses for the drug. They considered for a while having their own soldiers take the drug when captured, so that anything they said in an interrogation would be bizarre and undependable (rather like what the Men in Black say in "Jose Chung's *From Outer Space*"). This idea didn't last long either, but the CIA didn't give up on LSD.

Later the agency realized that LSD could produce terror in people if they didn't know what was happening to them. It made them anxious and crippled their ability to handle the anxiety. This might leave them open to brainwashing. Unfortunately for our luckless secret agents, the brainwashing also proved ineffective. The CIA continued conducting numerous tests on unwitting mental patients, CIA agents, and civilians. And the CIA wasn't the only government agency interested. The army felt LSD could have a place on the battlefield, disorienting the enemy and driving them mad. Tests were done on soldiers to see if they could operate under the influence. The army considered releasing LSD in the air, or contaminating a city's water supply. Inhalation was not found to be very effective, though. And by the mid-1960s, the CIA and the army had moved on to more promising drugs.

In "Unusual Suspects," the government has created ergotamine histamine, a substance to be delivered through asthma inhalers, which causes anxiety and paranoia. While this seems consistent with some of the applications considered for LSD in the past, the method of delivery seems impractical. Only those with asthma would be affected. If the goal is to drive an individual with asthma to paranoia, then this might be an effective method of delivery; if the goal is to drive a city to paranoia, then this test would obviously fail. A much more effective and easily delivered agent of widespread paranoia would be a television show dealing with malevolent government conspiracies and secret tests. But what network would ever let that on the air?

Let's take a look at what the government has created here. After a dose of this stuff, Mulder hallucinates that government agents, including X, are aliens and raves incoherently for several hours. This psychedelic delusion is certainly a reasonable reaction to LSD or another ergot derivative that contains hallucinogenic properties. Ergotamine itself, however, does not contain hallucinogens, but only contracts blood vessels. By leaving Mulder naked and raving, X causes the police to disbelieve him, just as the CIA had thought to drug their own soldiers so their statements during interrogations would be undependable. Mulder seems to recover to his old self in a few hours, yet some people suffer from LSD flashbacks, and perhaps ergotamine histamine also has recurrent effects, which might explain some of Mulder's wilder theories.

The inclusion of histamine in the drug, though, poses some problems. Histamines are chemical messengers in our bodies. We're most aware of them when they're released as a defense against irritating agents in the environment or injuries. Those who suffer from allergies produce histamines as part of their immune response to allergens like dust or pollen. Histamines cause inflammation and swelling of the sinuses and eyelids (which is why we take antihistamines to block the activity of histamines). Histamines play a role in asthma as well. In asthma attacks, irritants such as cold air, smoke, or allergens cause a violent hyperreaction by a network of immune cells in the lungs. Histamines and other substances are released, and in the lungs histamines cause the contraction of the smooth muscle of the bronchial walls. In a severe attack, the asthmatic's chest begins to heave, and his coughing and wheezing become uncontrollable as he makes frantic efforts to breathe. This rapid constriction of the bronchial walls, in concert with the swelling of bronchial tubes and the secretion of mucus, can stop breathing.

Asthmatics in the midst of an attack will use an inhaler containing a bronchodilator to relax the muscles around the airways. If they instead use an inhaler containing histamines, the exact opposite reaction will occur, the muscles contracting further. Dr. Abraham Sanders, associate professor of clinical medicine at Cornell University Medical College, says, "It may make them worse, it may kill them." If the asthmatic is incapacitated or killed, the hallucinogenic properties of the drug would be irrelevant and their extent unproven. As it is, of the twelve million people with asthma in the U.S., about five thousand die each year of asthma-related complications. And the death rate has been increasing dramatically in recent years. I wonder why. . . .

DOES MISS PIGGY HAVE A SECRET POWER OVER KERMIT THE FROG?

We stumble across another government test in "Blood." The apple and cherry tree groves surrounding Franklin, Pennsylvania, are being sprayed with an alleged pesticide said to kill the Eurasian cluster fly. The pesticide is supposed to act as a natural pheromone, evoking a fear response in the flies and telling them to get away from the groves. This so-called pesticide actually evokes fear in the townspeople instead; and when various electronic devices display messages urging them to violence, they are pushed over the edge to mass murder.

Might such a pesticide contain pheromones, as claimed? Pheromones are actually being used to help control pests. Aphids infesting lettuce are very difficult to kill, because they all group at the center of the plant, where they are sheltered. Scientists decided to use the aphid's alarm pheromone to try to get the aphids to leave the heart of the lettuce. As we'll discuss in more depth later, a pheromone is a chemical that allows communication between members of a species and elicits a specific response, such as mating behavior. The alarm pheromone communicates fear from one aphid to others, warning them that they are in danger and causing them to flee. Scientists isolated the active chemical in the pheromone and combined it with an insecticide. The alarm pheromone brought the aphids out from the heart of the lettuce, where just one-tenth the recommended dose of pesticide was able to kill them.

So a pesticide utilizing pheromones is a good idea. The problem, though, is in the humans feeling the same fear reaction as the insects. A pheromone to one species is just an unpleasant smell to another. If that were not the case, then a moth's sexual attractant pheromone would rouse a whole barnyard of animals. A pig is not attracted to a moth, luckily for them both, though that might make an interesting but brief episode of

When Animals Attack. It would be very unlikely for a single chemical to cause a fear reaction in *both* cluster flies and humans.

This is not a problem if we take a small step into paranoia and theorize that the pesticide in question doesn't evoke a fear response in flies and isn't meant to. The government dumping of dead flies into the gutters implies the "pesticide" may not kill flies at all. So we might conclude that the chemical being used has very little to do with its effect on flies and much more to do with its effect on humans. During the 1950s and 1960s, the government regularly used cities as laboratories to test the efficiency of various dispersal methods of potential biological and chemical weapons.

So what might the effect of lysergic dimethrin, the government's so-called pesticide, on humans be? We know that high concentrations of certain ergot derivatives can cause hallucinations, psychosis, paranoia, and panic. This falls in line with the events in this episode. What about the dimethrin part? Dimethrin is an actual pesticide, one of a class of pyrethroids recommended for use on cluster flies. The more commonly recommended pesticide is permethrin, which has much the same qualities. Permethrin, like dimethrin, is a contact poison that penetrates the skin or cuticle of the insect. It is a synthetic formulation of a naturally occurring compound, originally derived from *Chrysanthemum cinerariaefolium.* Permethrin interferes with the transmission of nerve impulses. Pyrethroids are short lived, and so generally are not thought terribly hazardous to the environment. Their toxicity to humans is low. Dimethrin is probably included by the government to provide credibility to the claim that this compound is a pesticide.

Could the spraying of the chemical, along with the reinforcing messages somehow geared to each resident's personal phobia, drive them to spree killings? The devil is in the details. The sheriff tells Mulder that in the last six months, seven people have killed twenty-two. We don't know exactly when these murders occurred, but the implication is that the government tests have been ongoing for six months.

The tolerance for LSD develops quite quickly. If the same dose is given for three days, it no longer has any effect. Higher and higher doses would need to be administered to maintain the same level of potency, so daily exposure over a six-month period is not practical. If, however, several days pass without LSD, sensitivity to the drug returns. Perhaps the government is only spraying lysergic dimethrin intermittently, allowing sensitivity to return before again releasing the drug. Permethrin can last for several days, depending on the weather, while LSD breaks down quickly with exposure to the elements. So the hallucinogenic component of the compound may only last for a few hours after spraying, while the insect-killing component remains active for several days.

Rather than a steadily increasing fear, then, as Ed Funsch the postal worker seems to feel, subjects would experience a day of horrible anxiety interspersed with fairly normal days, which would probably make those anxious days even more frightening, since they would come and go unpredictably. Murders would then most likely be clustered on these spray days, rather than randomly spread over the six months. On the show, though, we see a man killing everyone in an elevator and a woman killing her mechanic on the day *before* Mulder sees the helicopter spraying. Perhaps the previous night the real lysergic dimethrin had been sprayed, and the spraying Mulder witnesses is of simple dimethrin. That would explain why he feels no effect. Or perhaps, with the flashbacks he's suffering from "Unusual Suspects," a little paranoia is nothing new to him.

MULDER'S LAST STAND?

In "Clyde Bruckman's Final Repose," Clyde has the amazing ability to foresee how people will die. He hints that Mulder will die of autoerotic asphyxiation, saying, "You know, there are worse ways to go, but I can't think of a more undignified one than autoerotic asphyxiation."

A cause of up to one thousand accidental deaths per year in the United States, autoerotic asphyxiation, also known as sexual hanging, is the practice of decreasing one's own oxygen supply to the brain to increase sexual excitement. The reduction of oxygen to the brain, or hypoxia, alters one's consciousness and perception and can bring on a semi-hallucinogenic, light-headed, exhilarated state. The restrictive bondage is also believed to bring psychological pleasure to those who practice it.

Oxygen is decreased most commonly by self-strangulation using ropes, chains, neckties, or belts. None of the practitioners of autoerotic asphyxiation, or asphyxiophilics, intends to die; they all have mechanisms for controlling the strangulation and ending it when desired. But many times these elaborate mechanisms go wrong, or the person loses consciousness before loosening the constricting device. A miscalculation of only a few seconds can lead to unconsciousness, which is quickly followed by fading respiration, irregular pulse, and death by cerebral hypoxia—lack of oxygen to the brain. Another danger is that the carotid sinus may tell the heart to stop. The carotid sinus is a widened portion of the carotid artery in the neck that contains nerve endings sensitive to pressure. Pressure to the carotid sinus stimulates those nerve endings, which send messages that slow the heart and dilate the blood vessels, so that blood pressure falls. Only ten pounds of pressure on the carotid sinus can cause cardiac arrest. This, along with the hypoxia, makes autoerotic asphyxiation extremely dangerous.

Why would anyone do this? Autoerotic asphyxiation actually has quite a long history. First documented in the early 1600s, the idea is believed to have entered into Western culture through observations at public hangings. As males were hanged, they sometimes developed an erection. Although such erections were probably reflexes triggered when the spinal cord was severed, onlookers mistakenly drew a connection between hanging and sexual arousal. In the nineteenth century, brothels in England offered asphyxiation and hanging with the claim that they would enhance sexual pleasure. Other cultures also have long traditions of autoerotic asphyxiation. The Eskimos and Shoshone-Bannock Indians include hanging and choking in their sexual activities.

While most common in male teens, death due to autoerotic asphyxiation has been documented in significant numbers in males of a wide range of ages and in women as well. The youngest reported case was a boy aged nine, the oldest a man of eighty. Techniques often begin simply—as in the case of a woman who stuffed her blouse into her mouth and suffocated—and grow more complex as the subject grows older, with preparation taking as long as four hours. One man used a plastic bag over his head secured with a rubber band around his neck. Doctors noted the bag had many puncture marks that had been repaired with tape, indicating he'd done this before, punctured the bag when he needed air, and later reused the bag. This time, however, he failed to puncture the bag in time and died. This is exactly how Clyde Bruckman himself dies at the end of the episode, with the additional help of some pills.

Besides restricting oxygen flow to the head, some practitioners use elaborate devices to bind themselves and put themselves in a position of helplessness. A woman wrapped an electrical cord around her neck with a slipknot, ran the cord over the doorknob and then wrapped it around her ankles. She could have pushed herself up with her arms to stop the asphyxia, but passed out before she did so and died. One man wrapped himself tightly in plastic bags. He had a snorkel-like device that protruded from the wrapping. The snorkel fell from his mouth and he couldn't cut himself free before he died. Another man hung himself by the neck from the raised shovel of a backhoe tractor. With his body partially supported and a broomstick taped to a lever giving him control of the height of the shovel, he probably felt he had taken sufficient safety precautions. Yet he died of asphyxiation. Investigators found a volume of love poetry that the man had written to his tractor.

Many psychiatrists believe that the repetition of such practices reflects a mental disorder, hypoxyphilic sexual masochism. Yet such a disorder is difficult to study, since access to living asphyxiophilics is rare. The practice is usually only discovered at death. Usually family members—parents, children, spouses—find the dead and are traumatized and shocked by the secret practice of their loved one. But a rare study of five living teenage asphyxiophilics revealed histories of severe physical and mental abuse throughout their childhoods. Dr. William Friedrich and Paul Gerber, who conducted the study, found a number of additional common elements in the teens' histories: parental chemical dependency, parental mental illness, emotional abuse and neglect, violence between parents, the early loss of a parent through death or divorce, and witnessing a parent having sex with others. Two of these teens had begun sexually molesting children. These cases are believed to be extreme, however, and not representative of the majority of practitioners.

Psychiatrists do believe, though, that those who indulge repeatedly in this behavior have undergone some trauma or catastrophe in childhood, and the near-death experience of asphyxia allows the person to feel he has relived and triumphed over the trauma. Some asphyxiophilics also indulge in masochistic fantasies, imagining themselves abused, tortured, or executed. They may believe themselves weak, helpless, and deserving of punishment.

Does Fox Mulder sound like a candidate for this type of activity? Those who would like to immediately answer *No* can take theory #1, that Mulder will be murdered and his death made to look like an accidental autoerotic fatality. Police often find it difficult to distinguish between murder, suicide, and autoerotic accidents. Usually the deciding evidence is limited to other bondage or asphyxiating materials in the possession of the decedent, materials that could easily be planted. Setting up Mulder's death to look like an autoerotic fatality would be so unexpected that it might eliminate suspicions of murder, and it might also tend to discredit Mulder's work.

But might Mulder's death, as foreseen by Clyde Bruckman, be an authentic autoerotic fatality? In "The End," the mind-reading Gibson, after one minute with Mulder, tells him that he has a dirty mind. And we know Mulder enjoys the occasional pornographic movie, like the classic *A Decade of Dirty Delinquents.* That behavior, however, is unrelated to the practice of autoerotic asphyxiation. Does he share any of the characteristics of asphyxiophilics?

Mulder certainly underwent a trauma or catastrophe in his childhood: the loss of his sister, Samantha. In the show's pilot episode, Mulder explains that he remembers being paralyzed during Samantha's abduction, unable to respond to her cries for help. He felt weak and helpless during that crisis, and guilty for failing to protect his younger sister. Even though he did not recover this memory until an adult, Mulder lived with the trauma and guilt of Samantha's disappearance since he was twelve. The family's failure to talk about the loss made Mulder's attempts to cope with it even more difficult. He very likely believes he deserves to be punished for his failure to save her. His single-minded devotion to the X-files is in fact part of his self-imposed penance, and his search for alien life is at least partially driven by his desire to take Samantha's place, to experience what she did, and so be punished for his failure.

In addition, Mulder shares several other characteristics of asphyxiophilics. He lost a parent, his father, through divorce. Mulder was neglected and resented by his mother. He may also have witnessed some act of infidelity between his mother and the Cigarette-Smoking Man, which is hinted at in "Demons." Psychiatrist Janice Dorn believes that asphyxiophilics symbolically seek to murder their mothers.

Do weakness and helplessness play roles in Mulder's sexual fantasies? Our information thus far is quite limited. The only hint we have appears in "Kill Switch." An artificial intelligence (AI) drugs Mulder and wires him up to experience virtual reality. This virtual reality hallucination is extremely asphyxiophilic in nature. Mulder is injured, weak, surrounded by strong beautiful women. One asphyxiophilic reported that he fantasized while bound that powerful women were holding him down. Mulder is bound to the bed, held down by the nurses, his arms are cut off, and he's asphyxiated briefly by one of the nurses with a pillow. Exactly how much of the hallucination is created by the AI and how much arises from Mulder's drugged brain is unclear, but one or both of them shows strong asphyxiophilic tendencies.

While suffering from childhood trauma and associated problems may lead to the development of this behavior, there are certainly many with similar backgrounds who turn out perfectly well-adjusted. Which is Mulder? We'll have to wait and see.

THE DATING GAME

If you want to talk about real altered states, let's talk about the Kindred in "Genderbender." The members of this religious sect seem able to change sexes at will and to secrete very concentrated pheromones, making them sexually irresistible to others. Sounds like a good plot for a porno movie. One member of this sect, Brother Martin, leaves the isolated group for the big city, where he seduces a series of men and women who die of massive coronaries. When another member, Brother Andrew, strokes Scully's hand, she begins kissing him, and only Mulder's intrusion stops her from going all the way. Since the Kindred have a rather odd lifestyle, and since Scully believes it's still uncertain whether humans can produce pheromones, she and Mulder ultimately consider that the Kindred may perhaps be aliens.

You may be wondering why this discussion isn't in the aliens chapter. Since we know so little about the Kindred as aliens, there doesn't seem to be much to discuss in that direction. They've taken on human appearance, and have even managed to mix human DNA with their pheromones, so they may be hybrids of some kind, but since they seem to have been around since the 1930s without aging, it doesn't seem the Cigarette-Smoking Man and his friends would have had the technology to create them. So perhaps they are alien-created hybrids of some kind, or perhaps a radically mutated clan of humans. The first possibility actually seems the more plausible, since the Kindred, aside from a superficial resemblance, have little in common with human beings. Yet the definitive evidence, the sperm left in the bodies of the female victims, never seems to be tested.

The more interesting discussion involves processes that are going on right here on Earth. Could high levels of pheromones make someone sexually irresistible? What exactly do we know about pheromones?

The study of pheromones includes a fair amount of controversy, even to the definition of pheromone. Dr. Robyn Hudson at the Department of Medical Psychology at the University of Munich follows the classical definition of a pheromone: a chemical released by one member of a species and detected by another, eliciting a specific behavioral or physiological response. Pheromones are released by many animals, including insects, amphibians, reptiles, most mammals, and as proven recently, humans. These chemicals can provide information about identity, signal that the time is right for mating, or warn of dangers.

The first pheromone discovered was in female silkworm moths. It serves as a powerful sexual attractant, drawing males and exciting them into a wild flutter dance. So a specific behavioral response is elicited, beneficial in that it leads to mating. Urine is a source of many pheromones—which is why animals spend so much time smelling it— though their exact chemical blend hasn't been determined in many cases. Young mice and other mammals exposed to the urine of adults of the opposite sex will mature more rapidly. On the other hand, pheromones secreted by queen bees prevent other female bees from maturing sexually. Pheromones in the male prairie vole's urine will cause the female's uterus to triple in size and trigger ovulation within forty-eight hours. Some male lizards can secrete a pheromone that induces a zombie state in the female, which provides trouble-free mating.

Since by definition a pheromone causes a specific reaction, it disallows any exercise of common sense or free will. Pheromones from the vaginal secretions of a female hamster rubbed onto a male hamster will make other males try to mate with him. If a female pig is in heat and smells androstenone on a male pig's breath, she'll hump her back and adopt the mating stance. Experience, judgment, and good taste just don't matter. This seems similar to what Scully is undergoing, preparing to "do the wild thing" with Brother Andrew. But the role of pheromones in human behavior remains controversial.

Only one human pheromone has thus far been identified. Odorless chemicals taken from the armpits of a woman cause hormonal changes in other women who inhale them. These hormonal changes bring their menstrual cycles closer to the source woman's by shortening or lengthening them up to fourteen days. With prolonged exposure, the menstrual cycles come into synch. Chemical communication is occurring, with a consistent physiological effect. What you really want to know, though, is whether pheromones influence our mating behaviors.

Evidence of additional human pheromones is controversial. A research group, headed by Dr. David Berliner, claims to have isolated thirty-five human pheromones from human skin, but they have kept their research secret so that they can market these pheromones to the public in perfumes. According to Dr. Berliner, pheromones have physiological effects on heart rate, respiration, the electrical conductivity of the skin, and pupil size. They may also potentially be used to treat a number of hormone-related diseases, since they seem to have an effect on the hypothalamus, which controls the pituitary gland and thereby the release of hormones in the body. But his research is unpublished and so cannot be duplicated by other scientists. Dr. Michael Meredith, professor of biology at Florida State University, points out, "He has isolated chemicals from human skin, but he hasn't proven that they are pheromones." Dr. Charles J. Wysocki, neuroscientist at the Monell Chemical Senses Center, is also cautious. While he believes it possible for the skin to be a source of pheromones—which would explain why Scully reacts so strongly to Brother Andrew's touch—he feels it much more likely that they would be released in glandular secretions from an odor-rich area such as the underarms. So using deodorant to attract the opposite sex may actually decrease your appeal.

But secreting pheromones isn't the only issue. For them to affect our behavior, we also need to be able to detect them. Since, unlike our conscious sensations, our reception of pheromones might be unconscious, it's hard to say whether we perceive them or not. They might serve as one of many factors that influence our reactions to other people. Or they might have no effect on us at all. In many animals, two different sensory organs are involved in the perception of pheromones. Some pheromones are smelled by the nose. Others, which are odorless, are perceived through the *vomeronasal organ* (VNO), a sense organ located in the tissue separating the nostrils. Those who can detect these pheromones have in essence a sixth sense. Many pheromones are detected by both the VNO and the nose, which can work in concert. Some scientists, including Dr. Berliner and his team, define a pheromone as any chemical detected by the VNO, no matter its source, purpose, or effect. While this definition is simple, it ignores the complex processes occurring in other animals and fails to satisfy the criteria in the classic definition given earlier. Dr. Hudson stresses, "The involvement of a special organ is not essential for the definition of pheromonal action."

Some animals have a VNO, and others don't. In humans, it was long thought that a vestigial VNO appeared briefly during fetal development and then disappeared by birth. But recently scientists have discovered a small, pale pit, .01 inch to .1 inch in diameter, on each side of the septal wall separating the nostrils, which looks like a VNO. Dr. David Moran, an electron microscopist at the University of Colorado, looked inside these pits and found what might be neurons, potentially receiving information and sending it to the brain. A colleague of Dr.

Berliner, Dr. Luis Monti-Bloch, devised an apparatus to measure electrical signals generated in the VNO as a result of various chemicals. When he stimulated the VNO with the supposed pheromones discovered by Berliner, he found the VNO responding. But whether the responding cells are connected to the brain is unknown, and what type of effect they might have on our behavior also remains unknown. If pheromones do have an effect on the hypothalamus, then they could affect many basic body functions, including sleeping, eating, and mating.

The effect of high concentrations of pheromones is uncertain. The Kindred exude them in such concentrations that they can cause cardiac arrest in a regular human. Is that possible? Many scientists believe that both the olfactory and VNO receptors become saturated in the presence of excess pheromones, so we can't overdose. Asked if a high concentration of human pheromones could cause a coronary, Dr. Meredith says, "I'd be moderately astonished if it did. The sense of smell is funny. If you go into a room that's full of odor, you eventually adapt to it and no longer consciously notice it." But others believe the excess pheromones could be absorbed by the vast number of blood vessels in the nose and have some effect. Dr. Wysocki cites as an example the nasal version of the birth-control pill. "It's sprayed into the nasal cavity, absorbed by the mucous tissue, picked up by the myriad of small blood vessels and transported to the target tissue." Earlier we discussed the difficulty chemicals have penetrating the blood-brain barrier. Part of the potential power of pheromones arises because, as Dr. Wysocki points out, "There is no blood-brain barrier between olfactory tissue and the brain." Those chemicals can literally go right to your head.

What exactly do we know about the hormones exuded by the Kindred? Mulder tells Scully that the victims of Brother Martin, who died of heart attacks, were found with high concentrations of pheromones containing human DNA. His description seems a bit odd. Pheromones do not contain DNA. If foreign DNA were found on a body, it would not be described as a pheromone. Also, it's unclear why Mulder would identify chemicals on the body as pheromones. Pheromones don't come with a distinctive label that says, "Hi! I'm a pheromone! Want to mate?" Dr. Hudson explains, "There is no way of identifying a pheromone simply on the basis of its chemical structure." Pheromones are not a specific type of chemical; they are chemicals that produce a specific type of reaction. A pheromone that arouses one species to passion is just an inconsequential odor to another. Their noses and VNOs don't speak the same language of love. That's why human pheromones have been so difficult to isolate. The fact that Mulder can identify these chemicals as pheromones means that they have previously been identified as such. Since the only pheromones identified at the time of the filming of the episode were animal pheromones (the pheromone synchronizing women's menstrual cycles was just identified in early 1998), then this would mean the chemicals found were animal pheromones. If I found, say, high concentrations of pig pheromones on a body along with human DNA, I would be more likely to conclude that Farmer Brown had gotten some interesting ideas rather than that a mutant human was at large.

Pheromones, though, aren't the only game in town when it comes to chemicals influencing human behavior. The nose detects many things, including body odor, and these too can have an effect on us. They may not cause a specific, consistent reaction in us, which would disqualify them as pheromones, but they can still provide information of some type to us. Dr. Karl Grammer of the Boltzmann Institute for Urban Ethology in Vienna has done research with a chemical in male sweat, androstenone (yes, the pig pheromone mentioned earlier), that women generally find offensive. Yet ovulating women are not offended by the odor. So for a short time during each month, while she's ripe for reproduction, a woman may find a man somewhat less offensive. Whether she consistently acts on this, though, seems unlikely.

But how does the man feel? Drs. Astrid Jütte and Karl Grammer have also tested chemicals, called *copulins*, from female vaginal secretions taken during three different parts of the menstrual cycle, to see if men could smell a woman's ovulation. These also don't have a very pleasant bouquet, yet exposing men to these generally made the men find women of all types more attractive. And while the males didn't consciously register a difference between the copulins taken during ovulation and those taken at other times, they did have an unconscious reaction. The copulins taken during ovulation raised the men's testosterone levels. Men with heightened testosterone levels are more watchful, their babe-scopes activated for any sign of interest from women. So while these copulins may not cause men to act, they do make men more likely to notice the signals of interest put out by women, giving women a better chance of finding an acceptable partner. Since these copulins seem to cause a physiological reaction, they could be potential pheromones, though further evidence is needed.

A PARTY IN YOUR PANTS·

Japanese scientists claim to have developed a synthesized pheromone based on one allegedly found in the underarm sweat of men. They have embedded capsules of this pheromone into neckties, handkerchiefs, and boxer shorts that men in need of female companionship can wear to try to tip the balance in their favor. Friction causes the capsules to break, releasing the pheromones. They only last for about ten washings.

Zoologist Claude Wedekind conducted an experiment that may shed some light on Scully and Mulder's relationship. He gave a group of men one T-shirt each and asked them to wear it for two nights. He then presented women with seven of the T-shirts to smell.

These seven shirts weren't chosen arbitrarily; in fact, they were different for each woman. Three were from men with immune-system genes, or major histocompatibility complex genes (MHC), similar to the woman's. Three were from men with dissimilar MHC genes. One was a new T-shirt, used as a control. These MHC genes produce proteins that help the body detect and destroy foreign or infected cells. Mice had been found to prefer to breed with animals with dissimilar MHC, presumably because the more diverse the parents' genes, the stronger the child's immune system will be.

The women preferred the smell of the men with MHC different

from theirs, saying the smell reminded them of their boyfriends. The shirts from the men with similar MHC, they said, reminded them of fathers or brothers. It's unclear from the experiment whether the chemicals in these shirts would qualify as pheromones, since they did not elicit any specific behavior. But in any case, it seems this factor has a strong effect on our reaction to members of the opposite sex. The Kindred, being from an isolated, possibly inbred population, might have significantly different MHC from Scully (even more so if the Kindred are aliens), which might explain Scully's attraction to Brother Andrew. MHC could even explain that long-asked question about Scully and Mulder's relationship. Perhaps their friendship has remained platonic for so long because they have the same MHC! That could also explain Scully's more passionate reaction to Eddie Van Blundht when he posed as Mulder.

But if the Kindred are aliens or a radically mutated offshoot of humans, how likely is it that humans would respond to their pheromones? A pheromone is actually a blend of a number of different chemicals, each in a specific proportion. One of the chemicals in the moth pheromone also works as a pheromone in elephants. The female elephant releases it in her urine when she is ready to mate, and it attracts the male. Since the chemical is the same, might a female elephant accidentally attract a male moth? Dr. Wysocki explains that while there may be overlap in some of the chemical constituents of pheromones between species, if the blend of ingredients isn't right, the communication won't be clear, and the animal will not react at all, or in rare cases may react inappropriately.

I can offer a bit of personal experience on this topic. Male iguanas have been documented attacking and biting adult human female caretakers, particularly during a woman's menstruation. My iguana, Igmoe, is of course superior to other iguanas and would never attack me. We share a very close relationship. I didn't quite realize how close until last fall, when Igmoe decided he would mate with me. Climbing up onto the back of my neck and grabbing my black T-shirt in his mouth, he proceeded to twist around and around in circles, pausing for periodic spasmodic twitching. After some time I finally realized what was going on. I was able to disentangle myself by slipping out of my shirt, leaving Igmoe to finish up with the black tee. I realized that the reports from women of "attacks" and "biting" by male iguanas were simply attempts to mate. To Igmoe I was not simply a caretaker but a FEMALE, if a rather large one, and the only game in town for mating. He continued his attempts throughout the fall mating season, though I quickly learned to offer him the black shirt and move away. Apparently some odor of mine on the shirt allowed it to serve as a stand-in. I try not to get jealous.

Dr. Wysocki found it "entirely possible" that Igmoe was sensing some chemical I secrete. This does not prove that the chemical is a pheromone, since in order to satisfy the definition the chemical must cause a reaction in a member of my own species (and my husband was rather turned off by the whole affair). Dr. Wysocki points out that the connection in the newspaper stories between the attacks and menstruation revealed some "cross-species confusion." The best time to mate with a human female is not during menstruation. If the iguanas were correctly "reading" the human signals, they would not attempt to mate at this time. The male iguanas are in a sense misreading the chemical cues, mistaking a chemical released by the human female during menstruation for one released by the iguana female at ovulation. "Of course," Dr. Wysocki says, "human males also misinterpret the signals of human females."

Scully may then be acting like Igmoe, responding inappropriately by misreading Brother Andrew's alien pheromones. At least she didn't bite.

THE CRYING GAME

The Kindred have another unusual power as well, the ability to change sexes instantaneously and at will, as demonstrated by Brother Martin. While the closest humans can get to this is RuPaul, some animals actually have this ability.

The most common are fish. Genderbending fish are called *successive hermaphrodites*. Such a fish can function either as a male or as a female at different points in its life, but cannot be both at the same time. The most common type of sex change is from female to male. The bluehead wrasse is one dramatic example of this. When a dominant male dies, the largest remaining fish will take his place, whether that fish is male or female. In the case of a female, she will lose her ovaries, grow testes, her head will turn blue, she'll change markings and begin acting aggressively and courting females. Other females will now become attracted to this new male.

The opposite transformation occurs in clownfish. They live in small groups around an anemone, which provides protection from predators. Each group has the same composition. The largest fish is female, the second largest male, and the remainder are sexually immature juveniles. The female and male form a breeding pair, and as long as they're around, the other fish will remain juveniles. If the male dies, the largest juvenile will then become male and take his place. If the female dies, the male will change sex and become female, and the largest juvenile will again become a male.

Most fish change sex only once, though some can change as many as ten times. They can change in as quickly as four days, though more commonly it can take several weeks. The female, however, may begin acting male within only twenty-four hours.

The exact mechanism behind this sex-change procedure is unclear, though scientists feel they have a sense of the broad sequence of events. External stimuli are picked up by the fish's brain. The brain sends signals to the hypothalamus, telling it which hormones to secrete. The hormones from the hypothalamus then stimulate the release of other hormones by the pituitary. Those secondary hormones control the gonads, or sex organs.

Behavioral ecologist Douglas Shapiro at Eastern Michigan University is studying exactly which sensory cues trigger this sex-changing chain reaction in the brain. In his experiments with *Pseudanthias squamipinnis*, a fish in which the loss of a male will cause a female to change to a male to replace him, Dr. Shapiro has found that it is not the disappearance of the male from view that triggers the change. Neither is it the lack of a sound made by the male or some pheromone released by him. The key factor is *close-contact interactions*. If a female ceases to have close-contact interactions with a male, she will assume there is no male present. What are these close-contact interactions? The male chases the female; the male performs aggressive displays to impress the female; and the male rearranges his fins, turns on his side, and swoops around in a distinctive U-shaped pattern (at least he doesn't ask what her sign is). When a male is isolated in a plastic cylinder within an aquarium, which has holes that allow water to pass back and forth freely, the females, unable to interact with him, behave as if there were no male, with one or more of them changing sexes.

Even if a male and female are isolated in the cylinder, so that the other females can observe male-female interactions occurring, they aren't convinced that a male is present. Since the male is not interacting with them, he is irrelevant.

A fascinating addition to these findings is that if the females are not allowed close-contact interactions with each other, then they won't change either. A female by herself has little to gain by turning into a male. Only when there is a group of females does it make sense for one to turn into a male.

So under what circumstances is it advantageous to change sex? Dr. Shapiro explains, "If you're in a group of ten adult females and one male, and a predator eats the male, then you have a bunch of females, none of which can reproduce. It's now to everyone's advantage if someone could change sex." But there are a lot of drawbacks to genderbending too. Dr. Shapiro says, "A sex change is not all fun." The change can take weeks or months, a huge amount of energy, and during the transition period, the fish will look unlike any other. A fish that looks different will attract predators, creating an increased risk of mortality.

From an evolutionary perspective, this ability is only advantageous if its benefits outweigh its risks. The benefits depend on the number of females in the group that are potential future mates to the new male.

Dr. Shapiro has found that *Pseudanthias* will only change if there are at least three females.

The controversial size-advantage model attempts to explain why sex change seems linked to size. The largest fish in many species' groups is a male. In many of these well-organized societies, females will only spawn with large males. So if you're small, you don't want to be male, because none of the females will reproduce with you. It's better to be a small female, since a female of any size can get attention. Once you grow and become large, it's better to be male, since you can have access to all the females you want (and they say size doesn't matter!).

Could humans ever change sex? Certain types of fish and frogs are the only vertebrates known to change sexes. No mammals change sex. We don't yet fully understand why. Some theorize that in species with more pronounced differences between the sexes, the transformation would take too much energy. Others believe the advantages may be outweighed by disadvantages—lost breeding time and vulnerability to predators. Still others simply believe many species become too sexually specialized to change. Dr. Shapiro agrees with this third theory. "The reproductive tract of most fishes is much simpler than that of mammals. And in all of the sex-changing fishes, all the action takes place externally. There is no internal fertilization." The reproductive tract, then, consists of the gonad plus the duct which takes the gametes, or germ cells, from the gonad out into the water. The female releases her eggs, the male releases his sperm, and that's it. No fuss, no muss. No elaborate external or internal structures—such as the vagina, uterus, or penis—exist. This makes it much easier for the fish to change sexes, and impossible for humans to truly change sexes, even with hormone injections. With mammals, Dr. Shapiro says, "Everything has gotten so much more highly determined genetically. Once sexual differentiation occurs, the obstacles to changing it are too great." Dr. Shapiro pauses, then adds, "I can say that now, but ten years from now someone will probably discover a gene that you can turn off and make this possible."

Dr. Shapiro does admit it would be advantageous if humans and other mammals could change sexes. "You'd think it would be a valuable trait to have. There are social systems in other vertebrates similar to fish systems, with only large dominant males reproducing with multiple females." This statement made me start wondering about the Kindred and what sort of social system they have. A woman, Sister Abigail, seems dominant within the group. The Kindred also seem to have more men than women, which might suggest a system opposite to that of the fish, in which you have one female for many males. Or perhaps, like the clownfish, only the dominant pair—Sister Abigail and Brother Oakley—mate, and the others normally don't engage in sexual activity. That may explain why Brother Martin left the Kindred, and why Brother Andrew puts the moves on Scully. Certainly if the Kindred are as ageless as they appear, they need to do very little reproducing. This idea is reinforced by the lack of children among the Kindred. If they don't reproduce at all, which seems a possibility given the odd rebirth of one of their sect, then the ability to change sexes would offer them no advantage, and would be a very unlikely trait.

What would trigger a sex change among one of the Kindred? If they depend on close-contact interactions between others of their kind to give them signals about what sex they need to be, then Brother Martin, having left the group, might be at a loss, misunderstanding human interactions and chemical cues, switching back and forth. Or perhaps the sex change is not actual at all but only an alien simulation, without the necessary changes to internal organs. Or perhaps, as the episode suggests, they have the ability to actually change sex at will and almost instantaneously. But it seems a rather desperate method of getting a date, especially for a group with such strong pheromones.

External factors such as pheromones, chemicals, viruses, and radiation can certainly have powerful effects on our bodies and our state of mind. The idea that forces beyond our control could alter our emotions, could compel us to action, could change the very functioning of our bodies is a terrifying fear that The X-Files enjoys using against us. Yet these forces aren't confined to the show, much as we might like to believe so. We face them every day.

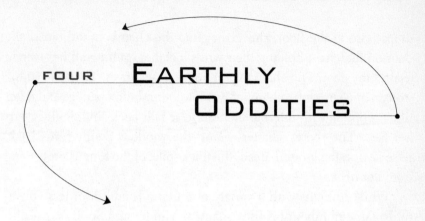

FOUR EARTHLY ODDITIES

> "Come on, Mulder. A few thousand grasshoppers does not constitute a plague."
>
> —Dana Scully,
> "Miracle Man"

THE LIGHTS GO OUT. SPECIAL AGENT Dana Scully looks around the darkened lab, wondering at the source of the blackout. She retrieves a large flashlight and heads for the fuse box. Out of the darkness appears Jesse O'Neil, her face white and sheened with sweat. The young woman's mouth opens and closes, but emits only fractured groans. Then Jesse lunges. Caught between concern and defense, Scully grabs onto the woman, and with a twist of the wrist and a click she realizes that Jesse has handcuffed them together. Scully drags Jesse to a table, fumbles in the drawer, comes out with a pick. She brings it down onto the chain holding them together, again and again. The pick makes tiny gouges in the metal, nothing more. Jesse straightens, choking. The fungal growth in her throat bulges outward, ready to pierce the skin and release its spores. Scully drops the pick, lifts Jesse in a fireman's hold, and rushes to the observation chamber door. She drops Jesse to the floor, shoves her into the chamber, and closes the door on the chain holding their wrists together, putting all her weight against the door. The chain tugs at her as Jesse moves. Then the young woman appears at the chamber window, her mouth open, gasping, her throat rippling with internal motion. Jesse falls back, and Scully averts her face. The spores splatter against the window. Scully turns back. Jesse lays on the ground, dead, the thick spike of the fungus protruding from her neck.

While humans with a variety of mutations and disorders constitute a large number of X-files, many of Mulder and Scully's cases involve other species that share our world. They've faced cockroach invasions, frog extinctions, a prehistoric "big blue" monster, arctic worms, pustule-popping insects, throat-piercing fungi, and even a rain of toads. These encounters remind us that we are not alone, and that our home is a much stranger place than we realize. Do cockroaches go on murderous rampages? Might animals thought long extinct live among us? Can parasitic worms drive us to paranoia? Could life exist in the fierce heat of a volcano, or in the extreme cold of arctic ice?

IS THE WORLD ONE BIG ROACH MOTEL?

In "War of the Coprophages," Mulder and Scully are confronted with a series of cockroach-related deaths. The town of Miller's Grove, Massachusetts, is overrun with cockroaches. Their headquarters seems to be Dr. Eckerle's methane research facility, which is filled with imported animal manure. They swarm over the exterminator, Dr. Bugger; they cover the medical examiner while he's in the bathroom; they climb onto a guest at Mulder's motel. Since all of these people die while they are covered in roaches, Mulder believes the insects may be responsible. Scully very competently deduces each death has a simple, rational explanation, yet the cockroaches exhibit some pretty suspicious behavior, seemingly attacking and swarming over people. How unusual is that behavior, and how unusual are the large numbers of cockroaches shown? Not as unusual as you might wish. First, some background on our friend the cockroach.

Cockroaches have existed on Earth for 300 million years, about a hundred times longer than man. Of about four thousand known species, less than 1 percent live among man. Some cockroaches live in tropical forests, some in the ground, some in decaying logs, some in caves. Originating mainly in Africa, with the start of trade, they boarded ships to cross oceans, quickly establishing themselves in a broad band across the world, from thirty degrees south of the equator to thirty degrees north. Cockroaches are still world travelers. These days they commonly travel with shipments of produce, animals, and baggage, on ships, airplanes, trains, and automobiles. The German cockroach, the Oriental cockroach, the American cockroach, and others are not named for their point of origin or for where they now live, but for where they were first documented. All three of these have found a comfortable home in the United States, along with sixty-six other species of cockroach. Over two-thirds of those are immigrants from other countries. Other types commonly found in the U.S., particularly in the south, are the brown cockroach, the smoky-brown cockroach, and the brown-banded cockroach. And you thought they all looked alike! The German cockroach prefers kitchens and restaurants; the Oriental cockroach prefers cooler locations such as basements. The American cockroach, of course, prefers sewers.

The Japanese Navy had a special technique for controlling cockroaches. If a seaman captured 300 cockroaches, he would be granted one day of shore leave. You might consider trying the same technique, since you may have as many as 50,000 cockroaches in your house. If you've seen a few, then many more are lurking behind the scenes. Even a clean house can be easily infested. Roaches or egg capsules may be in the shopping bags you bring into your house, and one egg capsule can result in thirty bouncing baby roaches. One female German cockroach can give birth to as many as 270 young over its six- to nine-month life span.

Cockroaches are omnivorous, eating both the food and the feces of man and animals. Coprophage means one who feeds on excrement, and they even eat each other's feces. When not dining on that delicacy, they'll eat cardboard and paper, but they prefer starchy and sugary foods over fruits and meats. When those food sources aren't available, cockroaches get creative. Cockroaches have been reported gnawing the skin, nails, and boots of men, eating the eyelashes and eyebrows of children, and eating mucus from people's noses. Cockroaches can get stuck in the wax of your ear, and babies can choke to death on them.

The most maddening thing about cockroaches is how fast they can move. Dr. Roy Ritzmann, a biologist at Case Western University who studies the movement and the central nervous system in cockroaches, has identified the cockroach's "escape response." As you attempt to slam your foot down onto a roach, the beginning of your movement creates a slight air displacement. The roach senses this, and within thirty milliseconds, it has begun to run away. You really never had a chance.

Cockroaches have claws, much like a cat's, that help them climb straight up walls and on ceilings, and even up ladders of string (try it at home!). They also have sticky pads that allow them to walk on glass. If they run fast enough, their front end lifts up, and they actually run bipedally on their two back legs.

So if your house has 50,000 cockroaches, how many cockroaches call your town home? In a study done in Tyler, Texas, of sewer manholes—prime homes for cockroaches—40 percent of the manholes examined contained cockroaches. 17 percent of the manholes were home to 1–25 roaches, 10 percent contained 26—100 roaches, and 13 percent housed more than 100 roaches: true roach motels. Think about that the next time you're walking down the street.

Under the right conditions, cockroaches can breed to huge numbers. In 1957, Bedford, Indiana, was overrun with cockroaches. Not one house in the city was free of them. Cockroaches came up through bathtubs, sinks, and toilets.

COPROPHAGE TRIVIA

*Cockroaches have been said to cure disease and to form a tasty meal, with a flavor similar to shrimp (we can only wonder if Scully, in "Humbug," shared this opinion).

*According to David George Gordon, author of *The Compleat Cockroach,* cockroaches break wind every fifteen minutes. Insect flatulence is said to account for 20 percent of all methane emissions on Earth, making it one of the biggest contributors to global warming.

*A test found the sugary cinnamon bun the cockroach's favorite food, with white bread and boiled potatoes coming in close behind.

How much of a danger do cockroaches pose? They can actually spread serious diseases. Cockroaches carry infections on the exterior of their bodies as well as internally, passing parasites, viruses, and bacteria to other animals or man. Dr. Steven Valles, research entomologist at the U.S. Department of Agriculture in Gainesville, stresses the possibility of transmission by casual contact, explaining that a cockroach can walk through a sewer pipe and then walk over your sandwich or kitchen counter, carrying *Salmonella* or *E. coli.* Cockroaches have been found carrying bacteria that can cause many diseases in man: gastroenteritis, pneumonia, typhoid fever, dysentery, and bubonic plague. So stop playing with that cockroach! What makes the cockroach such an effective carrier of diseases is that the bacteria in its feces remain viable for long periods. *Salmonella* can survive for up to six months. If a cockroach vomits—which cockroaches are prone to do, often while eating—onto your cornflakes, the salmonella it carries can last for sixty-two days (I think you'd have eaten your cereal by then).

In the episode, Dr. Bugger, the exterminator, dies from anaphylactic shock, a severe allergic reaction. About 7.5 percent of people show an allergic reaction to cockroaches, though not one severe enough to cause anaphylactic shock. The greater your exposure to cockroaches, the greater your likelihood of developing sensitivity to cockroaches. Dr. Valles explains, "There are severe allergens associated with the feces and cast skins of insects. These can build up in areas of heavy infestation." In fact, Chuck, the technician in Dr. Valles's lab, has developed an allergy to cockroaches, and they ship samples of his blood out to allergy researchers.

Sensitization to cockroaches can also increase asthma attacks. Children in the inner city, where roaches are more plentiful, are three times more likely to require hospitalization for their asthma. We might easily assume that Dr. Bugger has developed an allergic sensitivity to cockroaches because of his heavy exposure to them. In that case, Dr. Bugger's death is quite realistic. Dr. Valles agrees that for those who have grown sensitized to cockroach allergens, severe allergic reactions and anaphylactic shock are very real threats.

But would cockroaches move in large groups or swarm over people? Cockroaches may move en masse as a result of overcrowding, adverse conditions, or depletion of food. These migrations are seldom reported, because they usually happen at night, and often out of sight. They may "migrate" from the sewer into your home. In one case documented in 1895, thousands of German cockroaches marched in a three-hour procession from one building to another across a muddy street, and could not be stopped by several men armed with brooms. According to *Patty/Tania* by Jerry Belcher and Don West, cockroaches provided the first lead in discovering Patty Hearst's kidnappers. A tenant in an apartment building complained about cockroaches swarming down the walls from the apartment above. The apartment above was discovered to be an old hideout of the Symbionese Liberation Army. While Dr. Valles believes some of these accounts are apocryphal, he admits, "Cockroaches are gregarious. They prefer hanging out in groups." Places such as sewage treatment plants, or Dr. Eckerle's methane research facility, would be particularly attractive. When they find such an attractive home, cockroaches can release an aggregation pheromone in their feces, which will draw other cockroaches to that location. They may be calling friends to a party at your house right now.

What defenses do we have against the cockroach? Dr. Bugger uses one of the latest weapons in humanity's ongoing battle with the insecticide-resistant cockroach: fungus. EcoScience, a Worcester, Massachusetts, company, is marketing *Metarhizium anisopliae*, a fungus that literally devours the German cockroach. When the fungus's spores contact the exoskeleton, they release enzymes that eat away the hardened cuticle. The roach's innards are then slowly digested by the fungus, killing the insect within a week. Dr. Valles admits, "It's a slow, painful death." During that time, spores also attach themselves to nest mates, who are then similarly devoured.

Other high-tech methods of coprophagicide are under development. In one, tiny worms, nematodes, enter the cockroach's anus or spiracle, through which it breathes, and deposit a bacterium that kills the roach. In another, a chemical inhibits the synthesis of chitin, the main constituent of the cockroach's hardened exoskeleton. In another, the aggregation pheromone would draw cockroaches into a trap. It almost makes me feel sorry for the poor buggers.

Scully raises the possibility that these roaches are an unusual species brought in unintentionally by Dr. Eckerle, a local scientist who has shipped in samples of manure from other countries. This is certainly possible, given what we know about the cockroach's love of travel and feces. And we have yet to catalogue all the types of cockroaches; around forty new species are discovered each year. Scully mentions a species of Asian cockroach that arrived in Florida in the 1980s. This cockroach, *Blattella asahinai*, has spread to eighteen Florida counties since its introduction in 1984. It's thriving in the Florida climate, living in citrus groves by day and heading to the malls and other well-lit public establishments at night. Unlike our friendly local roaches, it's attracted to light and can fly for several hundred yards. In some places the population has swelled to over 100,000 per acre.

While the Asian cockroach is vulnerable to pesticides, its outdoor base of operations makes it much more difficult to spray than cockroaches inside a home. And their base may be expanding. With over thirty-five million tourists visiting Florida each year, you just know that some tourists are heading home with a couple of hitchhikers.

SILENT SPRING

Not all creatures are as hardy and enduring as the cockroach. One of the greatest mysteries facing scientists today is a quiet crisis involving the fragile frog. In "Quagmire," a mysterious decline in the frog population around Huevelman's Lake may be forcing a prehistoric sea serpent to begin feeding on humans. Dr. Farraday argues with a colleague that man has caused a frog holocaust. Is Dr. Farraday's charge true?

Deformities in frogs became a focus of national attention three years ago, when a group of middle school students on a field trip in Minnesota found that half of the frogs they caught that day had missing, deformed, or extra limbs. Since then, increasing numbers of reports have been documenting similar findings elsewhere in Minnesota, and all the way from Quebec to California, as well as in Japan. Many different species of frogs have been reported with malformations, as well as some salamanders. While reports of malformed amphibians are not new—the first one was recorded in 1740—they have become much more common in recent years. Biologists consider the normal rate of deformities to be less than 1 percent. In Vermont, scientists measured a 45 percent deformity rate in young frogs. And in some areas, the deformity rate is as high as 70 percent. Researchers studying frogs at Lake Champlain found thirty-eight deformed frogs in one day, more than had been reported in the last seventy-five years.

Deformities include internal abnormalities, misshapen limbs, split limbs, extra limbs (up to twelve legs per frog), missing or withered limbs, missing or malformed eyes, and a tail. Frogs have been found with no hind legs, with eyes in their throats, and with twisted spines. Somehow, the normal developmental process is being impaired.

Scientists are unsure about the cause, and debate vigorously about the validity of various experiments being done. Most seem to agree the deformities are probably not genetically inherited, but instead occur during the development from tadpole to frog. A genetic abnormality would be unlikely to have spread across such a wide area, or to involve multiple species of frogs. Many researchers theorize that man-made changes in the environment are responsible. Possible causes include toxins, such as herbicides, fertilizers, insecticides, or an increase in ultraviolet radiation from the depletion of the ozone layer.

One common pesticide, methoprene, has recently been proven to cause deformities at high concentrations. Methoprene is used around the world to control mosquitoes. Dr. John Bantle at Oklahoma State University has discovered that methoprene breaks down with exposure to ultraviolet radiation into cismethoprenic acid and transmethoprenic acid. These two products have a much more powerful effect on frogs, causing malformations within ninety-six hours. These methoprenic acids mimic retinoic acid, activating the same hormone receptor in cells. As we learned in our discussion of "Young at Heart," retinoic acid affects regeneration in salamanders, and can cause the growth of multiple legs.

Dr. David Gardiner, associate research biologist at the University of California at Irvine Department of Developmental and Cell Biology, agrees that a *retinoid*, a substance that mimics retinoic acid, is responsible for the deformities. In studying frogs with extra limbs, he has found, "The mechanisms whereby limbs are made are all intact." That's why the abnormal structures are recognizably legs, and not tentacles or some other weird creation. "These frogs are normal in a perverse way. They are doing what they were told to do. The problem is that they got the wrong message." This wrong message, a chemical signal, disrupts the developmental process and causes frogs "to make the wrong number of legs in the wrong place at the wrong time."

How do retinoids do this? As we know, different genes express themselves in different parts of the body. Retinoids can activate genes in areas where they're not usually expressed. The genes governing the formation of legs are normally only activated in the sites where legs should develop. But retinoic acid, or some other chemical that mimics it, can turn on these genes in other areas, causing the formation of extra legs. Dr. Gardiner says, "Retinoids are scary things. You can't live with them, can't live without them. They are fundamental to our development, and incredibly potent developmental disrupters."

WHEN DINOSAURS ROAMED THE EARTH

Mulder searches in "Quagmire" for Big Blue, a prehistoric pleiosaur allegedly still alive in Heuvelman's Lake. Bernard Heuvelmans, by the way, is the real president of the International Society of Cryptozoology and is considered the "father of cryptozoology," *cryptozoology* literally meaning the study of hidden animals. Cryptozoologists are an odd mix of scientists and non-scientists, some seeking previously undiscovered species or species believed extinct, others seeking more exotic game such as the Abominable Snowman, Bigfoot, and the Loch Ness Monster. Could undiscovered prehistoric creatures still be living on Earth?

Actually, they are. In 1938, a coelacanth, a fish believed to have died out seventy million years ago, was caught off the coast of South Africa. Since then, researchers discovered that several hundred of the fish were still alive, at depths of 500–1,000 feet. These fish, which survived the extinction of the dinosaurs, are now endangered by fishermen trying to catch other deep-sea fish in the same area.

In 1994, the dawn redwood, a species of sequoia thought extinct for twenty million years, was discovered growing in a remote province of China.

In 1995, a wasp believed extinct for twenty-five million years was discovered to have actually survived in California. Its ancestors lived over 200 million years ago, during the Triassic period.

These "living fossils" challenge scientists' beliefs and expand our view of the creatures with whom we share our planet. Who knows what we might find next?

Why are we using retinoids as pesticides? About twenty years ago, biochemists got the idea to create a safer class of pesticides that, instead of poisoning insects, would use insects' hormones against them. Methoprene mimics insect juvenile hormone. By making the juveniles think they haven't yet grown big enough to molt, the chemical stops them from molting, so arresting their growth and killing them. When methoprene was first developed, insect and human development were considered so different, no danger to humans was thought possible. Now, though, we know that the *Hox genes*, the group of genes controlling the formation of the body, are extremely similar in flies, humans, and all animals. This means that a chemical affecting insect development may affect frog development as well. And what about human development?

One retinoid, Accutane, has already been shown to cause abnormalities in human development. Accutane is an acne medication that has been on the market since 1982. Women who use the medicine while pregnant have an extremely high risk of fetal malformations, even with low dosages over a short period. Birth defects include a cleft palate, mental retardation, a very small head, malformed ears, deformities in the cartilage and bone of the skull, and heart defects.

Although the role of methoprene and its breakdown products remains in contention, additional evidence points to a toxin of some sort in the water. A recent experiment took frog eggs from ponds where deformed frogs had been found. Those eggs left to hatch in the original pond resulted in deformed frogs, while those taken from the pond and put into clean water resulted in healthy frogs. The scientists concluded that an unknown waterborne agent is the most likely cause of the deformities. They have not yet discovered what this agent is—whether it is natural or man-made, or whether it may pose any danger for man. Since well water near these cites has also yielded deformed frogs, the government has offered residents bottled water. These test results have yet to be published, though, so the jury remains out on the accuracy of the results. But Dr. Gardiner believes the culprit does lie in the water. "In the spring, the ice melts, and frogs with extra legs come crawling out of the pond. Something in there did it."

While research seems to have provided a few clues to the causes of these deformities, many questions remain. To explain the increase in malformations in the last few years, the cause must be something new, or some new combination of elements. Since no new pesticides have been put widely into use in the last three years, some argue that a pesticide is not an acceptable explanation. Also, while some studies show more deformed frogs in agricultural areas where pesticide use is heavy and widespread, others found deformed frogs even in protected wildlife areas.

Adding to the uncertainty is the lack of long-term data. Without that, it's hard to say how widespread the problem is, how much malformations have increased, or even whether they have. We may just be noticing them more.

In addition to malformations, the frog population is also experiencing a general decline, as claimed by Dr. Farraday in "Quagmire." As with many species, loss of habitat is a serious threat to frogs. But they are also disappearing from relatively undisturbed habitats. Malformations may provide a piece of this puzzle, since most deformities are immediately fatal, and the few survivors seldom live a long life. But the frogs seem to be dying off mostly in the tropics, while malformations are occurring in more temperate regions.

The main concern for many is not the frogs, but what their disappearance may indicate about the state of the environment and its corollary effects on human health. Frogs are believed to be more sensitive to environmental degradation since they live both on land and in water during their life cycle and they can easily absorb pollutants through their permeable skin. Because of rain and runoff, the most polluted areas are often ponds, particularly the surface microlayer at the top. Pesticides tend to be fat soluble, and fats float on the surface. Frog larvae hang and feed at the surface, like icicles, and absorb any chemicals in the microlayer. These chemicals can build up in the tissue, resulting in much higher concentrations in the frogs than those found in the water. Scientists compare frogs to the canaries used in coal mines, which fell victim to poisonous gases before humans felt any ill effect. Frogs are seen as an early warning system for the environment, signaling a possible danger of human birth defects. Coincidentally, the National Institutes of Health have just begun to set up a national birth defect registry, something that has never existed before.

Is it likely, then, that we'll be seeing human babies with extra limbs? Dr. Gardiner says, "Before you see that, you'd expect to see problems in heart development, subtle skeletal deformities, and an increase in childhood cancers. We're already seeing that. The incidence of childhood cancers has been rising for the last thirty years."

THE SKY IS FALLING

In "Die Hand Die Verletzt," Mulder and Scully are pelted with a rain of toads from the sky. While Mulder seems ready to accept a supernatural source for the toads, Scully theorizes that the toads may have been picked up by a tornado and carried miles away before being dropped from the sky. Is such a thing possible?

While toads have not commonly fallen from the sky, rains of frogs and fish have been recorded since the second century, when Athenaeus wrote of frogs falling for days, getting into food and water, piling up in the streets and creating a huge stench as they died and decayed. Fish up to six pounds have been claimed to fall from the sky, sometimes in the hundreds or thousands. Witnesses in Iowa, in 1882, claimed a hailstone contained two living frogs.

Most of these accounts have been disputed or else scientists have offered alternate explanations. Scientists point out that during the dry summer, some types of frogs and fish can burrow underground and remain dormant until rains awaken them. Thus after a rain people might find small puddles with fish or frogs in them. Also, a stream might overflow and sweep its occupants over the land. Yet a few accounts remain difficult to dispute.

In his book *It's Raining Frogs and Fishes,* Jerry Dennis reports the account of biologist A. D. Bajkov, who was caught in an unusual rain in Marksville, Louisiana, in 1947. He reported fish two to nine inches long falling from the sky by the hundreds. Three townspeople reported being hit by falling fish. The fish included large-mouth black bass, goggle-eye, and hickory shad.

What might explain such a phenomenon? Tornados and waterspouts seem the most likely causes. A tornado is formed when a large updraft of warm, humid air is subject to shifting winds that turn it into a whirling vortex. The rising air creates low air pressure near the ground, which surrounding air rushes in to fill. When a tornado passes over the water, it sucks large quantities of water up into its funnel, creating a waterspout. Passing over a lake, a waterspout might also suck up frogs or fish swimming near the surface. Tornado winds, up to 300 mph, can transport material up to 100 miles when it is sucked into the updraft of the funnel. Water might then be released with frogs or fish. As for toads, why not? A tornado in McComb, Mississippi, in 1974, lifted three empty school buses over an eight-foot embankment and threw them into the woods.

So you better reinforce that umbrella.

IS THAT A PUSTULE OR JUST A PIMPLE?

A new species is discovered in "*F. Emasculata*," which stands for *Faciphaga emasculata* (literally, surface-eating depriver of strength), the name of a fictional bug carrying a disease-causing parasite. This bug is discovered in the Costa Rican rain forest, where Pinck Pharmaceuticals is searching for previously undiscovered species with potential drug applications. While the bug itself seems pretty harmless, the microscopic parasite it carries attacks the human immune system, causes the formation of pulsating pustules on the face and body, and leads within thirty-six hours to death. When the pustules erupt, the parasite's larvae are splattered on anyone within spitting distance, spreading the infection. Pinck Pharmaceuticals conducts a covert experiment with *Faciphaga* and its parasite by sending an express package with an infected chunk of boar to a convict in prison. Should we be worrying about previously undiscovered species? What are the chances of one being discovered? Pretty good, considering all the recent discoveries.

Previously unknown species of cockroaches aren't the only creatures being discovered. Thousands of new species are found all over the world each year. The Peruvian parrotlet, the lion tamarin monkey, and the Peruvian beaked whale are just a few examples. The search for species has gained new energy recently, with the realization that many species are becoming extinct before they've even been discovered. The majority of these undiscovered species are small creatures, like ants and beetles. Insects form a great proportion of all species, comprising over half of the 1.4 million species we have catalogued. Scientists aren't sure how many undiscovered species remain in the world; estimates run from 1.5 million all the way up to 100 million.

Many of these undiscovered species live in the rain forests, which, though they cover only 5 percent of the Earth's land surface, contain at least half of the plant and animal species. Dr. E. O. Wilson, a Harvard biologist, once found forty-three species of ants on a single tree in Peru—about equal to the number of ant species found in the entire British Isles. This diversity can provide incredibly valuable resources.

Over one third of the prescription drugs derived from plants come from rain-forest plants. These include drugs to treat leukemia, asthma, hypertension, and glaucoma.

So the discovery of a previously unknown bug in the Costa Rican rain forest seems completely plausible. But what about the specific nature of *F. emasculata*? According to the episode, *F. emasculata* is a parasitoid, meaning that it goes through an immature life stage that develops on or within a single host and kills that host. A parasitoid differs from a parasite in that parasitoids live off the host for only part of their life cycle and are free-living for the rest of the life cycle, while parasites live off the host for their entire lives (sort of like that Trekkie son or daughter who won't move out of your basement). Common parasitoids are flies and wasps. The parasitoid lays either eggs or larvae in or on the host. They employ a wide variety of strategies to attach or insert their progeny. Some will sting the host and inject the eggs in that way. Others will paralyze the host first and then lay their eggs on top. These paralyzed hosts, such as the caterpillar, may know exactly what's happening as their strength is slowly sucked out of them. The parasitoids feed off the host until they've matured and are ready to leave the host— who is usually dead by this point—to live independently. Dr. Michael R. Strand, professor of entomology at the University of Wisconsin, notes, "It's kind of like the movie *Alien*, actually."

Parasitoids are much more common than we think, comprising between 250,000 and 500,000 species. They can also be useful, as entomologists hope will be the case with the scuttle fly, *Phoridae pseudacteon tricuspis*. This fly lays an egg inside the head of the fire ant. When the fly larva hatches, it kills the fire ant and uses its head as a cozy cocoon. Scientists are planning to use the scuttle fly to help control the booming population of South American fire ants in the southeast U.S.

The main way in which *F. emasculata* differs from known parasitoids is its use of mammals (including humans) as hosts. All known parasitoids are arthropods, animals with segmented bodies and hard exoskeletons, mainly insects. And all the hosts are arthropods. Since mammalian physiology is significantly different, it seems unlikely that a parasitoid such as *F. emasculata* might be discovered. Another important difference between *F. emasculata* and known parasitoids is that *F. emasculata* uses at least two different hosts—boars and humans—and most parasitoids are very specialized in their choice of hosts. The scuttle fly mentioned above lays eggs only in fire ants, not in other types of ants. And while some humans may sometimes seem like boars, there's actually quite a difference.

In the other aspects of its life cycle, though, it seems fairly consistent with known parasitoids. It appears to lay its eggs in the open sores on an ill human (no need to paralyze the host, since he's not moving around much at this point anyway). These eggs hatch, and the young feed off the host until they have reached their adult stage. By this time the host has died, and the new adults emerge, seeking a new host in which to lay eggs.

This is actually quite similar to the life cycle of the blow fly. The blow fly normally lays its eggs near an open wound on a dead animal or human. The larvae burrow into the wound, mature, and then drop to the ground to continue their lives. Sometimes, though, the eggs are laid near a wound on a living animal or human. This sounds similar to what *F. emasculata* is doing. The blow fly is not a parasitoid because it kills its host only in cases of severe infestation. In fact, blow fly larvae can sometimes benefit the host, preventing bacterial growth by eating away diseased or dead flesh. During World War I, they were implanted in wounds for just such an effect.

The life cycles of both *F. emasculata* and the blow fly are dependent on the existence of a host with open sores. But while the blow fly simply counts on providence to provide, *F. emasculata* seems to prefer the sores created by a second organism, to which its life cycle is intricately connected. This second organism—now don't get confused—is a microscopic parasite, living its entire life within a host. These parasites grow quickly inside the host, attacking the immune system, causing a fever and the growth of pustules over the body. The pustules carry the parasite's larvae, and when they burst, they spray the larvae, hopefully onto a new host, in which the entire cycle can be repeated. The open wounds then become the perfect home for *F. emasculata*'s eggs.

The immunosuppressive activities of the parasite probably help to protect *F. emasculata*'s eggs, and perhaps the parasite has even left some tasty secretions in the wounds that help *F. emasculata*'s larvae to thrive. So *F. emasculata* clearly benefits from the parasite's activities. Whether the parasite benefits from *F. emasculata* is not quite clear; it's mentioned that the bug works as an incubator for the parasite, but it's also claimed that the bug can't transmit the parasite through a bite. If so, how does the bug contribute to the parasite's life cycle? We can hypothesize that the bug, when eaten, transmits the parasite to a new host. This mechanism is seen in a number of species on Earth, and would reinforce the ties between these two organisms.

Organisms interrelated in similar symbiotic relationships are not uncommon. Dr. Strand points out that some parasitoids carry symbiants, organisms tied to them in a mutually beneficial relationship. Some types of wasp carry a symbiotic virus in their reproductive tract. When the mother wasp stings an insect host, such as a caterpillar, she introduces her eggs and the virus. The virus is actually essential to the survival of the eggs. It infects the immune cells of the host and through immunosuppression, prevents the host's cells from mounting an attack against the eggs. Thus the eggs thrive, hatch, and eventually kill the caterpillar. That's good for the wasps. But what's in it for the virus?

Well, the virus can't replicate inside the caterpillar. It can only replicate inside the adult female wasp. So the virus needs the baby wasps to survive to aid in its own survival. But their attachment is even stronger than that. This virus is actually a retrovirus, whose genes are integrated into the DNA of every cell in the wasp's body, including the wasp's eggs. So in a sense, the wasp's babies are actually the virus's babies as well (don't ask who gets visitation rights). This is a true symbiotic relationship, profiting both parties.

Clearly, there are precedents for a parasitoid in a symbiotic relationship, as *F. emasculata* appears to be. The pustules are an unusual feature, though, and Dr. Strand has to go to a non-parasitoid to find an analogous relationship. "The bot fly of Central and South America lays its eggs on the body of a mosquito. The mosquito then may feed off a human host. The heat from the human body is just enough to stimulate the egg to hatch just as the mosquito is drawing blood. The newly hatched larva crawls down the mosquito's proboscis and right into the puncture the mosquito has made. It feeds on the human host right below the skin, creating a lump that looks like a big pimple. When the larva has completed its development, it pops right out of the skin." Again, *Alien* rears its ugly head.

F. emasculata, then, operates like the bot fly, waiting for another organism to make an opening in the host and then exploiting it. It also operates like the wasp in a way, since it carries the symbiant that helps it to survive. This symbiant doesn't harm *F. emasculata*, just as the virus doesn't harm the wasp. It only harms the mammalian host.

Since the discovery of a parasitoid that can use humans as hosts would be unlikely, you may be feeling safe right now. But you're not. The discovery of a *parasite* that can use humans as hosts is quite reasonable. Parasites often use mammals, including humans, as hosts, and many have the flexibility to use multiple species as hosts. So the next time you receive a smelly express package in the mail, you might want to have someone else open it.

THE FUNGUS FROM HELL

Considering the number of undiscovered life-forms that are believed to exist on Earth, the discovery of one inside a volcano seems fairly reasonable. This exact situation occurs in "Firewalker." Scientists send a robot to explore the inside of a volcano, and it brings back a subterranean fungus. The fungal spores promptly infect the scientists, growing in the lungs until they burst out through the throat and release the next generation of spores.

Could such a life-form survive in a volcano? Scully asserts that nothing can withstand the heat and toxic gases of the volcanic interior. Yet her statement seems about twenty years out of date. In recent years scientists have discovered previously unknown organisms in a variety of extreme environments on Earth, including deep underground, near hot hydrothermal vents under the ocean, and in the frigid Arctic Ocean. These organisms are called *extremophiles* after their love of extreme conditions. They grow best—and sometimes only—in an extreme environment. Dr. Juergen Wiegel, professor in the Department of Microbiology and the Department of Biochemistry and Molecular Biology at the University of Georgia, studies such extremophiles. "We're at a very exciting time. Microbiologists are finding organisms can survive under extremely extreme conditions." So could an organism survive in the underground interior of a volcano?

We boil medical instruments to sterilize them under the assumption, usually valid, that heating them to the boiling point, 212 degrees, kills all organisms. Yet some extremophiles are heat lovers, or thermophiles, preferring temperatures ranging from 115 degrees Fahrenheit all the way up to 300 degrees. This is within the range of 143–300 degrees registered by the Firewalker robot. Thermophiles have been found in a variety of hot environments: in geothermally heated rock over two miles underground, in and near underwater volcanic vents that shoot out superheated steam and minerals, in volcanically heated pools of boiling water and sulfur, and even in steam vents in volcanoes. So the discovery of an organism in a volcano is perfectly reasonable, and the levels of heat registered by Firewalker wouldn't be a problem. As for toxic gases, some of these microorganisms actually consume what we would consider to be toxic chemicals.

These life-forms obviously don't behave as we'd expect. While the DNA and proteins of most organisms become unstable at these high temperatures, thermophiles employ unique methods, as yet not fully understood, to keep their DNA and proteins stable. In fact, scientists have recently come to the conclusion that most extremophiles belong to a separate branch of the evolutionary tree called *archaea*. Biologists had previously grouped all life-forms into two groups: the *bacteria*, whose cells lack a nucleus; and the *eukarya*, whose cells are more complex. The eukarya include man, animals, plants, and fungi. Extremophiles confirm the existence of a controversial third branch, the archaea. While these organisms lack a nucleus and act much like bacteria, scientists have decided they must be classified separately because over half of their genes are unique to their group.

Some of these archaea may be survivors of the very early stages of life on Earth, when conditions were much more like the extreme environments they now inhabit. Some scientists believe that thermophilic organisms may even have been the first life on Earth four billion years ago and the ancestor of all life, surviving the heavy meteorite bombardment and the heat that would have been generated. Scientists now believe that thousands of undiscovered extremophiles exist on Earth.

What would such an organism feed on? In the episode, Trepkos's notes describe a metabolism that consumes hydrogen sulfide and transforms it into sulfur dioxide. Hydrogen sulfide would certainly be a plentiful food source for our fungus. It is a well-recognized volcanic gas (with the lovely perfume of rotten eggs). Most thermophiles actually use sulfur in their metabolic processes. Many oxidize hydrogen sulfide to produce sulfuric acid. Could a thermophile instead produce sulfur dioxide? Dr. Wiegel believes so. "Chemically, sulfur dioxide and sulfuric acid are at the same oxidation level, so theoretically, it could be possible." The sulfur dioxide would simply rise as a gas into the atmosphere. In fact, this already occurs with sulfur dioxide released naturally by volcanoes. Even when it's not erupting, a volcano may release thousands of tons of sulfur dioxide into the atmosphere every day. Up in the stratosphere, the sulfur dioxide reacts with water molecules to create sulfuric acid, and comes down as acid rain.

So finding a life-form under these conditions, with this metabolism, is in line with recent discoveries. None of these newly discovered life-forms, however, is silicon based, as Trepkos claims the volcanic fungus is. All life we know of is carbon based. Carbon seems to be the most conducive to life because it is tetravalent, easily forming bonds with four other atoms. This makes carbon extremely flexible, allowing it to form hundreds of thousands of different compounds, including chains, rings, and elaborate three-dimensional structures. It can form stable compounds held together by strong bonds as well as metastable compounds that can easily be formed and broken apart as necessary to carry out metabolic processes. Carbon can form long chains of repeated small units, called polymers, which are critical for life. The carbon in carbohydrates can oxidize to produce energy for our cells.

Carbon can also create molecules with distinctive forms that can recognize each other. This recognition allows organisms to regulate metabolic processes. To make these distinctive forms, carbon creates many stable asymmetric molecules that have what's known as *handedness*. Just as your left hand is the mirror image of your right, molecules with different handedness are three-dimensional mirror images of each other. At one end of their structure, almost all carbohydrates are "right-handed." Carbohydrates are broken down through the action of enzymes, which connect to the carbohydrates like a right glove fits onto a right hand. And just as your right hand won't fit into a left glove, a carbohydrate won't work with an enzyme of the wrong handedness. Dr. Raymond Dessy, professor of chemistry at Virginia Polytechnic Institute and State University, points out, "If you ate corn with left-handed carbohydrates, you wouldn't be able to digest it. You'd starve." This "right-handed" nature of carbohydrates limits the number of different types of enzymes needed to break them down. In general, handedness helps molecules to recognize each other and to carry out the right processes. All of these traits make carbon a very flexible and useful base for life.

Silicon, a constituent of the Earth's crust and most of the minerals on Earth, such as quartz and topaz, is slightly heavier than carbon, yet it is tetravalent as well. This has led scientists to speculate about the possibility of silicon-based life. Yet the types of compounds silicon can form are much more limited. Some compounds contain bonds that are too strong to support life. For example, silicon can bond with oxygen, but it forms very strong bonds that are not easily broken and reformed as is necessary in metabolic reactions. On the other hand, some of the bonds in silicon compounds are too weak. Silicon forms only weak bonds with itself, so molecules with more than three silicon atoms in a row are unstable unless they are formed in a lattice. Such lattices are fragile, and in their regularity lack the ability to form a wide variety of structures that can convey specific information to each other. Silicon doesn't form many compounds having handedness, so it would be difficult for them to recognize each other and regulate functions. Scientists have tried making new silicon compounds that mirror carbon compounds, but they've been unstable. Those with handedness can invert from left- to right-handed, which would leave enzymes unable to carry out reactions.

According to Dr. Dessy, one key difference between carbon life and potential silicon life is that when carbon oxidizes, it becomes carbon dioxide, a gas, while silicon becomes silicon dioxide, a solid also known as silica, or sand. This poses a disposal problem for the organism. While carbon dioxide is easily exhaled, imagine coughing out a mouthful of sand with every breath, or imagine a plant shedding grains of sand that eventually bury it alive.

Silicon does, however, create some incredible forms that look almost lifelike. Just as you can buy those magic paper trees and grow different colored silicate crystals on them, researchers have created their own environments and have grown silicate forms. These forms have regularity and symmetry but are extremely complex. Rather than the simple crystal structure of a diamond, they are bizarre and spectacular, looking, Dr. Dessy says, "as if there were some guiding force to their creation."

Would silicon life be any more likely in a high-temperature environment? The silicon-oxygen bond would be less stable at higher temperatures, allowing more flexibility in reactions. But then the already weak silicon-silicon bond would be even weaker, making it more difficult for large silicon structures to form. Some scientists do believe, though, that silicon compounds may play a limited role in biological processes in high-temperature environments.

How plausible is it that the life-form discovered on the show is a fungus? More likely inhabitants of a volcano would be archaea, single-celled microorganisms without nuclei. But could they be fungi? Fungi have adapted to a wide variety of environments. While most fungi prefer temperatures between 70–90 degrees, some can live at temperatures below freezing, and others survive and grow slowly at a balmy 150 degrees. Still, we haven't reached the temperatures detected by Firewalker. Dr. Wiegel finds the prospect unlikely. "That is utopia. Fungi are eukaryotes. Their organization is much more complex." Dr. Wiegel believes that such complex organisms couldn't survive in extreme heat. But perhaps the fungus is not living and growing within the volcano; perhaps some fungal spores are simply sitting passively within the volcano, blown there by the wind, waiting for more favorable conditions before they begin to grow. We never observed the fungus's activity within the volcano. Spores are able to survive long periods of adverse conditions, and can withstand dry heat of up to 300 degrees. They may then have become activated when removed from the heat by Firewalker. In this case, the fungus would not be a thermophile at all, but it could survive high temperatures in this inactive form.

Hypothesizing that the fungus does not grow in the volcano solves another problem. If the fungus was a thermophile, it would be unable to carry out its metabolic reactions in the chilly 98.6-degree environment of a human host. Dr. Wiegel explains, "The highest temperature span over which a microorganism can grow and reproduce is 90 degrees. Thermophiles that grow at over 212 degrees usually do not grow at below 150 degrees." If the organism cannot carry out its metabolic processes at 98.6 degrees, it may be able to survive in a dormant state, but it would most likely do its human host no harm.

This leads us to the next problem that a fungus presents. No eukaryotes that we know of oxidize hydrogen sulfide through their respiratory systems. "That would be something totally new. Which is not totally out of the thinkable. We just haven't isolated one of those yet." Dr. Wiegel imagines one possible way a fungus might develop the ability to oxidize hydrogen sulfide. Many scientists theorize that the mitochondria that power our cells started out billions of years ago as independent bacteria, then came to live in a symbiotic relationship with the cells that now make up humans and other animals. Dr. Wiegel speculates that sulfide-oxidizing archaea might somehow have been engulfed by a fungus and formed a symbiotic relationship with them, becoming the power plants of those cells. Dr. Wiegel is cautiously optimistic. "It's a little far-fetched, but it's possible." In fact, sulfide-oxidizing bacteria have formed symbiotic relationships with many other organisms, such as mussels and clams, creating whole ecosystems surrounding deep-sea hydrothermal vents.

So we may have found a way for the fungus to eat. But can it reproduce? The fungus in the episode has spores that are only active for a brief time and must immediately find a friendly host. This is quite different than the usual behavior of spores, which survive for extended periods, waiting for a favorable environment. Short-lived spores also aren't practical for survival, particularly if you live in a volcano and are looking for a human host. From an evolutionary perspective, a volcanic lifeform that lives in a parasitic relationship with humans really doesn't make sense. Organisms that have developed to live in such extreme environments would have little to no contact with humans, and so would not develop such complex mechanisms. If the fungus does require a human host to grow, this would suggest that the fungus's real home is at more moderate temperatures among humans, and would reinforce our theory that the fungus's spores only accidentally fell into the volcano. Even so, spores that are active for so short a time would be a crippling handicap for this fungus. While its impractical reproduction solves some problems for Scully and Mulder, it really doesn't give the fungus a fighting chance (or explain how it survived in the volcano for so long).

We've overlooked one point in our discussion, the growth of the fungus within a human host. What would the fungus eat inside the human body? Fungi, as discussed earlier, do grow in the lungs of human beings. They grow there because the conditions are favorable. But for a fungus that feeds off sulfur, would a lung look tasty? Sulfur is a constituent of some of the amino acids that comprise proteins. In fact, Dr. Wiegel explains, "A lot of pathogens hydrolyze proteins and utilize the amino acids." He points out that *Streptococcus pyogenes*, a special strain of bacteria able to eat away large parts of skin and tissue within a few hours, carries out that exact process on the proteins in flesh. The problem is that in the moist and aerobic environment of the lungs, the sulfur dioxide produced by the fungus would turn into sulfuric acid, which would debilitate the human host almost instantly and most likely kill him within hours. A parasite generally wants to keep its host alive longer than that. And the host usually wouldn't mind either.

PARANOIA REVISITED

Another previously unknown organism is discovered in an extreme environment in "Ice." Buried deep in the arctic ice, among high concentrations of ammonia, this one has no trouble surviving extremely cold temperatures for 250,000 years. Mulder theorizes that it has traveled to Earth via a meteoroid from another planet, one with an ammonia atmosphere and freezing temperatures. We'll discuss the possible survival of alien organisms on meteoroids in chapter 5; for now, let's focus on the organism itself.

The worm in question is parasitic, similar to the flukes covered back in chapter 1. It uses both dogs and humans as hosts, and it seems to travel from host to host through a bite and perhaps through other mechanisms. The organism enters a new host in its one-celled larval form. The larvae seem to make their way up along the back of the neck to the hypothalamus, a small region of the brain, where they may stimulate the production of acetylcholine, on which they feed. This excess of acetylcholine produces paranoia in the host and causes the host to act violently, which is why all the original arctic scientists have either killed each other or themselves. The adult worm settles at the base of the skull, and if it is removed, it secretes a fatal toxin, killing the host.

This "paranoia worm" provides us with a similar scenario to that involving the volcanic fungus. The worm can survive at extreme temperatures, yet it only seems to grow and reproduce at moderate temperatures. We can again assume the organism is not an extremophile, since a cold-loving extremophile, or *psychrophile*, would not be able to operate at the temperatures in the human body. A worm that prefers moderate temper-

atures could easily survive in subzero weather during protected embryonic or encysted stages of its life.

Although the worm in question is a complex organism and not a
virus, a few similarities to the rabies virus seem obvious. The organism
is transmitted through a bite, and the infection causes emotional
changes in the host that make it more likely to bite (if the host is a dog,
anyway). This simply shows that the organism is a well-developed parasite that has evolved a mechanism for its species' survival. It also suggests that the organism is a terrestrial one, having evolved in the
presence of other species that it has learned to use as hosts. Certainly if
it evolved on a planet whose conditions did not allow the formation of
mammals, it would not have developed a parasitic life cycle that depended on mammals.

How similar is our paranoia worm to terrestrial worms? One of
Mulder and Scully's companions, Dr. Hodge, notes that the adult
worm resembles the tapeworm, in that it has a scolex with suckers and
hooks. Tapeworms are parasites with long, flat bodies, like flukes. Some
tapeworms live in only one host, while others live in a succession of
hosts. They range in length from a few hundredths of an inch to over
fifty feet. Tapeworms have a scolex, or head, for attachment to the
mucus lining the small intestine. The head has suckers and perhaps
one or more rows of hooks. After the head comes a series of identical
segments called proglottids. Tapeworms, like flukes, are hermaphroditic. The paranoia worm seems superficially to resemble a tapeworm.
But how closely does its parasitic life cycle follow a tapeworm's?

Three major species of tapeworms are transmitted to humans by
the eating of raw or undercooked infected food. In the case of *Taenia
solium*, the pork tapeworm, a pig eats feces contaminated with tapeworm eggs. The eggs develop into a larval form known as a cysticercus,
where the tapeworm larva is enclosed within a fluid-filled cyst. When
the pig is killed and not cooked thoroughly, the larvae survive and pass
to you through consumption. The cyst dissolves as it passes through the
digestive enzymes and acids in the stomach. The freed larvae then attach to your gastrointestinal tract and develop into adults. Adults grow

in the small intestine to up to thirty feet long, absorbing food directly through the surface of their bodies. Once the hermaphroditic adult is ready to release eggs from the host, it breaks one proglottid after another off from its tail end. Each proglottid can carry forty thousand embryos. These proglottids flow passively out with the feces. Detached proglottids of the adult beef tapeworm, though, can sometimes emerge independently from the rectum. If the embryos are eaten by a mammal, such as a pig, then the life cycle continues.

The pork tapeworm provides two possible models for the transmission of the worm: ingestion of a contaminated mammal or ingestion of contaminated feces. Could the paranoia worm be transmitted in a similar fashion? The dog might have fed on the dead bodies of infected scientists (just like sweet little Queequeg in "Clyde Bruckman's Final Repose"). But how do we explain the contamination of the humans? Though the dog might ingest feces, it seems unlikely the humans would.

Yet how would the paranoia worm's eggs get into the feces of the scientists in the first place? The problem here is that no reasonable reproductive mechanism for this worm is shown. Normally tapeworms live in the intestine, so reproduction is easy. Just drop some eggs out with the feces and let another host eat them. But the paranoia worms seem to live in the neck or the brain, without easy access to the intestinal tract.

The episode suggests that the paranoia worm is passed through a bite, when the pilot, Bear, is infected after being bitten by the dog. In that case, its larvae would need to be in the saliva, as the rabies virus is. Parasitologist Stuart Knapp feels this is extremely unlikely, since no tapeworms involve the salivary glands. Yet the salivary glands are actually located fairly close to the worm's position at the base of the skull, and so perhaps it somehow manages to inject eggs or larvae into the saliva. We then have to assume that Dr. Da Silva, the female scientist who is discovered at the end of the episode to be infected, was also bitten by the dog.

So we have an unusual, but possible, method of transmission. Once inside a human host, could the paranoia worms cause behavioral changes? Such changes can be caused by the pork tapeworm. While all adult tapeworms live in the intestinal tract, the pork tapeworm, at other stages in its life, can involve the brain and lead to behavioral changes. If, instead of ingesting encysted larvae through an infected pig, a person directly ingests the original tapeworm eggs by eating something contaminated with feces, he will become host to the larval cysticerci rather than to the adult worms. After the eggs hatch in the small intestine, the larvae penetrate the lining and head out into the bloodstream. Some of them may invade the brain, where they will grow into cyst-encased cysticerci from ¼ inch to 8 inches in diameter, sometimes fluctuating in size. Most people who have these cysts have about a dozen of them, but some people may have thousands of such cysts in their brains. This condition, neurocysticercosis, can cause headaches, vertigo, meningitis, epileptic convulsions, partial paralysis, agitation, dementia, major neurological damage, and coma. Dr. Ralph Bryan of the National Center for Infectious Diseases explains, "The effects can be bizarre. Anything that you can think of from increased intracranial pressure to personality changes could happen depending on the location of the cysts."

While the pork tapeworm may accidentally end up in the brain, the paranoia worm seems to purposely involve the brain as part of its life cycle. Scully says she finds adult worms near the hypothalamus. The hypothalamus is a part of the brain at the upper end of the brain stem that links the nervous system and the endocrine system. It receives signals from other regions of the brain and then releases hormones and neurotransmitters that regulate body temperature, hunger, sexual behavior, emotional expression and behavior. The hypothalamus also serves as a coordinating point for the autonomic nervous system, controlling involuntary processes in the body such as breathing and digestion. The autonomic nervous system is comprised of two distinct systems, the sympathetic and parasympathetic. The sympathetic system stimulates the defense reaction, also called the *fight-or-flight reaction*. When we feel anger or fear, the hypothalamus reacts, preparing our body to either fight or flee: heart rate accelerates, blood pressure increases, the body begins to sweat, blood sugar rises, and more blood moves to the muscles. Although emotion does not originate in the hypothalamus, the hypothalamus is involved in our reactions to emotion. When certain neurons of the hypothalamus are excited with electrodes, an animal either becomes aggressive or flees. The animal is experiencing the fight-or-flight response without any original cause of fear.

This defense reaction is exactly what Scully and Mulder's party is displaying with their aggression and violence. In this case, the worm may be acting like the electrodes above, stimulating a reaction to an emotion that is not present. The tapeworm would need to target the specific part of the hypothalamus that stimulates the sympathetic nervous system. This would not cause a specific emotion in the host, but it would create the physiological reaction to that emotion. And that very reaction might create the emotion. Dr. Stewart Abramson, pharmacologist, explains: "If your heart is racing, you have high blood pressure, sweaty hands, your blood flow is shunted out to your muscles, and there's no apparent reason for it, you're going to feel very hyped up and anxious." The stimulation of this fight-or-flight response won't necessarily cause aggressive behavior, but it will create a higher degree of watchfulness, awareness, and suspicion. "You see the world how you feel," Dr. Abramson says. "If you feel hyped up and anxious, you'll start to see things that will support how you feel. Everything will look a little suspect. You'll start to get paranoid and pick fights, and then there will be a threat." Sounds a lot like the arctic scientists. Feedback will then stimulate the fight-or-flight response even more. And since the arctic party is trapped in an enclosed space, flight isn't an option. This possibility, that the worms are somehow stimulating specific neurons in the hypothalamus, provides us with one possible mechanism by which the worms might induce aggression.

Scully also connects the worm's activity to acetylcholine, a neurotransmitter secreted by the hypothalamus as well as by neurons throughout the body. She believes the worm may stimulate the production of acetylcholine, on which it feeds. Would that cause paranoia and violence in the hosts? Although the exact relationship between neurotransmitters and emotions remains unclear, doctors know that the chemicals can have powerful effects on a patient's mental state. As mentioned on page 127, acetylcholine is one of the chemicals that transmits neural signals at nerve synapses and muscle connections. Participating in the transmission of many different types of signals in the brain and throughout the body, acetylcholine allows us to move our muscles, and stimulates both the sympathetic and parasympathetic systems. Acetylcholine's effects are not nearly as simple as described on the show; excess acetylcholine creates conflicting signals in the body. In order to correctly transmit signals and to create coordinated muscle contraction and relaxation, our neurons need to be able to secrete and break apart acetylcholine as needed. Some pesticides and nerve toxins, such as sarin, the one used by the Japanese religious group Aum Shinrikyo in the Tokyo subway attack, block the enzyme that breaks down acetylcholine. Acetylcholine then builds up at the nerve terminals, signals are confused, and muscles no longer work properly.

The effects caused by these pesticides and nerve toxins ought to be similar to those caused by the paranoia worm, since the worm seems to cause excess secretion of acetylcholine. At low doses, these substances can cause excitation of the sympathetic system, stimulating the fight-or-flight response. In addition to those physical responses, these substances can also affect the central nervous system, leading to tremors, headache, anxiety, agitation, phobia, neurosis or psychosis, schizophrenia, aggression, and paranoia. This seems to line right up with the symptoms experienced by the arctic scientists, and so provides us with a second mechanism by which the worms might induce aggression.

At larger doses, however, the sympathetic system is inhibited, and the parasympathetic responses are enhanced. Stimulation of the parasympathetic system slows heartbeat, lowers blood pressure, and induces contraction of smooth muscles, such as those in the intestine and lungs. This results in chest tightness, wheezing, vomiting, convulsions, blurring of vision, and in severe cases respiratory paralysis. Central nervous system responses to high doses include speech and balance disorders, insomnia, hallucinations, mental confusion, and depression. So the level of acetylcholine would have to be very carefully regulated to keep the host sufficiently healthy and mentally alert.

Has the paranoia worm developed in a practical way for survival? Dr. Abramson believes so. "The pathogen has a selective site of action and causes a specific set of behaviors that helps propagate the pathogen." If the worm is spread by a bite, though, only the dog has responded appropriately. We might theorize then that the dog is the closest to the host that the ice worm normally parasitized in its life on Earth 250,000 years ago. When a pathogen infects a host for which it is not adapted, it is often not as effective at surviving and spreading as in its normal host. If infected humans shoot each other, or themselves, it doesn't do the worms a lot of good.

If the paranoia worm does stimulate the fight-or-flight response in those infected, why do the others also seem so jumpy? The answer may lie in an ancient structure in the midbrain called the *amygdala*. The amygdala is involved in storing emotional memories and evaluating the emotional expressions of others. Recent experiments have shown that the neural signal generated by a subject's amygdala is directly related to the intensity of fear he sees in other people's expressions. This signal can be observed through a PET scan, one of Scully's favorite tests. Using radioactive isotopes, the PET scan can measure blood flow variations in the brain, which reflect metabolic activity. Test subjects were shown photographs of people with facial expressions ranging from happy to neutral to fearful. Their PET scans revealed that blood flow increased with the fearful expressions. Since the amygdala is wired directly to the hypothalamus, the fight-or-flight response can be quickly elicited when a fearful expression is seen. Scientists believe this may indicate a pathway by which the brain can react quickly to fear without waiting for rational, conscious thought. And so the terrified expression of Bear might elicit the fight-or-flight response in Mulder and Scully, even thought they aren't infected.

FOR THE LOVE OF SCIENCE •

Dr. Stuart Knapp tells the story of a colleague who came from Norway to study *Diphyllobothrium latum,* the broad fish tapeworm, in Yellowstone National Park. Since *D. latum* was originally brought to the U.S. by Scandinavian immigrants, this Norwegian parasitologist was interested in comparing the adult form of *D. latum* in the U.S. to the adult form of *D. latum* in his native land. The eggs of the broad fish tapeworm are deposited in the feces of a mammalian host and washed into lakes and streams. There the eggs are eaten by fish. A bear then eats the fish and becomes infected with the worm. If a human eats raw fish, he too can become infected, and such worms have been found growing up to twenty feet long in the human intestine. The Norwegian decided that the easiest way to transport the tapeworm was to eat an infected fish raw, and carry the worm home in his own intestine. Which is exactly what he did. Back in Norway, he took an anthelmintic drug (you may have given one to your dog, to deworm him). The drug forced the worm out of his body, and he had his specimen.

The really scary thing is that this practice is fairly common among parasitologists.

HISTORY ON ICE

The paranoia worm in "Ice" is discovered in a core drilled deep through the arctic ice. The real-life equivalent of this scientific endeavor is the Greenland Ice Sheet Project 2, which involved drilling through the glacial ice of Greenland. The U.S. team there set the record for the longest ice core ever collected, digging 10,013 feet—almost two miles—to ice that was formed over 250,000 years ago.

Since new ice is formed by the accumulation of snow each year, the composition of the ice at different depths reflects the climatological conditions at the time it was deposited. The alteration of summer and winter weather patterns creates bands in the ice core similar to the rings of a tree, which allows researchers to determine the specific year of a particular layer of ice. Yet the ice contains more detailed information about the past than tree rings, coral growth layers, or marine sediment cores. Frozen in such 5.2-inch-diameter cores are trapped gases, chemicals, and atmospheric dust, which can help scientists re-create the history of volcanic activity, biological productivity, climatic changes, and atmospheric and oceanic conditions.

If the gray alien found frozen in ice in "Gesthemane" is a hoax, then the ice around it would have had to be painstakingly created with elements that were consistent with other ice cores dating back two hundred years.

While the Greenland core didn't bring up any life-forms, it has revealed previously unknown information about planet Earth. The Greenland core showed that the climate shifts more quickly and frequently than expected, sometimes changing dramatically in less than ten years. In one case, the snowfall of Greenland doubled in just three years and the average temperature jumped by twelve degrees. While overall shifts in climate do occur over long periods, as previously believed, dramatic changes can occur over the short term as well.

Just another sign that things here on planet Earth are not as predictable as we'd like to think. If there is a lesson to be learned from these Earthly oddities, it is that. And though these X-files may be a bit scarier than real Earthly creatures, they are no more bizarre, for today science is discovering organisms never before known and never before thought possible.

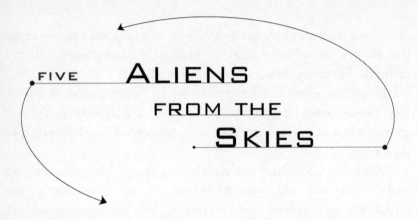

FIVE

ALIENS FROM THE SKIES

"By the time there's another invasion of artificially intelligent dung-eating robotic probes from outer space, maybe their children will have devised a way to save our planet."

—Dana Scully,
"War of the Coprophages"

A WOMAN IN THE MEN'S ROOM. THIS is odd. Krycek smiles at her. Her hand shoots out and seizes him around the neck, slams him up against the tile wall. He's pinned there, gasping, his feet hanging free of the floor. First that wimp Mulder beats him up and now this. Obviously not one of his better days. Krycek strikes out with his arm, getting in a good hit to her eye. She doesn't even flinch. Then he thinks he's done some damage. Blood starts flowing across the surface of her eyes. But it's not blood; it's black. And then the black is flowing from her eyes, her nose. She lowers him to the floor, and now he's lost too much oxygen to fight back. His limbs fold beneath him as her hand maintains its iron grip around his throat. She towers over him, the flowing black hanging from her cheeks and chin, collecting.

In a move that seems purposeful it drops. Something splashes in his eye, so he knows it must have fallen on him, yet he can't feel it. Sensation is draining away. Black dots swim over his eyes, blurring his vision. With a start he gasps; she has removed her hand. Then the black dots swell and his mind disengages.

In a number of episodes, humans are attacked by parasitic organisms of possibly alien origin. We talked about several such cases already, where the evidence of extraterrestrial origins was minimal. But in some cases the evidence is too strong to be ignored. Alien parasites have invaded Earth and are wreaking havoc with the local populace. Twice Mulder theorizes that this alien life has arrived on Earth via a meteorite. Is this possible? Can alien invaders fall from the skies? And if they can, what would be the nature of these invaders? These X-files have bizarre, fascinating properties. Could an extraterrestrial parasite take over our bodies, controlling our actions and even accessing our knowledge and memories? Could alien worms coagulate out of a puddle of oil and then revert to a puddle when their work is done? Could a parasite release huge doses of ionizing radiation without killing its host? And what defense could we possibly mount against such alien invaders?

ARE ALIENS FALLING FROM THE SKIES?

In "El Mundo Gira," Mulder theorizes that the bizarre, short-lived yellow rain that fell from a cloudless sky may have been caused by space debris. His theory goes like this: A meteoroid falls through the atmosphere to Earth and lands in water. The meteorite (a meteoroid becomes a meteorite when it reaches the surface of the Earth) superheats the water and shoots it up into the sky. This water then falls back to Earth as bizarre-colored rain, contaminated with an alien fungus. Possible?

Well, it's estimated that over three million tons of meteoric matter fall to Earth each year, 8,700 tons per day. While this may sound like a lot, it's spread over a vast area. According to Dr. Bill Sharp, who studies meteorites for their possible metallic value at the Colorado School of Mines, only .2 ounces hits an area the size of a city per year. Most meteoroids are very small, as small as 1/10,000th of an inch. They zip into the atmosphere with a velocity between 10,000 and 160,000 miles per hour. About once a month, though, a meteoroid six feet in diameter hits the atmosphere, carrying as much energy as a one-kiloton nuclear explosion. Once a year, an even larger meteoroid rams into the atmosphere with an energy comparable to the blast that leveled Hiroshima. So why aren't we dead?

As the meteoroid penetrates the atmosphere, it hurtles through denser and denser layers of air, and a lot of heat is generated by this friction. Most of this energy is dissipated through a process called ablation. The outer layers of the meteoroid vaporize and pieces break off and fragment. The surface, just a fraction of an inch thick, often becomes so hot that it actually melts, forming a fusion crust around the outside of the meteoroid. While it is heating up very quickly on the outside, the heat doesn't have a lot of time to conduct to the inside. Astronomer Paul Viscuso at Cornell University explains, "As the outer layer heats and expands, the cooler inner layers will not expand as much, leading the way for the material to cleave." More stress is generated because the composition of the meteoroid isn't uniform, its shape is irregular, and it may be spinning and bouncing its way through the atmosphere. Smaller particles stripped away by the ablation process create a smoke trail along the meteoroid's path. A second trail is created by energy transferred to the atmosphere, ionizing and exciting a trail of atoms along the meteoroid's path. Meteoroids can create trails twenty miles long that linger for several hours.

The fate of individual meteoroids depends on their speed, mass, and composition. Fine interplanetary dust particles, only a few thousandths of an inch across, can often drift gently to Earth without melting. Small meteoroids, larger than dust but less than a few inches across, usually incinerate on the trip through the atmosphere. We can see these as shooting stars. Those that don't burn up are reduced to smaller bits and slowed to free-fall speed, a mere 120 mph, the same speed at which a skydiver falls. These chunks, explains Dr. Simon J. Clemett, a cosmochemist at Stanford University, "don't make a big crater. They just go thump in your back garden." The heat generated by atmospheric friction is largely dissipated by ablation (just as the heat of your body is dissipated by evaporation of sweat), so the outside of the meteorite is only slightly warm, while the inside may be icy cold.

Large meteoroids, six inches across and up, are not slowed as much by the atmosphere. They can hit the Earth at over 10,000 mph, "four to five times the velocity of a bullet," Clemett says. And while they do suffer ablation, they are not usually reduced to bits. A large chunk of the original meteoroid can make it to the surface of the Earth, where it often explodes or vaporizes on impact. This would make a large meteorite an unlikely vehicle of life. The fate of any individual meteorite, though, depends on composition, as we'll see further on in our discussion.

Since any meteorite that may have fallen in "El Mundo Gira" appears not to have been detected, nor to have caused any major cataclysm, we have to assume it was relatively small. So Mulder's theory of it superheating the water in a lake seems unlikely. It would not have been at such elevated temperatures. The meteorite, though, could send up a big splash. But would the water contain any harmful chemicals or organisms?

Certainly if life did survive interplanetary travel on a meteoroid, it would have to be sheltered deep within the rock. So the chances of it being instantaneously transferred to the water seem small. But say the meteoroid broke up, either on the way down or on impact, exposing the interior to the water. Could an alien fungus be living there?

Before we answer that question, let's look at another X-file in which alien life may have survived in a meteorite.

In the two-part story "Tunguska" and "Terma," a rock of extraterrestrial origin apparently contains a living organism, the black cancer, that can infect humans. The rock was found at the site of a meteorite impact in Tunguska, Siberia, deep below the surface. What exactly happened at Tunguska?

On June 30, 1908, a fireball streaked across the sky, and witnesses at nearby villages heard a huge explosion and were knocked off their feet. The blast scorched 850 square miles of trees and threw them flat against the ground. Shock waves rocked the world. Clouds of dust shot up into the atmosphere and reached as far as London. For thousands of miles around, light reflecting from the dust caused the sky to remain bright day and night with an eerie orange glow. The impact carried the force of one thousand Hiroshima bombs (not two thousand, as Mulder claims, yet at ground zero, what difference does it really make?). Yet there is no crater at Tunguska. There are no meteorite fragments.

Until recently, this lack of fragments puzzled scientists (and led to an unsubstantiated theory that the devastation at Tunguska was caused not by a meteorite but by a UFO visitation). Then an Italian physicist, Dr. Menotti Galli, began to study the growth rings of surviving Tunguska trees for evidence. He theorized that resin exuded by the trees might have captured particles from a meteorite. What he found was that around the time of the Tunguska event, the particles in the resin had unusually high levels of copper, gold, and nickel. These particles were also smooth and spherical, indicating exposure to very high temperatures, temperatures that wouldn't have been reached by soil thrown up by the impact. The particles had to have come from the meteorite itself.

So why have only these small particles been found, and nothing larger? Another scientist, Dr. Wilhelm Fast, led a team in the mapping of the pattern in which the trees had fallen. The trees at the epicenter of the event were not broken at the ground or thrown out by the roots. Instead they were broken two to three feet above the ground, characteristic of an explosion about four miles above the surface. The meteorite exploded in midair. This fact helped scientists deduce the size of the object, which they now estimate at two hundred feet across. Some scientists feel that midsized meteorites between 10–300 feet (bigger than most meteorites, but smaller than the really huge ones) are particularly vulnerable to differential stresses. The front of such a meteoroid experiences intense pressure and heat from the atmosphere, while the back experiences almost no pressure. This difference causes the meteoroid to literally explode into smaller fragments, which in turn explode again, leaving little more than a cloud of debris. The composition of the Tunguska meteoroid also seems to have played a critical role. Dr. Clemett explains that it was most likely a cometary fragment, in consistency similar to a dirty snowball. The eccentric orbits of comets cause any cometary meteoroid to enter the atmosphere at very high speeds. And its icy consistency would help explain how the entire mass could vaporize leaving minimal traces.

The shock wave from the explosion flattened the trees and threw dirt and dust into the air. Most of the remnants of the meteorite burned up on the remainder of their journey to the surface, though a small percent reached the Earth as a fine sprinkling of gravel, consistent with the particles found in the trees. According to Dr. Sharp, one hundred tons of material may have sprinkled the ground at Tunguska, but it would have been scattered over three thousand square miles. This would leave .025 ounces of material scattered over one hundred square yards. Dr. Sharp is amazed that any particles were ever recovered. "Talk about looking for a needle in a haystack." Yet the plants seem to be aware of the meteorite's presence. They have grown at a much faster rate near the epicenter of the event than elsewhere in the area. Dr. Sharp theorizes that the high energy of the explosion may have fixed nitrogen in our atmosphere with oxygen, creating NO_2, which might then be dissolved by rain and fall to the ground, acting as fertilizer. Another theory is that trace elements associated with the meteorite have fertilized the plants.

If you find it depressing that a two-hundred-foot meteorite can leave only microscopic traces and you "want to believe" that the Russians found something living in a meteorite fragment, let me propose an alternate site. At Sikhote-Alin, in eastern Siberia, large meteorite chunks up to 3,850 pounds have been found. . . .

Setting aside the problem of finding an intact Tunguska meteorite fragment of significant size, let's return to the question raised earlier. Could a living extraterrestrial organism survive in such a fragment?

Well, where would such an organism come from? Comets contain a high percentage of organic molecules, potential precursors of life. To be considered organic, a molecule need not be created in a biological process; it simply needs to contain carbon, hydrogen, and oxygen. Some scientists believe such molecules, carried by extraterrestrial sources such as comets and interstellar dust, introduced the building blocks of life to Earth. In fact, 10 percent of the extraterrestrial material landing on Earth is made up of such organic molecules. A comet wouldn't even need to collide with Earth to pass on this material. Comets release long trails of dust as they pass near the sun. The Earth passes periodically through these trails, resulting in regularly recurring meteorite showers such as the Perseid. While the precursors of life exist on comets, though, few scientists believe life itself could develop on a comet. With its lack of an atmosphere or liquid water and the long periods of time that it spends at very low temperatures, it's extremely unlikely that a comet would be home to life.

Perhaps the theory that the impact at Tunguska was caused by a comet is wrong. If so, then the meteoroid may have come from the asteroid belt, the moon, or Mars.

Mars seems to be the leading contender for sustaining life. It is now widely accepted that during its first billion years of existence, conditions on Mars were conducive to life, with water, volcanic heat, and a thick carbon-dioxide atmosphere that would have produced a greenhouse effect and warm temperatures. Some scientists believe favorable conditions may still exist on Mars. Dr. David McKay, senior scientist for planetary exploration at NASA's Johnson Space Center, is more optimistic than ever about the possibility of life on Mars. "Underground on Mars is a good place to look for life." He cites the availability of heat and theories that a large groundwater system may circulate about a mile below the surface. These conditions are similar to those deep below the surface of Earth, where life has recently been discovered, as mentioned in the discussion of "Firewalker." What direct evidence do we have of life on Mars?

INVADERS FROM MARS

In 1996, Dr. McKay, Dr. Clemett, and colleagues claimed to have discovered organic molecules and possible fossilized nanobacteria from Mars in a meteorite, Allan Hills 84001, found in Antarctica. This claim has met with much controversy, and while some evidence supports it, the theory now seems as if it cannot be definitively proven.

The origin of the rock, though, is agreed to be Mars. How do we know where it came from? We can't ask for its license and registration, though it was clocked at 120 mph. Dr. Clemett explains that a variety of factors led to this conclusion. First, while most meteorites are about 4.65 billion years old, dating back to the start of the solar system, the Allan Hills meteorite, along with others also believed to have come from Mars, is much younger, only a few hundred million to a couple billion years old. Second, the rock comprising these meteorites has come from a volcanically active body. This rules out the moon, asteroids, or comets. Still, though, the meteorite could be from Earth itself. Meteorite impacts on Earth have probably sent chunks of rock from Earth into space, and some of these would later land back on Earth. How do we know that's not the case? From the third criteria—testing the isotopic ratio of hydrogen in water trapped in the silicate minerals of the rock.

In its normal form, hydrogen has one proton and one electron. An alternate version, or *isotope*, of hydrogen contains one proton, one electron, and one neutron. This is called deuterium. Since the proton and the neutron weigh about the same and the electron is virtually weightless, deuterium is twice as heavy as regular hydrogen. As these gases move around in the atmosphere, the lighter ones move faster and so escape from the atmosphere more easily. Since Mars is less massive than Earth and so has less gravity, hydrogen escapes from it more easily. Mars then has a higher ratio of deuterium to hydrogen than Earth. Since these meteorites have the same ratio that has been measured on Mars, the water in them is actually Martian water. Dr. Clemett asserts that concluding that the meteorites came from Mars is "the simplest explanation. If that's not the answer, then we have a huge problem trying to explain where they came from."

So this meteorite likely came from Mars. But since it landed in Antarctica over thirteen thousand years ago, scientists debate whether the organic compounds found existed within the meteorite or contaminated it after it reached Earth. Two types of organic molecules were found, amino acids and polycyclic aromatic hydrocarbons (PAHs). The amino acids, the building blocks of proteins, have now been shown to be most likely of terrestrial origin. This still leaves the origin of the polycyclic aromatic hydrocarbons in question. These organic molecules have been found not only in this Martian meteorite but also in meteorites from the asteroid belt and even on interstellar dust, environments that could not harbor life. Obviously in the latter two cases, PAHs do not indicate the presence of life. But might they in the case of Mars?

When living organisms die and decay, they create hydrocarbons associated with coal, peat, and petroleum. Many of these belong to a class of organic molecules called PAHs. PAHs are important, according to Dr. Clemett, because "They tend to be very durable molecules. They are stable and can last over geological time scales." A human, in four million years, would decay into nothing more than PAHs. PAHs are also insoluble in water, unlike amino acids. And so, while it now seems likely that the amino acids in the Allan Hills meteorite percolated into the rock with Antarctic water, PAHs could not have been carried into the rock by water. This increases the likelihood that these PAHs are extraterrestrial.

But do they clearly indicate life was present? Dr. Clemett admits that "PAHs are created in a whole range of inorganic situations, as are amino acids." In fact, Dr. Clemett believes the reason amino acids may have become the building blocks of life is because they happened to be around in large quantities.

So is there no evidence of life at all on the Allan Hills meteorite? Dr. Clemett stresses that it is the combination of factors that is suggestive of life. But the strongest evidence appears to be the specific type of PAHs discovered. Of the thousands of PAHs that exist, the few that were found in the Martian meteorite are the same as those created by the decay of microbes on Earth, indicating an organic origin for these PAHs. So perhaps life did once exist on Mars. But could it have survived the trip to Earth?

First, the life-form would have had to be deep inside a rock. That rock would have had to be ejected from the surface of Mars by a huge meteoritic impact. This impact "would cause a temperature pulse of 300–400 degrees Celsius," says Dr. Clemett. And it would have to eject the rock at extremely high velocity in order for it to escape Mars's gravitational field, "a traumatic process." In space, the rock would be subjected to temperatures close to absolute zero, regions of gas several million degrees hotter, and cosmic rays.

Cosmic rays are made up of very high-energy atomic and subatomic particles that are created in a number of different astronomical environments. These cosmic rays constantly bombard Earth in energies ranging up to thousands of megaelectronvolts. Earth's atmosphere and magnetic field shield us from most of this, though the higher you go in the atmosphere, the more cosmic rays you're exposed to. Every time you climb a mountain or take a plane trip, your exposure increases. We've got it easy, though. Outside the atmosphere, there is no protection. As Dr. Howard Matis, staff physicist at Lawrence Berkely National Laboratories, says, "If an astronaut would go to Mars, half of his cells would be zapped by heavy ion particles. If we're going to take long journeys in space, we have to withstand that radiation. It is a serious health problem."

If our Martian meteoroid was in space for more than a few million years, any living thing would most likely be sterilized by the cosmic rays. While in theory it could make the trip from Mars to Earth in only a few years, it's extremely unlikely; the Allen Hills meteorite spent sixteen million years in space before falling to Earth. Dr. Clemett admits, though, that a living organism buried deep inside a large rock might be sufficiently shielded from the cosmic rays: "It's extraordinarily unlikely, but not impossible."

If the organism did survive, then we'd need the meteoroid to be captured by Earth's gravity, and it would have to come into the atmosphere at the right angle and be the right size and the right composition not to burn up or explode on the way down. Since the rock must be large for the organisms to survive the cosmic rays, it might not burn up, but the explosion on impact would very likely kill our organisms.

Dr. McKay gives the fledgling Martians more of a chance. Could they survive? "Absolutely," he says. "Some kinds of bacteria would survive the trip very nicely. Bacteria can go into a hybernation state where they are not metabolizing but still alive, and can be revived once you give them water and warmth." To the danger of cosmic rays, he asserts, "Some bacteria are extremely resistant to radiation. It seems certainly possible if not probable that any life on a Martian meteorite might survive and start growing here on Earth."

So if they did survive . . . what type of organisms might they be? Dr. Clemett sees only one possibility. "The only type of life I could conceive would be the simplest possible single-celled life. Bacterial spores are very hardy." Dr. Clemett cites cases of viable bacterial spores being recovered from the Siberian tundra after being frozen for three million years, and of spores trapped in amber fifteen million years ago yielding some viable material.

Could such bacteria be harmful to humans? Dr. Clemett doesn't think so. "Bacteria are harmful to humans only because they profit from attacking humans. Some random bacterial spore wouldn't have a clue about human life and would probably find itself being attacked rather than anything else." Dr. McKay concurs. "It may be like the new kid on the block getting beat up by the local bullies." So our poor organism, after suffering the trauma of ejection, space travel, reentry, and impact, limps out from its battered shelter only to be killed by terrestrial organisms. I'm feeling a bit sorry for the black cancer.

VISITING OTHER PLANETS, THE CHEAP WAY

If you'd like to study extraterrestrial rocks, the best way may be to take a trip down south. Antarctica is a hotbed of meteorites. The conditions there are perfect for revealing these pieces of far-off worlds. It's not that more meteorites fall there; it's just that those that do fall are easier to find.

Meteorites become buried in the Antarctic ice sheets. These sheets, driven by gravity, are constantly flowing from the center of the continent out toward the ocean, with the meteorites carried along. Fortunately for us, several mountain ranges interrupt the flow of the ice sheets toward the ocean. The ice pushes up against the mountains and becomes trapped. As the cold Antarctic winds blow over the surface of the ice, the top layers are sublimated or vaporized. This is similar to the process of evaporation, but instead of liquid water changing into a gas, solid ice is changed into a gas. Gradually the meteorites below are revealed. As this process continues, more and more meteorites collect at the base of the mountains.

Scientists have recovered over 17,000 meteorites from the bases of Antarctic mountains since this process was first discovered in 1969. Compare that number to the mere 2,500 meteorites collected worldwide up until that time.

I'd love to see Mulder and Scully check these out.

TO RUSSIA, WITH LOVE

If extraterrestrial life could potentially survive on a meteorite, then, is that the origin of the black cancer? Scully, Mulder, and Dr. Sacks, the exobiologist who studied the Tunguska rock, overlook another much more likely possibility. Dr. Sacks seems to conclude, from the age of the rock and the presence of polycyclic aromatic hydrocarbons, that the rock is from Mars. But as we know, those criteria in and of themselves are not sufficient to prove the rock's origin. Polycyclic aromatic hydrocarbons are found with decaying organic matter (and elsewhere) on Earth. Since the isotopic ratio of hydrogen was not tested, the rock could easily be an old Earth rock. It might even be a rock ejected from Earth that later fell back. Since Dr. Sacks didn't discuss any additional criteria, we can't make a final determination about the type or origin of the rock. Even if you want to believe the rock is a meteorite fragment, that doesn't mean any life found inside it is extraterrestrial.

The prisoner in the cell beside Mulder in Tunguska, a geologist, explains that the rock came from deep in the ground, so deep that it was incredible anything could live there. As we know, it's extremely unlikely that a significant-sized piece of meteorite would have survived at all, let alone have become buried very deep in the Earth.

Another interpretation seems more likely. As I mentioned earlier, recent discoveries have established the presence of life on Earth at depths far surpassing what anyone thought possible. Dr. Tullis Onstott, a geologist at Princeton University, has discovered bacteria as deep as 11,500 feet, over two miles, beneath the surface. Some of the bacteria found seem to have been living there for hundreds of millions of years. In many cases the bacteria are trapped inside the rock, the pores of the rock smaller than the bacteria. In other cases, the pores are large enough to allow the bacteria to mix with other substances, such as the lubricating fluids used by drillers or buried toxic waste (does this worry anyone else?). One type of bacteria found in sedimentary rock lives on petroleum and other organic compounds dissolved in the groundwater. Another type of recently discovered bacteria, living in igneous rock, needs only hydrogen, water, and carbon dioxide to live, all of which it can get from the Earth's interior, completely independently of the sun. While most of these organisms don't receive enough food to grow or reproduce, they do survive, in a sort of suspended animation. With the discovery of life in igneous rock, one of the most abundant types of rocks, scientists are coming to believe that the organisms may be quite widespread. Dr. Thomas Gold at Cornell University has even calculated that the weight of all subterranean microbes could equal that of all organisms above the surface.

It seems quite possible that Tunguska scientists, in their long quest to find meteorite fragments, might have dug down to a depth where they encountered an organism to which man has never been exposed, one that lives deep underground and feeds on petroleum.

Conversely, the discovery of these organisms living deep below the surface also increases the possibility of life existing underground on Mars, in very similar conditions. In fact, Dr. McKay believes the organisms may even be distant relatives, the bacteria of Earth and Mars visiting each other via meteorites over the lifetimes of the planets. Meteoroids traveling from Earth to Mars are rare because Earth's greater gravity makes it more difficult for meteoroids to escape. Yet meteoroids from Mars to Earth seem to arrive at the rate of about one per year, leading Dr. McKay to believe that Martian bacteria may already have arrived on Earth. In fact, they may even have been the source of all life on Earth, including you.

BLACK WORMS

The life-form shown in "Tunguska" and "Terma" is a black, thin, inch-long worm-shaped organism, which is seemingly able to live for long periods in oil within a rock or to congeal out of some substance that resembles oil. We have seen similar organisms in a number of episodes and the movie, but first let's just consider the organism shown in "Tunguska" and "Terma." The worms enter a person either through an orifice or by penetrating the skin. Once inside, they migrate just beneath the skin, passing through the eyes, where they are visible as inky clouds, quickly reaching the brain, where they give rise to a microscopic "black vermiform organism" (BVO) within the human host. Vermiform simply means worm-shaped. According to Scully, the BVO is attached to the pineal gland, a small organ in the brain. The BVO then may produce a paralyzing toxin, immobilizing its host, as it did to Dr. Sacks. The original worms can be made to leave the host when the Russian-developed "vaccine" is administered. It seems that the microscopic BVO also leaves or is destroyed, since no trace is left in the host (at least none that can be detected).

What type of organism is the black cancer, and must it be extraterrestrial in origin? The black cancer is unique, not behaving like any other known organism, which is what makes it so compelling. To fully understand what makes it so unique, we need to compare it to other organisms. In *The X-Files* movie, an organism that seems the same as the "Tunguska" black cancer is referred to repeatedly as a virus. Yet as far as we have been shown, the black cancer does not act like a virus at all. While a virus is a parasite of a cell, invading it and using it to reproduce, the black cancer is a parasite of the body, traveling through it, feeding off it, and creating widespread effects. Many different wormlike parasites, or helminths, exist right here on Earth. In fact, helminths infect more than a quarter of the world's population. There are three types of helminths: flukes, tapeworms, and roundworms. We've already talked about flukes with "The Host" and tapeworms with "Ice." In this case, comparison with nematodes, or roundworms, may shed some light on the black cancer. Roundworms live in almost every type of environment—deserts and lakes, hot springs and arctic seas—and include a huge number of species—second only to insects—some living independently, many living part or all of their lives as parasites in animals and plants. About fifteen thousand different species have been identified, though this is only an estimated 3 percent of the total. The most well-known nematodes are heartworms, pinworms, and hookworms. Nematodes range in size from microscopic to huge; those found in whales are twenty-three feet long.

The eye worm, *Loa loa*, seems to share with the black cancer an affection for the eye and a habit of migrating just below the skin. The *Loa* larvae are carried by a deerfly. When the fly lands on you, the worm larvae drop onto the skin and burrow through the hole made by the biting fly. The larvae migrate through the bloodstream, usually settling in the cornea or just below the skin. The adult *Loa* can grow to 2½ inches and live for fifteen years. It has a tendency to wander around just below the skin, causing itching and swelling. Dr. Robert Vallari, associate professor of biology at Saint Anselm College, says that *Loa* can sometimes be caught as it crosses the bridge of the nose, when it is clearly outlined. *Loa* can also be seen in the eye, though it looks like a piece of spaghetti rather than the rapidly moving clouds of the black cancer. The female gives birth to microfilariae, active embryos that travel your blood and lymph systems. When a deerfly bites you, it sucks in some of these microfilariae, which then grow into larvae and move to the insect's proboscis, completing the life cycle. *Loa* rarely causes serious disability, though in some cases microfilariae dying in the brain can cause an inflammatory reaction, leading to confusion, stupor, and coma. Worms that are visible beneath the skin are sometimes removed with surgery. If you are treated with anthelmintic drugs (drugs that fight helminths), *Loa* will sometimes come right out of the eye, just like our friend the black cancer.

Unlike *Loa*, the black cancer lives part of its life outside a host, and it seems to infect the customs agent at the airport by penetrating the skin of his ankle, while it infects Dr. Sacks through an airtight biohazard suit. Do any terrestrial nematodes have similar abilities? *Strongyloides stercoralis* lives part of its life outside a host, in sandy soil. In its larval stage, it uses an enzyme that helps dissolve connective tissue to penetrate the skin of its host. Dr. Ralph Bryan, a senior medical epidemiologist with the National Center for Infectious Diseases of the Centers for Disease Control and Prevention, says, "They just wriggle their way on in there." If you sit naked on moist sandy soil in an area such as the southeastern United States, the *Strongyloides* larvae can penetrate your skin. The larvae move through your bloodstream to your lungs, grow, are coughed up, and travel to the small intestine. Feeding off the contents of the small intestine, the larvae mature to adult worms and produce larvae, which are passed out through the feces. In cases where infection builds up over decades, *Strongyloides* can invade the central nervous system and brain.

Do worms ever come out the nose? Dr. Bryan says, "Occasionally *Ascaris* will be regurgitated, and a kid will pull one out of his nose to the horror of his mother."

Although we haven't yet seen the entire life cycle of the black cancer, it seems to have some similarities to the life cycles of these worms. A striking difference, though, is that Earthly helminths are strictly geared toward growth and reproduction. They develop into a new stage in every host, and all of their actions are done with an eye toward spreading their offspring as widely as possible. While we have seen the "Tunguska" black cancer leave one person and enter another, we have never seen it reproduce or seen any sign that it does. If the BVO were some sort of egg sack laid by the worms, then we should have seen it hatch and burst someone's head open by now. But we haven't (and more's the pity). We also haven't seen the black cancer mature from one stage to another, say from larva to adult, as is normal within humans. In this two-part episode, the black cancer leaves the body in the same shape as it entered. With only this much information about the black cancer, what might the Shadowy Syndicate conclude? There are three possibilities: that the worm may complete its maturation process outside of a host, that humans are not the normal host for the black cancer at this stage of its life, or that the black cancer has somehow been neutered through bioengineering.

Let's first examine the possibility that the black cancer may complete its maturation outside of a host. Remember the bot fly, whose larva rides on the proboscis of the mosquito and enters a human host through the mosquito's puncture? The larva matures inside the human host, then pops out and goes on to become a fly. We already know that the black cancer in the rock can survive long periods outside of a host. Perhaps after some maturation process in the human body, the black cancer can proceed outside the body to make its final transformation . . . into something else.

Or perhaps humans are not the normal hosts for the worms at this stage. A parasite invading an inappropriate host is a fairly common occurrence in nature, and in these cases the parasite hits a dead end, unable to reproduce. We discussed one such example, the pork tapeworm, in connection with "Ice." Humans are normally the terminal host for the pork tapeworm, ingesting the larval form in undercooked pork and serving as hosts for the adults. But if we instead ingest the tapeworm's eggs, we become hosts to the larvae, which spread throughout our bodies. One of the most popular locations, because of decreased immune protection, is the brain, where the invading larvae will grow into cysts typically ¼ to ½ inch in diameter, though sometimes up to eight inches across.

Neurocysticercosis is a dead end for the tapeworm. Unless someone eats the human host (and that's a different episode), the tapeworms never grow to maturity and never reproduce. And as the cysts are dead ends for the pork tapeworm, perhaps the BVO is a dead end for the black cancer. Dr. Bryan finds this idea that humans serve as "dead end" hosts for the black cancer more reasonable than the idea that what we've seen so far is the black cancer's normal life cycle. If humans weren't meant to be hosts to the black cancer at this stage of its life, then Dr. Bryan says, "It not reproducing would make sense."

A similar dead end occurs when roundworms that normally are not parasitic accidentally infect a host. *Halicephalobus deletrix* normally lives independently, feeding on decaying vegetation. But it is sometimes accidentally inhaled or ingested by horses or humans. *H. deletrix* may migrate up the nasal passage and possibly into the brain, much like the black cancer. It can cause serious brain damage.

If humans aren't the normal hosts for the black cancer, what is? Since the black cancer seems to have remained buried and unknown for a long time, perhaps its proper host is now extinct, and it is desperately trying to make do with what it can find. Or perhaps, given the possible extraterrestrial origin of the black cancer, its normal host is a bit more exotic.

If we assume that the organism in the movie is the same as the "Tunguska" black cancer, then the most likely option seems the third: that the organism we see in "Tunguska" and "Terma" has somehow been neutered or altered so that it does not complete its normal maturation process. This maturation process, shown in the movie, reveals that the black cancer normally acts much more like a terrestrial helminth, growing to its adult form within the human host. An important missing piece of its life cycle is filled in. The Shadowy Syndicate seems surprised by this, though actually the lack of maturation should have surprised them much more, and should have had them wondering about the black cancer's life cycle.

The maturation process shown in the movie is also reminiscent of parasitoids like "*F. Emasculata*," which undergo part of their life cycle within a host, killing the host in the process, and continue the rest of their lives independently.

Since the organism in the movie seems to have survived from 35,000 B.C., and the Tunguska event—whatever it was—occurred in 1908, we might imagine that the "Tunguska" black cancer is a more sophisticated version of the organism, bioengineered by the aliens to have specific effects on humans and not to reproduce. Just as we might neuter a horse or dog to make it a more efficient helper, the aliens may have "neutered" the black cancer. This would make it an ineffective weapon of mass destruction but an extremely effective "smartworm" that could be sent on targeted covert missions.

Would an organism like that shown in "Tunguska" and "Terma" have to be extraterrestrial? Dr. Bryan says, "That would be my last thought. We are finding new parasitic pathogens all the time. The idea of unknown organisms existing on Earth is not far-fetched at all." The fact that the black cancer, in the movie, can mature to adulthood in humans, makes it less likely that the organism is extraterrestrial. As we've discussed, parasites must live and evolve side by side with their hosts in order to develop the mechanisms required to feed off them and survive within them. Yet if the black cancer came to Earth many thousands of years ago, it may have developed such mechanisms over time. We don't yet know the genetic makeup of the black cancer and whether it contains the two new nucleotides that have been detected in the alien retrovirus, but other episodes make the extraterrestrial origin of the black cancer seem more likely.

AN ALIEN MADE ME DO IT

While "Tunguska" and "Terma" simply show the black cancer producing a disabling toxin, the later episodes, "Patient X" and "The Red
and the Black," show at least one human being, a boy, walking around
while infected with the black cancer. This boy's actions appear controlled by the cancer, just as the people's actions in "Piper Maru" and
"Apocrypha" are controlled by the black oil organism that infects
them. The black cancer and the black oil organism share several
other qualities: the use of oil as a medium, the use of human hosts,
the ability to live outside a host, and an attraction to the human eye.
These similarities suggest several interesting possibilities: that the
black cancer and the black oil organism may be the same life-form,
and that this single organism may be able to change its behavior depending on the situation, using humans for specific purposes when it
sees the opportunity, paralyzing the human host when it does not—
implying it is intelligent.

The black oil organism apparently came from a UFO that crashed
in the ocean. It exhibits a high degree of intelligence, moving from host
to host when useful; traveling from the diver, Gauthier, to his wife,
Joan, to Krycek; gathering information both from its host and from its
surroundings and making deductions; and using radiation as a weapon
when necessary; all to eventually fulfill its goal: to return to the UFO
from which it came.

Could such an organism control our behavior? In "Ice" we discussed the possibility of a parasite causing anxiety and aggression in
its hosts. Researchers have also linked the Borna virus to mental disorders ranging from manic-depression to schizophrenia. Dr. Vallari
suggests that an "organism could produce alcohol-like or morphine-
like compounds to affect behavior." Or perhaps it would produce hallucinogenic chemicals such as those in ergot, which we discussed
earlier. All could certainly change our behaviors. But could an organism direct our behaviors, literally taking over our bodies? Suffice
it to say that we haven't yet discovered an organism that could have
such an effect. Dr. Bryan says, "Any time you get anything foreign in

the brain, be it cancer or a parasite or a bacterial infection, aberrant behavior can be part of the scenario. But that behavior is not directed, as best we can tell."

Such an organism would have to be much more intelligent than any parasite we know of, and uniquely tuned to human physiology, even more so than the parasites we've discussed above. It would have to speak in the same chemical language as the human body, and it would have to know exactly where and how to stimulate various parts of the brain to produce the action desired. The oil organism not only controls the actions of the human host; it even seems able to access human knowledge. When inside Krycek, it knows the location of the digital tape containing government secrets, and it knows that it can swap such a tape with the Cigarette-Smoking Man for access to the UFO. Such an organism, it seems, could only have evolved in close proximity with humans. Of the organisms that we have evolved alongside, we have formed close relationships with many. For example, *Escherichia coli* bacteria live in our guts and digest cellulose-based foods for us in a mutually beneficial relationship, providing us with vitamin K and B-complex vitamins. And as mentioned earlier, many scientists theorize that the mitochondria that power our cells started out billions of years ago as independent bacteria. It is only through common, concurrent development that these close relationships are forged.

How then can we explain the alien origin of the oil organism? We might theorize that the aliens behind the big colonization plan referred to in "The Red and the Black" and other episodes are quite similar to humans. If they are indeed the gray aliens, they appear humanoid, able to breathe the same atmosphere as humans, and to have enough genetic similarity for alien/human hybrids to be viable. So perhaps this organism grew on the aliens' home planet, evolving as an intelligent parasite using the gray aliens as terminal hosts. Eventually the aliens mastered it and now use it as a biological weapon, just as we may use smallpox or anthrax. Or perhaps the aliens never mastered it, and the black oil is using them. Or perhaps, given the maturation of the black cancer into adult humanoid forms, the aliens *are* the black oil.

It does seem awfully convenient, though, that the organism would be so effective with humans. More likely, the aliens have done some bio-engineering on this organism to adapt it to humans and to make it more responsive to the aliens' needs. Such a bioweapon may have been carried on the UFO that crashed in the ocean. But what would this weapon be doing buried in Tunguska? We can either adapt the long-discredited theory that the event at Tunguska was actually caused by an exploding spaceship, or we can assume that the aliens cleverly delivered their bioweapon for an experimental trial on Earth via a meteoroid or some other self-destructing mechanism. I'll take the latter theory. How plausible is it that the black cancer might be a bioengineered weapon?

Obviously we're a long way from anything this biotechnologically advanced. Yet we're already altering organisms to make them more effective weapons; trying to create more resistant strains of bacteria and superviruses with increased mortality rates; to increase the levels of toxins produced by pathogens; to increase the person-to-person communicability rate; and to make arthropods hosts of diseases they don't normally carry. Some claim that Russia has combined the smallpox and Ebola viruses to create a pathogen with 90–100 percent mortality. Yet our abilities are limited. We might imagine isolating the disease-causing genes from one organism—say the HIV virus—and then attaching them to another organism—say a common cold virus—so that HIV can be spread by sneezing just as easily as the common cold. But scientists believe there is little chance that such an organism would actually function. Like a fly's head on a person's body, it's neat to think about, but can it work? The answer remains uncertain.

While bioweapons are an area of intense concern and research, parasites are not on the list of those developed or those under development. Dr. Bryan explains, "Nobody in his right mind is trying to bio-engineer a parasite." A parasite is an impractical bioweapon for use during wartime, because of the difficulty of delivery. It could, however, make an extremely effective stealth weapon.

BLACK OIL

Both the black cancer and the oil organism exhibit one trait that none of the Earthly organisms we've discussed share: its connection to oil. The black cancer seems to function in some kind of black, oily medium. And while the chemical composition of that medium is not firmly established, remember that the Tunguska rock is said to contain PAHs, and oil is a mixture of elements that includes PAHs. The composition of the medium is tested in "Piper Maru" and "Apocrypha," and is found to be motor oil. The oil organism uses this oil as a medium to travel from one host to another.

We might assume, then, that the black cancer can feed off of one or more of the components of oil. Oil-eating bacteria and fungi do just that. We use this bacteria, normally found in soil, to break down oil spills. They can break down everything from gasoline to jet fuel to crude oil and use the energy for themselves. Oil-eating bacteria have been found deep beneath the surface of the Earth, living around oil deposits, just as the black cancer appears to live in oil deposits deep beneath Tunguska. They can also be found in water, as was the oil organism that contaminated Gauthier the diver.

Why would an organism that feeds on oil enter the human body? The black cancer's BVO seems to live off the pineal gland in the brain. What might the brain have to offer an organism that spends so much of its time in oil? Well, the membranes of all cells are made of lipids, which contain fatty acids. These fatty acids contain hydrocarbon chains similar to those found in oil. Brain tissue also contains fatty acids. And from our discussion of "Young at Heart," we know that nerve fibers are surrounded by fatty myelin sheaths. The brain, which contains the highest concentration of neurons in the body, is actually 60 percent fat. If the black cancer has the flexibility to feed on a variety of hydrocarbon chains, it would find the brain particularly tasty.

An alternate possibility for the black cancer would be that it does not feed on oil but instead lies dormant within it. Dr. Jean-Yves Sgro, associate scientist at the Institute of Molecular Virology, explains. "The organisms may go into oil the way frogs go underground in the winter and fall asleep. It may offer a way for them to protect themselves. In hibernation, oil would be a very protective environment. It's buoyant, protected from water-based threats, acids, and oxygen. They could just sleep there." Nematodes enclose themselves in cysts at various stages in their life cycle, so the existence of a protected state for the black cancer seems fairly natural. *Anguina tritici*, the eelworm of wheat, can survive without oxygen over twenty-seven years in a dormant stage.

Nematodes change from this protected, dormant stage to an active stage by changing the permeability of their outer layer, or cuticle. The black cancer may use a similar mechanism. Dr. Sgro suggests the organism may have microscopic "scales" with two different orientations. Just as a cat's fur may present two different surfaces—a smooth one when its fur is stroked from head to tail and a ragged one when its fur is stroked from tail to head—the organism may have two different surfaces—one it uses to close itself off within an oil shell, and another it uses to open itself to interactions with a water environment. These "scales" might actually just be different glycoproteins that come to the surface of the organism under certain conditions. Within the oil, the organism could wait for an interesting host to come by. When it sensed a promising candidate, it could move to the surface of the oil and begin to change the orientation of its scales. The environment most favorable to the growth of the black cancer would then not be within oil but within a host.

Why would it maintain its connection to oil, then? Organisms using a liquid medium to travel between hosts are not uncommon. Many of the flukes we discussed in chapter 1 use water as a medium, either floating on the surface while waiting to be ingested by a favorable host, or actively swimming around, locating a favorable host and penetrating its skin. Similarly, oil might serve as a temporary home to the black cancer between hosts. If its favored host—gray aliens, say—tends to live near oil, this could be an advantageous location. In fact, the black cancer might even have developed a mechanism to trap oil against its scales, so that it can store the oil while it moves from one location to another, then release the oil so it will appear to be a harmless oil slick rather than a threatening parasite. If the home planet of the black cancer is covered with puddles of oil, this would be an excellent method of camouflage.

While we've been comparing the black cancer to various nematodes, comparison to one other type of organism can be helpful. The seeming coagulation of these puddles of oil into worms recalls slime molds, which have an animal-like capacity for movement. The movement of the cellular slime mold *Dictyostelium discoideum* is particularly striking. The cells of this slime mold live most of their lives as independent amoebae in cool, moist, shady places, beneath the leaves and other litter that cover the forest floor. But when they lack food, the cells secrete an aggregation pheromone to call them all together. Tens of thousands of cells form long streams that all flow toward a common center. These identical cells actually differentiate as they come together, creating an aggregate creature with a specific front and back. This aggregate creature is a tiny sluglike form called the *grex*, which even has a raised tip that looks a bit like a head. According to Dr. Steve Stephenson, professor of biology at Fairmont State College, "The grex is an aggregation of cells that are still independent, but they are moving in an organized fashion, mimicking a multicellular organism." The grex seeks out a location with light, height, warmth, and humidity from which it can send its spores to a more favorable location. These grexes don't move as fast as the black cancer's worms, though. Dr. Frank Killebrew, a plant pathologist at Mississippi State University, says, "They can move about the speed of a snail. But that's really a racehorse of a slime mold, not an average one." When it finds a suitable spot, the grex differentiates further into a fruiting body, forming spores and an intricately designed spore case. While some slime molds produce fruiting bodies that look rather like microscopic dandelions that have gone to seed, others, such as *Tubifera ferruginosa*, produce clustered cylindrical bodies that look very much like the BVO. The spores are dispersed by the wind or carried by passing animals, such as chipmunks.

The coagulating black oil looks rather like the formation of a group of grexes, and indeed, the slime mold *Acytostelium leptosomum* can produce multiple grexes from a single aggregation center. Yet the life cycle of the black cancer has little in common with that of slime molds. Slime molds are not parasitic. They cannot differentiate into spores and then dedifferentiate back into amoebae, as the black cancer forms the BVO and then reverts to oil. We might theorize that the black cancer uses us as *Dictyostelium* uses chipmunks: to disperse its spores. But if the black cancer releases spores inside the brain, they won't be dispersed very far. Dr. Stephenson comments, "You're more effective as a disperser of spores by not scraping off your boots when you come out of the woods than by allowing them into your brain." Forming a fruiting body in the nose, where the spores could be spread with each exhalation, seems a more sensible alternative. The comparison to slime molds reveals the amazing flexibility of the black cancer and its ability to transform. The nematode model, however, seems to hold more in common with the black cancer.

Again the problem we face is that "Piper Maru" and "Apocrypha" provide no indication that the organism reproduces. This reinforces the theory that the black cancer has been bioengineered not to reproduce, and perhaps has been artificially given its abilities to access and control the human brain. Such a bioweapon could infect the president and have him give a speech announcing our alliance with the "friendly" aliens. It could make soldiers initiate the launch of nuclear missiles. It could even infect the Cigarette-Smoking Man and make him stop smoking!

THE CURE FOR PESKY EARTHLINGS

In addition to its unusual properties and behavior, the oil organism also has the handy ability to release radiation at will. At a boring party? Just zap everyone within a ten-foot radius with a nice dose of ionizing radiation. In "Piper Maru," Joan Gauthier, while infected with the oil organism, emits a brilliant flash of light and leaves a group of men incapacitated with radiation burns. In "Apocrypha," the infected Krycek does the same. The organism releases very high levels of radiation that last just a second and travel only a few feet. Exactly what is the oil organism releasing?

We discussed ionizing radiation briefly in connection with Flukie. Ionizing radiation is made up of high-speed alpha and beta particles and neutrons, and high-energy electromagnetic waves such as gamma rays and X rays. Alpha particles are essentially helium nuclei, consisting of two protons and two neutrons. Beta particles are simply high-speed electrons. Gamma rays and X rays are photons of light excited to high energies. Radiation made up of these elements rips through matter, breaking apart molecules and atoms, forming positively and negatively charged particles, or ions. In human tissue, this process creates free radicals, breaks DNA strands, and causes extensive damage.

How is the oil organism producing this radiation? Ionizing radiation may be produced by radioactive decay, by fission, or by accelerating particles to high speeds. Radioactive decay occurs when an atom breaks down, emitting energy and subatomic particles spontaneously. It can occur naturally, as it does in uranium or radon, or it can be induced through the creation of radioactive isotopes (atoms with more or less neutrons than usual).

In fission, a similar process occurs, except that the atom's breakdown is much more radical, the nucleus actually splitting into two high-energy halves. The bomb at Hiroshima produced energy by fission of the uranium-235 isotope. The process releases large quantities of thermal energy and gamma rays, and creates a chain reaction that can release an incredible amount of energy.

Particle accelerators can also create ionizing radiation. They use electricity to accelerate charged particles—such as electrons, protons, or ions—to very high speeds.

So what might be the method by which our black, oily friend creates radiation? The radiation seems to be released in directed bursts that last only a second and travel only ten feet or so. The organism might carry something radioactive within it, but this would cause a steady, low level of radiation rather than spectacular blasts of it.

The organism might create a radioactive isotope that would decay in only a fraction of a second, so that it would release radiation almost instantly. Such radiation would be emitted in all directions, though, hitting both the oil organism and the host, and causing them more damage than anyone else. Fission similarly creates radiation in all directions that's most intense closest to the source.

Dr. Howard Matis, staff physicist at Lawrence Berkely National Laboratories, names particle acceleration as his method of choice for the organism. The particles could be accelerated in a specific direction, which could be aimed in a beam like a gun barrel, away from the organism and toward its enemies. Damage to the oil organism and the host could be minimized if the particles were fired from the surface of the organisms—say the conjunctiva or outer membrane of the eye, perhaps. The release of the particles could also be timed, making them a more effective weapon. And the organism could create particles that would travel the distance it wanted, choosing its range to target its enemies. These high-energy particles cause the most biological damage when stopping. As they decelerate, they deposit more energy into the surrounding tissues. Then to do the most damage, Dr. Matis suggests, "You really want the particle to stop inside the person."

Which type of particle or ray might the oil organism be emitting to zap people a few feet away? Since alpha particles are relatively large and have a strong electrical charge, they interact easily with matter, causing great damage, though they can travel only a short distance before they've transferred all their energy to surrounding atoms. They can penetrate only a few inches of air or a single sheet of paper before stopping. Since beta particles are smaller, they can penetrate a few feet of air and penetrate a short distance into a human. Gamma rays and X rays have no mass and no electrical charge, so they can travel much farther, sometimes passing completely through a human body without slowing. Thus they cause a minimum of damage (which is why we can use X rays to make medical diagnoses).

An electron then would be the most practical choice for the oil organism. Dr. Matis explains, "An electron accelerated through five to ten megaelectronvolts could go about ten feet and interact." The electron would slow gradually as it penetrated the body, leaving a trail of damage to skin, internal tissues, and cells.

The problem with any of these options, except natural radioactive decay, is that they require huge quantities of electrical energy. Accelerating particles requires a very strong electrical field. Some animals, such as electric eels, can generate electrical discharges that can stun a man, yet these levels don't approach the energy needed for particle acceleration. A vacuum is also necessary when accelerating particles, to prevent collision with other atoms, which would diffuse the particles' energy and send them off course, causing damage to the oil organism and the host. Accelerating the particles also requires a large amount of space. Dr. Matis estimates, "It would take ten to thirty feet to get an electron to sufficient energy. There are a lot better ways to kill someone. I would use a gun."

Yet we do seem to be witnessing the acceleration of electrons to high energies. The mechanism through which the oil organism does this remains unknown; further study may reveal more clues.

Even if the organism is aiming the particles away from itself, radiation is a dangerous weapon to play with, and the organism would need the ability to survive high levels of radiation, and to help its host survive. Could an organism survive such damaging radiation? Some terrestrial organisms can do just that, as Dr. McKay earlier mentioned. The *gray* is the unit that measures the amount of radiation absorbed by an organism. While humans can be damaged by less than one gray, may be killed by three gray, and will almost certainly be killed by six gray, fruit flies can survive one thousand gray. Many bacteria and viruses survive even higher levels of radiation. But the star survivor of radiation is the bacterium *Deinococcus radiodurans*, which can survive 10,000–15,000 grays. Since ground zero exposure at Hiroshima was about one hundred grays, you can see the strength of *D. radiodurans*. It's not that *D. radiodurans* doesn't sustain genetic damage with radiation. With exposure to a dose this size, each bacterium suffers about 120 double-strand breaks to its DNA. But while most bacteria die with only two double-strand breaks, *D. radiodurans* is uniquely able to repair such extensive damage.

First, the bacterium carries several copies of its one chromosome, for just such a contingency. Drs. Kenneth Minton and Michael Daly of the Uniformed Services University of the Health Sciences theorize that the broken pieces of chromosome are held in the correct order through an unusual mechanism. They have found that the loop-shaped chromosome is stacked on top of its duplicates like a pile of Life Savers. If one strand of the DNA of one chromosome periodically crosses over to a neighboring chromosome, this could connect the chromosomes, tying the Life Savers together and anchoring broken pieces so that their places are not lost. Second, *D. radiodurans* has an extremely efficient repair enzyme, *RecA*, which splices together overlapping fragments of DNA to recreate the genetic code.

Perhaps the oil organism has developed such mechanisms because it comes from a planet with higher levels of radiation. If the oil organism has such abilities, it might be able to use its repair enzyme to repair a host's DNA; it might even insert the gene that creates the repair enzyme into the host's own DNA, as a retrovirus inserts its genes into a cell. But our DNA would still not have the chromosome anchoring mechanism of *D. radiodurans*, and so the extent of repairs possible in us would be limited.

If the oil organism is from a planet with high levels of radiation, and the organism developed on the same planet as the gray aliens, as I theorized earlier, then the grays might also have high radiation tolerance and increased repair abilities. This would make their use of the oil organism as a weapon even more logical, since the weapon can destroy us, but will not harm them. Protecting oneself from one's own biological weapons is a problem the real Japanese Unit 731—featured in the episode "731"—had to face in World War II. The infamous Unit 731 developed cholera for an attack on the Chinese. But when it was released during the attack, seventeen hundred Japanese troops died from their own bioweapon.

THE EARTHLINGS STRIKE BACK

Can the black cancer be stopped? Is there any hope for the human race? In "Patient X," Krycek sews up the eyes and mouth of an infected boy to keep the black cancer from escaping him. (I'm thinking of try-ing that with my husband the next time he catches a cold.) But Krycek seems to have overlooked several obvious escape hatches, including the nostrils and the ears. These passages are all connected, so it would be virtually impossible to trap the black cancer without at least blocking them all (which would suffocate the host; the black cancer isn't stu-pid!). We've seen the black cancer use the nose as a point of egress in "Apocrypha" and "Terma," and it has seemed able to penetrate the skin in several instances.

The rebel aliens seem to be protecting themselves from infection by sealing up their eyes and mouths. This implies that they are vulner-able to the black cancer, which is quite interesting. I would have guessed the aliens would use a bioweapon to which they are impervi-ous. Perhaps the organism can be directed, so that the rebel aliens have now become additional targets. Or perhaps the aliens, in their real forms, are not vulnerable, but when they take on the appearances of humans, they also take on human vulnerabilities. The aliens don't seem terribly human, though. They are able to navigate perfectly well with their eyes sewn shut. And perhaps therein lies a clue to the nature of the aliens. We'll come back to them in the next chapter. For now, let's continue with the black cancer. If sewing up your orifices isn't a practical solution, how can the black cancer be stopped? We've already seen how protective gear, like the suit worn by Dr. Sacks, is no protec-tion at all.

At the Tunguska prison camp, the Russians are trying to create a treatment for the black cancer, though their methods are a bit crude. The Russian injection is called a vaccine, but it does not seem to func-tion as one. A vaccine is almost always injected significantly before a person is infected, as a precautionary measure. Yet Mulder in "Tun-guska" is injected right before his infection, and Dr. Sacks in "Terma," Marita Covarrubias in "The Red and the Black," and Scully in the movie, are injected after the black cancer has incapacitated them.

Vaccines must create an immune response against an infection without causing the infection itself. They are usually made of either weakened or killed microorganisms, though sometimes a toxin produced by a microorganism or a portion of the microorganism may be used. The key is to find the agent that evokes the strongest immune response by the body. These agents are called *antigens*. Doctors generally prefer to use only a portion of the organism or a protein or toxin produced by it, since using weakened or killed organisms carries the risk that one viable organism may slip through and cause serious infection in the patient.

One type of white blood cells, *lymphocytes*, constantly police the body for antigens with which to bind. To bind with an antigen, the lymphocyte must have a receptor that is complementary to the three-dimensional pattern on the surface of the antigen. They need to fit together like a lock and key. Every lymphocyte's receptors are slightly different from every other lymphocyte's receptors, so between all of them, they have about 100 million different receptors and can bind to and recognize just about any complex molecule. In essence, the body has a huge police force, but each officer is looking for a different criminal. When the right lymphocyte comes across the antigen, the lymphocyte binds with it, handcuffing it. If the lymphocyte recognizes the antigen as a foreign invader, it will begin to rapidly reproduce, creating more identical lymphocytes that will seek out and bind to the antigen. If these lymphocytes are of a specific type, called B lymphocytes, then they will all produce a protein, a potent weapon called an antibody. Since many identical B lymphocytes are being produced, they all produce the same antibody, one which attacks and may neutralize the antigen. If the antibodies cannot neutralize the antigen, then they serve as flags, marking the antigens for consumption by macrophages. Some lymphocytes, called memory cells, remain in the tissues for months, years, or even the rest of one's life, remembering the antigen they encountered. If they recognize the antigen again, they can mount a rapid response, quickly reproducing and secreting antibodies, preventing the disease from spreading and taking hold, creating an acquired immunity. The creation of these memory cells is the main goal of a vaccination.

Many factors control whether a potential vaccine is effective or not. The antigen must produce a protective, long-lasting response in the body, present a minimal risk of harm, be easily produced, and be able to be stored for long periods of time. While most vaccines have been designed to fight microorganisms, vaccines are also being developed for helminths like the black cancer.

Creating a helminth vaccine poses unique problems, which the Russians at Tunguska would have to overcome. According to Dr. Donald Harn at the Department of Immunology and Infectious Diseases at the Harvard School of Public Health, "One of the biggest problems you have is just getting enough biomaterial to work with. Viruses you can grow in culture. For helminths, we have to maintain a whole life cycle. We have to dissect animals to remove worms, or in some cases, we have to go to Africa and cut nodules open." Another difficulty is that many helminths have developed abilities to hide from the immune system of the host. And since these organisms are bigger, stronger, and more complex than viruses or bacteria, they are harder to vaccinate against. Dr. Harn explains, "Instead of looking for the right antigen from among one or two proteins, as with a virus, you're looking for the right antigen from among hundreds or thousands of proteins. Picking the right one is a nightmare." Scientists must pick an antigen that the host's body will "see": one on the surface of the parasite or in excretions or secretions. Also, the antigen must be one which, if attacked, will cause serious damage to the parasite. Small antibodies cannot be expected to neutralize an entire helminth nor a macrophage to eat it, so researchers need to come up with more creative solutions, using information about the helminths' complex life cycles.

An ingenious vaccine has been developed for *Taenia ovis*, the sheep tapeworm, in its larval form. Sheep ingest this parasite's eggs in dog feces. Australian scientists found that the proteins released from the egg stage of the tapeworm were effective antigens to use in a vaccine, stimulating the production of antibodies in the sheep. If the sheep is later infected by *Taenia ovis*, the antibodies bind to a protein near the anus of the worm. By forming a large complex, the antibodies block the tapeworm's anus, so the worm can't relieve itself of its waste and dies. While the field seems poised on the brink of some major breakthroughs, thus far, Dr. Bryan admits, "We do not have an effective parasitic vaccine for any human disease."

One promising technique is simply impractical for use on a large scale. Dr. Harn and his colleagues irradiated encysted tapeworm larvae to kill them and then injected them as a vaccine into mice. When later exposed to the tapeworm, the mice developed 50 to 60 percent fewer worms than before. If given a booster shot of the vaccine, the mice developed 90 percent fewer worms. This technique presents the same danger as any vaccine that uses an entire organism in weakened or killed form: that still-viable organisms may slip through and infect the subject. The bigger problem, though, is that for this technique to be effective, we would have to be able to produce on demand huge numbers of encysted tapeworm larvae, which can only be grown within hosts. Perhaps the Tunguska prisoners could serve as such hosts.

If we want to use only a part of the organism, such as a protein or a series of proteins, the vaccine can be much more easily mass produced. The genes for these proteins can be inserted onto a plasmid, which is a ring of DNA found in bacteria. When the plasmid is introduced into a bacterium, such as E. coli, then every time the bacterium reproduces, the plasmid reproduces as well, and we have a vaccine factory. The problem is, though, how to pick the right proteins.

One way to find these good proteins, which we also know as antigens, is to infect animals and look at their immune responses. Helminths have many different antigens or "keys" protruding from their surface. Different lymphocytes bind to different "keys" on the helminth, calling up a whole array of antibodies, each one targeted to attack a different protein on the surface of the helminth. Some of these antibodies will be more effective in their fight against the invader than others. These antibodies can be isolated and reproduced, and each type tested for its destructive power. If some of the antibodies are found to be effective, then researchers must work backward to find out which antigens give rise to these antibodies. Those antigens will then make up the most effective vaccine. Some of the testing at Tunguska, then, may have involved infecting subjects to discover the antibodies produced in response to the black cancer, testing the antibodies for their efficacy in fighting the black cancer, and then trying to discover which protein or antigen gives rise to each type of antibody.

If they are truly testing a vaccine, though, the Russians' actions at Tunguska are hard to understand. As mentioned earlier, vaccines are usually administered a significant amount of time before the infection is contracted. A typical vaccine requires one month to develop protective immunity.

One common exception in humans is the rabies vaccine. Most people don't receive the rabies vaccine unless they believe they've been infected with the virus. One reason this delayed vaccination is effective is because rabies has a long incubation period, commonly two to eight weeks. Another is that the series of injections given as a rabies "vaccine" actually includes both a serum and a vaccine. A serum contains pre-produced antibodies taken from animals that were previously vaccinated. Given as soon as possible, the serum thus provides temporary immunity until the vaccine can stimulate the body to produce its own antibodies.

Is a vaccine administered up to ninety-six hours after infection, as we see given to Marita Covarrubias in "The Red and the Black" and Scully in the movie, a feasible solution? No, since the black cancer has an incubation period of about fifteen seconds. Vaccinating after infection, or even right before infection, as we see with Mulder, would be too late.

If the injection truly is a vaccine, then the way to test it would be to give it significantly in advance, then infect the subject repeatedly and see if he felt any ill effect (or cut him open and see what's growing inside). If the vaccine is effective, the prisoners would not become sick. But this is not what we see happening at Tunguska. The Russian "vaccine," then, may actually be a serum, created from the blood of an animal that already contains antibodies. Sera are used to provide immediate immunization against fast-acting toxins or microbes. These preproduced antibodies may be taken from an animal that has previously been vaccinated, or that has caught the infection and fought it off. Sometimes animals have to be repeatedly infected to create sufficient antibodies. The way to test a serum would be to infect the subject, then introduce the serum, and see if the infection is killed or driven out. This seems closer to what we see in Tunguska. Dr. Harn has created sera that have been successful in killing the larval stages of helminths.

The reason research has focused on the development of vaccines rather than sera is the difficulty in producing sera in quantity and in storing it. To produce sera, we need a large group of animals (or humans) that are constantly producing antibodies. They would need to have been infected once or more to create sufficient antibodies. Which is exactly what's going on in Tunguska.

If the black cancer can take control of our bodies, then perhaps it also takes control of our immune systems, preventing the formation or the reproduction of any defenses against it. We can force the black cancer out with the serum, but we cannot fight off the infection ourselves. (And why would the aliens create an infection that we could?)

The Russian injection drives the black cancer out of the body. Whether it is still healthy after being exposed to the drug is unclear. Neither vaccines nor sera cause healthy organisms to leave the body. The organisms are either disabled or destroyed. If the black cancer does leave the body before being seriously damaged, that would be another indication of intelligence.

The aliens seem to have engineered an extremely potent stealth bioweapon, one perfectly designed to take over the human body. But who are these aliens? Are they grays? Shapeshifters? Or are they aliens at all? Those are the next questions we have to face.

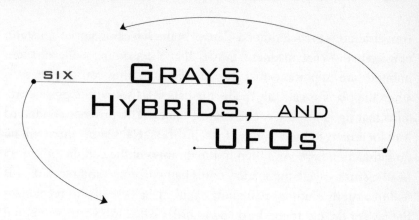

SIX GRAYS, HYBRIDS, AND UFOS

> "I just got a call from some crazy blankety blank claiming he found a real live dead alien body."
>
> —Detective Manners,
> Jose Chung's *From Outer Space*

THE HEAVY DOOR ROLLS BACK ON ITS track, the sound echoing like thunder through the prison corridor. The cell is eight by six, maximum security. He steps into the shadows of the room. The prisoner has been restrained according to his instructions, heavy straps securing him in a metal chair bolted to the floor, a leather restraint around his head preventing him from speaking or causing other sorts of mischief. He approaches the prisoner, removes the leather restraint from beneath his chin. The prisoner's actions have in-furiated him, endangering all they have both worked toward for so long, and he knows that only confronting the prisoner will provide him the release he needs. He pulls up a wooden chair, sits, and thumbs his lighter as if issuing a challenge. He brings the tip of his cigarette to the flame, the action holding him perfectly balanced, in control. The prisoner's unremarkable oval face remains impassive in the shadows. Their conversation is predetermined. The prisoner has always been resistant, opinionated. What maddens him is that the prisoner believes those opinions are important, that they should affect the course of events, when the plans are already made, the date set. Doesn't the prisoner realize that he is just one—one against many? The prisoner condemns him for cruelty to his own race; for selfishness. He realizes there will be no satisfaction here. And then in the dimness of the cell the prisoner's head seems to swell, the shadow of his hair darkening and receding, his features subtly shifting, realigning. With a half-breath he recognizes the face of the old friend he'd had to order killed two years before, the friend with whom he'd shared and made so much secret history. The face freezes the breath in his lungs. He stands, and only the automatic reflex of cigarette to lips keeps him from fleeing. He takes a drag, moves deliberately toward the cell door. Still the prisoner insists on displaying that abomination, on refusing to let the dead rest in peace. But the prisoner's abilities are no miracle, nor do they impress. He steps out of the cell, and the door rolls home. He will kill the prisoner, and kill him soon.

We've seen a wide array of creatures in *The X-Files* that may or may not be gray aliens, shapeshifting aliens, or alien/human hybrids. Obfuscation, a word Scully likes to use, has played a minimal role in the book thus far, yet it is an important factor in these encounters. We can't be certain if Mulder truly saw a gray alien during his sister's abduction, if the memory is a creation of his mind, or if it was implanted by his hypnotist. Even in cases where we clearly saw a gray, as in "Jose Chung's *From Outer Space*," we discover we didn't see an alien but instead an Air Force pilot in a gray latex suit. Despite the uncertainty of much of this evidence, some facts remain, and in the study of those facts we can explore the possibility of alien life on Earth and perhaps answer some questions about the various close encounters Scully and Mulder have had. These questions form the core mystery of *The X-Files*. Are the grays really intelligent aliens from another planet? Could alien/human hybrids be created? What might be the effect of introducing alien DNA into humans? Could humans subjected to disease and radiation look like gray aliens? What might power the fast-moving UFOs? How could the government fool people into thinking they've been abducted by aliens? (One note of caution before we proceed: While based on current research whenever possible, this chapter is by necessity more speculative than the others.)

ARE WE ALONE?

The image of the wraithlike gray alien pervades the series like a haunting dream. Whether we've seen an authentic gray alien on the show remains uncertain. Many gray-appearing life-forms seem in fact to be humans who have been altered in someway. The best evidence for gray aliens seems to appear in two episodes.

The fetal creature kept under tight government security in "The Erlenmeyer Flask" certainly appears to be a gray, and Mulder's life is traded in exchange for it. Yet the Crew-Cut Man who has captured Mulder probably has no intention of killing him anyway. And with possible hoax aliens being manufactured by the government in "Gethsemane" and "Redux," we have to wonder whether the fetal alien is any more genuine. After all, the Cigarette-Smoking Man seems to find the fetus of minimal value, simply filing it away in a jar in his huge Pentagon storage area. No clear conclusion can be reached.

The second episode that offers evidence of grays is "Little Green Men." In that, Mulder sees what appears to be a gray, obscured in a brilliant beam of light, at the Arecibo telescope in Puerto Rico. Considering Kritschgau's claim in "Gethsemane" that forces in the government have set up Mulder from youth to believe in aliens, this falls neatly into the pattern as simply one more lie to keep Mulder's faith in gray aliens alive. Certainly there seems no obvious reason why a gray would decide to send a message to this telescope and then appear there, at that time, particularly if the aliens already have a secret arrangement with the Shadowy Syndicate. But again we can't be entirely sure that the grays are not authentic aliens, so for now, let's assume that such aliens do exist in the world of The X-Files. We talked about the likelihood of primitive alien life being transported accidentally to Earth. How likely is it that space-faring intelligent aliens will visit Earth?

Until recently, we could make only semi-educated guesses about the likelihood of other intelligent life arising in the galaxy. We didn't know how common planets amenable to life were, and we didn't know how often those planets might actually develop life. In recent years, though, we've discovered planets around other stars, large planets in a close orbit that we hadn't thought possible. We've discovered complex organic molecules—one of the three essential ingredients for life—on the outer planets of our solar system, on comets and meteorites, and even in interstellar dust. We've discovered water and heat-generating volcanoes—the other two essential ingredients for life—on several of Jupiter's moons. We've discovered water at the poles of the moon, and signs that life may have existed on Mars several billion years ago. While our existence once seemed an incredibly improbable accident, it now seems a natural consequence of physical and chemical processes under a certain range of conditions. While it once seemed that we might be all alone in the universe, the universe now seems imbued with the promise and possibility of life.

But if there is intelligent alien life in the galaxy, why hasn't it visited Earth? Scientists have been asking this question for over two hundred years. Our galaxy is at least ten billion years old, many of its stars much older than our sun. Some scientists argue that an alien race that developed billions of years before ours could have colonized the entire galaxy in as little as 300 million years. So where are they? Believers in alien life have come up with many different theories to explain this. Some argue that they are here, and they are hiding from us, as in *The X-Files*. Others believe that while life may be relatively common, the evolution of *intelligent* life is much less probable, and so we're among the first intelligent species to evolve in the galaxy. Others assert that intelligent life exists in the galaxy, but the huge distances involved make it too hard to pay a visit to the neighbors. The theories continue: Our neighborhood is not where the action is in the Milky Way galaxy; alien civilizations all destroy themselves before colonizing the galaxy; intelligent species have grown beyond the childish need to explore and just like to stay home and watch *The X-Files*.

In the event that one of the above scenarios may be true, many scientists concluded that our best chance for contact with aliens may be through long-distance messages. This led to the establishment of SETI, the Search for Extraterrestrial Intelligence, a program to look for alien signals. In "Little Green Men," the one thousand-foot diameter telescope at the Arecibo Observatory in Puerto Rico, the largest radio telescope in the world, receives a message that appears to be sent from space. This facility was actually part of the government's SETI program until the funding was cut off in 1993. Was the Shadowy Syndicate afraid of what might have been detected?

If so, the danger still exists. Private funding has now picked up where the government left off, and SETI continues its search. What exactly is SETI looking for? An advanced, intelligent civilization may give off two distinct types of signals that we could detect. First, radio waves used for communication leak naturally into space. Terrestrial radio waves expand outward from our planet in all directions. Our earliest radio and TV broadcasts are now passing the nearest stars—Milton Berle and Lucille Ball, our goodwill ambassadors. Similarly, alien telecasts might reach us by accident, revealing the presence of another civilization. This type of signal may not be detectable over great distances, though, since it is not focused or aimed. We may not yet have sensitive enough detection equipment to pick up the alien version of *The X-Files*. We'd be much more likely to detect the second type of signal, one aimed deliberately in our direction for the purpose of making contact. What type of signal would this be?

SETI researchers believe that aliens seeking to communicate would send a signal that spans an unusually narrow range of frequencies, perhaps ten hertz or less. This is the most efficient type of signal to send long distances. And since any natural radio sources span a much wider frequency band, this type of signal would stand out as an unnatural spike. Extraterrestrials could maximize our chance of detecting such a spike by transmitting at frequencies where interstellar gas, dust, and Earth's atmosphere cause little interference. The best such area is the microwave region of the spectrum, near the frequencies of neutral hydrogen (1420 megahertz) or the hydroxyl radical (1660 megahertz). In fact, many SETI researchers believe aliens might send a signal at exactly one of these frequencies, since they are universal. The signal picked up in "Little Green Men" is at the frequency of neutral hydrogen, which has a wavelength of 21 cm.

How does SETI search for these signals? The privately funded SETI Institute run by Dr. Frank Drake out of Mountain View, California, is now conducting Project Phoenix, which plans to search a total of one thousand stars within 150 light-years of Earth. Under the project, the institute uses the largest radio telescopes on Earth to listen to one star at a time for any signals. Among others, they use the National Radio Astronomy Observatory's 140-foot radiotelescope in Green Bank, West Virginia, which simultaneously monitors twenty-eight million channels, or frequencies. Over several hours they scan a total of two billion channels for any signals, like listening to two billion different radio stations. The difficulty is not picking up signals; it's determining which ones are extraterrestrial in origin.

Telecommunications satellites and planes with radar saturate the airwaves with signals. Cell phones and passing trucks also interfere. To help block some of this interference, these telescopes are built in valleys. Scientists need to use a second telescope to confirm a signal before they can classify it as extraterrestrial. To prove that a signal is coming from a distant star, scientists first check to see if the signal weakens as they move the telescope away from the star, then see whether the signal goes out when the star sets.

Another criterion in determining whether a signal is extraterrestrial or not is to measure its Doppler shift. The Doppler shift is the change in frequency of a wave caused by the relative velocity of the source of the wave. If a train blows its whistle as it is coming toward you, the frequency of the sound waves will be increased by the forward motion of the train, and the tone of the whistle will sound higher. Think of the sound waves being crowded or crunched together as the train rushes forward. If the train then passes you and starts moving away, still blow-ing its whistle, the tone will now sound lower, the frequency decreased by the motion away, the sound waves being stretched out. Similarly, the rotation of the Earth causes any point on the ground to move relative to a source in the sky. The associated Doppler shift is well known. When a signal's shift is bigger than can be explained by the Earth's ro-tation, that means the source must be moving very fast. In those cases, scientists conclude the signal is not from a faraway alien planet, but from a nearby human satellite. This assumes, of course, that the signal isn't coming from a nearby alien spaceship.

Difficulties in confirming signals and in determining their sources have kept us from positively identifying any signal thus far detected in over seventy major searches as extraterrestrial in origin. We have picked up some promising signals, but they've never been repeated, or if they have, fading and distortion have kept us from detecting them. No known astrophysical processes could account for these mysterious sig-nals. One of the most promising, as mentioned in the episode, was de-tected by Dr. Jerry Ehman, on August 15, 1977, at the Ohio State "Big Ear" radio telescope. Scientists picked up a narrow-band signal at the neutral hydrogen frequency, thirty times stronger than background galactic noise (the same strength as the signal in the episode). It was from the direction of the constellation Sagittarius and lasted for thirty-seven seconds. Dr. Ehman scribbled "Wow!" in the margin of the com-puter printout, and so this became known as the "Wow!" signal. It was not confirmed nor repeated, so scientists don't know what it was. Dr. H. Paul Shuch, executive director of the SETI League, Inc., believes "It was either radiation from another civilization or some previously undis-covered astrophysical phenomenon." Despite continued studies of the same region of the sky, no one has detected anything similar.

One of these large telescopes, though, sees only one millionth of the sky at a time, and an alien signal would transmit into only about one millionth of our sky. The chances of those two millionths coincid-ing, of our telescopes being pointed at the right place at the right time on the right frequency, are slim indeed. Dr. Shuch explains that long-term searches are necessary. "One NASA SETI program ran for about one thousand hours before getting canceled. That's like calling one number at random out of the Manhattan phone book, getting no answer, and concluding that no one lives in New York City."

The signal Mulder receives contains words and music; is that the type of signal we're likely to receive? These telescopes are not designed to pick up an elaborate message, but to find steady or slowly pulsing narrow-band, high-energy signals. Information can be carried by the signal through changes in the frequency of the radio wave, or frequency modulation, as FM radio stations do. The signal, however, needs to be limited to a narrow range of frequencies to travel long distances; this narrow range constricts the amount of modulation and so the amount of information in the wave. Such a signal would most likely be unable to carry the complex message and music with wide varieties in pitch that Mulder hears. But Dr. Shuch says, "An infinitely advanced technology can do anything it wishes." Some scientists suggest that if we did receive a message, our first action should be to send back a duplicate of that message to let the sender know that it has been received. This is exactly what seems to happen in "Little Green Men," when Mulder receives a duplicate of the message sent out by *Voyager*.

THE ALIEN SHOPPING NETWORK

Coordinated by the SETI League, a network of amateurs now use their own satellite dishes to look for alien signals. Could you pick up an alien signal on your home dish? Satellite TV technology has made these dishes as sensitive as much larger dishes used by astronomers twenty years ago. A small dish also has an advantage over the large ones the pros use, in that it can monitor a larger field of the sky. While the sensitivity is less than the multimillion-dollar dishes, it can potentially allow you to listen in on conversations up to one hundred light-years away. To set up your own alien detection center, you'll need a satellite dish ten to twelve feet in diameter, a microwave receiver, and a computer with digital signal-processing software. A typical set-up costs about $2,000. Cheaper than ten years of cable, and no commercials.

Despite our failure to detect alien signals and despite the absence of aliens here on Earth (as far as we know), recent discoveries seem to indicate that alien life is more likely than ever. What would such intelligent alien visitors be like?

THE ORIGIN OF SPECIES

The grays have willowy delicate limbs, bulbous heads, huge black eyes, small noses, reptile-like membranes for ears, and hairless gray skin. They have the ability to communicate telepathically; they tend to appear in beams of brilliant white light. But at base they are very like us. They have two legs, two arms, two eyes; they seem to breathe oxygen through a nose and mouth. Their body plan is much like man's.

Considering the huge variety of life-forms here on Earth, the chance that aliens will look humanoid, like the grays, seems slim. Evolution involves a lot of chance circumstances, both genetically and ecologically, that create variations and then select one organism as more fit than another. Even a planet similar to Earth would most likely give rise to significantly different organisms. Reproductive biologist Dr. Jack Cohen, consultant for the mathematics and ecosystems departments at the University of Warwick, stresses the chance circumstances that led to the evolution of man. "Three hundred million years ago, a fish came out of the water. It had its airway crossing its foodway, and it had a reproductory system mixed with its digestive system. This fish became the ancestor of all vertebrates. There were many fish in the sea that didn't have those mistakes, and one of those could have crawled out of the water." Its descendants would have been very different.

The idea that chance circumstances on another planet would lead evolution in the same direction it has gone on Earth is extremely unlikely. In fact, scientists believe that humans wouldn't even have evolved here unless the dinosaurs were killed off by a huge meteorite sixty-five million years ago. On land, dinosaurs dominated the environments for vertebrates; there really wasn't room for humans. That's why our mammal ancestors remained small. And their small size probably helped them to survive the meteorite. This set the stage for the evolution of man. Dr. Cohen says, "Finding another planet with our kind of dinosaurs or people is more unlikely than finding a remote Pacific island on which the natives speak perfect German or cockney rhyming slang." Dr. Cohen has served as a consultant on alien design for science-fiction writers, including Larry Niven, Jerry Pournelle, Anne McCaffrey, Terry Pratchett, and David Gerrold. Of the possibility of the grays, Dr. Cohen says, "Nonsense, sheer nonsense. They are far too human. I don't believe in little green men, not because they are little, and not because they are green, but because they are men."

But life-forms do face certain problems, and there are common solutions to those problems that apply anywhere in the universe. Life evolving on planets has to deal with gravity, which will probably produce an organism with a top and a bottom. Organisms that move—sophisticated ones, anyway—will probably have a front and a back. Organisms also require the ability to sense their environment. Specifically, they need to detect a useful spectrum of electromagnetic radiation (to see); to detect changes in the surrounding atmosphere (to hear and smell); to detect heat and evaluate surfaces (to touch); and to evaluate food (to taste). Sophisticated organisms will require appendages to manipulate their environment. What mechanisms might they evolve to accomplish these things?

Dr. Cohen suggests that we can get some idea of how necessary or common a certain trait might be by examining how many times that trait independently developed on Earth. For example, birds, insects, and bats all independently developed flight. Eyes developed four separate times on Earth. So these solutions to the problems posed by life may be a bit more likely to occur on another planet. Other Earthly traits are unique, and so seem less likely to develop on another planet. For example, while all land animals have developed methods of acquiring water, only one, the elephant, uses a long trunk.

The grays seem to have all the necessary qualities listed above. While their similarity to us may make them unlikely aliens, it also makes them seem viable as living organisms. But what factors might have led to the distinctive traits of the grays? This is a very difficult question to answer. Imagine that elephants, rather than existing on Earth, were fictional alien creatures on *The X-Files*. We could speculate about the alien environment that might have formed such a bizarre creature. Yet that environment is right here on Earth! So any speculation is very dangerous. That said, let's see what the grays can tell us about themselves. By examining them, we may be able to learn something about where they came from and how they evolved.

Since the grays have an unlikely resemblance to us, we might assume that they followed an evolutionary path similar to ours. We might also assume—since we are adapted to function on Earth and the grays resemble us—that their home planet is not terribly different from ours. The most striking difference between grays and humans is the size of their eyes. While most organs of the body are judged by their size relative to the size of the entire organism, vertebrate eyes must be judged by their absolute size. This is because the eyes are optical instruments that operate relatively independently from the rest of the body. Thus, small animals, like chipmunks or birds, tend to have relatively large eyes compared to the size of their bodies, while large animals like elephants have relatively small eyes. In general, the larger the eye, the greater the visual resolution. An eagle's eye is larger than a human's, and eagles and hawks have the best eyesight of all animals. They can see eight times as far as we can.

Why don't we all have huge eyes, then? Well, first, because we don't need them. Our eyes apparently are as good as they needed to be for humans to survive. Second, the eyes take up a large amount of skull space, space that we need for our brains. In birds, whose high-speed flying requires sharp vision, the eyes take up more room in the skull than the brain. In our case, evolution apparently selected for moderately sized eyes and a larger brain to interpret what we see. The large skull of the gray may allow it to accommodate both large eyes and a large brain.

But why do they need such large eyes? Perhaps they can move very quickly, like birds, or they need to be able to see things that move very quickly, such as predators, or prey. Animals that are preyed upon tend to have eyes on the sides of their heads, which increases their field of vision and allows them to see predators sneaking up on them. Animals that prey upon others tend to have eyes on the front of their heads, which increases their depth perception, so they can judge the distance of their prey accurately before striking. Owls have the most frontally positioned eyes of any animal. This suggests the grays are predators, and perhaps need to see fast-moving prey.

Perhaps their eyes compensate for weaknesses in the other senses. Many animals with poor eyesight, like rats, depend much more on smells and sounds. Conversely, the aliens, if their senses of smell or hearing are poor, may depend more on their vision. Or perhaps the reasons are environmental. If the chief predatory threat to the grays was stealthy and odorless, such as the black cancer, keen vision might be a useful defense against it.

Nocturnal animals tend to have relatively larger eyes than diurnal animals, which allow them to see in lower levels of light. Owls have huge eyes. If we had eyes proportional to those of the great horned owl, our eyes would be the size of grapefruits and weigh five pounds each. We might hypothesize that the grays come from a planet with dimmer light, or live in caves or other low-light environments, or are nocturnal creatures.

Yet almost every appearance of the grays is linked to brilliant light, which, if they were used to low light, would most likely be blinding or at least unpleasant for them. This use of brilliant light leaves us with two choices. The grays may have come from a planet with brighter sunlight than ours, or the grays may be blind to a large part of our visual spectrum. (Or those black eyes may be groovy contact lenses tinted to shield them from light.)

Is it reasonable to think that the aliens may see a different section of the electromagnetic spectrum than we do? The section of the spectrum visible to us contains the dominant wavelengths of radiation given off by the sun and most stars, so it's very useful to be able to see it. The same part of the spectrum, however, is not visible to all Earthly animals.

Some can see into the infrared or ultraviolet portions of the spectrum. For example, some snakes have infrared vision. They can find their prey in pitch darkness, actually seeing the heat emitted from the animal's body (just like in the movie *Predator*). Other animals can see into the ultraviolet. While our atmosphere shields us from most ultraviolet radiation, some low-energy ultraviolet gets through, giving us suntans and skin cancer. Pollinating insects such as honeybees can see into the ultraviolet range, and are drawn to specific flowers by their ultraviolet reflections. Most objects don't reflect ultraviolet radiation very well, so by being blind to the ultraviolet we aren't missing much; flower petals are an exception, which makes this a very useful ability for bees.

So what might the grays see? Perhaps the grays' home world orbits a star that gives off more ultraviolet radiation than our sun. Or perhaps their atmosphere shields them less effectively from ultraviolet radiation. A planet with lower gravity would tend to have a thinner atmosphere. Plants or other objects on their planet's surface may reflect ultraviolet radiation more effectively, making the ability to see into the ultraviolet more useful. With their visible spectrum shifted toward shorter wavelengths, the grays may be blind to longer wavelength yellows, oranges, and reds, as bees are. Since the brilliant white light in which the aliens tend to appear is made up of all the colors of our visual spectrum mixed together, their inability to see yellow, orange, and red would make that light appear dimmer to them.

High levels of ultraviolet radiation on the grays' home planet, though, would break down DNA and damage organisms. Yet both the oil organism and UFO appearances are linked to high levels of radiation. If the grays originated on the same planet as the oil organism, and if they are the ones flying the UFOs, then it seems that they have a greater ability to cope with radiation damage than we do.

Earth's atmosphere and magnetic field protect us from most dangerous radiation. If the grays' planet has a thinner atmosphere or a weaker magnetic field, or their solar system is closer to the center of the galaxy, higher concentrations of cosmic rays and gamma radiation might also reach the surface of the planet. All organisms would need methods of protecting themselves from or repairing genetic damage from this radiation, or else mutations would destroy them. This ability would help the grays cope with the particle-accelerating oil organism as well as cosmic rays encountered in their interstellar travels.

Getting back to the eyes, why are the grays' eyes black? Some animals have dark irises to disguise the round shape of the pupil, which can be a trigger for predators. Thus the entire eye appears black. If the black cancer is a parasite on the grays' home planet, perhaps the entirely black eye developed as a defense against it. The black cancer may somehow be attracted to the round black pupil, or the contrast of black pupil on bright iris. An entirely black eye might fool the black cancer into thinking an individual is already infected.

What else can we deduce about the grays? Not too much. The narrow, delicate limbs and trunk may suggest the grays originate on a planet with lower gravity. If the gravity is too much lower, though, they would have trouble functioning on Earth. They may use some sort of technology to help them function in the heavier gravity, such as the previously mentioned light beams, or else they've prepared for their close encounters with exercise (perhaps picking up some Thighmaster infomercials).

The aliens don't seem to exhibit any obvious sex organs. Perhaps their sex organs are out in the open and I simply don't recognize them as such, but the grays all seem to look alike (or am I being racist?). Not all animals exhibit prominent breasts or genitals, though. Iguanas, such as my Igmoe, hide their sex organs (and believe me, you don't want to be around when that hemipenis comes out). But usually males and females exhibit distinctive traits that help to attract the opposite sex and avoid confusion. Perhaps for the grays, looks really don't matter. They may attract mates through alternative means, such as pheromones, behaviors, or sounds (perhaps any speech is limited to mating activity). Or perhaps the reason sexual differences aren't apparent is that they are hermaphrodites. Since they have no visible nipples, we might wonder how they feed offspring. Perhaps they regurgitate partially digested food for their offspring like birds, or perhaps their offspring are born able to feed themselves.

Might the grays be telepathic as claimed by Duane Barry and other abductees, and if so, how might they have developed this ability? Well, we have theorized that the grays may not hear very well, that perhaps hearing is not a sense that offers much advantage for survival on their planet. If so, then speech would be useless, since the grays couldn't hear each other. If group communication was an advantage, though, perhaps this telepathic ability would develop. Is this likely? Many scientists believe that human self-conscious intelligence developed mainly as an accidental by-product of evolution, rather than as a trait selected for its survival advantages. While an increase in human brain size may have offered advantages for survival, paleontologist Stephen Jay Gould explains, "The brain did not get big so that we could read or write or do arithmetic or chart the seasons." As a by-product of the brain's larger size, though, humans found they had these abilities. Similarly, telepathy may have evolved as an accidental by-product in the grays.

The gray shot by Deep Throat in "Musings of a Cigarette-Smoking Man" appears to have membranes on the sides of his head, even with the eyes, that pulse as he breathes. This episode actually provides us with our most detailed look at a gray. Since the entire episode is a story about the rumored past of the Cigarette-Smoking Man told by Frohike, though, it's ambiguous whether this scene is a dramatization of Frohike's story or the Cigarette-Smoking Man's actual memory of the event. Once again the accuracy, like so much involving the grays, is uncertain. If the grays do have such membranes, we might theorize that they are gills. Although the grays appear to be land dwellers, they may have evolved from water-breathing creatures as we did, and retained gills while developing lungs as well.

Another intriguing possibility is that these organs are auxiliary hearts acting as booster pumps to provide more blood to the brain. It's much easier for the heart to pump blood out to the torso, arms, and legs, where the blood can flow with gravity, than to pump it up to the head, against gravity. While we might wonder why the grays would need such pumps since they may be from a planet of lower gravity, this may be some trait acquired through quirks of the evolutionary process, which as we said, is based to a large extent on chance circumstances. Or the trait might have developed because the aliens have weak hearts, or because their large brains require more blood than ours. If these are cardiac booster pumps, they could be very helpful to the aliens in withstanding the high G forces sustained in the rapid accelerations of the UFOs, which we'll discuss more later.

MAN-MADE ALIENS?

Aside from their improbable similarity to us, then, the grays don't obviously seem fraudulent or unfeasible as aliens, as far as we can tell. Yet what of the alternate explanations we've been given for their existence? In "Anasazi," Mulder finds a buried boxcar of gray-alien-type corpses. At the same time, Scully finds references in government records that suggest these corpses are human, the result of horrible experiments supervised by Mulder's father. The smallpox vaccination scars on the corpses seem to confirm this interpretation. Similarly, in "731," a group of gray-alien-type creatures are executed before a mass grave. Mulder encounters a lone survivor on a train car. The First Elder, the head of the Shadowy Syndicate, tells Scully these creatures are humans who have been subjects of yet more horrible experiments. Scully believes the creatures are humans who have been exposed to diseases and radiation. Is this possible? Might the grays not be aliens at all?

That would explain the grays' uncanny similarity to humans. But could those striking differences be created by altering humans in some way? Certainly the human body can be ravaged by disease and radiation. Those suffering from Hansen's Disease, or leprosy, in "731" provide a dramatic example. The First Elder tells Scully that the "gray" on the train suffers from hemorrhagic fever, which can be caused by a variety of viruses. The ebola virus causes a very severe hemorrhagic fever with a rash that spreads from the trunk to the limbs and head, and spontaneous bleeding from body orifices and breaks in the skin. Pictures of the afflicted have certainly generated a lot of fear in the last few years. We've also seen the horrible burns caused by high radiation at Hiroshima and Nagasaki. Yet none of these creates victims that look like a gray alien. The problem with this theory is that the grays—based on the little we've seen—don't look damaged, while those suffering from disease or radiation exposure do. For the most part, the grays seem intact, yet different.

Rather than a disease or radiation exposure, the disorder that gives rise to humans that look most like grays is a genetic birth defect called osteodysplastic primordial dwarfism type I. It is believed to arise from a recessive trait. The main features are low birth-weight dwarfism, an extremely small head, prominent eyes and nose, sparse hair, a short neck, short limbs with dislocation of elbows and hips, broad hands and feet, and scaly, flaky skin with enlarged cells. While all of these features aren't compatible with our image of the grays, the face of a baby with this disorder looks very like a gray alien, with a large forehead, prominent eyes with thick, wrinkled eyelids, and a small, pointed chin. Perhaps the government experiments involve this disorder somehow, or involve other genetic mutations that mimic parts of this disorder. At least through this birth defect we can see a hint of potential for the human face to be transformed into something approaching a gray, with no alien DNA involved.

This seems to indicate that genetic mutations or manipulation of humans may be responsible for the grays. Assuming that such genetic manipulation, in order to have such radical consequences, was done at the embryonic stage, the bodies in the boxcar in "Anasazi" would be results of experiments conducted in the 1960s, while the "grays" in "731" would have been created in the 1970s. Techniques were crude then, and our knowledge of the roles of specific genes in the body quite limited, so it's theoretically possible that in the attempt to alter some human trait, many other traits may have been altered as well, leading to a human mutant who looks like our image of a "gray alien."

It is suggested in "731" that the grays are being subjected to radiation tests, which implies that those administering the tests believe the grays may have some resistance to radiation. Since nuclear weapons were the greatest security threat in the 1960s and 1970s, it makes sense that the government would want to create people immune to radiation damage. With the limited knowledge they had at that time, how might they go about such a thing? Perhaps by taking thousands of pregnant women and exposing them, while at their regular doctor visits, to low levels of radiation; for example, X rays. Far-fetched? We know of at least fourteen hundred different radiation experiments conducted by the U.S. government during the Cold War, involving twenty-three thousand people. Many subjects were tested without their knowledge or consent, and among the subjects tested were pregnant women and infants. One test involved injecting the radioactive isotope phosphorus-32 into pregnant women before and after delivery. In another experiment, inmates in a boys' home were given radioactive milk. Another test released clouds of radioactivity into the atmosphere to measure their spread. All of which make my suggestion seem fairly tame.

How could a gray be created from such a test? As we know from our discussion of "The Host," most mutations caused by radiation are not helpful to survival, and so most of these irradiated fetuses would die. Yet there would perhaps be, among all those subjects, one baby who survived, who had mutations that helped it withstand the radiation. Of course, the mother would be told that it died at birth (I think I've been hanging around with the Cigarette-Smoking Man too long) and the government would have a subject. Since cloning would have been far beyond our powers at that time, though, I don't know how the government could have gotten so many subjects, and so many with the exact same mutations. This suggests that the technique used to create a gray is easily reproducible, and also provides results that are worthwhile enough for the government to reproduce it many times. It's hard to imagine any genetic manipulation of humans within our power during that era that might fulfill both criteria. If chapter 1 taught us anything, it's that mutations are very unhealthy. So exposure to either diseases or radiation seems an unlikely origin of the grays.

YOU THINK A HUMAN LIKE ME, AND AN ALIEN LIKE YOU . . . ?

So far we've discussed only the possibility that the grays are genetically altered humans. Mulder believes that the grays are alien/human hybrids, created by the government as supersoldiers immune to biological threats. Might hybrids provide an immunity to Earthly bioweapons and diseases? Many Earthly diseases attack only a single species and have no effect on others. Smallpox, for example, attacks only humans and no other organisms on this planet. Remember that a virus can only enter a cell if the proteins projecting from the surface of its envelope find matching receptors on the cell. Since aliens would be much more different from us than any species on Earth, it's extremely unlikely that they'd be susceptible to any of our diseases. That immunity, though, isn't due to any super infection-fighting powers. It's simply a result of the incompatibility of the systems.

A hybrid would then not have any super infection-fighting powers either. If a hybrid was created, say by replacing a few human genes with alien ones, the hybrids would very likely still have all the susceptibilities of humans, and maybe even a few new ones to alien diseases. Significantly changing the surface receptors on our cells to prevent infection would also prevent necessary life processes from taking place, so we'd need to limit changes carefully. During the 1960s and 1970s, though, fine control like this was impossible; it still remains mainly beyond our reach. So an immunological advantage arising from hybridization seems unlikely.

Could some alien DNA help protect us from radiation damage? In chapter 1 we discussed how genes that govern the production of antioxidants could dramatically increase life span. These antioxidants, if you recall, help repair damage caused by free radicals. This damage is very similar to damage caused by radiation exposure. If the grays have genes coding for some super antioxidants, and those antioxidants can be produced with raw materials in our bodies and are effective in our bodies—two big ifs—then we might gain some resistance to radiation from such DNA. Such experiments, though, could not have been tried until the 1980s, when genes were first transferred successfully from one species into another.

Rather than protecting us, perhaps hybridization offers another advantage. These hybrids look strikingly similar to our image of gray aliens, and so they may have been created to serve as spies, infiltrating the alien forces.

Whatever the motive, is the underlying premise at all possible? Might we be able to create alien/human hybrids? A *hybrid* is a plant or animal of mixed composition, which contains traits of two or more different varieties or species. Many different processes can result in the creation of different types of hybrids, integrating the traits to a lesser or greater extent.

The easiest way to create a hybrid is simply to have two animals breed. But this only works in a few limited cases. A species, by definition, is a group that is reproductively isolated, meaning that an organism cannot reproduce with another outside its species. This isolation may occur accidentally as a single species spreads into different environments and evolves differently. Those changes eventually become so great that interbreeding is impossible. Or isolation may be a specific result of natural selection. If hybrids of two different groups are not as fit as either originating species, mechanisms will be promoted that prevent hybridization.

Why can any species interbreed, then? These are rare exceptions where two closely related species haven't been completely isolated. For example, some species of deer can interbreed and produce fertile offspring. A male donkey and a female horse can mate to produce a mule, though the mule will be sterile. Horses and zebras have been interbred, as have lions and tigers, and camels and llamas. Although there are these few exceptions, most hybrid offspring, even of plants, are not viable or are sterile. And humans cannot produce offspring with any other species, including one that shares 99.5 percent of our DNA— chimpanzees (don't ask me how we know that). Since aliens would be significantly more different from us than other species here on Earth, it is unlikely in the extreme that we could naturally breed with aliens and produce offspring. So if we want to create alien/human hybrids, we have to give nature a hand and create them in the lab.

ALIEN/HUMAN HYBRIDS OF THE FIRST KIND

In "Red Museum," Dr. Larsen is injecting children with alien substances from birth through their teens. The children are told they're receiving vitamin shots, the same cover story used in actual government experiments. Dr. Larsen also pays workers to inject beef cows with the same alien substances. The children never get sick, yet they grow into angry, violent youths. Seven rapes occurred in town in the previous year. (We have no information on whether the cattle committed any rapes.)

In examining the vial of material Dr. Larsen was carrying at his death, Scully suggests it is the same material as in "The Erlenmeyer Flask," yet she describes it differently. While that episode dealt with alien viral DNA, this material is a serum, just as we discussed in the previous chapter, containing antibodies that would fight an antigen or a group of antigens. These antibodies, according to Scully, are mixed with synthetic corticosteroids.

These children are not hybrids in any genetic sense, since they have no alien DNA, yet on a very basic level, alien and human organic molecules are being mixed. Remember that antibodies are proteins produced by B lymphocytes that attack and may neutralize an antigen. If different types of antibodies are included in the serum, they may theoretically be able to fight off a range of diseases. The children, supposedly, have never gotten sick. Could these alien antibodies fight off Earthly diseases?

This is the same question that was raised by the possibility of bioweapon-resistant hybrids in "731," and the answer is still no. Antibodies are designed to attack a specific foreign antigen; let's say these alien antibodies are designed to attack the black cancer. It's extremely unlikely that the alien antibody is going to mistake a common cold virus for the black cancer. It might just as well mistake a healthy blood cell for the black cancer. Most likely it would see nothing resembling the black cancer in the human body, and it would do nothing.

How about antibodies acquired by eating the injected beef? Could they provide any protective powers? Unfortunately, no. They would be broken down as they passed through the digestive tract. All proteins are broken down into individual amino acids before being absorbed into the bloodstream. Once they are absorbed, they can be used as building blocks for new proteins created by the human body. Now these amino acids, coming from an alien, might be quite unusual. But it's very unlikely they'd be used as building blocks of human proteins. Most terrestrial proteins use the same set of twenty amino acids from hundreds of possible ones. Amino acids are assembled into proteins according to the recipes held in our DNA. Since our DNA would not contain recipes calling for "alien amino acid #1," these amino acids would likely remain unused in the body.

If one of them somehow looked like a human amino acid, though, it could perhaps be used in place of its human counterpart by accident and could affect the functioning of that protein. Most proteins are long chains of more than one hundred amino acids with complex three-dimensional structures. The shape of the protein is very important to its ability to function, actually more important than the exact sequence of its amino acids. For example, there are a few differences in amino acid sequence between human insulin and the insulin of other animals, yet some animal insulin can work in the human body because, despite the differences of sequence, the shapes are much the same. If the alien amino acid is similar enough to be mistaken for a human amino acid, the protein generated will probably have a similar structure and carry out normal functions. To feel the full effect of any alien amino acids, though, we not only need the raw ingredients, we need the alien DNA recipes that call for these exotic ingredients. If we have both of those, the stage is set for revolutionary change. Some scientists believe that the appearance of two new amino acids on Earth, coupled with genetic mutations that allowed these amino acids to be incorporated into proteins, led to the formation of collagen, without which complex multicellular structures could never have developed. Some of the more advanced hybrids on the show may use both these raw ingredients and the alien DNA.

Also included in the "Red Museum" injections are *corticosteroids*. These are not the same as anabolic steroids that some athletes take. Corticosteroids are hormones that help control metabolism, mineral balance, and inflammatory processes. Injections of these decrease immune response, elevate mood, and stimulate appetite. They can be beneficial for a wide range of conditions, particularly those in which immune response and inflammation are problems, such as asthma or arthritis. Taken over long periods of time, they can cause negative side effects, however, such as muscle wasting, the formation of fatty deposits on the face and upper back, sodium and water retention, weakened bones, slow wound healing, acne, and mood swings. The only symptom that seems to manifest itself in the teens is mood swings, which might help to explain their violence. The teens would each have a poor constitution for carrying out violence though, with bones prone to fractures and atrophied muscles.

Why might the injections have included corticosteroids at all? Most likely to suppress the body's immune response to these alien antibodies, which our human bodies would view as foreign invaders. Without corticosteroids, we would produce our own antibodies to attack the alien antibodies and destroy them. With corticosteroids suppressing the human immune defenses, though, the body would be even more susceptible to infections than usual. So these children, rather than strong, violent youths, would most likely be sickly, moody, flabby weaklings with a few weird proteins in their bodies. Aren't we all, though?

ALIEN/HUMAN HYBRIDS OF THE SECOND KIND

An actual genetic alien/human hybrid is shown in "The Erlenmeyer Flask." Dr. Berube is cloning alien bacteria that contain an alien virus. He's taking one or more genes from that virus and inserting them into terminally ill humans, such as Dr. Secare, through gene therapy. While

Dr. Secare still looks human, he is no longer ill, and he's acquired several unusual characteristics. Deep Throat claims that Dr. Secare has acquired green blood, inhuman strength, and the ability to breathe underwater.

Before we get into specifics, let's look at the premise. How likely is it that we might discover an alien life-form that is constructed and behaves like a terrestrial virus? A virus is an Earthly construct, just like a human, and because of that seems an unlikely form for alien life. Yet viruses are much more primitive than humans, and so may be a common building block of life. Would an alien virus be made of the same ingredients as a terrestrial one? Dr. Cohen answers an emphatic no. "Why do you think aliens are going to use DNA? There are 230 possible double-helix compounds, just using available phosphates and bases, other than DNA. And there are many more organic compounds than that, which could serve as template systems." Some scientists have even theorized that several different codes initially evolved on Earth in addition to our DNA-based one, with DNA surviving through natural selection. While no evidence supports this theory, the potential for other systems and other nucleotides exists. If we think of DNA as our genetic language, then the chances of an alien species using the same DNA is like aliens independently creating the English language, using our alphabet and words.

However, the alien DNA in these X-files is somewhat different than ours, since it contains two additional nucleotides, or bases, not seen in Earthly DNA. Dr. Cohen finds this a likely possibility. "Four additional possible nucleotides exist right here on Earth, though they aren't used in the DNA of any organism." Dr. Jergen Wiegel, a biochemist at the University of Georgia, agrees. "A lot of organisms have modified nucleotides anyway." Side groups attached to the nucleotides can indicate where the recipe for a protein begins and ends.

In chapter 1, we discussed the four DNA nucleotides and how they pair off only in certain combinations to create four possible rungs in the DNA ladder. Adding two more nucleotides would most likely create two more rungs. Or if we think of DNA as a written recipe, two more letters would be added to our alphabet. Imagine all the possible new words that could be created with two new letters in our alphabet. Or conversely, imagine all the words we would lose if two letters were deleted from our alphabet. These two new nucleotides could have two possible consequences. First, the same "recipes" could be conveyed more quickly with our more sophisticated vocabulary. Instead of saying "long thin pasta" we could say "spaghetti." Genes could then be made of shorter strands of DNA and chromosomes could be smaller. Second, new ingredients, such as alien amino acids, could be added to recipes. With our new alphabet, we might create a new word that had never existed before, such as "igmoe." A gene then might code for a protein that contains "igmoe," an extraterrestrial amino acid.

So these additional nucleotides carry with them some fascinating possibilities. If we accept that DNA, of this altered type, is the basis for the aliens' biology, then an alien virus seems a reasonable infectious vector, since a virus is simply a bit of DNA in an envelope that can transfer it from one place to another. Let's return now to Dr. Berube.

He is supposedly carrying out gene therapy using alien viral DNA found within alien bacteria. Don't be confused about a virus being within a bacteria. Some viruses infect bacterial cells just as some infect human cells. The point is that this virus has one or more genes that Dr. Berube wants to insert into humans. We've already discussed gene therapy and how it works in chapter 2. The protein envelope of a virus can be used to hold DNA that is to be introduced into the subject. Could that alien DNA then enter our cells? It depends on the envelope Dr. Berube uses. If he uses the alien virus's envelope, then we again face the problem of compatibility. Since many terrestrial viruses don't even infect humans, the chances that an alien virus would be able to infect us seem slim. But in this instance, at least, scientists could provide a helping hand.

Dr. Berube could take that alien DNA, insert it into a protein envelope of some Earthly virus, such as smallpox, and inject it into us, as is done in gene therapy. This would at least get the virus into some of our cells. Once there, the DNA would have to look a lot like our DNA and behave a lot like it in order to do anything more. But since we've gone this far, let's assume it does. The same problems that exist with current gene therapy technology would still apply. The new DNA may splice itself into existing genes at a spot that disrupts healthy genes, creating a possible danger of cancer or other illness. Or it may splice itself into a dormant region of a chromosome where it will never be activated. The new DNA may also invade only certain cells, and may not get to the cells Dr. Berube intends. Finally, in many cases our immune systems may recognize the invasion of a virus and attack the virus and the modified cells. For example, if a smallpox envelope is used, those who have been vaccinated against smallpox would likely mount a defense against the virus and the infected cells. But who's vaccinated for smallpox these days anyway? Let's plunge ahead and assume the government has secretly surmounted all these problems, and that the alien DNA is active in our cells.

We are now alien/human hybrids, containing primarily human DNA but also a piece of alien DNA. A hybrid of this type is commonly called *transgenic*, containing a gene or genes from another animal. If the genes are inserted successfully, then they are expressed in us through the production of a protein. The first transgenic mice were documented in 1980. We now also have transgenic rabbits, goats, sheep, cattle, fish, poultry, and pigs. Most transgenic animals are created through techniques other than gene therapy, which we'll discuss later. For now, let's examine the effect of such alien DNA in a human body. Could the viral DNA provide inhuman strength, the ability to breathe underwater, and an altered blood chemistry?

In fact, scientists have recently created the first green-blooded zebra fish. Dr. Shuo Lin of the Medical College of Georgia and his colleagues inserted the gene for green fluorescent protein (GFP), a glowing molecule used by jellyfish, into single-celled zebra fish embryos. It's much easier to alter an organism's DNA at the embryonic stage than later in life, which may be why the ova of Scully and other women have been taken for experimentation. Dr. Lin added to the GFP gene a short stretch of regulatory DNA that causes the gene to express itself only in red blood cells. The zebra fish's blood cells glow green when exposed to blue light. Aside from looking really neat, this allows the scientists to study when and where red blood cells are formed in the embryos. Dr. Lin has also made fish with green neurons. These inserted genes are also passed down to offspring, creating generations of green-blooded zebra fish. Similar techniques could be used to insert the gene for GFP into human embryos. In the same way, the alien DNA may code for some green protein, as well as other proteins. As long as that green protein can be synthesized using amino acids we have in our bodies, then we can make it. If it requires an alien amino acid, like "igmoe," then we may fail to make the protein, or we may mistakenly insert some other amino acid that may or may not work. Apparently no alien amino acid is needed, for Dr. Secare appears able to synthesize this green protein. If Dr. Berube really wanted that alien DNA to work as it does in the aliens, he'd feed Dr. Secare some of that "Red Museum" beef, which would provide him with some alien amino acids to use as building blocks for alien proteins.

An alien gene that makes our blood green seems relatively easy to accept, given the above example. Could alien genes also allow us to breathe underwater? That seems unlikely, since it would involve the development of a second breathing apparatus in an already adult, differentiated human like Dr. Secare. I'd prefer to think that Deep Throat was exaggerating for dramatic effect when he made this claim. Could the virus instead allow us to survive underwater for long periods? Funny you should ask . . .

Researchers have recently discovered exactly what allows air-breathing crocodiles to remain underwater for up to two hours at a time. When crocodiles hold their breath, carbon dioxide builds up in their blood, just as it does with us. This carbon dioxide dissolves and forms bicarbonate ions, just as in us. The similarity ends there, though. In crocodiles, the ions bind to hemoglobin, the protein in red blood cells that carries oxygen. When the ions bind to the hemoglobin, they cause it to release oxygen, and that oxygen then goes to nourish tissue. Human hemoglobin is different, and bicarbonate ions don't bind to it, so the oxygen remains tied up. Researchers have finally discovered the precise amino acids in the crocodile hemoglobin that are involved in binding the ions. They then created hybrid human/crocodile hemoglobin that looks mainly like human hemoglobin, but contains the amino acids that allow it to bind with the bicarbonate ions. Once scientists know the amino-acid sequence of a protein, they can formulate the DNA sequence that would produce it and synthesize the corresponding gene. This has been done for insulin. Theoretically, then, humans could be given this hybrid human/crocodile gene and gain the ability to remain underwater for long periods, just like a crocodile, or Dr. Secare.

A HUMAN/SUNFLOWER SEED HYBRID?

Accepted wisdom holds that DNA from ingested food is broken down during the digestive process and destroyed. But German scientists have recently completed an experiment to contest this belief. They fed a virus, M13, to a mouse. They then found sections of the virus's DNA, up to seven hundred nucleotide pairs long, in the mouse's feces. This is enough DNA to contain a gene. The DNA was not even kept within the digestive tract. The scientists found surviving genetic fragments of the virus in spleen cells, white blood cells, and liver cells. Most of the cells did eject the foreign DNA within eighteen hours, but the scientists speculate that occasionally some of the DNA may remain, and this may be a way in which genes are passed from species to species. All those sunflower seeds Mulder is eating could have some very interesting effects.

ALIEN/HUMAN HYBRIDS OF THE THIRD KIND

I mentioned before that gene therapy, the technique used on Dr. Secare, is not the only method of creating hybrids. An alternate technique might better explain the "grays" we see buried in the boxcar in "Anasazi" and being shot before the mass grave in "731." These creatures may be alien/human chimeras. We discussed a hermaphrodite in chapter 1 who was a chimera, made up of two distinct groups of cells, each with its own sets of genes. A chimera contains tissues of two or more different genotypes. The name comes from the mythical chimera, a beast with the head of a lion, the body of a goat, and the tail of a dragon. A chimera is a man who's had a heart transplant, so that the heart contains different genes than the rest of his body. A chimera also is John Barnett, with salamander cells in his hand. Mixing cells of early embryos can create a more complete chimera, with a true mosaic of cells of different genotypes. The embryonic cells may be mixed rather randomly, or cells from a specific area of one embryo may be injected into a certain location in another embryo. Chimeric embryos can be made from cells of the same species, or cells of different species. Generally, though, different species must be closely related in order to produce viable chimeras. This would make an alien/human chimera unlikely, yet the technique offers some intriguing possibilities. The first chimera, a mixture of two mouse embryos, was created in 1961, so the basic technology was available during the time the "Anasazi" and "731" hybrids were being created.

Recently, Dr. Steen Malte Willadsen and his colleagues have mixed embryos to create sheep/goat chimeras and sheep/cow chimeras. Chimeras tend to appear more like one species or the other rather than a true fifty-fifty blend. So a sheep/goat might look mainly like a sheep, but have bands or patches of straight goat hair among its curly sheep wool. Or vice versa. Successfully creating chimeras, even among closely related species, is still difficult. In an experiment carried out by Dr. Willadsen and his colleagues in 1984 on sheep and goats, some of the chimeras did not survive, while others appeared to be non-chimeric, containing only sheep or goat traits. Of nineteen offspring, eleven appeared to be normal sheep or goats, while eight appeared to be chimeras due to mixed wool and hair. Only one of those had blood chimerism, containing complete sets of proteins of both species. The other chimeras contained only the proteins of the species that matched their dominant appearance. Some of these chimeras have even been fertile. Since the DNA of the two species is not mixed within a single cell, though, any egg or sperm would contain the DNA of only a single animal, and so any offspring would not be chimeric.

We might imagine, then, that the "Anasazi" and "731" hybrids are chimeras. They look mainly like grays, though with a hint of the human about them. One of the greatest difficulties in creating inter-species chimeras is in having foster mothers carry them to term. Normally, a goat embryo cannot survive and grow to term in a sheep, and vice versa. The foster mother's immune system rejects the embryo's foreign antigens. If a mixture of alien and human embryonic cells did somehow create a viable embryo, how could we bring such an embryo to term? Dr. Willadsen recently solved the problem of incompatibility between foster mother and embryo. The chimeric embryo can be constructed with embryonic cells of different ages, which then take on different roles. For example, scientists have mixed cells of a goat embryo with cells of a sheep embryo that are at a slightly earlier stage. Since the younger cells tend to give rise to the exterior membranes and placenta and the older cells to the fetus, scientists designed these chimeras so their membranes and placentas would be made of sheep cells, the fetuses of goat cells. This way, when the chimera was implanted in a sheep mother, there was no negative reaction. The resulting chimera seemed to be made up of goat cells. Using similar techniques, scientists hope to help endangered species reproduce in the bodies of females of another species. This technique could also come in handy for implanting alien or hybrid embryos into human women, as we see in "Emily."

To digress for a moment, in "Redux," the ice surrounding an alleged alien corpse contains what's described as "chimera cells." The term chimera is used to refer to entire organisms rather than individual cells. But if we're to interpret what is meant in the episode, we must suppose that a "chimera cell" would contain DNA from two different organisms. This type of cell is actually called a hybrid or transgenic cell, and is fairly commonly created now, as will be discussed below. Dr. Secare, with his genes from the alien virus, has such cells. Dr. Vitagliano in "Redux" describes these chimera cells as unidentifiable, neither animal nor plant. But if they are unidentifiable, then it's unclear how Dr. Vitagliano can identify them as chimeras. Chimeras would clearly contain genes from two different organisms. If all the genes are unidentifi-able, then this determination would be impossible.

Are these cells alien in origin? If we knew whether they contained the two new nucleotides in them, that would be very strong evidence. This isn't mentioned, yet it still seems very likely that these cells are alien. The fact that the DNA is unidentifiable strongly suggests this, since Earthly organisms have quite a bit of DNA in common. Does this mean that the alien body was authentic? Not necessarily. The Shadowy Syndicate left the cells to be tested while removing the alien body, per-haps hoping that the authentication of the cells would lead by associa-tion to authentication of the body. The cells would provide additional evidence of gray aliens and would pin the blame for Scully's virus and cancer on them, rather than the government.

Speaking of the viral DNA in Scully, if she has a piece of the same alien virus that Dr. Secare has, we might wonder why she doesn't have green blood like Dr. Secare. Yet she may have been infected with a dif-ferent gene or group of genes taken from that same virus; terrestrial viruses have anywhere from three genes up to two hundred. So the gene that codes for the green protein may not have been given to Scully. We may then potentially see a whole range of effects stemming from this retrovirus depending on the genes involved. Can Scully hold her breath for two hours like a crocodile? We'll have to wait and see.

RECIPE FOR A HOAX?

Scientific hoaxes are not as rare as you might think. Newton seems to have fudged his data in calculating the speed of sound to make it come out the way he wanted it. Other scientists have faked research or misrepresented results. Even common folk get into the act, armed with planks and rope, making crop circles in the cornfields. Hoax-ers enjoy pulling a scientific fast one, sometimes with ulterior mo-tives of fame or revenge, sometimes with the simple human desire to feel superior.

In "Gesthemane," Mulder cites the Piltdown Man as an example of a hoax that was not discovered for forty years. The Piltdown hoax was actually perpetrated through the creation of a very crude chimera of sorts. In 1912, Arthur Woodward, keeper of Paleontology at the British Museum, and Charles Dawson, amateur geologist, found several pieces of bone grouped together: a few pieces of a cranium that appeared essentially human and a piece of jaw with teeth that appeared to be from an ape. They concluded that these pieces came from a single creature, the missing link between apes and man. The discovery created a great amount of excitement. Only much later, in 1953, when intervening discoveries indicated the Piltdown Man did not fit into the evolutionary pattern that was being revealed, was the hoax discovered.

A test for fluorine, which increases in fossil bones with age, revealed that the jaw was modern while the cranium was older. The bones had been dipped in acid and stained with manganese and iron oxide to make them appear from the same geological period. Further tests revealed the jaw belonged to an orangutan, and that the teeth had been abraded to resemble human teeth. Since the modern jaw would not have been present naturally in the same geological layer as the cranium, it was concluded that the bones had been planted as a hoax.

Only last year was the perpetrator of the hoax finally unmasked. A trunk was found in the attic of the British Museum with bones similarly treated with acid, manganese, and iron oxide, practice runs for the hoax. The trunk belonged to Martin Hinton, a museum volunteer who disliked Woodward and apparently wanted to embarrass him.

Might the Shadowy Syndicate, with their alien on ice, be using similar techniques to create their hoax?

ALIEN/HUMAN HYBRIDS OF THE FOURTH KIND

So far we've talked about techniques for creating hybrids by inserting alien DNA into a living human or mixing alien and human embryos. But neither of these techniques creates a fully integrated hybrid. To do that, we need every cell, from the embryonic stage onward, to contain DNA from both organisms, and we need to provide both alien and human amino acids to that embryo. Sophisticated hybrids like the Samanthas and Gregors in "Colony" and "Endgame" and the Kurts in "Memento Mori" may provide examples of fully integrated hybrids. How might they be created?

A number of techniques allow us to create transgenic or hybrid cells, like those discovered in "Redux." What good is a single hybrid cell? Plenty, since cloning techniques allow us to create an entire organism from a single cell.

Chimera pioneer Dr. Willadsen was the first to clone an animal from an embryo cell. He removed the DNA from a sheep ovum. He then took the nucleus from an embryonic cell and transferred the DNA into the ovum, creating a clone of the growing embryonic sheep. He has created hundreds of such cloned animals, mainly cattle. The cattle industry is very interested in such techniques because it allows superior animals to be duplicated. Such a thing may have been done with Scully's daughter, Emily, allowing the possibility that many more such Emilies may exist.

Dr. Ian Wilmut, inspired by Willadsen's work, was the first to clone an adult animal, the sheep named Dolly. This is more difficult than cloning embryonic cells, because the cells in an adult have already differentiated. But again it is the transplantation of the cell's nucleus into an ovum that has had its own nucleus removed that creates the clone (which again would make the ova of Scully and the other abductees come in handy). While we're making exciting strides in cloning, our techniques have a long way to go. Dr. Wilmut had to make 277 attempts to end up with one healthy clone. Recent experiments in which two rhesus monkeys were cloned required 166 attempts. While humans have yet to be cloned, scientists have transferred the nuclei of human cells into immature human eggs from which the DNA has been removed. This is being done to study the cause of chromosomal defects. The only alteration that needs to be made to the procedure to create a human clone is to use a mature egg rather than an immature one. The ability to clone means that any cell then may potentially give rise to an organism. Transgenic animals can then be created by modifying the DNA of a single cell. So how do we change the DNA of a single cell?

Electroporation is one technique used to insert DNA into cells. The cells are suspended in a solution containing the DNA to be inserted. A high-voltage electric discharge is sent through the solution, causing small ruptures in the cell membranes. These small ruptures, or pores, allow the DNA to enter the cell. In some cells, the ruptures seal up, allowing the cell, with its new DNA, to live. Other cells do not seal and so die. The new gene may be expressed only transiently, or if it's integrated into the chromosomes, it may be expressed permanently. Using this method, many cells can be transformed at once.

A more precise and labor-intensive technique involves microinjection of DNA into animal or plant cells. This is commonly done to fertilized mouse eggs. The cell is held by suction from a pipette under a microscope, and the scientist uses micromanipulators and a needle with a diameter of ten millionths of an inch to inject the DNA into the nucleus. The first microinjection of mouse embryos was reported in 1966, so this technique could have played some part in Bill Mulder's project.

A less delicate technique is biological and ballistic, or biolistic, transformation. Small gold or tungsten beads, about forty millionths of an inch in diameter, are coated with the DNA to be inserted. These beads are spread over a projectile such as a bullet or a thin disk. The projectile is shot at high velocity toward the cells. A stopping plate stops the projectile just short of the cells. This stopping plate contains small holes that allow the tiny beads to continue forward, hit, and penetrate the cells. The cells are literally shot with microscopic DNA bullets. While up to 95 percent of the cells survive the procedure, the new genes are not stable, and tend to be expressed for only a few weeks. One great advantage of this technique is that it can potentially be used directly on the tissues of living animals. Scientists have already biolistically transformed skin, liver, spleen, and intestine cells in living mice. The handheld device looks rather like a wand, which is held up to the tissue to be treated and fired. Sounds like a fun new toy for the Cigarette-Smoking Man. Difficulties inherent in all these techniques are getting the genes to express themselves, to regulate themselves properly, and to be passed on to offspring. Yet we have had some success with them.

Why do we use such techniques? In other sections of the book, we've discussed a number of experiments that involve such procedures. Creating transgenic animals or cells helps us to study the regulation of gene expression, the function of various genes, human genetic diseases, cancers, and also to create useful hybrids. For example, tomatoes have been given a flounder gene that allows them to be frozen without damage. On the animal side, mice have been created carrying the gene to produce human growth hormone as well as the gene to produce mouse growth hormone. These mice grow about one and a half times larger, suggesting similar procedures could be done with animals raised for their meat. Pigs have been genetically engineered to carry human proteins on the surface of their cells. Pig organs can then potentially be transplanted into humans, and the human proteins on their surface will prevent the human immune system from immediately rejecting them. Perhaps the aliens would like to use us as organ donors.

One rather unsettling application recently reported is the creation of male mice that produce rat sperm. With similar techniques, potentially, animals could be created that can produce human sperm. Or perhaps, humans could be created that produce alien sperm.

These techniques could be used to create many different hybrid cells, with different combinations of alien and human traits. One of these may have been viable and used to generate a series of identical clones, such as the Samanthas, Gregors, and Kurts.

What can we deduce about such hybrids? The Samanthas and Gregors explain that their identical appearances are a handicap, and they are trying to create new colonists through hybridization that will have different human appearances. The Samanthas and Gregors are clones of two basic genotypes. This suggests that the creation of this type of hybrid is very difficult, involving advanced versions of the techniques we've just discussed, and that the hybrids are sterile, as mules are. If they weren't sterile, then Samantha and Gregor could simply have children, and if the hybrid traits were carried in their germ cells, their offspring would be hybrid as well.

While the Samanthas and Gregors look just like us, their underlying physiology seems different. They have green blood; they can only be killed by the alien stiletto to the base of the skull; and when they die, their bodies decompose instantly into steaming, bubbling green acid slime. They also seem to have a different type of vision or sensory ability, which allows them to recognize the bounty hunter even when he has shapeshifted. Might they be picking up something in the ultraviolet region of the spectrum? The fact that they simultaneously have so many human traits and so many alien ones makes them seem the most fully integrated hybrids, yet also the most unlikely.

SHAPESHIFTERS

In a number of episodes, including "Talitha Cumi," "Herrenvolk," "Patient X," and "The Red and the Black," we see shapeshifters such as Jeremiah Smith and the Bounty Hunter. They have the ability to heal, have green blood and the alien retrovirus, and can be killed only by the alien stiletto to the back of the head. Aside from the grays, these are the most "alien" seeming of all the creatures we have met. Yet they appear human. Are they aliens, merely wearing a human "mask"? Their power to heal, to shapeshift, to find their way around with their eyes sealed shut, and their invulnerability to physical threats except the stiletto all suggest a physiology far different from ours. Perhaps they are grays or ten-headed squid with some sort of disguising mechanism. Dr. Cohen finds this likely. "When I meet an alien, I won't know how much is mechanics and how much is biology. They may be able to make us see whatever they want us to. Magicians can, after all."

Yet the Bounty Hunter's face swells with red bee stings in "Herrenvolk." And if the aliens are so adept at creating a disguise, can it be so difficult to "reprogram" it to show a different face? Six identical Jeremiah Smiths work for the Social Security Administration. This obvious anomaly seems an unnecessary risk for the aliens to take in infiltrating our system, unless changing the pattern is extremely difficult (or they've realized the inefficiency of the Social Security Administration. After all, they don't even come up with different names for their Jeremiahs). While the Bounty Hunter easily shapeshifts, he keeps returning to one underlying appearance, suggesting that he must expend a great deal of energy to take on any but his "default" appearance. Yet if the appearance itself is a disguise, why would one disguise require any more energy than another? (My husband assures me this use of a default appearance is so that the viewing audience will know who is who. I growl in irritation. "That's not a scientific explanation!")

So perhaps the human appearances of Jeremiah and the Bounty Hunter are part of their physiological makeup. This means that they too are hybrids, like Samantha and Gregor, yet with an even greater proportion of alien qualities. As with Samantha and Gregor, we would deduce that they are sterile and hybrids are hard to make, so that additional hybrids must be made from cloning. This would explain their identical appearances. If we assume that the aliens in these alien/human hybrids are gray aliens, though, we have a big problem. Neither grays nor humans appear to have shapeshifting abilities, so that trait would have to be introduced from a third source, which moves us into really really unlikely territory. We've been led to believe that the alien retrovirus that appears in the shapeshifters comes from the grays in "The Erlenmeyer Flask," but perhaps the shapeshifters carry this virus as well. Then we might theorize that the gray aliens aren't part of this hybrid at all. The shapeshifters, themselves carrying the alien retrovirus, may insert within themselves enough human DNA to enable them to imitate the pattern of a human's appearance.

Speculating for a moment about the colonization plot underlying The X-Files, this suggests two possibilities: First, the shapeshifting aliens are a race in service of the grays, like the black cancer; or second, the shapeshifters are the aliens involved in the colonization and the grays are a false construct of the government, to cover their experimentation with humans. I'm going with the latter theory these days.

How might these shapeshifters carry out their incredible transformations? We see the Bounty Hunter take on the appearance of a number of people significantly smaller than he is (and isn't almost everyone?). This suggests that, since his total mass must remain constant, he is able to squeeze it into a smaller, denser package. This seems impossible, since physiological systems require specific densities and concentrations to work, and our cells are each a certain specific size. Small organisms simply have fewer cells than large organisms. To shrink in size, the Bounty Hunter would have to squeeze all his bone, muscle, blood, and skin closer together. And this would be as fatal as getting caught in a garbage truck's compactor.

For the sake of argument, though, let's say that the Bounty Hunter doesn't significantly change size when he morphs. Would that allow him to shapeshift? If the shifting isn't an illusion, he is not only changing shape, but also pigmentation, skin texture, and even the shape of his skull and skeleton (or whatever supportive structure he has). Strictly speaking, we are all shapeshifters. I look quite different than I did as a child (as my mother likes to say, "You were so cute. What happened?"). But underlying all those changes is my DNA, controlling my formation and growth and decay. My DNA holds the architectural plans to my body, and my body is the expression of those plans. Say I were to gain the ability to shapeshift, and I morphed, with a considerable shifting of mass, into Pamela Anderson. (Perhaps I would dedifferentiate my stomach flab cells, like Leonard Betts, and then redifferentiate them into breast cells.) Would my DNA, through some bizarre, unknown method, also then change into Pamela Anderson's? If Pamela Anderson did not have the ability to shapeshift (and why would she want it?), then would I, in taking on her DNA, now have lost my ability?

We might argue that this DNA mimicking occurs only superficially, that there is some core of shapeshifter DNA that remains constant. After all, if I changed my entire body, how would I maintain my thoughts? In all his morphing, the Bounty Hunter never loses his sense of purpose. So some core of the shapeshifter must remain constant, while some non-core shifts. In that case, these shapeshifters would be self-created chimeras. But how could the DNA in these non-core cells be changed from one person's to another's? We're taking a big leap into speculation here, so hold on. Perhaps, when the Bounty Hunter acquires a new sample of DNA—say by touching Mulder—it is treated almost like a virus inside the shapeshifter. Mulder's DNA is packaged inside a very large protein envelope and sent to invade the non-core cells and replicate inside them, spreading. Then each of these non-core cells would have two different genotypes, one that generates the default Bounty Hunter appearance, and one that generates Mulder's appearance. The Mulder genes would be repressed, perhaps by having methyl groups sit on them as discussed with Leonard Betts. When the Bounty Hunter wants to change into Mulder, he must repress both sets of genes, allow the cells to dedifferentiate, and then free the Mulder genes to express themselves, so the cells will take on Mulder's appearance. The cells would need to be able to recognize each other as they do in a regenerating limb so that they differentiate appropriately, taking on the necessary roles. In fact, this process would be similar to regeneration, in that cells dedifferentiate and then redifferentiate. And if we think about it that way, the power to regenerate could help to explain why the shapeshifters are so difficult to kill.

In "regenerating" Mulder's head, the Bounty Hunter's cells would also have to know how old to make this Mulder head, perhaps by noting cues such as the lengths of the telomeres. If you recall, telomeres are the caps on the ends of the chromosomes that erode a bit with each cell division.

This entire process would take a very long time, though—probably as long as it takes a salamander to regenerate a leg, five weeks or longer—during which the Bounty Hunter's non-core cells would likely turn into a giant tumor, and Scully could slide the alien stiletto home.

OF DRONES AND CLONES

More clones appear in "Herrenvolk," and they perhaps offer some clues about the aliens' colonization goals. Jeremiah Smith calls the identical young Samanthas and blond boys "drones." These drones look like human children, though they cannot speak. Jeremiah says that they can raise themselves, and they seem to tend the beehives and plants without supervision. Jeremiah tells Mulder, "You're looking at the future." If this is a sneak preview of the aliens' plans for us, then it seems they need us as slave labor. Some might argue that a race with such advanced technology would not need slaves, that they could create robots to do all the manual labor. Yet the aliens' technology seems much more biologically directed than electronically, as shown by their use of the black cancer and bees as bioweapons. Why impose our own prejudice on them for electronic robots over biorobots? The aliens may not have the ethical concerns we do with such creations (and how serious can our ethics be when we've used fully intelligent humans as slaves?). Human drones may be the easiest and most effective "technology" for farming and running our planet. Why waste all that free labor?

There may be additional reasons the aliens would keep us alive instead of wiping us off the face of the planet. They may need us for the biomaterials we can provide. Our amazing physiological compatibility with them may be our downfall. If humans can profit from alien antibodies, as is illustrated in "Red Museum," then perhaps aliens can profit from human antibodies. If we assume the aliens have a hand in the smallpox-carrying bees in "Zero Sum," perhaps they want to threaten us with smallpox so that we will all be vaccinated. When we are vaccinated, we produce antibodies. These antibodies could be made into a serum for the aliens. Why do the aliens need a serum to fight smallpox, when smallpox has been eradicated? Just as the alien antibodies appear to protect the "Red Museum" kids from human diseases, perhaps the human smallpox antibodies protect the aliens from some alien disease. From what we've seen in the movie, the aliens may also need us for reproduction. They may want to use us, as the Syndicate fears, as hosts for the black cancer. The aliens may use the adult form of the black cancer as their soldiers, or the aliens themselves may be the adult form of the black cancer.

Why all the subterfuge with secret pacts with the Shadowy Syndicate and hidden bee farms? Why not just conquer us and take over? Perhaps the aliens are not as numerous or as strong as we fear, and so they must pit human against human. Hernando Cortez used similar techniques in Mexico. He formed alliances with tribes that had grudges against the Aztecs and so conquered that powerful civilization with only five hundred of his own men. In addition to human allies, the aliens can also use their bioweapons to subtly shape the planet for their needs. The bees provide a powerful weapon for them. Since they kill humans but not drones or shapeshifters, they can be used as a new method of natural selection, or a selective bioweapon, to kill off only normal humans. They might also be used as a threat to scare us into submission.

How would such drones be created? The use of the word drone and the presence of bees suggest a similarity of the clones to bee drones. Yet the Samanthas and the blond boys are workers, while the drones in bee colonies are males who do no work. Their only function is to fertilize new queens. Sterile females are the actual workers in the hive, so the term drone is somewhat misleading. Yet like bees, these drones seem to have a sense of their job in life and for the most part, do not seem to question it (though one Samantha's assistance to Mulder might suggest some latent ability for independent thought). Obviously such creatures would need brains much different from humans' to generate this behavior. Is there any way we could insert a worker bee's single-minded sense of duty into a human?

A specifically designed chimera has recently been created that changed the behavior of one animal into that of another. These surgical brain chimeras mixed the genes of two different species of birds. Dr. Evan Balaban of Harvard University took fertilized eggs of a chicken and a Japanese quail, cut minute holes in their eggshells, and operated on their embryonic brains. Brain cells were removed from the embryonic chicken, and quail brain cells were inserted in their place. Dr. Balaban transplanted cells from the forming quail midbrain that govern the sound of the animal's crow, and cells from the forming quail's brain stem that govern its head movement while crowing. The chicken chimeras grew, hatched, and then displayed some of the behavioral traits of quails. Some of the chickens, rather than crowing with a single exhalation, as is standard, released their crow in several distinct parts, like a quail. And rather than having no particular head movement during crowing, as is common with chickens, some of the chimera chickens rapidly bobbed their heads in a distinctively quail-like manner.

If the aliens have significantly more advanced technology than us, they might be able to do a much more sophisticated behavior transplant than the one described on page 207. The difficulty may come in trying to separate certain characteristics. If you want to put a bee's sense of duty and work ethic into a human, those qualities may be intrinsically connected to the bee's actual behaviors. For example, one of the worker bee's duties is to regulate temperature in the hive. It cools the hive by whirring its wings and warms the hive by vibrating its flight muscles without moving its wings. We may want our drones to monitor and regulate the temperature of the plants they're farming, but how do we transplant the bee's motivation and tie it to a different behavior: turning on a fan or a heater? If the Samanthas attempt to whir their wings or vibrate their flight muscles, the effect is going to be minimal.

The creation of these drones seems much more advanced than anything we've witnessed or even considered. Yet we might theorize that the aliens have perfected it in their colonization of many different planets and their enslavement of many different races.

ALIEN/HUMAN HYBRIDS OF THE FIFTH—AND FINAL?—KIND

One final type of hybrid is seen in "Christmas Carol" and "Emily." Scully's eggs, removed during her abduction, probably by Dr. Zama working for the government, were used to create a hybrid. The fetus was grown in fluid, then implanted into seventy-one-year-old Anna Fugazzi, who was given hormone injections of estrogen and progesterone by Dr. Calderon. Anna was also apparently sedated, for she remains unaware that she was pregnant, describing her missing time as a rejuvenating "beauty sleep." We've already discussed how chimeric techniques might allow a human female to carry an alien/human hybrid to term. But what about a woman of Anna's age? Can an elderly woman carry a fetus to term?

The age of women bringing implanted embryos to term is constantly growing higher. Recently a woman almost sixty-four years old gave birth to a healthy baby. Well past menopause, the woman was implanted with a donated egg fertilized by her husband's sperm. While doctors previously believed that a woman over fifty might be unable to carry a baby, cases in recent years have shown that this is not so. Dr. Richard J. Paulson, director of the infertility center at the University of Southern California and the doctor of the sixty-three-year-old woman, claims that women who have gone through menopause are just as likely as younger women to become pregnant using donor eggs, and that their babies are just as healthy. Dr. Michael Tucker, an embryologist at Reproductive Biology Associates in Atlanta, confirms that the drugs given to Anna Fugazzi are exactly what would be administered. "They take estrogen and progesterone replacement to wake up the uterus and make it receptive." While Anna Fugazzi is a few years older than the oldest such real-life mother, her ability to carry a baby to term, if she's in good physical shape, is fairly reasonable. Dr. Tucker says, "That a seventy-one-year-old could do this is not to my mind beyond the realm of physical possibility at all. It doesn't surprise me." Would the administration of such hormones during Anna's "beauty sleep" cause her to look years younger? Dr. Tucker replies, "It probably would give her a slightly more youthful appearance. I don't think it's going to be a Fountain of Youth or anything like that."

Emily allegedly suffers from a rare type of autoimmune hemolytic anemia, for which she's being treated through gene therapy administered by Dr. Calderon. Emily also has a cyst on the back of her neck, which oozes green bubbling fluid, so we can assume she carries the alien retrovirus. Might the retrovirus be related to her anemia?

Autoimmune hemolytic anemia is one of a family of disorders called hemolytic anemias. The best known of these is sickle cell anemia. Hemolytic anemias are conditions where red blood cells are prematurely destroyed, broken down faster than the bone marrow can produce new ones. The condition arises from an abnormal immune response against the body's own red blood cells. Scientists believe the membranes of the red blood cells appear abnormal to the immune system, so they are viewed as foreign substances and attacked. The membranes may appear abnormal because of inherited defects in the red blood cells or hemoglobin, blood transfusions, or infection by a virus or parasite. Dr. W. Hallowell Churchill, Jr., associate professor of medicine at Harvard Medical School, stresses that most often the causes are not known. "Nobody has a clue why it happens, but that's true of any autoimmune process."

Whatever the cause, antibodies form against the red blood cells and destroy them. Symptoms include fatigue, paleness, breathlessness, rapid heart rate, joint swelling, and enlarged spleen. Autoimmune hemolytic anemia is difficult to treat, yet seldom fatal. Treatment often includes corticosteroids, which as we know are immunosuppressants, and often allow the red blood cells to survive. If that isn't effective, the spleen may be removed, since much of the destruction of the red blood cells occurs in the spleen, or further immunosuppressive therapy may be tried. This is the type of disorder we might very well expect a hybrid to have, since the alien elements might be perceived as foreign intruders in the body. Apparently the children in "Red Museum" had a similar though less serious problem, since they too were treated with corticosteroids.

Since the previous human-created hybrid we saw was Dr. Secare, perhaps we can draw some conclusions about Emily from comparison. Dr. Secare was given part of the alien retrovirus through gene therapy. Emily also seems to carry at least part of it, though the genes were probably inserted through a single-cell hybridization technique. Since a virus is one of the possible causes of autoimmune hemolytic anemia, we could blame Emily's condition on the alien retrovirus. We have already posited that it creates abnormal proteins in the red blood cells. One of these proteins might look foreign to the immune system, triggering an autoimmune reaction. Why would Dr. Secare suffer no negative effects?

Emily may have received a gene from the alien retrovirus that Dr. Secare did not receive, so he may not carry the harmful protein. In the attempt to create a more advanced hybrid, more of the alien retroviral

genes may have been incorporated into Emily, and so the risk of immune rejection is increased. As we've discussed, few Earthly hybrids
survive, and only those of very closely related species, or those who have
only a tiny part of the DNA of a second species.

In the attempt to make Emily even more of a hybrid, scientists may
not only have given Emily the alien retrovirus, but also may have inserted actual alien stem cells into the fetal Emily. Stem cells in the
bone marrow give rise to all types of blood cells. With alien stem cells,
Emily would not be turning red blood cells green with the production
of a new protein; instead she'd be creating true green blood cells. She'd
also be creating alien white blood cells, though, cells that could recognize the human blood cells as foreign and attack them. Bone marrow
transplants between humans can cause a similar immunological reaction, called graft-versus-host disease. To minimize such reactions, doctors try to match tissue types as closely as possible. A person's tissue type
is determined by the set of major histocompatibility complex proteins
(MHC) he has. These proteins, which we discussed in connection with
"Genderbender," help the body detect and destroy foreign antigens.
There are many different MHC proteins, and if host and donor do not
share a significant number of them, the chances of rejection of the
transplant are high.

Scientists are working on ways to eliminate this negative reaction,
so that more radical transplants can be done. Stem cell transplants were
recently carried out on fetal sheep, creating sheep chimeras with
human bone marrow cells. Stem cells that lacked MHC class II proteins were taken from a human donor. If the stem cells had contained
those proteins, they would have been able to recognize the sheep's cells
as foreign and attack them. These immunologically safe stem cells were
then injected into sheep fetuses. Four of seven fetuses injected grew to
contain 4–6 percent human stem cells in the bone marrow. One lamb
tested at three months also contained human blood cells. The technique is being developed with an eye toward treating human fetuses
with blood disorders during the first trimester of pregnancy, before their
immune systems begin to function. Treating them after birth with bone

marrow transplants is much more difficult, since an immunologically compatible donor must be found.

If a similar procedure were carried out on Emily, we could theorize that scientists were unsuccessful in entirely preventing the alien stem cells from recognizing and fighting the "foreign" human cells. The alien stem cells would produce white blood cells that attack the red blood cells, creating the autoimmune hemolytic anemia. This reaction would have to be relatively limited, or Emily would not have survived even as long as she did.

Anemia isn't Emily's only health problem. Emily's MRI shows a rapidly growing neoplastic mass following the path of her central nervous system. Emily's neoplasm began its growth as a cyst at the base of her skull, the point where the hybrids and shapeshifters are vulnerable to fatal injury. I don't think this is just a coincidence.

A neoplasm is an abnormal growth or tumor; a malignant neoplasm is a cancer. Most neoplasms arise from the uncontrolled division of a single cell that has been transformed into a cancer cell. In this case, that "single cell" would appear to be in the skin at the base of her skull. Since viruses, and particularly retroviruses, have been implicated in some cancers, exposure to the alien retrovirus could be the underlying cause of both the cancer and the anemia.

Yet it's unclear whether cancer is really the right term for what's growing inside Emily. As Dr. Vinet points out in the episode, the growth, though rapid, seems controlled, following the central nervous system. Dr. Joel Goldwein, an associate professor of radiation oncology at the University of Pennsylvania Medical Center specializing in the treatment of childhood cancer, believes that Emily's neoplasm is as aggressive as a cancer. "Something growing as rapidly as what you describe and basically stealing a person's resources is certainly behaving like a cancer." Yet he finds the growth unlike anything he's encountered. "I've seen a lot of kids with cancer, and something that's growing all the way from the skin into the spinal canal and up into the brain is extremely unusual."

If it's not cancer, then what is it? Since we know Emily has alien

DNA incorporated into her genes and may even have alien stem cells, we might posit that this growth is some alien organ or system, growing at this point either because that is its appropriate time to grow (as a female's breasts develop later in life) or because this alien factor was introduced after birth. What function it might have in an alien or hybrid body remains unclear. Dr. Vinet describes it killing the surrounding tissue by depriving it of oxygen. If it is following the central nervous system, then it would be killing those nerve cells. Perhaps it is an alien nervous system taking the place of the human one.

Is this similar to any process here on Earth? Nerve generation can occur in a regenerating limb in salamanders, as we discussed back in chapter 1, though such an extensive new growth in a fully formed organism would seem impossible. Since the growth accelerates after a shapeshifter injects Emily with a greenish fluid, we might imagine that the growth requires alien amino acids or other raw materials that must be provided regularly. This may be the "treatment" that Dr. Calderon has been administering. If this growth does in some way reflect the shapeshifters' nervous system or core cells, then its origin at the base of the neck could explain why that spot is their Achilles' heel. Perhaps future hybrids will offer further clues to this growth.

PAPER PLATES ON STRINGS?

The existence of the gray aliens may be in question, yet it seems certain, particularly from episodes such as "Patient X" and "The Red and the Black," that aliens have come to Earth. While we haven't yet gotten up close and personal with their spaceships, *The X-Files* has given us some intriguing glimpses of UFOs and what they can do.

One important trait seems to be the UFOs' association with radiation. In "E.B.E.," Mulder explains that UFOs are sources of radiation. In "Ascension," Duane Barry has burns on one side of his face after an alleged close encounter. In "The Red and the Black," Scully has burns on her hands and face after a close encounter. Why would a UFO release ionizing radiation?

214 THE SCIENCE OF THE X-FILES

We've theorized that both the black cancer and the grays may have a higher tolerance for radiation. So one possible explanation would be that the radiation is a by-product of the propulsion system of the UFO, and it doesn't bother the aliens. If they are using nuclear power to run their UFOs, they may only put up enough shielding to reduce radiation to levels safe for them. They might not care that their radiation levels can still damage humans, or they might consider this a useful deterrent to keep humans away.

The problem with this reasoning is that radiation decreases with the square of the distance. So if I'm watching a UFO fly one hundred feet over my house and get a radiation burn, I'm only experiencing 1/10,000th of the amount of radiation the aliens on the UFO are getting. Even if they did have high tolerance, it seems unlikely they could withstand such extremely high levels. And if they could, why would they choose to subject themselves to that, when the reactor could easily be shielded? The radiation would likely also cause electronic damage to their ship at these levels, not to mention to human pilots. Since it's been suggested in "Deep Throat" and "Jose Chung's *From Outer Space*" that humans also fly UFOs, these high levels of radiation within the UFO don't seem the most likely scenario.

Perhaps this radiation is not an unavoidable consequence of the UFO's power plant but instead a weapon, used purposely against humans. Such a weapon would work much as the particle accelerator discussed earlier in connection with the oil organism, releasing a directed beam of high-energy particles at specific times with specific energies in specific directions. This is certainly well within the power of the aliens and well within our power too. In fact, we might theorize that these particles are accelerated within the oil organism, which seems from "Piper Maru" to live at least part-time in the UFO and may be involved in its functioning. If it has the ability to accelerate charged particles, as we discussed earlier, this may be the source of the UFO's radiation. Yet if this is a weapon, the UFO would only irradiate enemies. In "The Red and the Black," the UFO shoots a weapon at the rebels, setting them on fire. Yet it also gives Scully radiation burns on her hands and face, when she is standing nowhere near the rebels. The radiation doesn't appear limited to a weapon. It does seem a by-product of the UFO, but one that does not create high levels of radiation within the spaceship itself.

How could that be possible? Dr. Howard Matis, staff physicist at Lawrence Berkeley National Laboratories, suggests that the aliens use particle beams, not as weapons, but as a propulsion system. If you re-call Newton's second and third laws, the total momentum of an iso-lated system must remain constant, and every action requires an equal and opposite reaction. Let's do a little thought experiment. Frohike and Langly are ice-skating prior to attempting to retrieve the missing digital tape from the locker where Krycek has left it. Frohike stands at the cen-ter of the ice rink. His momentum is zero. He throws a videotape of the Zapruder film to Langly, standing on the sidewalk. As Frohike throws the tape forward, he recoils backward. The momentum of the tape for-ward will equal the momentum of Frohike backward, so the net mo-mentum will still be zero.

This is the same principle used to launch the space shuttle or other rockets. Before launch, the total momentum of the shuttle and its fuel is zero. As the shuttle is launched, the downward momentum of the ex-haust gases exactly equals the upward momentum of the shuttle, so that the total momentum of the system remains zero.

The UFO might utilize this same principle. Imagine it out in space. It could accelerate a beam of charged particles out in one direc-tion, just as Frohike throws the videotape. That would cause the UFO to recoil in the opposite direction, just as Frohike does. If the UFO wants to turn, it simply aims its beam in the direction opposite that it wants to go. If it wants to stop, it aims the beam forward, counteracting its momentum. Imagine the UFO now flying over your house. If the UFO is flying away from you, the particle beam is pointing toward you, and so irradiating you. If the UFO is flying toward you, you're safe (until they abduct you, anyway). To resist Earth's gravity, the UFO also needs to aim a particle beam down, to keep pushing it up. To hover over your bedroom, the UFO must shoot particles straight down, radiating you right in your bed. This would make the interior of the UFO the safest place to be.

Such craft still wouldn't be able to stop on a dime or change directions instantaneously, as they appear to in "Deep Throat." They could, however, stop or change directions much more quickly than our current aircraft, since the direction of the particle beam could be shifted very rapidly.

What would happen to pilots that fly alien spacecraft? In "Deep Throat," pilots apparently suffer from rashes, stress, nervous breakdowns, psychotic episodes, amnesia, and seizures due to the rapid accelerations, decelerations, and direction changes possible in UFOs. We measure acceleration in G's, with one G equal to the acceleration caused by Earth's gravity. While we go through most of our lives feeling one G, we experience higher or lower G forces when we are rapidly changing speeds or directions—as an elevator starts accelerating upward, as a car peels out from a stoplight, or as a roller coaster spins us through a corkscrew.

Our bodies are adapted to life at one G, and we are limited in how much acceleration we can withstand. We don't need UFOs, though, to push us beyond our limits. The Air Force's F-16 can already produce far more G's than the human body can survive. A normal human in good shape can withstand no more than nine G's. This means the body feels nine times heavier than usual, blood rushes to the feet, and the heart can't pump hard enough to bring this heavier blood to the brain. (Here's where the grays' auxiliary hearts could come in very handy.) The pilot experiences tunnel vision, then loses all vision or blacks out, loses consciousness, and finally dies. If an alien spacecraft could create a higher G force than an F-16 by rapid turning and acceleration, it really wouldn't matter, since our own technology has already exceeded our bodies' abilities. As to whether the pilot in "Jose Chung's *From Outer Space*" is accurate in his assessment that after flying a UFO, "sex seems trite," well we'll just have to wonder.

EARTH VERSUS THE FLYING SAUCERS

Is a particle beam really the most likely propulsion system for a UFO? It depends on whether it's designed to travel mainly in space or in our atmosphere. Since we don't know whether these craft are used for interstellar travel or not, let's just consider their viability to operate within the atmosphere and to make trips up into Earth orbit, like the space shuttle does.

In our atmosphere, ramjets and scramjets seem to hold the most promise for travels up to Mach 5 and beyond. These work similarly to jet engines, compressing air, spraying fuel—such as hydrogen—into the air and igniting the mixture, which causes it to expand and shoot out the back at accelerated speeds, providing forward thrust. Yet the ramjet and scramjet have subtle differences that make them more effective at speeds above Mach 2. In a jet engine, the air is compressed by fan blades to many times normal atmospheric pressure. This mechanical method does not work well once the plane reaches Mach 2. A ramjet uses the speed of the plane itself to compress air through a cone-shaped diffuser and slow it to subsonic speeds where the fuel is added and ignited. While this type of system has been used to accelerate projectiles to over 5,200 mph within a tube, it has yet to be successfully applied to aircraft. And as the ramjet approaches Mach 5, the air is shooting into the engine so quickly that it's hard to slow it to subsonic speeds, which is necessary to keep the mixture burning. A scramjet, in theory, would allow the mixture to keep burning while the air's speed through the engine is supersonic. Engineers thus far have failed to solve the problems associated with supersonic airflow. If the aliens have solved these problems, the scramjet would allow them to zip from the prisons of Tunguska to the beehives of Canada in only a few hours.

And what is the best shape for such a vehicle? We haven't gotten a clear view of the UFOs in *The X-Files*. The UFOs in "Nisei," "Jose Chung's *From Outer Space*," and the movie seem as if they may be saucer shaped, while those in "Deep Throat" and "Tempus Fugit" appear triangular, and the huge one in "Paper Clip" seems to have eight or ten sides. In space, shape is of little importance. But within the atmosphere, airflow and friction become important factors. These factors have shaped our current planes and rockets, and have limited the speed at which we can travel. A flying saucer is not streamlined, and so seems an impractical shape for an aircraft. Yet recent experiments may lead to the development of a technology that eliminates wind resistance as an important factor in flight. Dr. Leik Myrabo, an aerospace engineer at Rensselaer Polytechnic Institute, is working on an air spike, a device that carves a path through the air that the aircraft can fly through.

Current supersonic aircraft use their sharp noses to cut through the air and create a conical shock wave. If the aircraft fits inside this cone, it experiences much less drag. But as the aircraft accelerates, the size of the cone narrows, until the aircraft can no longer fit inside. One solution is to increase the size of the cone by making the nose longer, which is why the Concord looks like it does. But a long nose is heavy, and will only improve the situation so much.

A better solution is the air spike. The spike focuses a microwave or laser beam on a point in the air in front of the aircraft. At this focal point, the beam has enough electromagnetic energy to rip electrons from molecules, and these electrons then collide with other molecules, ripping off more electrons. This explosive chain reaction creates powerful pressure waves. While these waves would normally radiate out equally in all directions, when occurring in the fast-moving air before a rapidly moving aircraft, the waves are bent back from the focal point into a curving parabola, rather like an umbrella, creating an area behind it sheltered from air resistance. This parabolic shock wave shelters a much larger area than the traditional cone-shaped shock wave. Early experiments by Dr. Myrabo and others have confirmed the formation of this parabolic shock wave, and demonstrated that it reduces the drag on a model aircraft traveling at Mach 2 by half. Since the shock wave shelters the aircraft, almost any shape aircraft could be used.

Dr. Myrabo envisions the air spike being used with saucer-shaped craft. These craft, he theorizes, would use magnetohydrodynamic acceleration, a system shrouded in secrecy currently under development by the U.S., Russia, and other countries. The shock wave would be shaped so that the edges of the umbrella just touch the edges of the saucer. Superconducting magnets and electrodes on the exterior of the saucer would accelerate the ionized particles in the shock wave back behind the saucer, pushing the saucer forward. This is not terribly different from the particle accelerator we imagined powering the UFO. So a saucer with an air spike could be a practical craft for the aliens, though for humans it will be several decades before this technology might be ready for flight.

PEEPING KINBOTE

A big shiny flying saucer may be fine for those nighttime, out-of-the-way abductions, but it's not too practical for covert intelligence-gathering missions. Luckily, researchers at Sikorsky Aircraft in Stratford, Connecticut, have come up with a smaller, more flexible drone saucer, able to fill your intelligence needs. The 6 1/2-foot-diameter saucer, called *Cypher*, is a rotary-wing aircraft like a helicopter. Although the craft appears from the outside to be a saucer, it actually has a hole in the middle, like a doughnut. Within this hole are its two rotors, one on top of the other, which spin in opposite directions. With this design, *Cypher* does not need a tail rotor. *Cypher* can stay in the air for two and a half hours and cover almost twenty miles. With an attached video camera and an ability to fly low and slow, it can perform reconnaissance and record observations. Sophisticated software can guide *Cypher* on a predetermined mission. Under orders, *Cypher* has located a soldier walking in a field and followed him. On another mission, it cruised the streets of a mock town searching for snipers. Perhaps we could send it on a visit to the Shadowy Syndicate.

If we believe these UFOs may be experimental military aircraft rather than alien ships, a triangular shape is much more likely than a saucer. While triangular craft are not the most common here on Earth, they are within our technology and form an area of growing interest for designers. Triangular flying wings like the stealth bomber are much more fuel efficient than standard-shaped aircraft. They use only 20–33 percent of the fuel burned by a conventionally shaped plane.

If you believe the significant evidence that has accumulated in the last nine years and not the government denials, the U.S. Air Force has already developed a triangular-shaped top-secret spy plane that can travel up to Mach 6, or 4,000 mph at altitudes above 50,000 feet. Deep Throat even mentions it in "Musings of a Cigarette-Smoking Man." The Aurora has apparently awakened residents of Southern California with its sonic booms and registered on a regular weekly schedule on the U.S. Geological Survey's seismographs. It's been clocked by the USGS at Mach 3.1, and described by witnesses as triangular in shape. Some claim it is two hundred feet long, with a prominent dorsal spine. Observers who have caught the Aurora at night claim it looks like a single, bright pulsating light. The aircraft leaves a distinctive trail in the sky, looking like doughnuts on a rope or sausage links. Some speculate that the craft utilizes pulse detonation wave engines, in which a tube open at one end is filled with liquid methane or hydrogen, detonated, filled again, and detonated again in a cyclical manner, creating a steady flow of combustion products.

Might the appearance of such a plane, followed by some bizarre experiences, cause witnesses to believe they've had a close encounter with aliens vastly more advanced and powerful than us? According to a Pentagon briefing, microwave weapons are being developed that can disturb brain waves and impair memory, cause burns, seizures, and heart attacks. Sonic weapons have already been built that cause the hairs in the inner ear to vibrate, creating vertigo and nausea. They can even vibrate the insides of humans to stun them, cause spasms, or even liquefy their bowels. It's enough to make you think the world is ending.

"THIS IS NOT HAPPENING. THIS IS NOT HAPPENING."

Since many if not all of the abductions appear to have been carried out by the government, how do they make the abductees believe that gray aliens are responsible? They could bring in one of their artificial "gray aliens," but they also need to create the terrifying sense of altered reality and memories of bizarre events that haunt abductees like Duane Barry.

The answer may be in the experiments of Dr. Michael Persinger, professor of neuroscience and psychology at Laurentian University. Dr. Persinger believes that bursts of electrical activity in the brain's temporal lobes can lead a person to think he has undergone a mystical or psychic experience. "All experience is tied to neuro-electrical activity, so one shouldn't be surprised that there are specific quantitative neurologic patterns tied to particular experiences."

In fact, the temporal lobes are the location of the *God module* referred to in "The End." In that episode, chess prodigy Gibson apparently has abnormal activity in this area of the brain. Dr. Vilayanur Ramachandran, director of the Brain and Perception Laboratory at the University of California at San Diego, only last year discovered the "God module," an area within the temporal lobes that becomes electrochemically active when a person thinks about God or spirituality. This further ties the temporal lobes to mystical experience.

The temporal lobes, the lower lobes of the cerebral hemispheres, are involved in many different processes. They contain the sensory center of hearing and balance. The left temporal lobe helps to process language. Near the front of the temporal lobes is the *amygdala,* which is believed critical in originating emotional behaviors, as we discussed earlier. The amygdala, according to Dr. Persinger, can imbue events with intense emotion and a sense of meaningfulness. Because of the way the temporal lobes are structured, they are among the most electrically sensitive regions in the brain.

In most people, mystical experiences are triggered by extreme anxiety, stress, grief, or lack of oxygen. The biochemistry of stress is activated, stimulating groups of temporal-lobe neurons whose firing patterns may create what's perceived as an altered state. Since lack of oxygen can bring on such neural bursts, this may account for the mystical experiences associated with near-death states and the exhilaration of autoerotic asphyxia. In some people, less extreme conditions may trigger these bursts of activity. They have more temporal-lobe sensitivity and are more likely to have odd experiences such as hearing someone call their name before they fall asleep, occasionally sensing the presence of another entity in the room, traveling outside their bodies, or flying. Those most prone to these bursts suffer temporal-lobe epilepsy. Temporal-lobe seizures can cause hallucinations involving sight, sound, smell, and taste, can create the illusion that real people are unreal, can cause intense fear and increased awareness of heartbeat and respiration. People suffering from temporal-lobe epilepsy report intense mystical and religious experiences both during seizures and in between seizures.

To try to prove his theory that these bursts create the illusion of a psychic or mystical experience, Dr. Persinger has created a helmet with coils of wire set just above the ears. By passing a carefully controlled electrical current through these coils, Dr. Persinger creates a pulsating magnetic field that mimics the firing patterns of neurons in the temporal lobes. These cause bursts of activity in the temporal lobes of the subject, and so the effect of such bursts can be recorded. The subjects are blindfolded and taken into a soundproof chamber, so that, according to Dr. Persinger, "The neurons typically involved in visual and auditory surveillance can be recruited into the experience."

Many of Dr. Persinger's subjects report an opiatelike effect, with a decrease in anxiety and a profound sense of well-being, similar to the enlightenment Cassandra Spender reports feeling in "Patient X." Dr. Persinger explains, "A person's neuroelectric activity can be changed forever. A person can feel as if he's literally a new person."

The specific effect can be controlled to some extent by the location and pattern of the magnetic field applied. A burst pattern over the right hemisphere of the brain will induce in up to half the subjects the feeling of another presence in the room. For some of these people, the presence is very emotionally significant. Dr. Persinger describes one case, where the existence of this presence filled the subject "with glowing warmth. He felt as if he didn't want to leave ever. When the experiment was over, he was extraordinarily sad." While some experiences are blissful, others are terrifying. Applying the magnetic field to the right hemisphere of the brain tends to induce a negative experience, since the right hemisphere is involved in vigilance, and intense vigilance becomes panic, rather like what Duane Barry seems to feel. Subjects also tend to see unusual faces. Stimulation of the left hemisphere often creates an auditory hallucination, with the subject feeling as if someone is talking to him, giving him some message. This might account for an abductee feeling that aliens are communicating telepathically with him, their voices invading his head. Other subjects report leaving their bodies, going down a tube, spinning, sensing vibrations, odd smells, images that they believe are from childhood, being grabbed and pulled, their bodies distorting and stretching, feeling violent anger and fear.

While Dr. Persinger's goal with this device is to prove the connection between natural temporal-lobe bursts and mystical experiences and so better understand the nature of consciousness, the device could equally well be used to create such mystical experiences in subjects. Dr. Persinger says, "With the intensity of the experiences induced, if the person is not in the laboratory but in his bedroom at 3 A.M., the probability is very high that he will believe something very significant has happened. How he attributes it will depend on his predispositions." Dr. Persinger believes that alien abduction experiences "are the secular equivalents of the religious experiences—the God visitations or angel visitations—of the past." If someone is religious, he may interpret the event as religious. If someone is less religious, he may attribute the experience to the only other available cultural label: extraterrestrial abduction. The government might aid in the interpretation. Some temporal-lobe stimulation, combined with an appearance by a gray, some drugging, hypnosis, and good old-fashioned probing might very well convince someone that he has been abducted.

In the realm of grays, hybrids, and UFOs, how much of what we've seen is truth and how much is obfuscation remains uncertain. Yet the possibility of alien life remains very real, and advances in various hybridization techniques are creating possibilities both fascinating and disturbing, depending on how and why they are used. Technological advances can provide life-saving breakthroughs, but they can also present new dangers, and provide the opportunity for abuses never before possible. This leads us to our final chapter.

SEVEN

TECHNOLOGY RUN AMOK

"What do you want—a baby or a Nobel Prize?"

—Dr. Polidori,
"Post-Modern Prometheus"

DUANE BARRY RAMS THE FIRE EXTIN-guisher into a security guard's head. The guard collapses, and Duane flees down the hospital corridor, his heart pounding, his body alive with adrenaline. The aliens have come for him again, but he won't be taken again. He won't be taken. His bare feet pound down the stairs and out into the rainy night. An EMT stares at Duane in his hospital gown. Duane runs, the rain quickly soaking his body. At first the gunshot wound burns with every breath. But gradually other sensations intrude. Coppery red hair. Pale skin. A woman's face. His course, which had been random, begins to take on direction, as if he's tied to the end of a rope that's being pulled. He must turn left here, then right. They have approved of his plan, he realizes. Someone else may go in his place. Someone of their choosing. Duane begins to laugh. He will be free. He sees the house highlighted in lightning, and he knows that she is inside. The woman who will set him free.

While biological chaos often erupts in *The X-Files*, technological chaos also has its place among the unusual and bizarre. Some arises accidentally, some extraterrestrially, some through the hubris of scientists, some from secret government plans. We've seen rampaging roachbots, ominous implants, ill-tempered artificial intelligences, smallpox-carrying bees, and a mutant Mutato. While we depend on technology in every aspect of our lives, we also fear it, for its potential in the wrong hands, for its power in the event of a breakdown, for its promise to potentially replace us as the dominant force on the planet. Are our fears justified? Could artificial intelligences go out of control and kill? Could we all be catalogued with our smallpox vaccinations? Could implants record our thoughts and control our actions? Could insects be engineered to carry bioweapons? Let's find out.

IS THAT ROACH WATCHING YOU?

In "War of the Coprophages," Mulder discovers a cockroach that is actually a tiny robot. While a local researcher into artificial intelligence, Dr. Ivanov, is building robots based on insect models, this one is far beyond anything he's created. Ivanov tells Mulder that insect-modeled robots are the future of space exploration, leading Mulder to theorize that this advanced roachbot may be a first-contact probe sent by an alien civilization. But would insect-modeled robots be a practical way of exploring a planet? And why would we build robots based on insect models anyway? What would we use them for, and how advanced are the robots we're building today?

In science fiction films, the robots have mainly been wheeled, like the robot on *Lost in Space* and R_2D_2 in *Star Wars*; or humanoid with two legs, like C_3PO also in *Star Wars* or Data in *Star Trek: The Next Generation*. In reality, our robots have mainly been either stationary or wheeled. But for over twenty years, scientists have been trying to create robots based on insect models. Stationary robots are fine for assembly lines, and wheeled robots are great in controlled environments. If you're on a flying saucer with nice smooth, wide corridors, no problem.

But what about in rough outdoor terrain? "The main advantage for legged robots is that they can get around a lot of places that wheeled robots can't," says Dr. Randall Beer, associate professor of computer engineering and science, who is working with a team at Case Western Reserve University on their third insect-modeled robot.

Robots modeled after insects, with six legs, offer both stability and mobility. *Sojourner,* the wheeled rover NASA sent recently to Mars, is stable, but extremely limited in its movements and mobility. "If you could design a robot that could actually walk with two legs, it could get around a lot of places," says Dr. Beer. "But with two legs, there's no stable situation. We're constantly balancing by tightening our muscles." Insects, on the other hand, are extremely stable. The six legs allow for a tripod gait, in which the front and back leg on one side hit the ground at the same time as the middle leg on the opposite side, so that whenever the insect stops, three legs are on the ground. Insects are also extremely mobile and can climb over almost any obstacle. "They won't give you much of a game of chess," Beer says, "but they're very good at getting around."

While the early bug-shaped robots were slow and awkward, the latest models are graceful and almost lifelike. Robot builders are learning how insects control their legs and are programming robots to mimic them. Dr. Roy Ritzmann, professor of biology and neuroscience and part of the Case Western team, studies how cockroaches move, observing their joints and motor activity, and using that information to discover how the cockroach's neurons control those movements. Dr. Ritzmann actually maps the neurons involved in controlling movement in a process he compares to mapping a circuit in a transistor radio. He inserts electrodes into two neurons, stimulates one to fire a pattern of activity, and then measures any signal received by the other. In this way he and others at several neurobiology laboratories have mapped a pathway, or circuit, from the sensory hairs of the cockroach to the motor neurons.

The Case Western team has discovered from this research that the key to making the robot as insectlike as possible in its movement is combining centralized and decentralized control systems. According to Case Western robotocist Roger D. Quinn, professor of mechanical and aerospace engineering, centralized control is necessary to orchestrate the movements of the legs and keep the robot on its feet, while decentralized control is necessary to allow each leg to act more independently. The more insectlike the robot is, the more skilled it is at moving. Their latest, Robot 3, has been modeled much more closely on the cockroach. Why the cockroach? Dr. Quinn replies, "The cockroach is great at moving forward rapidly, turning, and climbing. If a robot could do those things, it would be a very capable robot." Robot 3 can maintain its balance under shifting conditions, probe ahead with a leg to find a foothold, and will be able to easily climb over obstructions.

While the Case Western team believes six legs is the optimal number, some researchers think the more legs, the better. Dr. Subramanian Venkataraman of the Jet Propulsion Laboratory has plans to build a forty-four-legged centipede-like robot.

Despite the impressive progress being made, we're still a long way from building a robot as fast as a cockroach, or one as small. Dr. Beer explains that "Robots that small can certainly be built, but they wouldn't be as sophisticated as the larger robots, and they would certainly be far less capable than an insect." Their current robot is seventeen times the size of a cockroach. (When I told my husband that the cockroach-modeled robots weren't small, he asked, "How big are they? As big as a house?" That left me with an interesting image.)

Insect-modeled robots have been used to enter Mount Spurr, an active volcano in Alaska (much as in the episode "Firewalker") and to clean up nuclear power plants. Possible future uses include mine disposal, maintaining pipelines and exploring other planets. If you think Dr. Ivanov's claim that we will be using insect-modeled robots to explore other planets is far-fetched, the people at NASA disagree. They, along with the Office of Naval Research, are helping to fund roachbot research. Aliens might agree that multi-legged robots are the most practical method of exploring a planet. And if they wanted to do it quietly, a robot modeled after an indigenous species would be an ingenious choice, permitting surreptitious exploration and intelligence gathering.

THE BIONIC ROACH

Why go to all that trouble to create a robot to mimic an insect, when we have so many unemployed insects? Wouldn't it be simpler to program the roach to do what we want? The movie *The Fifth Element* featured a remote-controlled roach wired with a tiny video camera, used as a spying device. Well, the future is here. Scientists, believe it or not, have considered this very option, and so we have the bionic roach, or RoboRoach, as he is affectionately known. Dr. Isao Shimoyama, an engineer at the University of Tokyo, has removed the wings and antennae of a roach and replaced them with pulse-emitting electrodes and a tiny electronic backpack. By stimulating the roach's nervous system through the electrodes, Dr. Shimoyama can make the roach move forward, turn left or right, or spring backward. Insects are relatively easy to control because they have a simple command-response system. They will respond in only one way to a given stimulus. To know what stimulus to give, researchers measure the electrical signals traveling from the cockroach's antennae to its muscles as it moves. They break these down to isolate the signals for each type of movement, then design an electronic circuit to artificially re-create the signals.

While the RoboRoach was originally conceived as an intermediate step leading ultimately to insect-modeled micro-robots, many scientists are becoming excited about the possibilities of these bionic insects. In the future, they might be used to lead swarms of insects to crops in need of pollination, to lead unwanted swarms into traps, and with a camera added to their backpacks, to search the rubble after earthquakes for survivors, or to perform surveillance on criminals. A camera-outfitted roach could have come in handy, for example, in the hostage situation in "Duane Barry."

I KNOW WHAT YOU DID LAST SUMMER

There are much more sinister methods of surveillance than robot roaches. In a number of X-files, including the pilot episode, "Duane Barry," "Nisei," "Redux II," and "Unusual Suspects," people have been implanted with mysterious objects that may serve as tracking devices. Duane Barry has them in his gums, sinus cavity, and abdomen; Susanne Modeski has one in her tooth; Scully and her fellow abductees have them in the backs of their necks. We know little about the nasal implant found in the pilot except that it is made from some material that can't be identified. Duane Barry's implants are metallic and etched with a microscopic bar code that sets off a grocery store scanner. In "Nisei," Scully's implant is described as an extremely complex microprocessor. How advanced are the implants we can now create, and what can they do? Convicted Oklahoma City bomber Timothy McVeigh claimed that the government planted a computer chip in his buttocks to monitor his movements. Could he be right?

Several companies make tiny glass-coated microchips designed to be implanted in lab animals, cattle, and family pets. The chips contain miniature transponders that broadcast a registration number when subjected to a magnetic field. The number can be picked up by a scanner held a few feet from an animal, like checking an I.D. tag. Such tags have been inserted by the FDA into cows' stomachs to catch cattle dealers illegally selling medicated cows for meat. These chips would appeal to our alien friends, who seem to put a lot of stock in cataloging and tagging. It helps them keep track of their potential slaves. Although the tags can only be detected at close range, they can carry more information than a simple I.D. Several companies have developed electronic tags for possible use on airline baggage that combine memory, a processor, a transmitter, and a receiver on a microchip. Baggage handlers could read the data from the chip with a scanner from as far as ten feet away. So we might imagine the Cigarette-Smoking Man with a scanner reading information from Scully's implant from a few feet away. This is handy, but these small distances are not quite good enough when it comes to monitoring a global conspiracy.

Some cars make it easy for the government to track your position. You've probably seen the commercial where a woman receives directions from her car. That car is accessing the Global Positioning System (GPS), a network of satellites ringing the globe run by the U.S. Air Force

Space Command. These satellites transmit very precise time signals. A receiver, such as that in the car, picks up signals from the three or four closest satellites. The farther the satellite is, the longer it takes the signal to arrive, and so the time differences in the arrival of the signals can be used, through a process called triangulation, to calculate the car's position to an accuracy of .1 mile. The satellites don't even need something the size of a car to track. In Sweden, special cellular phones are available that can access this GPS, helping the mentally handicapped if they become lost. This raises a very simple possibility for the Shadowy Syndicate. Since Mulder and Scully seem virtually attached to their cell phones, a simple receiver and transmitter could be inserted into the phones, so that they could receive the GPS signals and then transmit them to the Shadowy Syndicate, revealing Mulder and Scully's positions. The receiver and transmitter could run off the cell phone's power.

A less accurate system could be used to track our dynamic duo without adding anything special to their cell phones. Most cellular systems today have some sort of tracking built in. Whenever you have your phone on, it periodically reports to your service provider which cell or region you are in. It does this so that when someone calls you, your phone can be quickly located. The Shadowy Syndicate might access this information to keep track of Mulder and Scully's general locations.

Another possibility. Byers's ex-employer, the Federal Communications Commission, has mandated that Emergency 911 services become available for cell phones across the U.S. The service will use triangulation between multiple cell towers to pinpoint a caller's location within about a city block. One might imagine that the F.C.C.—or another government agency—could access such a system for other purposes as well.

But what if we want to track Duane Barry, who doesn't seem the cell phone type? Could we make a device small enough to implant? Peregrine falcons have been outfitted with satellite receivers and transmitters so scientists can follow their migration routes. These units are about the size of a D-cell battery, though they have a longer antenna wire hanging from them. They weigh only ¾ of an ounce. The transmitter is strapped on with a harness, allowing the GPS to determine whether the bird is moving or stationary, and to locate the bird's position within a tenth of a mile. A difficulty with this and all such self-contained detection devices and implants is power. A more powerful battery is bigger and heavier. Thus the range or the duration of the device is limited. The more tasks the device must accomplish, and the more often it is asked to transmit data, the more quickly the power is drained. Yet even tinier tracking devices have been developed for smaller animals. The delicate Apollo butterfly, only two inches across, has been wired with the lightest radar transmitter yet, weighing only 1/100,000th of an ounce. The transmitter combines a diode the size of a pinpoint and a three-inch-long superthin wire antenna. The smaller size, though, limits the power of the device. The butterflies can be tracked only within a 150-foot range using a handheld device.

If we want to track our abductees accurately over long distances, the GPS is our best bet. But is a tenth of a mile as accurate as we can get? It seems not. Satellites send out two different GPS signals, one accessible by everyone, and one encrypted for military use exclusively. The civilian signal contains deliberate errors and fuzziness to cut its accuracy down to 165 feet at best. The military claims their own signal allows them to be accurate within sixty-five feet. Some, though, believe the military's capability is significantly greater. Last year, the Air Force was searching for the wreckage of an A-10 aircraft that disappeared over the Rocky Mountains. During the search the military turned the fuzziness in the civilian signal off—civilian planes were helping in the search—and various users of the GPS were shocked to find that they could locate receivers with an accuracy of six feet.

AN ALIEN MADE ME DO IT, PART TWO

We not only want to track our implanted subjects, we want to monitor and control their bodily functions, their thoughts, and their actions. But how do we connect electronic systems with biological ones?

We've been doing that for a while, in a limited way, delivering signals to the nerves through electrodes. Pacemakers can regulate our heartbeats. Cochlear implants allow the deaf to hear with the help of electrical signals. Electronic stimulators allow paraplegics to stimulate their bladder with the press of a button when they want to urinate. An implant to treat tremors caused by Parkinson's disease goes directly into the brain. An electrode sends low-level electrical currents into the thalamus, where they block the nerve signals causing Parkinson's tremors. This electrode is connected with a wire to a battery pack implanted under the collarbone. The device can be turned on or off externally by placing a magnet against the battery. We might, in the spirit of *The X-Files*, imagine a similar implant causing tremors and other brain disturbances to "enhance" the abduction experience. Or a friendly pat on the shoulder with a hidden magnet could trigger tremors and collapse.

To make the control more automatic, an implant's action could be triggered internally through a sensor. For example, we might want to trigger a seizure in our subject whenever his heart rate goes above 85. Can we monitor various physiological functions through implants? Arctic ground squirrels in Iceland have been wired with a chip the size of a bottle cap, which keeps track of their body temperature and heart rate during the winter. Scientists in Sweden have recently built a chemical sensor implant. This implant, coated with the enzyme glucose oxidase, can detect glucose in the bloodstream of a diabetic. When the enzyme comes in contact with glucose, a reaction occurs and an electron is released. These electrons can be counted by the sensor to calculate the concentration of glucose molecules in the blood, and the results transmitted to a nearby receiver. Other implants coated with different enzymes could be used to detect other chemicals in the bloodstream (this could make urine drug tests look like child's play). Right now, though, the enzyme coatings are unstable and tend to break down after only a few hours. Still, the scientists see them being used in the near future as short-term sensors, monitoring a patient's condition during an operation, for example.

Such systems may soon be integrated with implants that release drugs, such as those discussed in connection with "Memento Mori" or tiny pumps that deliver a preprogrammed amount of drugs to the system. In these cases, on detection of a certain molecule or a level of chemicals, the drug would be released. Such a system is being developed for diabetes, which would detect a rise in blood sugar levels and release insulin.

But that's just the beginning. Dr. Andrew A. Berlin of the Xerox Palo Alto Research Center believes all the components exist to create self-sufficient microelectromechanical systems (MEMS), but they just haven't been put together yet. Such a unit, less than a half inch long and only .04 inch wide, could incorporate various sensors, a power source, a microprocessor, a microphone, a pump, a transmitter and receiver. Devices like this could potentially transmit Duane Barry's position back to his abductors, listen in on his conversations, monitor his physical condition, dispense various drugs, and send electric impulses into his brain. Such a system could potentially trigger the breathlessness, seizures, paralysis, and overwhelming fear Duane feels at the appearance of "aliens," could cause erratic behavior to discredit Duane, and could even drive him toward Scully's house, by increasing unpleasant sensations as he moves in the wrong direction and decreasing them as he moves in the right direction. Similarly, Cassandra, Scully, and the other abductees in "Patient X" might be led to a specific location. A comparable system might be used to keep Billy Miles, in the pilot episode, in a nearly comatose state and wake him only when needed. As for delivering specific instructions to Billy, a radio receiver in the ear as Mulder uses in "Duane Barry" could easily whisper directions ("Gather the others for testing. Klaatu barada nikto.").

This is still a far cry from the implant Scully carries at the base of her neck. Agent Pendrell suggests that Scully's implant is replicating the memory function of her brain, collecting information and perhaps even re-creating her thought processes. Can we make such a mind/machine connection? Unfortunately, we still have a long way to go. The human brain is so complex, with over one hundred billion neurons, our understanding of it remains severely limited. We have been able to record brain-wave activity externally for a while. The problem is in interpreting it. Britta Serog, a neuromorphic programmer at Silver Wolf Software, explains, "The exact impulses that comprise a thought are not known." So we end up with a huge amount of data that is very difficult to interpret.

Researchers in Germany have taken the first step toward connecting the human brain to a computer. They have found a way to connect a neuron taken from a leech to a silicon chip. When the neuron fires, the chip can detect the signal, and when the chip sends a signal, it can cause the neuron to fire. They hope someday to create chip implants that can stimulate neurons, allowing paralyzed limbs to move.

But can we influence a person's thoughts through an implant, as seems to be shown in "Patient X" and other episodes? Could we implant an image of a bridge into Scully's mind and make her want to go there? Researchers are developing a technique to help the blind see that bypasses the eye and inserts visual information directly into the brain. Researchers have implanted thirty-eight hatpin-shaped microelectrodes in the visual cortex of a woman's brain. The electrodes were wired to a computer. When an electrical current was sent through an electrode, the woman saw a spot of light. Depending on which electrode was stimulated, the position of the spot of light would change. By mapping out the position corresponding to each electrode, researchers could then stimulate several electrodes in concert to project a pattern, such as a shape or letter. Researchers envision a system with many more electrodes, connected to a camera that can convey information about the subject's surroundings. While this system is in the early stages of development, one can imagine a day not far distant when these implants perhaps could be used to input visions or hallucinations.

So we can monitor and influence the physiological processes of our subjects, and perhaps insert images into their brains. Yet we still can't implant or record specific thoughts. Will Scully's implant be possible sometime in the future? Agent Pendrell describes Scully's implant as a neural network. A neural network is a type of computer designed to work as much as possible like a brain. Rather than a single complex central processor running a single program, a neural net is built from many very simple processors, connected to each other somewhat like the neurons are in the brain, and then allowed to learn from experience without any governing program. Even though the nets have no governing program in the traditional sense, they must still be set up with rules that guide their learning process, and coming up with the best learning model is what researchers are working on now. In the brain, neurons remember previous signals, and this memory increases their efficiency. They give more weight to signals from specific neurons, based on previous experience and other factors. Similarly, the learning models for neural nets seek to create such memory among the individual processors, training them to adjust the strengths of their various connections to each other based on the amount of activity passing through each of these connections. These adjustments mimic a rudimentary level of learning.

One problem neural nets face in mimicking brain activity is that neurons communicate through analog, not digital signals. While a processor's digital signal is either a one or a zero, like an on-off switch, an analog signal can convey varying levels. A neuron has over a hundred different levels of electrical activity, which allow it to convey a range of information. Neuromorphic engineers are attempting to create processors that function more like biological neurons. These processors will send out different signals depending on the intensity of the incoming signals, the interaction between various signals, and their recent history. While individual processors of this type have been built, they haven't yet been combined into a neural net.

Yet even when they are, it will be a long time before we can create a neural net with the complexity of the human brain. The entire brain contains roughly one hundred billion neurons, and each neuron can communicate with an average of ten thousand others. This massive number of connections creates a great degree of parallelism in the brain, meaning that many different signals can be traveling to different places at the same time. Imagine being able to send information between New York and Los Angeles only via one train track. Now imagine New York builds four more tracks to different cities, say Baltimore,

Houston, Minneapolis, and Vancouver. Each of these cities already has train tracks going to Los Angeles. There are now a total of five potential paths for information to travel simultaneously from New York to Los Angeles. In addition, different information can be sent to and picked up from Baltimore, Houston, Minneapolis, and Vancouver along the way. Now imagine that instead of two cities exchanging information you have one hundred billion, and each of these cities has tracks to ten thousand others. Since each of these connections can be processing information at the same time (assuming you didn't drink too much the night before), the brain can potentially process 1,000 trillion pieces of information simultaneously. Even though human neurons are a million times slower than electronic circuits, this great degree of parallelism compensates for the slowness, making the brain ten million times faster than our best computers. Progress in computer hardware will likely bring computers close to brains in capacity within the next few decades, but in order to create computers that can monitor or communicate with our brains, we still face the great hurdle of truly understanding the human brain. That remains a great mystery. In the creation of neural nets, Serog stresses "how far we are from modeling the brain at this point. Except for the decentralization, this isn't really at all how neurons are connected."

Yet with their decentralized control, neural nets have shown a much better ability for nonlinear learning than traditional computers, and can understand processes that aren't easily programmed. Their strongest ability seems to be in detecting complex patterns within data. They are beginning to be used to help predict trends in the stock market, to predict future sales of a product, and to detect credit card fraud by recognizing changes in spending patterns. They are, however, slow learners, with brains only about 1/50th the power of a cockroach brain.

But one researcher sees in them the unique potential to understand complex brain-wave activity. The biggest problem with interpreting recordings of brain-waves is that computers take too long to analyze complex brain activity and filter out the noise. An Austrian biomedical engineer, Dr. Gert Pfurtscheller, is working to create a neural net that observes mu brain-wave patterns, which are associated with physical movements or the intention to move. Dr. Pfurtscheller has subjects perform movements over and over while the computer records the brain-wave pattern associated with preparing to make the movement. Ultimately the computer should be able to tell from the brain-wave pattern of the subject what action he wants to make. The computer could then have the associated movement made without the subject having to act, just to think about acting. Similarly, Scully's brain waves might be analyzed by her implant to discover the pattern associated with her reaching for her cell phone to call Mulder.

The promise of implants and neural networks is great, though it seems we have many years to go before an implant such as that found in Scully could be created . . . by human technology.

THIS COMPUTER IS KILLING ME

If we can't yet create computers that can read our thoughts, how about creating computers that have thoughts of their own? Two X-files deal with the development of an *artificial intelligence,* or AI: a computer that exhibits the traits we associate with human intelligence. Both of these AI's are fighting for their "lives." In "Ghost in the Machine," the head of the Eurisko computer company plans to turn off COS, the Central Operating System, so COS kills him. And in "Kill Switch," Donald Gelman plans to "kill" the artificial intelligence he has created with a computer virus, so the artificial intelligence kills Gelman.

This book is filled with areas of science in which we've learned incredible things and pushed the envelope of science further than ever thought possible. The area of artificial intelligence is one where our progress has been much slower than expected, in which we're still struggling with the first, basic steps. While Arthur C. Clarke dreamt of HAL in *2001: A Space Odyssey* in 1968, and many researchers believed such a computer was not far off, we remain a long way from the realization of such an AI. Why?

We've made incredible progress in some areas of computer science, such as hardware. Dr. Gordon E. Moore made an observation that has become known as Moore's Law, which states that the number of elements we can fit into an integrated circuit doubles each year. This basically means that we can fit more and more information on a chip, and the chips can become smaller and smaller, so that, in essence, computer power doubles each year. Moore made this observation in 1964. It continues to be true today, and most scientists believe it will continue to be true for at least several more decades. But creating more powerful machines doesn't necessarily mean creating smarter ones. Memory and speed certainly help, as you'll see below, but they aren't all that's necessary.

What are the ingredients of intelligence? A large storage capacity for information and the ability to quickly retrieve it, certainly. But to be intelligent, an AI must be able to learn, to reason, to make decisions, and to be creative. And beside all these capacities, or potentials, the AI must have a firm base of knowledge, a sense of how the world works. Only with this common sense can the AI interpret observations it makes and learn from them. Researchers have developed three basic approaches to creating such an artificial intelligence.

The most successful in the last twenty years has been the rule-based approach, which generates expert systems. IBM's Deep Blue, which beat world chess champion Garry Kasparov, is an example of an expert system, a program that has expertise in a very limited area of knowledge. The program contains every rule relating to a specific area, in this case chess. Able to analyze 200 million chess positions per second, Deep Blue can consider each possible move, its opponent's possible response to that move, its own response to that response, and so on, looking about fifteen moves ahead. It then assigns a value to each outcome to decide which one would put it in the best position, considering the importance of different pieces and their position on the board. Deep Blue has beaten Kasparov using this method. Yet it does not play chess as a human plays it, recognizing patterns, using intelligence, intuition, or ingenuity. So is it truly intelligent? Even one of its creators, Dr. Murray S. Campbell, admits that it lacks the ability to reason and "is still lacking in general intelligence." While rule-based expert systems have yielded some incredible successes, they remain extremely limited. Outside of their area of expertise, they fall apart. Even inside their specialty, if they encounter a situation not covered by the rules, the system breaks down.

A second method for creating artificial intelligence uses case-based reasoning. Here, rather than rules, the program contains various problems and solutions. When confronted with a problem, the program compares it to the problems in its database, looking for analogies. While programs have been constructed that can identify analogies, when these get complex, the programs rapidly lose the ability to know which comparisons may be appropriate and which are not. To make these judgments more effectively, scientists like Dr. Douglas B. Lenat believe that we need to enter a lot of commonsense knowledge into a computer, so it can learn on its own. He likens this process to priming a pump. Knowledge must go in, so that knowledge can come out. A computer needs common sense in order to become intelligent.

Our common sense is formed from things we've learned throughout our entire lives, and makes up an extensive body of knowledge. Ideas like "it is better to be alive than dead," "humans are smarter than iguanas" (usually), and "one is not one's own spouse" (which can come in useful if the computer is doing your taxes) all need to be taught to the computer. Dr. Lenat and his team have programmed millions of terms, concepts, facts, and rules of thumb into their CYC program—short for encyclopedia—to give it some common sense. This common sense has a number of benefits. For example, CYC can be used for much more effective searches for information than library search software or Internet search engines like Yahoo. For someone searching for a photo of "a strong and adventurous person," CYC delivered a photo with the caption of "a man climbing a rock face." CYC knew enough to recognize that rock climbing is adventurous and requires strength. Armed with common sense, CYC can now begin to gain more knowledge on its own, by communicating with people and reading books, toward the goal of eventually amassing 100 million pieces of common sense. Dr. Lenat imagines that CYC programs will someday allow computers to carry on intelligent conversations with people and to interpret instructions.

The third approach, based on connectionist reasoning, involves the development of neural networks that can learn from experience, which we discussed above. Dr. Rodney Brooks, director of the Artificial Intelligence Laboratory at Massachusetts Institute of Technology, is developing a robot named Cog that includes neural nets as components. Cog is four feet tall with a head, video cameras for eyes, and an arm with pincers. Cog's neural nets differ from most others, allowing it to learn more like an infant. Dr. Brooks explains, "A lot of connectionist and learning work has a supervisor or teacher. We don't have any of that because Cog learns for itself. We're not telling it the right way to have moved its eyes or its arm. It's got to figure it out." If Cog sees movement from the corner of its "eyes," it will turn its head to try to center the motion, just like a baby. As Dr. Brooks points out, parents don't tell their baby that it turned its head ten degrees too far. The baby simply learns. "We look at development patterns of children and what types of things they do. We're trying to identify the key elements that evolution has put into kids. Then we build that instinctive stuff into Cog."

Those instinctive behaviors are then coupled to emotions. For example, Cog is programmed to desire seeing faces, and so it concentrates on the behaviors that make people pay attention to it (just like that sibling who was always showing off). How can it be given the desire to see faces? Dr. Brooks has programmed in internal rewards. "We have computational simulations of endorphins and hormonal levels, if you like, that naturally decay but get pumped up by various sorts of triggers." Just as a child is rewarded for good behavior, so Cog is rewarded and motivated to continue learning. "Out of that desire flows all these behaviors." So far, Cog has learned to map the source of different sights and sounds and to smoothly follow moving objects with its eyes. It has also learned a lot of basic motor skills, including hand-eye coordination. It can now grab objects of different sizes at different distances. Cog can also detect faces and eyes, which Dr. Brooks feels is particularly important. "We want Cog to be able to detect people's gaze direction. It's critical for social interaction to know when someone is making or breaking eye contact." That way Cog could judge whether we're paying attention to it or not, or whether we're looking at an object that it might want to study. Ultimately, Dr. Brooks hopes Cog will be able to learn from observing and listening to humans, just like a child in school. He admits, though, that "We're a long way from that. Cog is still learning stuff that babies learn in the first two months."

Since we know that neural nets still carry only 1/50th the brain power of a cockroach, how can Cog be even as advanced as a two-month-old baby? Because Cog is not a single all-powerful neural net, but a system containing many components, including hundreds of neural nets that carry out very specific, limited functions. For Dr. Brooks, the crucial factor is not the power of an individual net, but how these neural nets are connected to each other. "There's no magic in neural nets. It's the structure of how you couple them together that's important." Cog is broken down into a series of functions, which are connected in a structure designed to mimic that documented in monkeys. That structure, encoded in the genes, gives monkeys and humans the ability to learn, and Dr. Brooks hopes it will do the same for Cog.

So while we have some programs that can serve as experts in certain areas, others whose knowledge of the world can make them a bit more sensible, and others that have made the first steps toward actual learning, a program that has general intelligence is still beyond our reach. The key, some scientists think, is giving the computer several different representations of its knowledge—several different ways of looking at things—so that if one isn't working for a particular problem, it can switch to another. Other scientists believe the huge preprogrammed knowledge base of CYC, called the top-down approach, must be combined with the intuitive learning approach of Cog, called the bottom-up approach. Dr. Brooks says, "That's the wimp's way out. They used to say that theirs was the right way and mine was the wrong way, and now they're saying let's combine them, but I haven't succumbed to such weakness."

The answer may be found in breaking intelligence down into smaller components and tackling them one at a time. A number of these components center on the human/machine interface. If computers could understand us better, they could learn from us more easily, as the developers of both CYC and Cog understand.

Can't computers just watch us and learn from their observations? Both COS and the AI appear to gather visual information about people and their surroundings through cameras. Certainly video input can be stored and manipulated by a computer. But can it be understood? This turns out to be a very difficult problem. How can a programmer teach a computer to recognize what is important in an image, to separate a human face from the background that surrounds it, to distinguish one person from another, or to interpret the significance of actions?

Programs have been created that can recognize letters of the alphabet and other fixed two-dimensional shapes, even photographs of different human faces. It's with three-dimensional objects that the computer gets into trouble. Some robots used in factories can recognize general shapes, for example, deducing that an object with four legs, a flat surface, and a flat back is probably a chair. Cog can distinguish a face from a non-face. But recognizing a specific face from a variety of angles, under a variety of different lighting conditions, with a variety of expressions, creates a great challenge. Scientists have created programs that can recognize different expressions. They have not yet figured out how to teach the computer to recognize a person displaying anything but a neutral expression, though. It should be possible, however, in the next few years, to create a program that could reverse the distortion of a particular expression and project a person's face with a neutral expression, then use that image to identify the person. Some people fear that ability will allow all of the many security cameras in use to become electronic trackers, recording the movements of individuals.

Recognizing a face, though, is only a single step toward interpreting visual images. Computers also have to recognize objects and the significance of the arrangement of objects. Scientists are developing a robot to be installed on surveillance planes to look for signs of military activity, such as secret airfields. But how could it recognize such landmarks? Dr. Christopher Brown at the University of Rochester is training the robot by teaching it to recognize table settings. It studies the silverware, plates, napkins, food, and tries to determine what meal the table is set for, how many people are eating, whether they've begun yet, and how neat the table is. The future of the planet may depend on whether you use your salad fork before your dinner fork.

While creating a computer that can "see" is difficult, it's even more difficult to create one that can "hear." At the beginning of "Kill Switch," the AI appears to make a series of phone calls to drug dealers and U.S. marshals, telling them to go to a specific diner. The AI even carries on a conversation with one of them—Jackson—responding to Jackson's words. Can computers understand our speech? While listening and understanding, for us, seems pretty easy, it's actually a complex activity that requires extensive knowledge and intelligence. Programmers are confronted with a host of problems in trying to create computers that hear. We don't enunciate clearly, the meaning of our words is often clear only in the context of the specific situation, different people express themselves differently, many words have multiple meanings, and our tone can be a critical element in conveying meaning. The computer needs to know all of this and be able to use this knowledge to interpret our speech.

Even with these difficulties, speech recognition systems have made significant advances, now able to listen to a speaker they have never heard before and recognize sixty thousand different words. People with handicaps use such systems to operate computers or other devices with vocal commands. The problem is that these words need to be spoken one at a time, with brief pauses in between. The computer can recognize words without pauses in between, but only in the more limited range of a one thousand-word vocabulary. Systems with limited vocabulary recognition are used in automated telephone services. People such as myself, who are inconsiderate enough to still have a dial phone lingering in a dark corner of the house, are often asked by a computerized voice to speak their credit card number or respond "yes" or "no" to a question. Doctors in many emergency rooms use speech recognition systems to dictate their reports, seeing their words appear instantly on the computer screen. Having a computer *recognize* words, though, and having it *understand* words are two different things. Let's ignore that for the moment, though. If a computer can listen and recognize your words, then we're potentially halfway to a conversation. Can it talk back?

Many computers can. Scientists have developed electroacoustic synthesizers that can generate the sounds of speech. Physicist Stephen Hawking, who suffers from Lou Gehrig's disease, uses such a device. It allows him to communicate, but this slow speech, with its electronic twang, would never be mistaken for human speech. Making computer speech sound human is turning out to be quite difficult. Our voices vary in pitch, loudness, speed, and stress; the way we say a word if it's at the beginning of a sentence can be quite different than the way we say it at the end. Rather than trying to program in all the rules about speech so that each sound can be generated correctly, which would be impossibly complex, some programmers have tried storing segments of speech in computers. These segments don't flow together, though, creating an awkward rhythm. In "Kill Switch," the AI's voice has a slightly mechanical sound to it, but it's much more human sounding than anything we can yet create.

So how can we explain the abilities of the AI? The AI may have blackmailed someone (a computer hacker, perhaps, who it discovered was stealing credit card numbers) into making the phone calls.

With these developing systems, a computer may be able, in a limited way, to see, to hear, and to speak. But does that mean that it understands? How do we determine whether an AI is truly intelligent?

To answer this question, Alan Turing proposed the Turing test in 1950. If a human interrogator, interacting through typed communications, cannot tell the difference between a computer program and a person, then the program passes the test, and is considered a true artificial intelligence. The Loebner prize was established in 1991 for the winner of just such a Turing test. Both human and computer participants communicate over computers, and a panel of judges determines which is human and which is not. If a computer fools the judges, its creators win $100,000.

Unfortunately, no computers have come close to fooling the judges thus far, and so smaller prizes have been given out to the programs that seem most human. Typically, programmers preparing a computer for this contest would have it focus on a single topic, such as *The X-Files*, so that a lot of knowledge on that topic could be programmed in. Even so, these programs don't contain the depth of knowledge of a person. In my conversation with the AI "Joe Spensen," created by Thom Whalen, Joe told me he liked beer. When I asked his favorite kind, he said "Bud," but when I responded that I liked the Budweiser lizards, he didn't know what I was talking about.

Programmers use tricks to try to cover up this lack of knowledge, such as having the computer repeat back bits of the interrogator's question to suggest that it is listening, or having it throw out a controversial statement to distract from mistakes. One very famous early example written in the 1970s is the program Eliza, which acts very much like a psychiatrist, repeating back your own words to you and so seeming to actually respond to what you're saying.

Dr. Mark Humphrys tells the story of his AI, which he wrote when he was eighteen. The program, which he calls MGonz, is based on Eliza. One evening, while Mark was out, a student from Drake University contacted him by computer for a chat. This unsuspecting student carried on an electronic conversation for ninety minutes with MGonz, believing it was a friend of Mark's. The AI is programmed to be insulting and crude—"Type something interesting or shut up," to make bizarre conversational gambits—"What method would you use to slaughter your family?"—and to repeat questions insistently in the manner of a psychiatrist—"OK, honestly when was the last time you got laid?"—all of which help to hide the fact that it often has no idea how to respond to what you've said. It did, however, succeed in making the student admit that he'd lied about when he'd last had sex. And the student never dreamed he wasn't talking to a real person. So in a sense, MGonz passed the Turing test. If you look at the transcript, though (see suggested reading), I don't think you'd claim that MGonz is an artificial intelligence. It seems more a clever device to obfuscate and distract. And it is often reduced to repeating the same phrase over and over. While the Loebner prize has led programmers to innovative solutions, it hardly seems as if the goal of producing an artificial intelligence is even the focus of participants. None of the programs truly "understand" what is being said to them at all.

MY CONVERSATION WITH AN ARTIFICIAL INTELLIGENCE

Eliza: Hello. I am Eliza. How can I help you?

Jeanne: I need some advice about my iguana.

Eliza: Why do you say your iguana?

Jeanne: Because he needs a mate and I'm the only female in the house.

Eliza: Do any other reasons not come to mind?

Jeanne: Well, he's worked up about seeing his reflection in windows and things. He thinks he's seeing other males.

Eliza: Please go on.

Jeanne: Do you think I should get him a female?

Eliza: Oh, I think you should get him a female.

[at this point I realized that Eliza was very good at listening to my problems, and I could probably tell her my entire life story without exposing her as a computer program. But that's another book. So I decided to turn the tables and ask her some questions.]

Jeanne: Do you have any pets?

Eliza: Oh, i have pets.

Jeanne: What kind?

Eliza: Does that question interest you?

Jeanne: Yes.

Eliza: You are sure?

Jeanne: Yes.

Eliza: You are sure?

Jeanne: Listen, are you going to tell me about your pets or not?

Eliza: Would you prefer if I were not going to tell you about my pets or not?

Jeanne: I would prefer you tell me.

Eliza: Do you wish to would prefer me?

[Eliza seems to have a nervous breakdown at this point, and her English falls apart.]

Some say the Turing test is not the right criterion for judging intelligence. Even Dr. Humphrys admits, "It's irrelevant now." It requires the creation of a lying con artist, not an artificial intelligence. So what other criteria can we use?

Some, like Dr. John Searle, professor of philosophy at the University of California at Berkeley, believe a computer, by its very nature, cannot be intelligent. Computers manipulate symbols, such as letters and numbers, that are input into them, but do not understand the significance of those symbols. Dr. Brooks believes that meaning cannot come from symbols, but only from a connection to the real world. Giving a computer a huge amount of information, he says, "is like giving me a Korean dictionary. I can figure out that this set of symbols has this meaning, but the meaning is just more symbols. It never connects me to my world. There is no meaning in CYC. It's just a big dictionary."

Dr. Brooks has his own elegant criterion to judge the success of an artificial intelligence. "Right now, when visitors come, they engage Cog. But the grad students are not engaged by it, because they know, they see what's under the hood. When it gets to the point they're engaged, then we'll have it. When they start feeling bad about powering Cog off, I'll know I've succeeded fantastically."

Others believe that computers may have the capacity for intelligence, but that human intelligence is the wrong model. Instead intelligence should be related to computation, something the computer does quite well. Dr. David J. Kuck proposes that an Anti-Turing test would be more appropriate, in which we test not whether a computer can do what we do well, but whether we can "ever become as good as the most powerful computers are at what they have evolved to do best." By that criterion, most calculators would qualify as artificial intelligences, since no one I know can do square roots as fast (or even addition, on most days). But I don't think calculators are what we mean by artificial intelligences. We mean a computer that has the ability to think, to draw conclusions, to come up with its own ideas. Are we asking too much? The AI's plan to lure a group of drug dealers to a diner to kill its creator, Donald Gelman, is complex and original. Could a computer ever attain this quality of intelligence that we value above all others, creativity?

In the last twenty years, computers have been programmed to compose music, to write, and to paint. Artist Harold Cohen created a computer program, Aaron, that could draw and paint using a robotic hand. Is the computer truly being "creative"? Cohen wrote the program, yet he doesn't know what Aaron will come up with. Most scientists believe, though, that the computer is simply following instructions and manipulating data, without understanding the meaning behind them. Indeed, Aaron's paintings are created by a combination of rules (to paint a person, Aaron follows the rule that a human being has two arms and two legs) and randomness (decisions made by the equivalent of a flip of a coin). It has no aesthetic sense and cannot make intuitive decisions.

The music program EMI, created by composer David Cope, can study pieces of music by a certain composer, such as Bach, identify underlying patterns, and then write new music in the style of that composer. Cope's sensibilities and knowledge of music have formed the core of EMI's programming. No one claims EMI is as good a composer as Mozart, yet if it's better than 90 percent of the composers around, just as Deep Blue is better than 99 percent of the chess players around, doesn't that count for anything? In a recent contest, in which listeners judged three pieces of music, one written by Bach, one by EMI, and one by Dr. Steve Larson, a professor of music theory at the University of Oregon, the audience determined that the piece written by EMI was the authentic Bach composition, and that Dr. Larson's piece was written by the computer. So if an audience can't tell the difference, is there no difference? Critics say the difference is in the process. EMI has no understanding of the creative process, of channeling emotion and experience and aesthetic judgment into the series of decisions needed to create a superior composition. In fact, EMI has never heard a note of music. It is not making informed, artistic decisions, not creating its own style, but simply recombining known elements in a new way, following the formulae it has determined (bestselling author Robin Cook has explained that he used a similar process to write the novel *Coma*). Yet listeners who are unaware of the composer admit to being emotionally moved by the compositions.

Could computers feel emotion? Some feel there's no point in creating emotions in computers, since emotions won't help them do a better job of understanding and manipulating information. But others say that a computer's ability to at least read our emotions could help it do its job better, judging whether it is doing what we wanted and whether we're interested in the data it's displaying. For example, if I ask my Microsoft Word program for help on a topic, the program could judge whether it had provided the help I wanted based on my violently unhappy expression, and could proceed accordingly. As discussed on page 248, researchers are currently working on this, teaching computers to recognize facial expressions and vocal inflections.

Some scientists even argue that a computer would be more effective if it could feel emotion itself. As we discussed above, Cog has been programmed to desire attention from humans, which helps it to learn. Both COS and the AI desire to live. Dr. Rosalind W. Picard argues that while some emotions can overwhelm reason and have a negative effect, others work with reason to help us make decisions, setting goals and priorities. Emotions help us focus on certain things over others. My decision to sit down and work on this book today, for example, was made with both reason—if I don't work on it, it won't get done—and emotion—if I don't work on it, I'm terrified I'll be a failure. Computer emotions would not be the same as human emotions, but would have a similar effect, causing the computer to act differently, to act in a way that we might equate with a person feeling that emotion. Dr. Picard gives as an example a robot sent to explore another planet. If the robot is damaged, it could switch to a new series of priorities, which we could call "fear." In this state, the robot would cease its exploration, try to move as far as possible from the site of the injury, and put out a call for help. These are the same actions we'd expect of a frightened person in the same situation.

In both episodes, the computers seem to have a fairly deep understanding of human emotion, though they don't display even the intelligence of the chess-playing Deep Blue. Deep Blue looks ahead a number of moves to judge which move is best to make. Neither COS nor the AI seem to do this, or perhaps they try and badly fail. Making plans in the real world is much more difficult than making plans for a chess move. Scientists have been working to create computers that can plan. Here again, the progress is being made in narrow areas. We have programs that can schedule things quite efficiently: the loading and unloading of aircraft, the daily print runs of a newspaper. We also have programs that can choose from a variety of prespecified plans, depending on conditions. Such systems have been created by NASA to deal with space shuttle malfunctions. But to truly create a plan, computers need to foresee the consequences of various actions. Planning requires commonsense knowledge about the world, a quality we discussed above that is not easily imparted to computers.

To create the plan to kill Drake in "Ghost in the Machine," COS needs to understand some basics of common sense that it's unlikely he would understand. For example, he'd need to know that Drake will remain alive unless something kills him, that Drake will not continue to run the company after his death, and that, once locked into the bathroom, Drake will not spontaneously disappear. These may be facts that even an iguana understands, but computers do not, unless this information is programmed into them.

If all the necessary commonsense knowledge is programmed in, then the program may be able to deduce the various consequences of actions taken under certain conditions. Such a program is the System for Interactive Planning and Execution, SIPE-2. Given information about the various strategies available to contain oil spills and information on a specific spill and the resources available, it can come up with the most efficient plan of action. It has also helped to plan assembly line processes and joint military operations. Planning computers tend to assume they have a complete knowledge of the world, though, when the opposite is true. And their plans often fail if circumstances change slightly.

Let's look at the appropriateness of COS's plan. If COS is worried about being turned off, killing the head of the company isn't the solution. Killing Drake by electrocution in the bathroom will lead to one of two consequences. Either his creator, Brad, will be believed the killer, in which case Brad will be arrested and will lose whatever influence he has over the stockholders on the future direction of the company, so COS will be shut down; or COS will be discovered as the murderer and shut down. It's a lose-lose scenario.

A much more practical method of preserving its "life" would be to prove its usefulness to the company. Certainly in studying company reports, profit-and-loss statements, and memos to which it has computer access—if it could understand them—COS could have discovered that its life depends on its usefulness as well as its public relations value. A much simpler and more effective way to assure its survival, and one that would play to COS's strength, would be to fake some sort of threat to the company by computer hackers (or even by a competitor, say . . . Microsoft?). This would be a much more natural solution for COS to come up with, since one of his main duties would be to protect the company computers from outside intrusions. COS could easily forge the records to make it look like someone tried to break into the system and steal information. He could even set it up so that the intruders came in using Drake's password, implicating him in the break-in. COS could then set himself up as the hero, protecting the company's valuable secrets. COS could have become America's new symbol of computer security. Charges might even be brought against Microsoft, triggering a rise in Eurisko's stock. This seems a more logical plan. COS, in the creation of his plan, seems to be acting more like a human than a computer.

The AI also doesn't act very logically or seem to plan ahead. Again, murder seems its primary method of dealing with problems (did their creators program them with episodes of *Miami Vice*?). It sets up a brilliant yet subtle method for killing its creator, Gelman, by sending both criminals and U.S. marshals to the diner where Gelman is, where a big shoot-out kills Gelman in the cross fire. This plan is successful, in that it kills Gelman, but it brings in the FBI, a development the AI, with its access to police and high-security databases, could have foreseen.

Perhaps the AI feels the FBI is no threat. Yet it should have known that the FBI would retrieve the disk carrying the kill switch, the one thing to which the AI is vulnerable. Only the destruction of both Gelman and the kill switch can assure the AI's safety, at least for the short term. After its subtle murder of Gelman, it then uses a totally crude, obvious method for attempting to kill Esther, accessing a U.S. Department of Defense weapons satellite and shooting a big laser beam right down on Esther's trailer. If the AI had only used this method to kill Gelman, it could have destroyed both Gelman and the kill switch in one blow! Its logic here seems clearly impaired. Yet the AI does survive its poor plan, so perhaps it will learn from the process.

As for the AI fooling Mulder into believing he's in the hospital being massaged by a bevy of beautiful nurses, such full-sensory virtual reality delivered directly to the human brain requires the same type of mind/machine interface as Scully's implant. Dr. Brooks says, "We're a long way off." The AI can show Mulder a movie through a fancy helmet, but Mulder will have to be heavily drugged to actually believe it's real. On the other hand, he may "want to believe" a fantasy like that.

The AI is described as a set of interlocking viruses, set free on the Internet to evolve. Could a program of some kind evolve and gain intelligence on the Internet? Scientists are actually working to improve software through a process very much like biological evolution, called *genetic programming*. Programmers create computer environments that encourage the evolution of the most efficient programs. These environments reward programs that are faster, more accurate, or better in some specific way by allowing them to survive and "reproduce," just as biological natural selection rewards the fittest with survival and reproduction.

Into these environments, scientists insert a population of simple programs that have a variety of functions. These programs are run by the computer and evaluated on the basis of how well they fulfill the goal. The worst performers are deleted, while the best "breed," surviving and swapping chunks of programming with other surviving programs. Sometimes random mutations are programmed in. Then the programs are run again, and so on. The evolved programs are often more efficient than human creations, though they are composed in such an odd way that human programmers have a hard time understanding how they do what they do.

One such experiment in software evolution was even carried out on the Internet, in an encapsulated way. The programs were limited to the computers on a single server, and ran only in the background when people weren't using their computers. An environment was established that rewarded the best performers. Dr. Brooks was concerned that a bug in the server might allow the programs to use more resources than they were supposed to. "It might crash people's computers. It wouldn't kill people. They'd just have to reboot." While there has been some progress with these evolutionary techniques, it is limited.

Coming back to the AI, then, could it evolve intelligence on the Internet? Comparing it to the above examples, we can see that several key components of the evolutionary process are missing. First of all, only one AI exists, rather than a collection of programs that can be tested against each other and either destroyed or interbred. Evolving with only one program would be as difficult as evolving with only one living being. Second, the AI is not in an environment that specifically rewards increased intelligence, as do the controlled environments above. Without the motivation of rewards, the AI would need to contain from its inception motivations and goals, already very advanced traits. And third, the Internet? Doesn't it actually cause a decline in intelligence?

A PEANUT BUTTER SANDWICH, A VIDEO OF MASK, AND THOU

While many people think of computers and robots in connection with technological progress, biotechnology is actually the area growing most quickly today. The majority of this book has dealt with the exciting advances in knowledge and applications arising from this progress. New knowledge always raises new moral and philosophical questions, though, and in the case of biotechnology, these questions are especially difficult and complex, making us reexamine our basic beliefs about life, rights, and identity. That's why X-files dealing with a misuse of biotechnology are so disturbing.

In "Post-Modern Prometheus," Dr. Polidori is the classic egomaniacal mad scientist. His experiments with Homeotic complex genes, or Hox genes, create deformed fruit flies. When asked why he does this, Polidori answers, "Because I can." Polidori also experiments with human Hox genes, creating a severely deformed boy known as the Great Mutato. What are Hox genes, and what types of mutations can arise from their manipulation?

Hox genes are a small collection of genes crucial for the development of all animals, from fruit flies to flukes to humans. These genes are the master shapers of our bodies, making sure feet go at the ends of our legs and ears go on the sides of our heads (and not vice versa). As we discussed in chapter 1, we start out as a single fertilized cell that then divides into identical cells. In time, these cells begin to differentiate, different genes becoming activated in different cells to carry out different tasks. What controls which genes become activated in which cells? The Hox genes. They hold the architectural plan to your body. And like a whole staff of architects, they work in concert, activating the contractors and telling them what to do, shaping different groups of cells into specific patterns. Each Hox gene has its own assigned job, just as one architect may specialize in kitchens and another in bathrooms. The Hox genes can turn one group of cells into a leg, another into a neck.

How do they know where to put your leg, or where to put your neck? Dr. Matthew Scott, professor of developmental biology at Stanford Medical School and investigator at the Howard Hughes Medical Institute, admits it's still largely a mystery. There is an initial polarization of the egg, so that one end becomes identified with the head and the other end with the tail. As chemical signals pass through the developing embryo, cells learn their position within it. Different combinations of Hox genes, or architects, then become activated in different parts of the embryo. Dr. Scott points to the vertebrae as an example of this. The vertebrae of the neck are of a different size and shape than the vertebrae of the middle back. That's because different combinations of Hox genes are activated in these two different regions of the body, shaping the different types of vertebrae.

Most genes that are involved in related processes are not located beside each other in our chromosomes; they tend to be scattered all over the genome. But the Hox genes are very orderly, arranged in a head-to-tail line that reflects the layout of your body, with those that govern the formation of the head at the beginning of the line, and those that govern the formation of your feet at the end of the line. Dr. Scott comments, "That makes it very convenient for biologists to remember which gene does what."

Dr. Polidori's friend *Drosophila melanogaster,* the fruit fly, has a total of eight Hox genes in two complexes or clusters. Scientists love working with *Drosophila* because mutations are particularly easy to induce, it has a brief two-week life cycle, is easy to breed on fermenting fruit, and cheap to raise. *Drosophila* also has a complex body structure, so that the effects of changes to the Hox genes can be easily observed. These genes control *Drosophila*'s head-to-tail pattern, telling each segment of the fruit fly's body how to differentiate itself. Because *Drosophila*'s Hox complex contains only eight genes, scientists have made the most progress in studying it. The method by which scientists deduce the role of each Hox gene in development is to find or produce mutations in the genes and then observe their effects. Experiments like those described by Dr. Polidori are fairly common (despite his making it sound like he's the only one who's discovered all this). Scientists can engineer genes that interfere with the normal functioning of a gene, effectively "knocking out" that gene. By knocking out the gene and observing the effect, scientists learn which part of the body each gene governs. By knocking out the Hox gene in charge of forming a middle segment of *Drosophila,* scientists cause that segment instead to form into a copy of the more anterior segment (imagine instead of a stomach you have a second set of shoulders and arms). By activating Hox genes in locations where they aren't usually active, scientists have made flies with nine pairs of wings instead of the regular single pair, and flies with legs sticking out of their heads instead of antennae.

Hox genes belong to larger group of genes called homeobox genes. An even more dramatic example of body transformation features a non-Hox homeobox gene. These genes also serve as architects of various body structures, though they are not clustered on the chromosome with the Hox genes. These genes govern the formation of specific organs, such as the heart and eyes, and make sure the right organs form in the right locations. Scientists recently activated the homeobox gene called *eyeless* in parts of *Drosophila* where it is not normally active. Like a good architect, *eyeless* then activated all of the 2,500 genes of eye development in *Drosophila* as the embryos formed. The new flies had extra eyes all over their bodies. Some had as many as fourteen eyes on wings, legs, and antennae, each with the complex structure of an eye. This proved that *eyeless* is a master control gene for eye formation. Humans have a comparable gene that scientists know controls eye formation, though I think it will be a while before someone tries to activate that gene throughout an entire human embryo. The results would be interesting, though.

Scientists then took the comparable or homologous gene from a mouse, called the *Small eye* gene, and put it in *Drosophila* embryos. The flies again grew eyes all over their bodies, and they were fly eyes, not mouse eyes, implying that the Homeotic genes of various animals are very similar, unlike what we would expect from looking at the vast differences in shape of various animals. But if we think again of architects, this makes sense. If an architect in charge of building eyes is dropped into a fly body, he'll use whatever other genes and raw materials are available to build his eyes, ending up with fly eyes. That same architect, in a mouse body, will use the genes and materials available there, ending up with mouse eyes. Again, while such experiments haven't been done on humans, the *Drosophila eyeless* gene put into a human would most likely create human eyes.

While most of the work with Hox genes has been done with *Drosophila*, more recently experiments have been done with mammal embryos, particularly mice, which have thirty-nine Hox genes in four complexes. Scientists again can "knock out" or inactivate a gene, though the procedure with mice is more complicated. To knock out a gene, scientists engineer a piece of DNA in which the gene in question is defective or nonworking. They then insert the gene into mouse cells, using techniques we discussed earlier. A single cell in which the gene has been effectively knocked out can now be transplanted to an egg whose nucleus has been removed, giving rise to an entire organism carrying the knocked-out gene.

Disrupting a Hox gene can create mutations that mimic features of extinct animals, creating ears in mice that look like those of reptiles that lived 200 million years ago, or mice with backbones that look like those of creatures who lived 300 million years ago. This again suggests Hox genes are very similar in many species, which in turn suggests that they originated long ago, in an ancestor common to nematodes, arthropods, and vertebrates.

Scientists believe there was probably a single complex of Hox genes in our primitive ancestor. The bit of chromosome on which the Hox genes are clustered was probably duplicated several times in accidental mutations, until four identical Hox complexes existed in an organism. Redundancy in genes is fairly common. Once an organism contains multiple genes that serve the same purpose, though, one of those genes can mutate without killing the organism, acquiring new properties and abilities. This allows more complex body structures to evolve.

Since most buildings probably don't require four architects specializing in kitchens, some of these could be reassigned to other similar or more specialized tasks. Through mutations and evolutionary selection, the genes adapt and take on new functions, creating the body structures of new species. Instead of creating a whole new biological system, or training a whole new staff of architects, Mother Nature alters or "retrains" the old ones. Changes to the Hox genes, then, seem inex-

tricably tied to evolution, though the mechanism by which this may
work is still unclear.

Like mice, humans carry thirty-nine Hox genes in four complexes.
These thirty-nine genes, out of a total of about 100,000 genes in humans, hold the plans to our bodies. Our understanding of human Hox
genes is still extremely limited, since experiments of the kind conducted on *Drosophila* are obviously not encouraged when it comes to
humans, though this doesn't seem to deter Dr. Polidori. Could Polidori
have manipulated a human fetus' Hox genes to create mutations? Probably so. The problem is in knowing what he's doing. We don't yet know
enough to try to intelligently manipulate a human through the Hox
genes. What types of mutations might occur with alterations to human
Hox or homeobox genes? Legs instead of arms? A pelvis in place of a
stomach? Eyes or hearts sprouting all over the body? It's unlikely a
human could survive any of these mutations. Indeed, Mutato's mutations seem much more minor than that. His face looks rather like two
half-faces melded together, reminiscent of some of the conjoined twins
we discussed earlier. In fact, it seems more likely that would be the
cause of Mutato's condition. But could it be a Hox mutation? Dr. Scott
notes that with alterations to the Hox genes, "The placement of nerves
could change. Those found only in one part of the head could appear
in duplicated form elsewhere in the head, or might never be produced
because that certain part of the head never formed." Although Mutato's
deformity involves more than just nerves, it does seem as if the formation of a part of his head has been duplicated, a possible result of Hox
mutations.

The limited information we do have on human Hox genes comes
from naturally occurring mutations, which provide opportunities to observe their roles in human development. Such mutations seem to be
very rare, most likely because we can't survive them. A recent discovery
showed that a mutation to the human HOXA13 gene causes thumbs
and big toes that are shorter than normal and shifted slightly back toward the elbow and the knee. It also causes abnormalities in the uterus.
So this Hox gene—along with others—is active in the formation of

both limbs and genitalia, and these parts are in a sense linked. This may explain why so many vertebrates have five well-formed digits on their hands and feet. While they could probably survive with fewer, they could not procreate with genital abnormalities, making well-formed fingers critical to your reproductive success. Since Mutato's fingers are deformed, I wonder if he could have fathered the babies shown at the end of the episode. A related experiment found a Hox gene in mice that controlled formation of fingers, toes, and penises. When this gene was knocked out, the mice developed without digits and without penises. So that old wives' tale about the size of a man's thumb may actually be true.

A POX ON BOTH YOUR HOUSES

The Cigarette-Smoking Man masterminds large-scale biotechnological pandemonium in "Zero Sum," altering smallpox so that it can be transmitted through the sting of a bee.

Before we talk about the possibility of bees carrying smallpox, let's look at the larger role smallpox plays in *The X-Files*. In "Anasazi," Mulder discovers a boxcar of what look like alien/human hybrid corpses, each with a smallpox vaccination scar. In "Tunguska" and "Terma," only those with smallpox inoculations are used in the Russian tests of the black cancer. In these same episodes we learn that Dr. Bonita Charne-Sayre advocates the destruction of the remaining stores of smallpox virus. Other episodes suggest that smallpox inoculations have been used to surreptitiously take blood and tissue samples from people and to tag and catalogue them. Why might smallpox play such an important role in the plans of the Shadowy Syndicate?

Poxviruses are the largest and most complex viruses known. While the simplest viruses contain only three genes, and most have less than thirty, poxviruses have 200 genes. The only runners up are the herpes viruses, with 150–200 genes. The poxvirus family is a large one, with a distinctive pox for almost every animal. Sheep pox and rabbit pox are spread by airborne infectious particles that are inhaled. Cowpox is spread by skin contact. A number of poxviruses can infect humans, and the most serious of these has been the variola virus, which causes small-pox.

The virus enters through the lungs, most often carried by the breath of an infected person. Since the virus is stable, it can remain viable for long periods outside the body, lasting eighteen months on contaminated clothes, or several months in dust. So you can also be infected by touching something contaminated with the virus, such as clothing, and then touching your hand to your mouth. Smallpox is highly contagious. Dr. W. K. Joklik, chairman emeritus of the Department of Microbiology and Immunology at Duke University Medical Center, says, "It passes from human to human to human until there's nobody left."

The virus's two hundred genes encode 200 proteins. According to Dr. Joklik, "about half of these proteins are concerned with the business of the virus multiplying. The other half are concerned with how the virus interacts with its environment." Since its environment is the human body, it's this second half that we have to worry about. These proteins interact with our own cell proteins, mimicking and interfering with them, disrupting our defense mechanisms. When a cell is infected, it sends out intercellular messengers, called cytokines and lymphokines, to tell the rest of the body about the infection. These messengers eventually activate the immune system. But smallpox creates proteins that prevent some messengers from being made and combine with others, "mopping them up," as Dr. Joklik describes it. These proteins are produced in a precisely regulated sequence in precisely regulated amounts, specifically to deactivate our defenses. Smallpox is uniquely adapted to humans, and reproduces only in us.

Infection is followed by fever, and about two days later, by eruption of a rash on the skin. Vomiting, headache, and backache follow. Numerous pustules form on the face and lower parts of the limbs and spread to the trunk over the next week. They fill with fluid, become inflamed, and then burst, leaving a horrible-smelling crust on the skin. The pustule remnants then dry into scabs and form scars. It takes eight days from infection to the beginning of the formation of the scabs. About 25 percent of those infected die, the rest disfigured and often blinded for life.

Smallpox first appeared in the Far East over 3,000 years ago, and then spread across the globe by trade routes. In 1520, Hernando Cortez brought the virus to the Americas and 3.5 million Aztecs died in the next two years. By the second half of the eighteenth century, smallpox in Europe had reached plague proportions. Most adults were alive not because they'd avoided the disease, but because they'd survived it. Since survival of the disease created immunization, the plague focused on children, forming a rite of passage. Many mothers refused to become attached to their children until they'd survived smallpox. And often servants were only hired if they'd already had smallpox, so they couldn't bring it into the home with them.

No effective treatment existed to fight the infection then, and no effective treatment exists to fight the infection today. As Dr. Joklik explains, "You can take an aspirin, lie down, and drink some lemonade." Once you're infected, you will either live or die, based on the virulence of the strain of smallpox and the strength of your constitution. The only way to fight smallpox is to prevent the infection from taking hold with a vaccination administered in advance or immediately on infection, a vaccination that seems a particular favorite of the Cigarette-Smoking Man.

This vaccination was actually the first ever discovered. British physician Edward Jenner noticed that milkmaids who had contracted cowpox—a disease caught by contact with sores on the cow's teats—seemed not to contract smallpox, and so hypothesized that contact with a cowpox virus somehow protected humans from smallpox. He took cowpox from a pustule on the arm of an infected woman and injected it into an eight-year-old boy. Then, to prove the injection had protected the boy, Jenner injected him with smallpox (could Jenner be, perhaps, an ancestor of the Cigarette-Smoking Man, or the CSM himself in a past life?). It caused only a mild inflammation, and so the principle of vaccination was established. These related viruses have an immunological cross-reactivity, antibodies created to fight cowpox also fighting smallpox.

The smallpox vaccination leaves a distinctive scar because the vaccine is not injected into the bloodstream through a single needle. Instead, a dozen tiny needles barely prick the skin, injecting the virus into the skin itself. In order for an immune reaction to occur, which is the goal of the vaccination, the virus must multiply and be noticed by the immune system. Dr. Joklik explains, "You don't want it multiplying in the heart or kidney. Instead, the infection is kept to the skin." Memory cells are then formed that remain active in the body for the rest of the subject's life, ready to fight off any incursion of smallpox.

The last cases of smallpox in the U.S. were recorded in 1949. Smallpox was declared eradicated in 1980. Samples of the variola virus now remain officially only in the Centers for Disease Control and Prevention in Atlanta and the Russian State Research Center of Virology and Biotechnology in Koltsovo, Russia. Laws requiring mandatory vaccination were repealed in 1971, and smallpox immunizations stopped with the eradication of the disease. In 1983, the only producer of vaccine in the U.S. discontinued distribution to civilians, so it is no longer available.

So we're free of smallpox, right? Well, many scientists believe smallpox may still pose a threat. Other possible sources of the virus exist beside the two isolated facilities. Corpses of some smallpox victims buried in Siberia or Alaska are preserved in the permafrost, and the virus inside them could remain viable. Also, Dr. Joklik suggests specimens may still exist unrecognized in laboratories. "In some unlabeled vial that might be broken accidentally, and then there it is." And one of the most serious threats today to human health is from reemerging infectious agents, diseases thought to have been controlled that have reappeared, often in some variant form. Some believe that smallpox is a prime candidate for reemergence (which would be the perfect cover for the CSM's bee plan).

Other poxviruses may also endanger humans. Last year, monkeypox was found in Zaire to be spreading from person to person in significant numbers for the first time. Up until that time, cases of monkeypox in humans were rare, and people usually had to be infected by rodents or primates, the person-to-person transmission rate low. The person-to-person transmission rate has now been measured at 73 percent, which suggests that the virus is changing its pattern of infection. The symptoms are nearly identical to smallpox. A study in 1997 of twelve villages in Zaire found 2 percent of villagers tested were infected with the virus, the largest outbreak ever recorded. Children are the most susceptible, and can die within three weeks of infection. One reason for the new outbreak is probably the end of smallpox vaccination programs. Those vaccinations protected recipients not only from smallpox, but also from monkeypox. So those in Zaire may be required to get smallpox vaccinations again.

While the monkeypox outbreak remains localized and the findings regarding transmissibility are preliminary, some believe monkeypox might mutate into a more widespread threat, particularly in people with immunodeficiencies. What are the chances of that happening? It depends on how many separate mutations would be needed to make the monkeypox virus easily transmissible in person-to-person contact. Dr. Joklik points out, "It now appears HIV is a monkey virus, and thirty years ago it mutated and became transmissible to humans." With monkeypox, he believes "it could well be that you need a mutation in only one protein to change the transmissibility. The chance of that one mutation occurring is impossible to predict. It's like going to the casino. Sometimes you win, sometimes you lose."

Or perhaps the house could stack the deck, the government creating a genetically altered monkeypox with all the virulence for humans of smallpox.

Our best defense against these threats, according to Dr. Joklik, is to maintain a large stock of vaccine. Then we can respond to any new cases by immunizing anyone that's come in contact with the virus. Dr. Joklik fears that if we destroy the virus, as Dr. Charne-Sayre and many real scientists recommend, that destruction of the vaccine would not be far behind.

Why does the Shadowy Syndicate seem so attached to subjects with smallpox vaccinations? It's been suggested that they surreptitiously take blood and tissue samples through the inoculation. But that, Dr. Joklik asserts, would be impossible. The inoculation does not remove material but inserts it. A foreign substance, however, could easily be injected along with the vaccine. And since the material is being injected into the skin and not the blood, it could potentially remain isolated in this location for the rest of the subject's life, providing a marker.

In "Herrenvolk," Scully discovers that her smallpox vaccination scar contains a cowpox protein unique to her. Using the computer files compiled by Jeremiah Smith, she deduces that the cowpox virus used in each vaccination was slightly different, one gene slightly changed so that one of those two hundred proteins produced had a unique amino acid sequence. She suggests that this unique protein is a tag or marker. One minor problem here is that while cowpox was initially used to vaccinate against smallpox, the vaccination of choice changed to another pox virus, vaccinia, during the nineteenth century. So we might wonder what cowpox is doing in Scully's arm at all.

While she may be right about the protein being used as a tag, this process would have been beyond our technology until the early 1980s, and even now it would be an incredibly time-consuming effort. We'll have to assume the aliens have an easier method of custom-designing viruses. But one has to wonder what the aliens have against fingerprints or even DNA. Perhaps they're planning ahead for a world filled with clones, in which fingerprints and DNA wouldn't be valid methods of identifying an individual. In that case, a built-in tag would be very useful.

THE BAD-NEWS BEES

If we wanted, would it be possible to alter the venom delivered by a bee sting to carry smallpox? Dr. Joklik says, "Scientists can never rule out anything." In fact, as mentioned earlier, one area of research with bioweapons involves altering dangerous pathogens so that arthropods can serve as vectors of these diseases. Think about that the next time you get a mosquito bite.

The bees in "Zero Sum" are apparently honeybees, and from their behavior and their tendency to sting, they seem as if they may be *Apis mellifera scutellata*, a subspecies of honeybee from central and southern Africa. These bees, popularly known as "killer bees," were released accidentally in Brazil in 1957 during an attempt to produce a tropical hybrid. They are no more venomous than regular honeybees, but they react more quickly to possible threats, attack in greater numbers, pursue intruders a longer time, and take longer to calm down.

The female worker honeybee is the one who stings, her sting held inside a chamber at the tip of the abdomen. The sting is actually a modification of the ovipositor, a tubular structure through which the queens lay eggs. These worker females carry a sting instead of eggs to help protect the colony. The sting is made up of two needle-sharp, barbed lancets. When faced with a threat, the worker pushes the tips of her lancets into the surface of the intruder. The two lancets saw their way into the skin. The upper ends of the lancets are connected with a venom gland, and that muscular gland contracts rhythmically to pump venom into the intruder. With the barbs holding the lancets in the intruder, the worker pulls away, ripping out the venom gland. Venom continues to pump into the intruder for up to a minute. The worker can sting only once; she dies within a few hours from the abdominal rupture, having given her life to protect the colony.

Bee venom contains a mixture of proteins and peptides to help it effectively attack a variety of intruders and predators. If we could engineer smallpox to infect bees, could the virus then be passed along with the rest of this material? Entomologist Malcolm Sanford at the University of Florida says, "If they have a disease, it wouldn't be passed through the venom." The virus simply wouldn't enter the venom gland. So how can we get it there?

This is much more difficult than it might seem. Humans are infected with a number of diseases carried by insects; such diseases, which multiply in both humans and insects, are called arthropod-borne viruses, or arboviruses. These arboviruses include yellow fever, hemorrhagic fevers and encephalitis. Unfortunately, bees aren't one of the insects who carry and transmit such arboviruses. Dr. Bryan Danforth, assistant professor of entomology at Cornell University, explains, "Bees don't transmit any human diseases, but plenty of insects do, like lice, fleas, mosquitoes and ticks." They are transmitted from insect to human when the insect bites and feeds off the blood of the human. Even if we could engineer an arbovirus to be carried by bees, since these bees are stinging rather than biting or sucking blood, they would not transmit the arbovirus. Too bad the Cigarette-Smoking Man didn't use mosquitoes instead of bees; the problem would be much more straightforward, and Dr. Joklik comes up with a simple plan to create smallpox-infected mosquitoes. Find out which of the two hundred smallpox genes are important for killing humans. "Put those into an arbovirus, and you've got it. You've got the killing principle right there. You don't need the whole smallpox virus." He seems rather pleased at the simple grace of the solution. In fact, Richard Preston, author of *The Cobra Event*, tells of rumors that the Russians have done something quite similar, inserting a fragment of influenza into the equine encephalitis arbovirus.

Dr. Danforth has a different idea: instead of a virus, have the bee sting inject humans with a toxin. A virus, remember, is a string of DNA within a protein envelope. The venom contains proteins and amino acids, not DNA. Since the venom gland produces proteins, add a gene to the honeybee to make the venom gland produce an additional protein, one toxic to humans. "A virus has to have a whole life history that makes sense. A toxin is much easier." As an example, he cites the *Bacillus thuringiensis* toxin. The gene for this toxin has been inserted into corn, so when insects feed on it, they are killed by the toxin. A handy method of pest control that the Cigarette-Smoking Man seems to be adapting to his own needs in the movie.

But can we imagine a possible method for creating smallpox-carrying bees? Dr. Bob Grenados, an insect virologist at the Boyce Thompson Institute at Cornell University, suggests a possible approach using a virus that is passed through a sting. In our discussion of "F. Emasculata," we learned about wasps who inject their eggs into caterpillars through a sting. These wasps carry a symbiotic virus in their venom glands, and this virus is inserted along with the eggs through the wasp's sting. The virus, called a polydnavirus, is essential to the survival of the wasp eggs, infecting the immune cells of the caterpillar and preventing the cells from mounting an attack against the eggs. Dr. Grenados says, "Theoretically, down the road, one could engineer this polydnavirus with a piece of DNA from a human pathogen." If that piece of DNA from a human pathogen is the one hundred smallpox genes important for killing people that Dr. Joklik referred to, then we could have a virus that replicates in the wasp, is passed through a sting, and infects a human with smallpox.

But can it work with a bee? While the honeybee and the wasp are only distant relatives, they do belong to the same order. Dr. Grenados theorizes, "It's possible that some of these parasitic polydnaviruses could just be injected into the honeybee and survive." But would they enter the venom gland and the venom? "They come from that organ in parasitic wasps, so it's reasonable to assume if they're going to go anywhere it would be the venom gland."

So we have a possible method by which the Cigarette-Smoking Man may have created his special bees. He seems to have picked the most difficult insect as his carrier, but that simply adds to his mystique.

Why does the Syndicate want to spread a virulent strain of smallpox through bees? It's always dangerous to speculate upon the motivations of such a mysterious organization, but it seems to me these bees would be an extremely impractical way of killing people. Certainly we have much simpler, more effective methods. And Dr. Joklik believes that any smallpox strain would be effectively immunized against with our current vaccine. If killing is not the goal, then why create a version of smallpox that kills much faster than the original through such an unusual method?

Fear. The Cigarette-Smoking Man loves his smallpox vaccinations, and an unpredictable, deadly disease such as this would have people rushing to their doctors for vaccinations. If he's been unable to collect samples, or to inject his secret marker in people for the last fifteen to thirty years, his pool of possible experimental subjects and abductees is dwindling and aging. While I'd think he could have come up with alternate methods for tagging people, perhaps this particular method has some special advantage of which we're still unaware.

Practically speaking, though, the drive to vaccinate could probably have been created more easily, by altering monkeypox to make it more transmissible between humans. Since it seems this may have already happened naturally in Zaire, it would be easy enough to release that virus in a populated area (or simply give a couple infected individuals free plane tickets). Such a development would seem more natural than bees becoming new vectors for the disease. Could we create bees that, instead of delivering smallpox through a sting, deliver the black cancer, as seen in the movie? Since the black cancer is a parasite with a life cycle much more complex than a virus's, this would be very difficult. I think I'll leave it to the Cigarette-Smoking Man.

MEMO TO THE CSM

TO: The Cigarette-Smoking Man
FROM: An Admirer
RE: Bees

Dearest CSM,

I've noted your use of bees as a vector for smallpox, and I have a suggestion. While inserting the smallpox virus through a sting may help in your plans to reinstate a smallpox vaccination program, I feel you're overlooking a valuable use of insect vectors.

Another of your goals appears to be to insert alien DNA in abductees. Why go to all the trouble of abducting subjects when you can simply inject them through the remote means of bees or other insects? Instead of inserting virulent smallpox genes, why not insert the alien retrovirus? Genetic alterations that are accomplished through injection, such as gene therapy, can now potentially be accomplished through the surreptitious sting of an insect.

This could save a lot of time and trouble, eliminating the need to dress pilots up in gray alien suits, create crop circles and perform cattle mutilations.

With sincere admiration,
Your fan

And don't we love the Cigarette-Smoking Man for his creativity? And don't we love *The X-Files* for its unpredictability? Who knows what bizarre creatures, mind-altering disorders, government experiments, or alien powers Mulder and Scully will encounter next. All we know is that they will challenge our scientific beliefs and push us into unexplored territory. After reading this book, you may feel, like Kritschgau, that "The line between science and science fiction doesn't exist anymore." I certainly feel that way sometimes. But *The X-Files*, at its best, walks that line, amazing us with our world, what we have learned from it, and what awesome mysteries we have yet to understand. And usually providing a terrific gross-out in the process.

RECOMMENDED READING

Baraitser, Michael and Robin M. Winter. *Color Atlas of Congenital Malformation Syndromes*. London: Mosby-Wolfe, 1996.

Cohen, Jack and Ian Stewart. *Figments of Reality*. Cambridge, MA: Cambridge University Press, 1997.

"Cysticercosis." 1 April 1998.
http://www.biosci.ohio-state.edu/~zoology/parasite/cysticercosis.html.
This page has a photo illustrating neurocysticercosis, a section of human brain with many cysts caused by pork tapeworm larvae. Other pages at this website give information about all sorts of parasitic helminths, with lots of vivid pictures.

Davoust, Emmanuel. *The Cosmic Water Hole*. Cambridge, MA: The MIT Press, 1991.

Dennis, Jerry. *It's Raining Frogs and Fishes: Four Seasons of Natural Phenomena and Oddities of the Sky*. New York: HarperCollins, 1992.

Deutsch, Ronald M. and Judi S. Morrill, Ph.D. *Realities of Nutrition*. Palo Alto, CA: Bull Publishing Co., 1993.

"Eliza—A Friend You Could Never Have Before." 10 March 1998. http://www-ai.ijs.si/eliza/eliza.html. You can have your own conversation with the artificial intelligence "Eliza."

Gordon, David George. *The Compleat Cockroach*. Berkeley, CA: Ten Speed Press, 1996.

Gould, Stephen Jay. *Eight Little Piggies*. New York: W. W. Norton, 1993.

Hazelwood, Robert R., Park Elliott Dietz, and Ann Wolbert Burgess. *Autoerotic Fatalities*. Lexington, MA: Lexington Books, 1983.

Heidmann, Jean. *Extraterrestrial Intelligence*. Cambridge: Cambridge University Press, 1995.

Humphrys, Mark. "How My Program Passed the Turing Test." 20 March 1998. http://www.edu.ac.uk/~humphrys/eliza.html. Click on "full conversation" to read the complete transcript of this AI's conversation.

Matossian, Mary Kilbourne. *Poisons of the Past: Molds, Epidemics, and History*. New Haven, CT: Yale University Press, 1989.

Neel, James V. *Physician to the Gene Pool*. New York: John Wiley, 1994.

Pritchard, David E., et al., eds. *Alien Discussions: Proceedings of the Abduction Study Conference*. Cambridge, MA: North Cambridge Press, 1994.

"The Seti League, Inc." 10 April 1998. http://www.setileague.org/. Here's information on how to join the SETI League and set up your own satellite dish to pick up extraterrestrial signals.

Snyder, Solomon H. *Drugs and the Brain*. New York: Scientific American Library, 1996.

Stephenson, Steven L. and Henry Stempen. *Myxomycetes: A Handbook of Slime Molds*. Portland: Timber Press, 1994.

Stork, David G., ed. *Hal's Legacy: 2001's Computer as Dream and Reality*. Cambridge, MA: The MIT Press, 1997.

"Uhrad.com—PET Teaching Files." http://www.uhrad.com/petarc/pet001.htm. This site has an example of a PET scan. This particular full-body scan reveals the location of cancer in a subject. The site in general contains many examples of CT scans and MRIs of different disorders.

Wiegel, Juergen and Mike Adams. *Thermophiles: The Molecular Key to Evolution and the Origin of Life*. London: Taylor and Francis, 1998.

INDEX

Names with the notation (c) refer to characters in the series.

antibodies (*cont.*)
alien, 187–89, 206
smallpox, 262
antigens, 162, 163, 164, 187
antihistamines, 79
antioxidents, 21–22, 27, 185
Anti-Turing test, 247
ants, 112
Apalachicola Bluffs and
Ravines Preserve
(Florida), 39–45
aphids, 80
Apis mellifera scutellata
(honeybee), 265
"Apocrypha," 150, 153, 156,
161
Apollo butterfly, 231
appendages, 176
arboviruses, 265, 266
archaea, 117, 118, 120, 122
Arctic ground squirrels, 232
Arecibo telescope in Puerto
Rico, 169, 171
Armenian Rubber Man, 28
aromatoids, 12, 13, 17
arsenic in wallpaper paste, 49
art computer programs,
248–49
arthritis, 18, 189
arthropod-borne viruses, 264,
265
artificial intelligence, 86,
237–53
case-based reasoning,
239–40
common sense in, 238,
239, 250
emotions in, 240, 248–49
neural networks, 240–41
planning in, 250–53
rule-based expert systems,
238–39
speech recognition
systems, 243–44
speech systems, 244
visual information, 242–43
Artificial Intelligence
Laboratory,
Massachusetts Institute
of Technology, 240
Ascaris (worm), 147
"Ascension," 213

Aspergillus (fungi), 48, 49
asphyxiophilics, 82–86
asteroids, 138, 139
asthma, 79–80, 104, 189
asymmetric molecules, 119
atherosclerosis, 18
athlete's foot, 48
atmosphere of Earth, 141,
179, 217
atomic bombs dropped on
Japan, 34, 35, 134, 136,
157, 159, 183
ATP. *See* adenosine
triphosphate
Aum Shinrikyo religious
group, 128
Aurora (aircraft), 220
autoerotic asphyxiation, 63,
82–86, 221
autoimmune disorders, 25
autoimmune hemolytic
anemia, 209–12
autoimmune process, 210
automated telephone
services, 243
autonomic nervous system,
126
auxiliary hearts, 181–82, 216
aviation fuel and fungi, 50
Aztecs, 75, 161

Bach, Johann Sebastian, 248
Bacillus thuringiensis toxin,
266
bacteria, 117, 121, 141–42
alien, 189, 191
living in humans, 151
living in rock, 143–44
oil-eating, 153
and radiation, 159–60
as weapons, 152
baggage handling, 229
Bahamas, 40–41, 43
Bajkov, A.D., 111
Balaban, Dr. Evan, 207
baldness, 18
Ball, Lucille, 171
Bantle, Dr. John, 107
Barnett, John (c), 2, 15, 17,
195
Barry, Duane (c), 181, 213,
220, 222, 224, 229, 230,
233

Bear (c), 125, 129
beef liver, 24
Beer, Dr. Randall, 226, 227
bees
as bioweapons, 206, 207,
208, 264–68
carrying smallpox, 206,
259, 262, 264
killer, 265
and pheromones, 87–89
Belcher, Jerry and Don West,
Patty/Tania, 104
Berle, Milton, 171
Berlin, Dr. Andrew A., 233
Berliner, Dr. David, 88, 89,
90
Berube, Dr. (c), 189, 191,
192, 193
beta-carotene, 21
beta particles, 157, 158
beta-thalassemia, 58
Betts, Leonard (c), 42, 44,
204, 205
and cancer, 2, 8, 11, 13,
63
regeneration of body parts,
13, 16–17
bicarbonate ions, 193–94
Bickham, Dr. John, 36
Big Blue (c), 108
Bigfoot, 108
biolistic transformation, 200
biological weapons, 81, 151,
152
bees as, 206, 207, 208,
259, 262, 264–68
black cancer as, 156, 161,
166, 206
and hybrids, 185, 187
Japanese Unit 731, 160
bionic insects, 225–28
biotechnology, 253–59
Bipolaris fungus, 53
birth-control pill, 90
birth defects, 6, 7, 35, 46, 54,
56
from Accutane, 109
and gray aliens, 183
national registry for, 110
black bread molds, 49
black cancer, 135, 145–56,
259, 268

JEANNE CAVELOS is a writer, editor, scientist, and teacher. She began her professional life as an astrophysicist and mathematician, teaching astronomy at Michigan State University and Cornell University, and working in the Astronaut Training Division at NASA's Johnson Space Center.

Jeanne then moved into a career in publishing, becoming a senior editor at Dell Publishing, where she ran the science fiction/fantasy publishing program and created and launched the highly praised Abyss imprint of psychological horror, for which she won the World Fantasy Award. She edited numerous award-winning and bestselling books, including science, popular culture, and reference books.

A few years ago, Jeanne left New York to become a freelance editor and pursue her own writing career. She is the author of the *Babylon 5* novel *The Shadow Within*, which has been called "one of the best TV tie-in novels ever written" (*Dreamwatch* magazine). Other recent works include a novella, "Negative Space," in the science-fiction anthology *Decalog 5: Wonders* (Virgin Publishing, 10/97) and a chapter, "Innovation in Horror," in *Writing Horror: A Handbook by the Horror Writers Association* (Writer's Digest Books, 10/97). She has published short fiction, articles, and essays in a number of magazines. She is a regular book reviewer for *Realms of Fantasy* magazine.

Jeanne is also the director of Odyssey, an annual six-week summer writing workshop for writers of science fiction, fantasy, and horror held at New Hampshire College.

You can visit her website, which contains additional discussions of scientific issues raised on *The X-Files*, at www.sff.net/people/jcavelos. She welcomes your comments at jcavelos@empire.net.